# THE ACADIANS

## ONE ACADIAN FAMILY AND LES MAUDITS ANGLAIS (THE DAMN ENGLISH)

### SAMUEL ANDRE AUCOIN

Black Rose Writing | Texas

ISBN: 978-1-68513-464-8
LIBRARY OF CONGRESS CONTROL NUMBER: 2024933034
PUBLISHED BY BLACK ROSE WRITING
www.blackrosewriting.com

Printed in the United States of America
Suggested Retail Price (SRP) $23.95

*The Acadians* is printed in Minion Pro

*As a planet-friendly publisher, Black Rose Writing does its best to eliminate unnecessary waste to reduce paper usage and energy costs, while never compromising the reading experience. As a result, the final word count vs. page count may not meet common expectations.

# THE ACADIANS

# PROLOGUE

There they were. My friends. My comrades. Their names carved into a 493-foot long, polished black granite, V-shaped memorial to a lost cause. I remembered their faces, our conversations, the battles won and lost in the war. I was back there with them in my mind until I felt a squeeze on my seventy-nine-year-old hand. My name is Samuel Andre Aucoin and I was with my nineteen-year-old granddaughter, Chloe Zerga, a college sophomore majoring in history. She was especially interested in the Vietnam War and had asked me to take her there.

"It's magnificent, isn't it, Grandpa? The Wall?"

It wasn't a question really, but I nodded and squeezed her hand.

"It's such a simple design, but it takes your breath away."

"Yes. I've been here several times over the years, and it continues to have a profound impact on me."

"You served in the Army with several of the men listed here, didn't you?"

She knew the answer, but I didn't mind that she was humoring an old man, inviting me to talk. "Yes, but one stands out to me. Roger Robichaud. I only knew him briefly, but we formed a strong bond."

"Do you remember where he is on this Wall?"

"Well, he died in 1965, and the names are listed by year of death, so it shouldn't be too difficult to find him."

We slowly made our way down the Wall, Chloe reaching out periodically to trace a name with her fingers. When we drew close, we scanned the granite surface. Chloe, crouching down, said, "Here he is. Can you tell me about him?"

I nodded, needing a moment before I could speak. "I know a lot about him and his ancestry. The story, however, is quite long. Are you sure you want to hear it?"

She rolled her eyes. "Are you kidding me? Of course, I do. But if it's long, we should get out of this heat. The humidity is killing me."

"Let's go back to that ice cream shop we passed on the way here. You're right. I can feel the sweat trickling down my back. We'll be much more comfortable in that air-conditioned shop."

On the way, Chloe said, "How did you meet your friend, Roger Robichaud?"

"We met in jump school at Fort Benning, Georgia."

"Jump school? Is that where the Army trains its paratroopers?"

"Yes. Roger and I were there at the same time, in January 1964. We were the only two in the class with French-Canadian names, so we became friends since neither of us knew anyone else. He was from Louisiana, and I was from New Hampshire. We were both eighteen years old."

"That's young. He died in 1965, just the next year. That's so sad."

"Yes, there are over 58,000 sad stories on that Wall."

She didn't ask me anything else until we reached the ice cream shop. I was grateful for the silence as the memories filled my mind with images, emotions, words, and regrets.

Chloe and I ordered our favorite treats and sat down at a table with comfortable chairs.

"When I first arrived at Fort Benning, what do you think I saw?"

"I don't know. What, Grandpa?"

"Thousands of robins all over Fort Benning! I finally knew exactly where many of them went in the winter. Roger told me Louisiana was the same—very few in the summer, but thousands in the winter. That was my first time in the South, and I was fascinated with the differences.

"But what I saw was nothing compared to jump school. It was only three weeks long. Roger and I had no trouble learning all the skills the instructors made us repeat over and over again: the parachute landing fall (PLF), assuming a fetal position and counting to four as we exited the aircraft, and more pushups than I'd done in my life. The first week was spent almost entirely on learning the PLF. Unlike what you see on TV with sky divers, we were forbidden from landing standing up. We had to hit the ground lightly with our feet, shift our bodies to one side, go into a roll and then come up standing. 'Hit, shift and rotate,' the instructors kept repeating.

"We soon mastered all the required skills and successfully made our five jumps from a Hercules C-130 aircraft. That probably means little to you, but that airplane was a big part of my life. It was then, and continues to be today, the major workhorse of the Air Force. It can land and take off on relatively short runways carrying significant payloads. And it can carry forty paratroopers.

"We graduated and waited for orders telling us where we would next be assigned. There were one hundred of us in our graduating class. They posted the orders on the bulletin board for ninety-seven of us. All ninety-seven were going to Okinawa to join the 173rd Airborne Brigade. Roger was one of the ninety-seven, but not me. They left the next day. I was upset. I wanted to go with my buddy Roger, but there I was stuck in the barracks with two other graduates I didn't know."

"Wow! Why weren't you on that list, Grandpa?"

"You'd never guess. I didn't find out for several months. Orders assigning me to an airborne unit in Germany finally came down. I don't know where the other two guys went. I jotted down Roger's new unit from his orders and wrote to him after I got to Germany. He was in Okinawa for less than a year and then his entire battalion was shipped to Vietnam. He was killed in mid-1965 when the vehicle he was riding in set off a large mine in the road. He was twenty years old."

"That's only a year older than I am now." Chloe's eyes got big.

"It is," I said, nodding. I took another scoop of my ice cream, trying to think of a way to lighten the mood. "Did I tell you Roger and I were both Acadians?"

"No, what's that?"

"Well, long ago, in the northeast of America, there was a land called Acadia. Roger and I both have ancestors traced back to that specific land."

"So, that makes me Acadian?"

"Yes, you are part Acadian. Want to hear about them?"

"Yes, I've never heard of Acadians. I've read American history from the Jamestown colonists and Pilgrims of Massachusetts through modern times. Not once have I read the word Acadian anywhere."

"I'm not surprised. The English-speaking authorities at the time, both American and British, were not especially proud of what happened to the Acadians."

"The story begins a very long time ago in France."

# CHAPTER 1
# THE BEGINNING –
# PROVINCIAL FRANCE

Jean-Claude Landry was quite happy with how things were going on his little farm. All but his two youngest children worked in the fields alongside him. They grew three main crops: wheat, beets, and turnips. On that beautiful, blue-sky day in October, all three crops were doing very well and would be ready to harvest in a week or so.

Jean-Claude was weeding the beet patch when he caught a whiff of something burning. He stood up and immediately saw heavy, black smoke just west of the farm. A group of the *sieur*'s men on horseback came galloping toward the smoke on the road bordering the farm. As they passed, they yelled *"Les maudits Anglais sont arriver, cachez vous!"* ("The damn English are here, hide yourselves!")

Jean-Claude frantically yelled to his children, "Back to the house, quickly! The English are coming!" As they raced to the house, he saw that the western edge of his fields was now on fire. As he rushed into the house, he exclaimed to his wife, Marie, "The fields are on fire! Everyone into the cellar!" With that, he lifted the trapdoor, and everyone piled in, closing the trapdoor after them. It was musty and pitch black. No one said a word. Marie held the four youngest, while Jean-Claude and the three oldest held hands. They all listened and soon heard the sound. It was like wind through the maples. But this was no friendly wind. The sides of their house were made of fieldstone, but the roof was thatch—very dry thatch. The sound of the wind soon grew to a roar.

If they could have seen it from a distance, their house resembled a torch, the four grey walls holding up an immense flame. The framework for the thatch was made of saplings, just large enough to hold the weight of the fifteen-inch thickness of thatch. Some of the saplings gave way, and the family heard it crash onto the trapdoor above accompanied by the popping sound of the fiery thatch that came with it. Fear gripped everyone in the cellar.

"Hail Mary, full of grace, the Lord is with you," Marie said and continued the prayer. The children soon caught up to her, and even Jean-Claude, not especially religious, joined in. The roar of the fire subsided as the thatch was used up. The sound soon changed to a lighter crackle.

Jean-Claude was aware of the periodic raids by the English that had been going on for many years. France and England were natural enemies. It was common for the English to raid French coastal villages, sink or steal whatever ships they found, and plunder the villages themselves – taking everything of value. But this was the first time they had caused any harm to his immediate family or the land he farmed.

"We need to get out now," Jean-Claude said and pushed up the trapdoor. The roof was gone, and the boys' bed in the corner, consisting mostly of thatch, was on fire. The boys' second set of clothes was also on fire, but hanging on hooks set into the fieldstone wall, the fire there caused no further damage. Before helping anyone out of the cellar, Jean-Claude surveyed the surroundings and determined the worst of the fire was over. He threw the kitchen water onto the boys' bed and was able to save the frame.

The children and Marie scampered out of the cellar and quickly escaped outside to avoid the smoky, acrid fumes when Jean-Claude soon joined them. Glancing past their house, the view of their fields took their breath away. There was nothing left of the wheat and beet tops. The fast-moving fire simply consumed everything in its path. The turnip tops, however, fared much better. Only the four or five rows closest to the beets were burnt to the ground. The most devastating loss, of course, was the wheat. Bread would be hard to come by for the coming winter. Losing all the tops of the beet plants and some of the turnip tops was a major loss since the tops were edible and the source of much needed, scarce nutrients for the family. A slight source of consolation—the underground beets and turnips were unharmed.

Marie fell to her knees, made the sign of the cross, and thanked Saint Mary for having seen them safely through this ordeal. She was gentle and Jean-Claude knew she would willingly forgive whoever started the fire, maybe considering it an accident. But even so, the loss was hard to accept.

"What a waste," she said, "It looks so pitiful." She sighed, stood up straighter, and said, "But it is part of God's plan, and all will work out for the best." The five oldest children dutifully made the sign of the cross with her, but not Jean-Claude.

"*Les maudits Anglais!*" ("The damn English!") snarled Jean-Claude. He was talking to himself, as he often did at moments of high emotion, but his words were clearly heard by Marie and the children. He saw the raid as a direct attack on his family. Enraged, he looked at the devastation of his fields––months and months of hard work down the drain, certain he could remember every hour of hoeing and weeding, planting, thinning, and chasing off animals. His savings were meager––just a few francs in the jar in the kitchen. Behind the rage was a gnawing fear: how would they survive the coming winter? Winter was inevitable and unpredictable. It could be colder and longer than usual. The children could get sick. Jean-Claude was normally slow to anger, easygoing by nature. He enjoyed spending time with and helping his friends and neighbors; and especially enjoyed having a little extra so they could celebrate the holidays with pies, cider, and full bellies. This attack, however, brought out the worst, or depending on your perspective, the best in him. He would fight to the death anyone who attacked his family.

Jean-Claude had farmed ten acres on the estate of René de Menou d'Aulnay, *Sieur* (Lord) de Charnizay for all his adult life. He had lost his first wife to a smallpox epidemic in 1632. His three children at the time, fourteen-year-old Perrine, and ten-year-old twins Antoinette and René, were ill as well but survived. He soon married Marie Aucoin (née Sallé). Her husband of fifteen years, Martin, died in the same epidemic. They had farmed a ten-acre plot on the same estate and had three children: François, 15, Michelle, 14. and Jeanne 2. Jean-Claude and Marie, with the *sieur*'s permission, gave up Marie's plot and continued to farm Jean-Claude's together. A son was born to them in 1634, and they named him René (the younger).

Jean-Claude looked to the east and saw the fire racing directly for the chateau of Monsieur d'Aulnay, just a mile away. He knew he needed to hurry there and render whatever aid he could, but he was hesitant to leave his traumatized family. He heard the galloping of horses and saw the *sieur*'s men returning from chasing the raiders and heading for the chateau. As they passed, they shouted that the marauding English had left the coast and were no longer on French soil.

"Go," said Marie. "We'll be fine here until you return."

They nodded to each other, both knowing they had little choice. The *sieur* ruled over his lands and could easily replace them with another family should he see fit to do so.

"Papa, I'll go with you," said François, the oldest boy.

"*Non!* I need you to stay here and watch over the family."

François was big for his age. Already, he was as tall as Jean-Claude and only a few pounds lighter. As he and Jean-Claude exchanged glances, it was clear his feelings regarding the raid were much closer to Jean-Claude's than his mother's. He had no love for the English. For most of his life, he'd heard the stories of the English raids and how they purposely selected the poorly defended French inhabitants for their wrath, and consequently, had grown to detest anything English. Often, he had spoken with Jean-Claude, wondering what the future held for him. François couldn't quite imagine spending the rest of his years in this one spot, though he knew that was the most likely—it was what his parents had done and their parents. But one thing was certain he would never forgive or trust the English.

Jean-Claude put his hand on his stepson's shoulder, aware of all that was going through his head.

"Go on," Marie said again. "We'll be fine."

Jean-Claude nodded and grabbed his long-handled shovel and ran to the chateau. When he arrived, he was relieved to see the fire had done no harm to the home and was now burning itself out well to the east. Most of the other tenant farmers had gathered to help, among them his cousin Pierre Chiasson.

"Pierre," Jean-Claude said, "How are your fields?"

"Very little damage," said Pierre. "The winds were from the south and kept most of the fire away from my fields. I could see your fields were not as lucky. *Désolé!*"

"*Merci.* I lost all my wheat, all the beet tops, a third of my turnip tops, and the roof of my house. We sheltered just in time. Fortunately, no one was injured."

The *sieur*, a stocky middle-aged man with a look of anger in his bright blue eyes, came out and addressed his sharecroppers.

"We have eyewitnesses who confirmed that an English raiding party came ashore this morning and set fire to the fields. Unfortunately, they all escaped before my men could engage them. I have sent word to King Louis informing him of this cowardly act." The *sieur* made eye contact with each of his sharecroppers and continued. "Some of your fields were spared from the fire. Others were devastated! We will all share equally in this loss." In this regard, the *sieur* was ahead of his time. Above all else, he was a businessman. The running of his estates was his primary business, and over the years, he had learned that treating his tenants firmly but fairly was in his best interest.

The *sieur* was a powerful noble, well-acquainted with the king, and used to ruling his domain. The sharecroppers knew he could be vengeful if slighted. He was a hard taskmaster yet was a fair one. To a man, they feared but respected him. "Over the next few weeks, you will all be harvesting your fields. My accountant will come to each of you and record your harvest. Those of you with losses from the fire will receive crops from those who have a bounty. I expect all of you to cooperate in this matter. Crops will be taken from some of you and given to your neighbors. After all the adjustments have been made, you will then provide me with my share as usual. Since the total is now less, we will all receive less. Return to your fields. We will all do what we can to absorb this loss."

Jean-Claude turned to Pierre and said, "If you have any extra roof saplings, I could use them to rebuild my roof."

"I have a few, and I believe Padé has some. We'll bring the saplings to you later today and help you rebuild your roof."

"*Merci*," replied Jean-Claude.


Padé Robichaud was another cousin; twenty-four years old, tall and lean, recently married, and although he did reasonably well with his ten acres, he was not happy with his tenant farmer status. He longed to farm his own land and had ideas about which crops to grow, dreaming about improvements he could make with the extra money if he didn't pay rent.

When Pierre and Padé arrived with the saplings, Marcel Béliveau was already there with a cart filled with thatch. Marcel brought his sixteen-year-old daughter Yvette. It was well known by the surrounding families that François and Yvette were in love and intended to marry the following year.

While the men rebuilt the roof, Yvette helped Marie prepare the evening meal. "Yvette, have you and François decided on any plans for after your wedding?" Marie had tried to have this discussion with François on several occasions but received very little information from him. He'd always make a joke about how she was trying to get rid of him. She thought it was more likely the converse. François was the eldest of seven and had not enjoyed even the meager freedoms of 17th century childhood for quite some time. Yvette was similar, the eldest of eight. Of course, they now wanted the respect and privacy of the adult life whose responsibilities they'd shouldered for some time. The normal sequence would be for the newly married couple to move away from their parents and set up their own household, hopefully not too far away. The parents, however, were sharecropper peasants and at the mercy of the landlord. Marie's biggest fear was that François and Yvette would decide to move to a faraway city like Paris or Marseille.

"We know we can't stay with our parents. We hope the *sieur* will provide us with a plot of our own."

Marie felt relieved. She wanted the same thing, for the *sieur* to provide François and Yvette with a plot of their own. The options available to a newly married couple, especially from the peasant class, were very limited. Becoming an apprentice to a tradesman, such as a carpenter, baker, miller, or such, was a possibility, but such positions were usually quickly filled through family networks. At least now she knew François would accept a plot on the estate.

Approaching the *sieur*, however, was not without consequences. His decisions were absolute. This matter required careful planning. Jean-Claude would be the one to approach the *sieur*, and he needed to voice his request as a solution and not as a problem for the *sieur*. Although only seventeen, François appeared to be in his early twenties and was strong, handsome, and intelligent. These attributes had not missed the eye of the *sieur*'s eighteen-year-old daughter, Claudette. She knew the farm routine well and made sure she was on hand on those occasions when François helped his stepfather deliver beets and turnips to the chateau. The *sieur* had many informers and was therefore aware of his daughter's interest in François.

Marie was unaware the *sieur*'s daughter was romantically interested in her son and how that interest complicated things for the *sieur*.

The following spring, after the planting was complete, Jean-Claude saw, to his surprise, one of the *Sieur*'s plots was idle. He didn't know why it was vacant. Perhaps the former tenants had passed away or were evicted, but then why hadn't the *Sieur* replaced the former tenants? The idle acreage was five or six farms away from his and close to his cousin Pierre's site, so Jean-Claude visited his cousin to ask about it.

After greeting his cousin, Jean-Claude got right down to business. "Pierre, do you know why your neighbor's plot is idle?"

"Yes and no," said Pierre. "My neighbor, Jean LeBlanc, was assigned to that spot two winters ago. He and his wife were newlyweds and struggled with the spring planting, so I helped him with it and with the fall harvest. He did okay for that first year and ended up with a decent harvest. But in early March of this year, the *sieur*'s men came to his house and spent considerable time talking to him. The next day, they came back with a wagon and loaded Jean, his wife, and all their belongings into the wagon and left. I haven't seen them since."

Jean-Claude didn't know what to think. Was Jean LeBlanc evicted? If so, it seemed like an overly harsh response from the *sieur*. The idle plot seemed perfect for François and Yvette, but would they suffer the same fate as LeBlanc? Why was the plot still idle? Was something wrong with the plot? Jean-Claude had more questions than answers.

After returning home, just in time for dinner, Jean-Claude informed his family what he had learned from Pierre. Marie was stunned that the *sieur* would evict a tenant without clear cause.

"It makes no sense," said Marie. "I know the *sieur* can do whatever he pleases on his land, but to evict a good tenant and leave that plot idle just makes no sense. There must be more to this story."

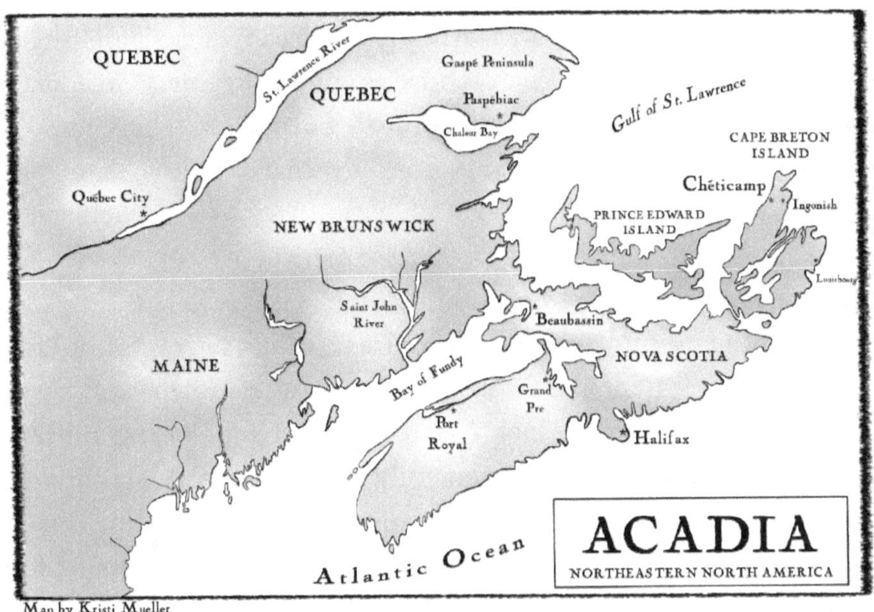

Map by Kristi Mueller

# CHAPTER 2
# LOUIS XIII, KING OF FRANCE

In early 1636, the King of France appointed the *sieur*'s son, Charles, to be the new governor-general of Acadia. Acadia consisted substantially of all the land south of the Gulf of St. Lawrence to the Saco River near modern-day Portland, Maine. It included all the modern-day Canadian provinces of Nova Scotia, Prince Edward Island, and New Brunswick, as well as eastern Québec and northern Maine.

In his appointment, the king made it clear he wanted Charles to focus on agriculture. He was to settle the new land with farmers, including their wives and children—as many farmers as possible. The king knew he was in a race with England for control of Acadia. On and off, France and England had been at war with each other for hundreds of years, and the English were his major adversaries for colonization of the West Indies and North America. Already, the English had significant colonies in Massachusetts and Virginia. Acadia, by comparison, was sparsely populated with Europeans. The king's plan was to develop an agricultural economy that would become self-sustaining. It could then support other ventures, and particularly his soldiers in Acadia. He could then exercise control over Acadia and keep the English out. The king's prior appointees in Acadia had focused on the fur trade and lumber. These ventures had made some appointees rich but proved marginal at best from a national perspective, principally because of the high cost of constant supplies from France. As well, fur and lumber were generally the trades of single men who could move easily, so they did little to populate the new land.

The king summoned the *sieur*. "Thank you for coming so quickly," said the king's assistant.

"My pleasure, anything for the king," replied the *sieur*. "I assume this meeting relates to my son's recent appointment?"

The *sieur* was proud of his son's new position as governor-general of Acadia but had mixed feelings, especially since Acadia was so far away. His expectation had always been that his son would take over the running of the estates. The *sieur* was in his late fifties, and the king's appointment was a major blow to the *sieur*'s succession and retirement plans. Father and son debated this matter at length. Charles was also conflicted, but in a quite different way. He felt an obligation to help his father, but the honor of the king's appointment and the excitement and lure of exotic Acadia were heady feelings for a young man and too much to pass up. Both also understood that refusing the king was risky. In the end, father and son agreed Charles would accept the appointment.

"You are correct, Monsieur d'Aulnay. The king is very pleased with your son's efforts so far and appreciates your contributions in this matter. He is currently in a conference with several of his ministers, but I will let him know you have arrived. I'm certain he will want to meet with you before the end of day."

"The king will see you now," announced the king's assistant a short time later. "He's in the garden and wishes for you to join him there."

"*Merci*," replied the *sieur*. As he entered the garden, he noticed the king was in deep conversation with another gentleman whom the *sieur* did not recognize.

Upon noticing the *sieur*, the king dismissed the other gentleman and motioned for the *sieur* to join him.

"René, my good friend! I'm so happy to see you. I trust your journey here was a pleasant one. I realize you're amid spring planting at your various estates, so I appreciate the sacrifice you've made in coming."

"I'm always at your service, my king," replied the *sieur*. "I will do whatever I can to help you."

"You've always been one of my most loyal and competent allies. I only wish I had many more like you. Look around you, René, and tell me what you see."

"I see the beautiful chateau you've built here at Versailles, and I see the magnificent landscape you've created."

"Look deeper at the surrounding countryside and tell me what you see."

"I see many productive fields. Wheat and perhaps cabbages, to name a few."

"Yes! That's exactly it. The small chateau I've built here is well-supplied by those fields. The surrounding farms and village are self-sustaining. In fact, the farms surrounding the village of Versailles produce an annual surplus, especially in wheat, that is sold in Paris for a considerable profit. My goal is to export this model to Acadia. I want our colony there to become self-sufficient as soon as possible, and I need your help to make that happen."

"I am at your service, my king. How can I help?"

"Your son sailed for Acadia in March with two vessels loaded primarily with settlers. I am now preparing two more vessels to join him. I expect these vessels to sail next month, fully loaded with competent settlers. My administrator tells me it's very easy to load two vessels with the dregs of society: beggars, laggards, prostitutes, criminals, and so on, but competent settlers such as farmers, carpenters, masons, millers, and the like are much harder to find. I need your help, René, in identifying farmers for this trip."

The *sieur* was shocked. In March, he had assisted his son by helping him find farmers for the two vessels. He had even convinced several of his own tenants to join the venture, leaving idle farm plots on his estate. It now seemed the king expected him to find even more farmers, likely resulting in more idle plots. On the one hand, he resented this adverse intrusion into his business. On the other hand, he was pleased the king sought his help. He would do whatever it took to maintain the king's goodwill. "Yes, your majesty. I'm sure I can find competent farmers to help fill your ships."

# CHAPTER 3
# ACADIA

In 1603, Henry IV, King of France, granted patents to a Protestant nobleman, Pierre du Gua, *Sieur* de Monts, which named him viceroy and captain general on sea and land in La Cadie, Canada. La Cadie was the old Micmac Indian name for the area. La Cadie was soon referred to as Acadie by the early French settlers. The Micmac were, and continued to be, the dominant Indian tribe in Acadia. In the early 1600s, their numbers are estimated to have been 30,000 strong—much less in modern times, unfortunately.

Port Royal, on the Bay of Fundy in Acadia, was founded in 1604 by Pierre du Gua, Jean de Biencourt, *Sieur* de Poutrincourt, and Samuel de Champlain, the famed navigator and explorer. This initial group totaled seventy-five men, half of whom perished that first winter from exposure, malnutrition, and scurvy on St. Croix Island, at the mouth of the St. Croix River in Passamaquoddy Bay, Maine, on the western shore of the Bay of Fundy. They chose the island because they believed it would be easier to defend against the unknown and possibly hostile native people. The natives looked on in curiosity. They realized these white men would find it difficult to survive the winter on a small island lacking adequate resources. They would have gladly provided help. The white men, however, did not seem friendly, so they left them alone. Winters in Acadia proved to be longer and far harsher than those in France.

The following year, on May 13, 1606, the *Jonas* sailed from the port of La Rochelle, France, with forty men to replenish the fledgling colony that had moved from the unforgiving St. Croix Island to the much more promising Port Royal, on the eastern shore of the Bay of Fundy. That was seven months before the departure of English colonists for Jamestown, Virginia, and fourteen years before the landing of the *Mayflower* at Plymouth Rock. The French had a head start in settling the New World but were destined to squander it.

In 1613, the Virginia pirate Samuel Argall swept up from Jamestown and sacked and burned Port Royal. Acadia, as a French settlement, almost completely vanished until the end of the 1620s.

In 1621, King James of England granted to Sir William Alexander of Scotland all the territory between the St. Croix River and the Gaspé Peninsula, including the modern-day Nova Scotia Peninsula, Cape Breton Island, and Prince Edward Island. That France and England were not at war and the international community already recognized France as the legal owner of said lands made no difference to the English king. Like most important documents in those days, the new English grant was written in Latin and provided that Alexander's new domain should forever be known as *Nova Scotia* in America (New Scotland).

It took a while, however, for Sir Alexander to get his affairs in order. Not until 1628 was he finally able to resettle Port Royal with seventy-two men and two women, mostly from Scotland and England.

In 1632, under a new treaty between France and England, France regained clear title to Acadia. Louis XIII, King of France, then sent new settlers to Port Royal and evicted all the illegal Scottish settlers.

•   •   •

Charles de Menou d'Aulnay de Charnizay landed at Port Royal in May 1636 with his two hundred settlers. He was twenty-eight years old, single, tall and athletic, with blue eyes and blond hair. As he disembarked, he received an enthusiastic reception.

"Welcome, my friend!" said an imposing native man in French. "I am Pasquideux, grandson of the great Membertou, a long-time friend of your king. I am the leader of all the Micmac people in this area. I will now help you as my grandfather helped your French kinsmen. I grant you and your company permission to make your homes here. All the land as far as you can see belongs to me. If the English come here to disturb you, I will immediately have them removed."

Charles, not expecting this warmth, was taken aback. He was six feet tall, and the man before him was the same height. The man was well-muscled, with broad shoulders and narrow hips. Three leather pouches were strung around his neck. Several more pouches were tied to his waist. Charles saw that a French captain of the guard was standing about ten feet away, waiting his turn to address him. Pasquideux had about forty men with him—all armed with knives and hatchets, and some of them also carried European firearms. Those forty men, Charles knew, would be no match for a company of British regulars. What he didn't know was that Pasquideux could summon 400 such warriors on very short notice. Those warriors were all battle-hardened, having fought many battles against neighboring Indian tribes and even against the English. Before coming to Acadia, Charles was led to believe the natives were correctly referred to as savages. They did not believe in God and had no religion, no morals, and no ambition, other than killing and desecrating the bodies of their neighboring tribes. They could be helpful but were not to be trusted.

"Thank you for welcoming me," replied Charles. "I have some gifts for you onboard. Perhaps we can meet again later, once I am settled, and I can present them to you."

"You and your captains will join me tonight for a feast in my lodge," announced Pasquideux. "Your Captain Bastarache here knows this land well. He will show you the way to my village. *Adieu!*" And with that, Pasquideux and his men left the area.

"Welcome, governor," greeted Captain Leopaul Bastarache. "I hope you and Pasquideux can become good friends. He has been, and continues to be, most helpful to this struggling outpost. Without his help, many of us here would have surely perished this past winter."

"Thank you, captain! How many soldiers do you have under your command? And what is the total number of civilians here at Port Royal?"

"I have nine men under my command. The civilians comprise seventeen men and three wives. The three wives are Micmac women. The three married couples have eight children."

Charles was shocked at the small number. "I expected to find over one hundred French colonists here. What has become of them all?"

"Most left for either the fur trade or the fishery. Many of the men initially sent here are now in the fishing village at Canso, about two days sail from here. The two priests sent here left to minister to the natives."

"How safe are we here, and what exactly is the purpose of this outpost?"

"With Pasquideux nearby, we are quite safe, sir. Our primary purpose is to provide a protected place for the fur traders to store their pelts until they accumulate enough to fill a ship for return to France. We currently have enough pelts on-hand to fill about half a ship. Most of the civilians here sort and prepare the pelts for shipment. The three married families cultivate the land. Last year, we had about twelve acres planted. The fields are very productive. It seems whatever we plant does well. While your company disembarks, let me show you the grounds, buildings, and your quarters."

Pasquideux's village was about two miles south of the Port Royal outpost. Along with Captain Bastarache, Charles brought the captains of the two ships and Guillaume Trahan, a leader among the new colonists. As they approached the village, Charles saw it was surrounded by a stockade fence about eight feet tall. The fence served two purposes: to contain the young children within the compound so their mothers need not worry as the children played throughout the village, and to make it difficult for the wild beasts, both four-legged and two-legged, to enter the village. The entrance was guarded by two burly men. As he entered, Charles took note of the thirty or so wigwams surrounding a large lodge in the center of the compound. Each wigwam was a round hut constructed with arched poles, the base of which had a diameter of about twelve feet, with a ceiling about six feet high. Animal hides, mostly deer and moose, were sewn together and stretched over the poles. Each wigwam housed a family group of eight or nine people. The lodge was a significant structure that easily held over one hundred. It was circular in shape and built with poles and animal hides. The ceiling was twice as tall as any man, and it boasted plenty of light and excellent ventilation. It was larger than any structure at the Port Royal outpost.

"Welcome to my village," exclaimed Pasquideux. "Have you been to a Micmac village before today?"

"*Non,*" replied Charles. "This is my first day in this country."

"The wigwams you see here were designed over countless generations of Micmac to be the best possible housing structure for this land. When strong winds come, as they do every year, they blow harmlessly around our wigwams, unable to cause harm from any direction. Those same winds frequently take the roofs off your buildings. You would be wise to adopt the structure of our wigwams for your housing units. My grandfather made this same recommendation to Monsieur Poutrincourt and Samuel de Champlain many years ago, but I have yet to see a single French-built wigwam." Pasquideux smiled and continued, "I understand your reluctance to switch and am not offended. Your housing unit also evolved over many generations. I wish you well with your homes!"

"I am impressed with the efficient design of your village," replied Charles. "It seems like a wonderful place to spend the summer."

Captain Bastarache had informed Charles that Pasquideux's group of Micmac came together at Port Royal every summer, and then left in the fall for their winter quarters. Many other groups of Micmac basically followed the same process. They came together and spent the summer near the large rivers and bays. In the fall, they broke into smaller family units and returned to their winter quarters deep in the woods.

Charles presented Pasquideux with the gifts he had brought: a finely engraved knife, a hatchet, about twenty steel arrowheads, three wool blankets, and a large copper cooking pot. "I hope these gifts will please you," said Charles.

"I am pleased," replied Pasquideux. "Thank you, my friend. These are wonderful gifts!"

•   •   •

The Micmac had been trading with various white groups: Basque, Spanish, French, Portuguese, and English for well over one hundred years. All these groups arrived every spring to fish for cod on the nearby Grand Banks, the most productive fishery in the world. The cod was split and dried on wooden racks on shore. Late in the season, if there was not enough time to dry the cod, it was salted and stored in barrels to prevent it from spoiling. The ships then returned to their home ports in the fall with their holds filled with dried or salted cod. But before they left, when the fishermen were on shore drying the cod, the natives contacted them.

The Micmac traded furs to the white men for metal products and textiles. Watching those strange invaders, something soon became clear to them. The white groups were often at war with each other. The Micmac themselves were no strangers to war; they often fought with the neighboring Abenaki, Mohawk, or Iroquois. But Pasquideux's grandfather decided that, to become stronger, his people needed to ally themselves with one of these white groups over all the others, but which one? All the groups came ashore to dry their fish, but none ventured inland until the French arrived at Port Royal in 1604. Pasquideux's grandfather was pleased and decided then and there to ally his people with the French. The Micmac depended now on the French for a continuing supply of manufactured products. Those goods made life much easier for the Micmac. The French benefitted by having a strong ally in place, and of course, the continuing source of valuable furs.

The early French colonists consisted entirely of men, many of whom married native women. Those blood alliances further strengthened the bond between the French and the Micmac. The offspring of those alliances were referred to as Métis, which is the French word for mixed or half-breed. The Métis are one of three recognized indigenous peoples in Canada, along with the First Nations and Inuit. Canada's 2016 Census of Population resulted in over 580,000 Canadians self-identifying as Métis.

·  ·  ·

As they entered the lodge, Charles was impressed with its spaciousness and at the amount and variety of food assembled. There was venison, turkey, cod, salmon, trout, lobster, and crab, as well as other shellfish and many assorted vegetables, both fresh and dried. What was missing was furniture of any kind. The floor was covered with fine animal skins. The food was on platters on the floor down the center of the lodge. Pasquideux guided Charles to the two seats of honor, one for each of them. These seats faced each other and were on the floor, like all the others, but featured large rolled-up bearskins that served as backrests.

"Thank you again for the wonderful gifts," said Pasquideux while holding the copper cooking pot. The Micmac had received many such copper pots over the years. But it was unlikely that one, other than the one he now held, could be found in any Micmac village. The warriors cut the copper pots into small pieces that were then fashioned into arrowheads. The traditional stone arrowheads of the Micmac were effective and deadly but very labor intensive. In the same time it took a warrior to produce ten stone arrowheads, he could produce over one hundred from a large copper cooking pot. Charles did not know that when Pasquideux gazed at the pot, he did not see a fine stew simmering over a fire. He saw arrowheads.

"I will return the favor this fall with provisions to assist you in getting through the winter. To survive in this land, much of the summer must be used to prepare for the winter. My men will hunt deer and moose all summer. The meat will then be cut into small strips and dried in the sun. We will do the same thing for the fish that we catch. All summer, the women will gather other foods from off the land. Mushrooms, berries, and other edibles will be dried and stored in large deerskin sacks and taken with us to our winter compound. Wild carrots and onions are very plentiful, if you know where to look. And near our winter quarters are many nut trees: chestnut, beechnut, hickory, and others. We gather these and store them in large deerskin sacks. We never consume all the nuts. We leave some in the bottom of the sacks and, in the spring, we add a little water. Soon they sprout and we plant them in our winter range. The oak trees provide us with acorns. They are the most plentiful of all the nut trees. Raw acorns are very bitter, and just a few will make you very sick, but if they are prepared properly, they are sweet with a nice nutty flavor, and you can then eat as many as you like."

"I have much to learn," replied Charles. "I will appreciate whatever help you can provide to assist my new colony to survive and grow." Charles was amazed at how well adapted these native people were to their land, more so, he thought, than many Frenchmen. After just one day, they no longer seemed like savages but simply very different. That was a distinction that not only appealed to his imagination but agreed with what he had already learned about the human tendency to judge. He no longer believed what he had initially been told about the Micmac. He was in a new land, in a new position. He would pay attention and make up his own mind about things.

As the feast was ending, a Micmac messenger arrived and spoke in hushed tones to Pasquideux, who soon became agitated. He moved away from the food and summoned his counselors to join him. Together, they discussed this new matter and within a few minutes arrived at what appeared to be a unanimous decision. All the counselors left the lodge. Pasquideux returned to his seat and informed Charles that the Abenaki had attacked a Micmac village across the bay and killed two men and a woman. Raids between the Abenaki and Micmac near their border were quite common. These raids usually resulted in supplies and perhaps even a canoe or two being stolen. They were typically conducted by young men coming of age, a sort of rite-of-passage, and were tolerated by both sides, providing no one was seriously injured. It was therefore rare for anyone to be killed during such a raid.

"My men and I will leave tonight to avenge this attack," said Pasquideux. "I'm sorry this feast to welcome you must end on such a sour note. I wish you and your company well and will see you again in a few days." With that, Pasquideux left the lodge.

As Charles was returning to the Port Royal outpost, he noticed several good-sized sailing vessels tied up on shore. Two of them were being readied. "Captain Bastarache," he said, "do those belong to the Micmac?"

"Yes, they do," Bastarache said. "The Micmac were quick to adopt our sailing vessels as their own and have been sailing for many years. Their vessels, of course, are much smaller than ours but can each easily hold twenty men plus their supplies. They use them on the bays and open ocean, but they still use birchbark canoes on the smaller rivers and lakes."

The following morning, after spending the night aboard the ships, the passengers again disembarked. Charles gave orders for the fruit trees to be brought to shore. The previous evening, he had met with Trahan and several other leaders among the colonists to determine how best to allocate the farm plots and fruit trees. They had transported about forty young fruit trees, mostly several varieties of apple, but also some pear and plum trees. The plan was to create an orchard near the outpost with ten trees. The other thirty would then be divided among the farmers. The farm animals they brought—sheep, cattle, oxen, and chickens—would be kept in a central location until they could multiply. Their offspring would then be allocated to the farmers.

"Trahan, as we discussed last night, you and your men will mark off fifty farm plots with the stakes we brought with us. Each plot should contain about twenty acres of land, including several acres of woods."

"Yes, governor," said Trahan.

Charles now directed his attention to the assembled carpenters and masons. "I need you to prepare corrals for the sheep, cattle, and oxen. All these are young and still small, so the initial corrals need not be overly large. You can increase the size of the corrals later when the animals gain weight. And we'll need an enclosure for the chickens. The existing buildings here need repairs to make them habitable. Once repaired, we can begin moving people off the ships. After the corrals and existing buildings, I want you to build housing units on the marked-off farm plots. All the houses should be about fifty feet from the woods. We can then build a straight road to run between the woods and all the houses."

"Thank you, sir, we will make you proud of our work," replied Joseph Theriault, the leader of the skilled workmen.

Charles next met Captain Bastarache. The old fort was in ruins and had been abandoned many years ago. "Captain, why hasn't this fort been rebuilt?"

"It's location here is not optimal," replied the captain. "The fort's cannons were no match for those of the English ship that entered the basin and destroyed the fort."

"What do you suggest to defend this colony properly?"

"We need a much larger fort with more and larger cannons. We need a sub-fort with additional cannons to control the entrance to the basin. As you know, the entrance is quite narrow and over a mile from here. A few strategically placed cannons of sufficient size could easily control the entrance and discourage all enemy ships from entering. Ideally, we should do both."

•   •   •

Pasquideux took twenty-five men with him and was met with twenty more from the Micmac village that was attacked. When they reached the Abenaki village, they found it had been hastily abandoned and several wigwams were left behind. It took a full day to catch up to the fleeing Abenaki a group of about seventy individuals—including men, women, and children.

The first Micmac weapon to find its mark was a copper-tipped arrow that entered the back of an Abenaki and went through his heart. Pasquideux was in a fury, and his hatchet caught an Abenaki in the neck with a mortal blow. His next swing severed an Abenaki's forearm. As he was about to strike another man standing before him, two Micmac arrows entered the man's chest, killing him. A woman, protecting her three small children, made the fatal mistake of brandishing a knife. A hatchet-blow to her neck nearly severed her head. It flopped to one side—a bit of skin and neck muscle kept it from leaving her body as her children were sprayed with her blood. Two other women with knives met similar ends. The battle was over in a few minutes. The remaining women and children were spared. The Abenakis fought bravely, but their men were outnumbered and no match for the Micmac warriors.

Pasquideux saw the terror in the eyes of the children. He knew they were now scarred forever. When they themselves became warriors, they would remember this day and take their vengeance on the Micmac. But Pasquideux had no solution for the dilemma. It was how it had always been. Blood led to more blood. Every time he vanquished his enemy in battle, his immediate euphoria was soon followed by an emptiness of spirit that accompanied the violent deaths. It was his way of life. He reminded himself it was what men do, that there was no other way to be a man. Before leaving the area, the Micmac performed one further act of terror. They scalped all the Abenaki dead, including the three women. The scalps were then attached to the Micmac waists—a sign of bravery and success in battle.

The Micmac gathered all the steel knives and hatchets and took several sacks of food from the Abenaki. Among their own casualties were one dead and five wounded. The worst of the wounds was an Abenaki arrow embedded in a Micmac shoulder.

Besides being the leader of his people, Pasquideux was a renowned medicine man. His grandfather and father before him had been medicine men. The knowledge of medicinal plants, common and not-so-common ailments and their cures, was passed down from generation to generation, usually in the same family.

About two miles away from the battle scene, the Micmac tended to their wounded. When the arrow was pushed through the man's shoulder, Pasquideux noted the arrowhead was stone. It was removed, and the shaft was then pulled back out of the shoulder. The wounds were cauterized with a heated knife, and Pasquideux applied a poultice from one of his leather pouches to each side of the shoulder. These were tied with several thin leather straps that were wound around the man's chest. Pasquideux then brought another leather pouch to the man's lips. It contained dried powder made from the inner bark of the willow tree. The man was given water and made to swallow a good quantity of the powder. The poultice would prevent infection while the willow powder, modern-day aspirin, would reduce pain and inflammation.

•   •   •

It took all day for Trahan and his men to measure and mark-off the fifty plots, in part for the thirty-one farm families aboard the two ships. The three mixed couples said they were satisfied with the land they now farmed and just asked if it could be divided into three parts and assigned to them.

The following day, Charles assembled all the colonists before him.

"Today, we will assign the farm plots at random. Each head of household will pick a slip of paper from this container. The slip will provide you with your plot number. Jean LeBlanc will record your name and plot number in this journal."

Jean LeBlanc, the former tenant of Charles's father, was one of the few colonists who could read and write, hence his assignment as the scribe.

# CHAPTER 4
# THE DEPARTURE

The *sieur* addressed his tenants, who were now assembled in front of his chateau. "The king has decided to expand his colony in Acadia and has recently appointed my son, Charles, as the governor-general for this new colony. For those of you interested, the king promises large farm plots and no rents for five years to any new colonists."

The *sieur* then introduced Monsieur Louis Hébert, one of the king's scientists who specialized in agriculture and was very familiar with Acadia. Hébert stated he was in Acadia thirty years ago with Monsieur Poutrincourt and Samuel de Champlain, that the climate there was like the one in France, and the land was well-drained with many rivers and very productive. He explained he was there for over two years and conducted many agricultural experiments. Near their outpost at Port Royal, he planted wheat, cabbages, turnips, and several other crops. All of them exceeded his expectations. The wheat, for example, he said, grew thirty percent taller than theirs in France with much fuller heads. The following year, he planted the same crops in the same place adding no fertilizer. To his surprise, all those crops were as good as the first year. This spoke to the excellent fertility of the land.

"How much forest needs to be cleared?" a tenant asked.

"And what about rocks in the soil?"

Hébert responded, "There is no forest to clear. The bays and the rivers that empty into the bays are bordered by very large meadows as far as the eye can see. These meadows produce a thick, luxurious grass that would quickly fatten your farm animals. And the soil in the meadows is devoid of rocks. In several places, I was able to dig down over three feet before hitting any rocks."

The tenants talked among themselves. Could it be that good?

"I have one more question," one of them said. "I've heard about savages in this new land. How safe will we be?" The group grew silent. Given their current situation, safety was a very real concern.

Hébert cleared his throat. "The native people in Acadia belong to the Micmac nation and are, by nature, a very gentle people. They love the French colonists and assist them in every way. Many of them speak French and have converted to our Catholic religion. I assure you; the colonists have nothing to fear from the native population."

Padé Robichaud, the not-so-happy tenant farmer, was very excited. This opportunity seemed to be exactly what he was looking for—a chance to farm his own land. He looked at his wife and declared, "We will volunteer for this opportunity and make our home in Acadia."

His wife's face was knit with concern. "Are you sure, Padé? I will follow your decision, but we will have no family there to help us."

Before he could respond, the *sieur* continued. "The king is readying two vessels for departure near the end of this month. And the king has furthermore stated that any colonists in Acadia who are not satisfied after three years may return to France at no cost to themselves. And I will make my own promise to you. If any of you volunteer and then decide to return, I will provide you with farm plots. If not here, then on one of my other nearby estates."

"But by the time the vessels arrive in Acadia, it will be too late to plant crops. How will we survive the winter?"

"You are thinking well," the *sieur* replied. "The vessels will have enough food and supplies to see you through the first winter. In addition, the king had recruited many carpenters, masons, millers, and other tradesmen for this voyage. They will assist you farmers in building houses and other structures and making this new colony a success. Please return to your homes," said the *sieur*, "and discuss this matter among yourselves. Later today, my men will come to each of your homes to see if you are interested."

As the tenants began leaving, one of the *sieur*'s men approached Jean-Claude and said the *sieur* would like a word with him. Jean-Claude immediately doubled over slightly. He felt as if he'd just been gut punched. He had never been summoned by the *sieur*.

• • •

"Landry, you have been one of my best tenants for many years, and I hope you will remain one for many more," said the *sieur*.

"Thank you, my lord," replied Jean-Claude.

"I know that your stepson, François, is your right arm and a big reason for your success. I know he is now a grown man and in need of his own farm plot. I can think of no better opportunity for him than to join this voyage to Acadia. As I mentioned earlier, if he's not satisfied with Acadia, he may return in three years."

Jean-Claude was alarmed at the interest the *Sieur* took in his family. He managed a very soft, "Thank you again, my lord. I will discuss this matter with François as soon as I get home."

When Jean-Claude arrived home, he gathered everyone around the kitchen table and informed them of his conversation with the *sieur*.

Marie spoke first. "Why did he single you out? It seems he specifically wants François to join this voyage, but why? Why François over any other tenant from his estate? It makes little sense!"

"I don't know," replied Jean-Claude. "I was shocked when he summoned me and then further stunned when he mentioned François by name."

"I, too, am at a loss," said François. "I'm surprised the *sieur* even knows my name."

Marie then said, "We must be very careful with our response. His men will be here soon. We must decide what to say. Jean-Claude, was there any sign from the *sieur* that he knew François and Yvette plan to marry soon?"

"*Non*, there was no such sign."

François spoke up. "After the wedding, Yvette and I hoped the *sieur* would grant us our own farm plot. We would prefer to remain nearby, but how can that happen now? Before today, I had never heard of Acadia. I prefer to remain here, but I do not want to cause any harm to my family."

François was clearly not happy with this change of plans. "Before today, I'd been reasonably certain the *sieur* would grant me and Yvette a nearby plot of our own. I am certain Yvette and I would succeed on the estate. But I fear that is no longer a possibility. Acadia appears now to be our destiny." Anxiety was written all over his face.

"But what of the sea?" Marie said. "The savages? The strange new world?" She reached out a hand to her first born, and Jean-Claude put his hand on her shoulder.

Jean-Claude could almost read the thoughts in his stepson's features. They shared a deep contentment of a good harvest, family around them, the way every dip in the land, every cluster of trees was known to them. What would it be like to live without that? Then something rippled across François' face, fear perhaps? Excitement?

"I don't know, Father. I've never contemplated such a gigantic change in fortune, and I can't even imagine all the dangers, or all the opportunities." He shuddered.

The three sat in silence for some time, but gradually François sat up straighter, and his whole demeanor calmed. Jean-Claude noticed the change that came over him, but Marie was not watching her son's face, struggling with her own fears.

"To defy the *sieur* is a major risk, but I cannot agree with sending any of my children to Acadia or any other faraway colony," said Marie.

"Mama, I know nothing of Acadia, but I will go there to keep the rest of you safe here on this estate. Certainly, there is a scary element to this move, but I am confident I can make the most of this upheaval. I must inform Yvette. She and her father may decide to call off the wedding when they hear of Acadia. I love her, but with or without her, I will go to Acadia. Protecting this family is of top importance to me."

•   •   •

"François Aucoin and my wife, the former Yvette Béliveau," said François to the ship's agent in mid-May 1636 as they boarded the *Saint-Joseph* for transport to Acadia. Their belongings included a kitchen table with two chairs from Yvette's father, two feather pillows made by Yvette, three wool blankets, two bed sheets, and some towels, plus various dishes and kitchen utensils given to them by François's parents. The ship's crew stored the larger items securely in the ship's hold, and the agent informed François as to his living space in another part of the hold.

Seventeen family groups had been assigned to that part of the ship. Besides the passengers, quite a few farm animals were aboard: sheep, pigs, cattle, oxen, chickens, and geese. On their way to their living space, François and Yvette noticed many young fruit trees had just been delivered to the ship.

"I'm so happy Padé and his wife are coming on this voyage," said Yvette. "I wish they could have been assigned to the *Saint-Joseph* like us."

Yvette loved François and knew he was the right man for her. She would follow him wherever he led rather than be left behind. Acadia, however, stirred her worst fears. Acadia meant wilderness, savages, untold hardships. Her husband might die in some way she couldn't even picture, or she might die far from her parents and siblings. She had always known she might die giving birth, as women did, but when she imagined such a thing, her mother was there, her priest was there. She had set her mind from an early age to marry a good man, a good provider, and raise her family in a secure environment, where if misfortune struck, her family would help. She was now faced with a forbidding Acadia, and she had many doubts. But François was determined, and she would stand by François.

"Yes," replied François, "it's a shame they were assigned to the other ship, but at least we'll all be together in Acadia. It will be nice to have some family there."

The passage across the Atlantic took six weeks, and fortunately no major storms hampered their voyage. The crossing was calmer and more pleasant than usual. Many of the passengers, however, still became seasick. Some became sick on day one and stayed sick for the entire voyage. Every available container was quickly filled to overflowing with vomit. The sickly smells permeated the entire hold. Those passengers who were able carried the containers up on deck and dumped the contents overboard. As soon as the containers came back down, they were quickly filled again. Yvette became sick early in the voyage and stayed sick for eight days whereas François stayed well. He tended to her as best he could. When Yvette finally felt better, she said, "François, promise me if Acadia is at all livable, we will remain there. I never want to cross this ocean again!"

An unexpected benefit from all the seasickness was that plenty of food was available for anyone who wanted it. The seasick passengers ate very little, and even after recovering, they continued to eat very little for fear of getting sick again. The ship's cook kept a large pot of soup simmering on the stove in the galley. The soup was thick with some meat and many vegetables and quickly became François' favorite. He ate several bowls every day and never tired of it. The cook baked bread every other day, and the smell of fresh baked bread was wonderful. While growing up, François never went to bed hungry. They always had enough to eat but no excess—just enough. Here, there was more than enough, and François was fascinated and very appreciative. He and Yvette spent as much time as possible on deck with its fresh air, or in the galley, with its delicious aromas from the kitchen.

The two ships arrived at Port Royal together on June 30, 1636. When François and Yvette finally disembarked, they saw Padé walking towards them. He was pale, unsteady on his feet, and had lost a lot of weight.

It was easy to agree that returning to France and enduring another sea voyage was not an option for them. This new land would become their home, and they were determined to learn all they could about this new place. Possessing the right skills to earn a living from the land and being young and healthy, success was the most likely outcome. And, most importantly, helping each other would become a way of life. Based on their abilities and force of will, they were determined to not only survive, but prosper.

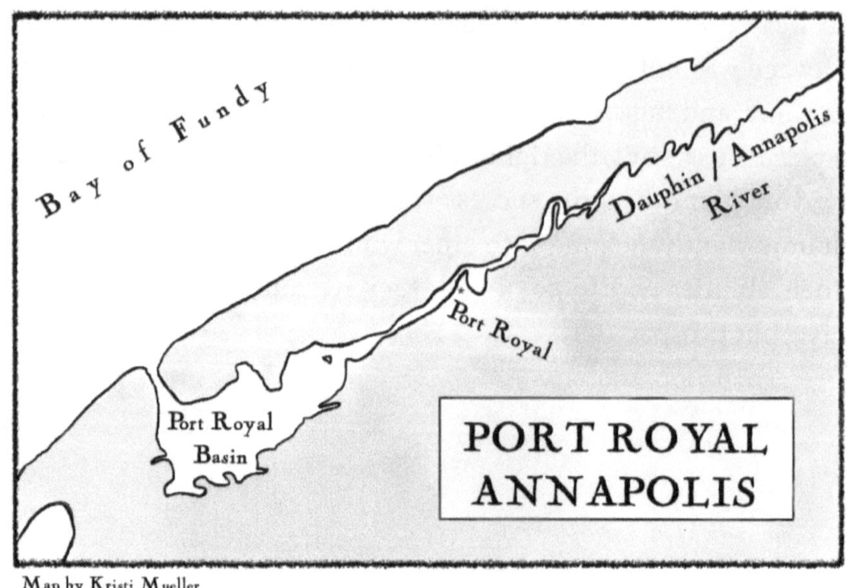


Map by Kristi Mueller

# CHAPTER 5
# PORT ROYAL

When the *Saint-Joseph* and its sister ship docked at Port Royal, Charles was there to greet the new colonists. He welcomed them and informed them their houses were in the final stages of being built. They would be moved into their new quarters as soon as possible. In the meantime, he invited them to explore the new settlement.

After visiting all the nearby buildings, François wanted to visit an occupied farm plot. The closest one was about a quarter of a mile away, so he and Yvette headed that way. When they arrived at the house, a woman with two small boys came out to greet them. François saw that the woman's husband, who had been working in the fields, was headed their way. The man was in his mid-twenties, of average height and weight, with a ruddy complexion. He seemed happy to have visitors.

After exchanging greetings, François asked the man how it was working on this farm plot.

Excited and pleased to describe his efforts, the man said, "The land seems to be very productive. The wheat I planted is already several inches taller than I would expect at this time. So far, I have about five acres planted, half in wheat and half in turnips. Everything is going well. The fertility of the land is amazing. I have not yet added any fertilizer, and you can see how well everything is growing."

"Yes, you have certainly done well. How large is your plot?"

"I have about twenty acres. It includes several acres of woods over there, above the road, and then all this broad meadow down to the high-water mark on the bay. All the plots seem to be about the same size, and each plot includes a fruit tree. I planted mine next to the house. So far, it's doing well."

François didn't want to offend the man, but he noticed much of the plot was not planted. He nodded toward the uncultivated area, "Is that part yours?"

"Yes. We got a late start this spring. I was only able to prepare five acres in time for planting. Next year, I intend to have my entire plot planted. As I'm sure you know, it's now too late for planting. When you get your plot, I suggest you turn over the soil closest to the high-water mark first. The grass is not as thick there, so it's much easier to work the soil."

"Thank you. My wife and I have much to do and much to learn about this new land."

"One other thing, in case you have not yet noticed. The tides here are enormous. Whereas in France, the difference between high tide and low tide might average about six feet, the difference here is well over forty. At low tide, six or seven more acres of land will become exposed below the high-water mark of your plot. The exposed land is loaded with several varieties of clams. If you decide to dig the clams, be careful not to venture too far down from the high-water mark. The tide comes back quickly, and it's easy to become stuck in the mud. A family further down the bay lost their eight-year-old son to the tide. The boy and his father were digging clams, maybe a little too excited by the bounty, and didn't notice the tide was coming back. They were about ten feet apart and both stuck in the mud. By the time the father freed himself, the water was already up to his chest and rising quickly. He couldn't see his son and just barely saved himself. The boy's body was never found."

"That's terrible!" said Yvette. "The parents must be devastated!" François could tell Yvette was shaken to the core by this sad story and put his arm around her. Losing babies was sadly common, but to lose an eight-year-old child was unthinkable. Yvette looked into his eyes. "No such tragedy will ever happen to one of our children. We must teach our children about these dangers—dangers of the sea, its tides and whatever other perils this land holds."

François nodded. There was so much to learn.

"Yes, this tragedy happened over a month ago and the entire community was, and remains, devastated. Even the chief of the local Micmac Indians visited the family and offered his condolences."

"Does the chief speak French?" asked François.

"Yes, his name is Pasquideux, and although I've never spoken with him, I've heard he speaks French well. The Micmac are friendly. I'm not aware of anyone having any problems with them."

•    •    •

Pasquideux was in his lodge in the middle of a war council. Two of his top lieutenants requested the council which, besides Pasquideux, included five lieutenants and three village elders. Sasniwah, his top lieutenant, was the first to speak.

"The arrival of these two ships with more colonists is unacceptable! We must attack and drive these foreigners away from our land. Soon they will overrun the land and force us away from our camp and hunting grounds."

"Your words are true and spoken from the heart," replied Pasquideux, "but attacking the French is not the answer. Our survival as a nation depends on our alliance with them."

"Our survival!" exclaimed Sasniwah. "You seem to forget it's the French that brought smallpox, measles, plague, and many other new diseases that have killed many of our people. We have lost skilled warriors to these diseases and must act now before we lose any more."

"I agree our people have suffered greatly from these new diseases. But if not from the French, the diseases would have surely come from the English, Spanish, or other groups that now frequent our shores. We cannot compete successfully against the warships and iron of the white man. My grandfather knew for our people to survive as a nation, we needed to ally ourselves with one of these white groups. As you all know, he chose the French."

"Not all of us believe in this strategy. There are many warriors who would gladly kill the French and all other foreigners to regain our land."

"The French are a means to an end," replied Pasquideux. "And, as you all know, the French have readily married our women, and many such mixed families now live in our villages. Three of these families even live at Port Royal with the French. These marriages are accepted on both sides and help to strengthen the bond between our people and the French. The Abenaki, by comparison, are frequently at war with the Bostonians on their border. There is no alliance there and no marriages. To survive, the Abenaki will eventually need to join our alliance with the French."

The war council continued its deliberations for several more hours. The issue at hand was whether to evict all French from Micmac lands. As was their custom, a vote on the matter was not taken until each council member had his say. When the vote was finally taken, Sasniwah's proposal was defeated, which ended the matter. Had his proposal been approved, Pasquideux would have been required to form a grand council that included all the Micmac villages. The grand council would then take up Sasniwah's proposal and, after due deliberations, would vote on the matter. The vote of the grand council would be binding on all the Micmac.

•  •  •

François and Yvette settled well into their new home. Their assigned plot was easy to work and quite fertile. All the crops they planted—wheat, cabbage, beets, turnips, carrots, and more—thrived. At low tide, they were able to gather many clams and other shellfish – a good source of fresh protein along with the plentiful fish in the bays and rivers. Padé's plot was less than a mile away, and the two couples often visited each other.

Neither François nor Yvette could read or write, but after their first year in Acadia, they wrote to their parents with the help of Jean LeBlanc, the local scribe, one of the few colonists who could do so. They told their parents of the large, fertile plots, of the bountiful harvests, plentiful fish, and the friendly Indians.

Two years later, in 1640, François and Yvette were surprised to see François's mother, stepfather and all their children arrive in Port Royal.

"Mama, I'm so happy to see you and all the family, but how is it possible you are here?"

François' mother was forty-three years old, his stepfather forty-four. No longer young but in good health, they still had many good years ahead of them. The letter they received from François and Yvette extolling the benefits of Port Royal got them thinking. Their *sieur* was under constant pressure from the king to find farmers for Acadia, and the *sieur*'s tactics to find volunteers became more aggressive. As a result, life on the estate became less pleasant as their friends and neighbors moved to Acadia. The final straw was when the *Sieur* increased his percentage of the harvest. Jean-Claude said to Marie, "Do you miss François?"

"Why do you ask? You know I do."

"I think we should go to Acadia. It sounds like the land where a man can get ahead."

Marie did not argue. She had never imagined adventure would be part of her life, but now that it was, she found herself happy. Her son's letter had stirred a deep curiosity about this New World—and, of course, she missed him.

The following year, in the spring of 1641, François' sister, Michelle Aucoin, married Michel Boudrot, and in 1648, François' other sister, Jeanne Aucoin, married François Girouard. These newlyweds, as well as many others, quickly established their own households further up the tidal rivers of Port Royal.

•　　•　　•

In 1638, on one of his return voyages to France, Charles married Jeanne Motin, the daughter of a prominent, well-to-do, family in France. They had eight children, four boys and four girls, and lived in a large house near the renovated fort in Port Royal. As recommended by Captain Bastarache, Charles increased the size of the fort and armed it with more and larger cannons. He maintained good relations with Pasquideux and the Micmac, considering Pasquideux a good friend who he frequently invited into his home. For reasons unknown to Charles, Pasquideux moved his summer quarters from the Port Royal area to Beaubassin, about one hundred miles further up the Bay of Fundy. When Charles questioned the move, Pasquideux's answer was vague. He mentioned the need for a change of scenery, better hunting grounds, and easier contact with other Micmac groups. He didn't mention that some of his people saw the growing French presence at Port Royal as a threat to the Micmac way of life.

•　　•　　•

"It's good we moved our summer quarters here," said one of Pasquideux's lieutenants. "Port Royal is far too crowded with whites, and their fort is an affront to our sovereignty. I understand we must maintain good relations with them, but we need not share the same space."

"I agree," replied Pasquideux. "Their leader, Charles, is a good man and a good ally. Our two peoples have much in common, but there are many differences. It's best if we live apart."

Pasquideux would have preferred to keep his summer quarters in Port Royal. He enjoyed his relationship with Charles. Pasquideux was married with four children of his own, and he especially liked bringing his wife and children to Charles' house for dinner. The whites cooked differently, and though his wife criticized their cuisine, he found it an interesting change. He also liked to hear Charles talk about France with its stone castles and old cities. He was aware, however, of the uneasiness his people felt with so many whites around. His oldest son, Pasquitrois, was now thirteen, well accustomed with the French and destined to take over leadership of the Micmac. Pasquideux's wish was that his son would not only continue the alliance with the French but strengthen it.

•   •   •

"Sir, will you be gone long?" asked Charles's assistant. "You have an appointment this afternoon with Monsieur Trahan. His proposal to dike more land further up the Dauphin River needs your approval."

"I'll be back in plenty of time. It's such a pleasant day I'll take the canoe up the Dauphin to see this new land for myself."

The Dauphin was the main river that emptied into the Port Royal basin. As Charles paddled up the river, he was fascinated to see a family of beavers cutting aspen trees on the shore and taking them up a brook that emptied into the Dauphin. As he watched them, he failed to see the log coming down the Dauphin that slammed into and overturned his canoe. The water was very cold and deep, and Charles was not a good swimmer.

Charles de Menou d'Aulnay de Charnizay, Governor of Acadia, drowned in the spring of 1650. He was forty-six years old. At about the same time, smallpox broke out in Pasquideux's village. This outbreak killed about one third of the villagers, including Pasquideux himself. His son, Pasquitrois survived. After Charles's death, considerable infighting occurred among various French nobles as to who should take over as governor of Acadia. In 1651, the king finally appointed Charles de la Tour as governor. La Tour married Charles' widow, Jeanne Motin. His reign, however, was short-lived. In 1654, the New Englanders attacked Acadia and took over control. By this time, François and Yvette were well established on their farm plot.

•  •  •

"The wheat seems to be doing even better this year than last and last year was the best ever," said Yvette as she and François sat on their porch one evening overlooking the refulgent Dauphin River valley.

"This is fine country," replied François. "A young land, not worn out as France is becoming. After building the dikes to hold back the tide, our plot grew from twenty acres to almost twenty-four. Did you ever imagine we would own twenty-four acres of such productive land?"

The Acadian dikes were built differently than any in Europe. These dikes, for example, had one-way tunnels built into them. The tunnels had a clapper on the bay side that allowed water to drain from the meadows back into the bay but snapped shut when the tide came back. After several years of rain and snowmelt to flush the salt back into the bay, the reclaimed land was then ready to plant. Building the dikes was a community project. All able-bodied Acadians assisted in this effort, which benefitted the whole. This community effort, their reliance on extended family, their knowledge of the Micmac way of reaching village-wide decisions, and their own experience with self-governance helped shape these French colonists into a new Acadian people.

Besides his twenty-four acres, François owned eight sheep, two cows, some pigs and chickens and an ox to help plow the land and pull his wagon. His orchard contained six apple trees, two pear trees and three plum trees. He had a large barn to house the animals and hay over the winter. They had six children—three boys and three girls. The oldest was Pierre, seventeen years old. Next came the three girls—

Louise, fifteen; Pauline, twelve; and Marcelle, ten. The middle boy was Martin, born in 1651, now three years old. The youngest was one-year-old Joseph.

One beautiful spring morning, Yvette said, "That looks like Padé riding his horse towards us."

"Yes," replied François. "I'll bring another chair out for him."

When Padé arrived, however, he had no time to socialize. He quickly delivered his grim message. "Trahan wants every head of household to meet at his barn tomorrow by mid-morning. The English have taken over control of all of Acadia and demand that all Acadians sign an oath of allegiance. We will discuss this matter in the morning at Trahan's. I must go now to inform the others." And with that, he quickly galloped away.

"The English in control? How is that possible?" exclaimed Yvette.

"I don't know. I was not aware any new conflict had developed with the English. Last week, when I delivered produce to the garrison at the fort and stopped by the village store, no one said anything about a conflict."

•   •   •

When François arrived at Trahan's barn the next morning, he saw that most of the Acadian heads of household were already there, including his good friend Leopaul Bastarache. After his military term was over, Leopaul remained at Port Royal instead of returning to France. He then married Ethel Doucet, a young widow whose husband had died a year earlier. They now had eight children. Leopaul was highly regarded in the community. As a former captain of the guard at the fort, he had dealt closely with the governor and therefore had a broader view of affairs impacting Acadia. He was also one of the few men in the colony who could read and write.

After greeting him, François asked, "Leopaul, do you know how the English are now in control?"

"I know very little, but it seems the English force that overwhelmed us was made up entirely of New Englanders. No one has seen any British warships or British regulars."

Guillaume Trahan now addressed the assembled Acadians.

"As you have all heard, the English are now in control of Acadia. Governor de la Tour surrendered Port Royal without firing a shot after he heard that all other French outposts in Acadia had already surrendered. Yesterday, I met with Major Sedgwick, the English commander. He says we can remain here and continue to practice our religion unmolested, providing we each sign an oath of allegiance stating we will not bear arms against the English. The penalty for anyone who violates this oath is death. Anyone who refuses to sign the oath will be forced to return to France. A ship is now being readied to return de la Tour, his officials, and his soldiers to France. Any of us may join that ship."

"If we stay here, what can we really expect from the English?" someone asked.

"Major Sedgwick seemed sincere. He wishes us no harm, only that we continue to farm peacefully on our land."

François, like the other Acadians, was alarmed at the English takeover. He had never forgotten the burning of his home and crops in France at the hands of the English. If need be, he was ready to fight for his family and land. He couldn't understand why de la Tour surrendered without firing a single shot. Had he stood his ground, the Acadians and Micmac would have come to his aid. Perhaps the French were not entirely on the side of the Acadians. They, in fact, abandoned the Acadians to the English. François knew he couldn't always trust the men in charge—his stepfather had had a good relationship with the *sieur* but trod carefully around him. "Trust in God," his mother always said. "Trust in family," said his stepfather.

After another hour or so of deliberations, all the Acadians agreed to sign the oath. No one wanted to return to France. After eighteen years in Acadia, they knew their standard of living was considerably higher than that of the tenant farmers in France.

•   •   •

The English controlled Acadia for the next sixteen years, from 1654 to 1670. Other than a small English force stationed at the fort, there was very little change for the Acadians at Port Royal. They quickly grew accustomed to governing themselves. They found that trading with the New Englanders was much more convenient and profitable than trading with the French had been. The New Englanders were eager to purchase Acadian wheat and cattle as well as other farm products. In return, the Acadians received many goods they could not produce themselves such as cooking pots, needles and thread, cotton clothing, gunpowder, firearms, and rum. Almost every week, a New England trading ship arrived at Port Royal.

By 1670, François and Yvette's two oldest sons, Pierre and Martin, had each started their own farms side-by-side, directly across the river from their parents' farm. The three daughters were married and on their own new farms further up the Dauphin River. The remaining son, eighteen-year-old Joseph, lived at home with François and Yvette and would take over the family farm.

Joseph rushed into the house early one morning. "It looks like Uncle Padé's son, Roger, is riding towards us in a hurry."

Just as François and Yvette came outside, Roger Robichaud rode up and breathlessly said, "The French have taken over control of Acadia and the English garrison has left Port Royal. Monsieur Trahan wants every head of household to come to his barn tomorrow by mid-morning so we may discuss this matter."

"*Sainte Marie!*" exclaimed Yvette, as Roger galloped away. "Now that we are used to the English, they are gone! I hope the new French governor will be as easy to deal with."

Soon after François arrived at Trahan's barn the next day, he saw that his two oldest sons and his brother-in-law, François Girouard, were together and discussing this matter. He joined them, but it soon became obvious no one knew anything regarding this new development.

Trahan then addressed the assembled Acadians. "Yesterday afternoon, the English commander at the fort summoned me and informed me that France and England had agreed whereby France gave lands in the West Indies to England, and in return, England gave back all of Acadia to the French. The English commander's orders instruct him to return to Boston with his entire garrison and all English officials now stationed at Port Royal. The ship from Boston that brought him this information is now in the process of loading the entire English complement. I expect them to sail back to Boston sometime tomorrow."

The assembled Acadians were concerned with the departure of the English. After many years, they had grown accustomed to dealing with them. Someone asked, "Is there any news from the French regarding this matter?"

"*Non*! I've heard nothing from the French. We can assume a French contingent is on its way here. After the English leave, I will make sure the vacated buildings are maintained and made ready for the French officials."

Someone else asked, "What about trading with the New Englanders? As you know, Monsieur Nelson in Boston is a ready buyer for our farm products. We currently have an order from him for ten head of cattle he was to pick up next week in Port Royal."

"Yes, I'm aware of our agreement with Monsieur Nelson. I will do all I can to maintain it. We'll have to wait and see what the French view is on trading with the New Englanders."

The following week, Nelson's boat tied up at the Port Royal dock as scheduled and picked up the cattle as well as other products. A week later, the French contingent arrived with the new governor Hector d'Andigné de Grandfontaine. He quickly decided he did not want to live at Port Royal. Instead, he established his headquarters on the mainland at Penobscot Bay in modern-day Maine. Penobscot Bay was at the heart of the fur trade in Acadia, and that's what really interested him. He delegated authority over Port Royal to his assistant, *Sieur* Le Borgne de Bélisle.

Two days later, shortly after sunrise, a knock sounded on the door of Wilfred Chiasson's house. Wilfred's farm was the closest one to the village center of Port Royal. Wilfred quickly opened the door and was greeted by one of the new French officials.

"*Sieur* Le Borgne de Bélisle orders you to deliver four fresh eggs to his residence every morning at this time starting tomorrow. For today, I will deliver the eggs."

Wilfred was taken aback by this order but didn't miss a beat. He called his eight-year-old son and told him, "Louis, go fetch four fresh eggs for the Monsieur." Wilfred had a large henhouse and for many years had provided the village center and the garrison with fresh eggs. When the eggs arrived, he gave them to the French official and said, "These four fresh eggs are a gift from me to Monsieur de Bélisle. If he wants more eggs, however, the price is one cent per egg. I will not deliver just four eggs. If that's all he wants, he will need to send someone here to pick them up."

"This is an outrage!" cried the official. "It is the *Sieur*'s right to order you, and your duty to obey!"

"Perhaps in France," replied Wilfred, "but not here!"

Angered, the official left in a hurry with the eggs.

Later that afternoon, Wilfred met with Trahan and informed him of the incident with the eggs.

"I'm not surprised," said Trahan. "I met with Bélisle yesterday and informed him I was the spokesperson for the Acadians here. He laughed derisively and said he had no need for such a person, that my duties in that regard were over. He then dismissed me. He seems to be set in his way of doing things."

"Well, he'll get no more free eggs from me."

"Be careful, Wilfred, we don't yet know exactly what we are up against."

The following morning, someone again came to Wilfred's door. When he opened it, he saw the same official but this time, accompanied by three soldiers. The official said, "Will you deliver the four eggs to the governor?"

"*Non!*" replied Wilfred.

"Arrest him and take him to the fort!" demanded the official. With that, the soldiers forcefully removed him from his home and quickly left with Wilfred as their prisoner.

•   •   •

When Trahan heard of Wilfred's arrest, he immediately called for all the heads of household. When they were assembled, he informed them of the egg incident and of Wilfred's subsequent arrest. He likewise informed them of his dismissal by Bélisle as spokesperson.

"This is absurd!" someone shouted. "We cannot let them treat us this way."

"I agree," replied Trahan, "but our highest priority right now is to get Wilfred released from the fort."

"Perhaps we can ask our Micmac friends to join us in a show of force," someone else added.

"It may come to that, but first, I suggest we try a softer approach. I suggest a less threatening group of us, perhaps five or six unarmed men, approach Bélisle and request Wilfred's release."

All in agreement, the group reluctantly returned to their homes.

Later that day, Trahan knocked on Bélisle's door accompanied by five other Acadians.

Upon seeing them, Bélisle demanded, "Why are you here?"

"Governor," replied Trahan. "We understand one of our farmers, Wilfred Chiasson, inadvertently offended you and has been taken prisoner. We request you release him in our custody. We will see to it Wilfred learns how to behave, and that this offense is not repeated."

"How dare you question my authority! I should arrest the six of you as well! Chiasson will be tried by the garrison tribunal two days from now. My recommendation is that he receive ten lashes and thirty days confinement for his arrogant and insolent behavior. If you do not know how to show respect to your superiors, I will certainly teach you." With that, Bélisle slammed the door shut on them.

Two days later, before sunrise, one hundred armed men gathered by the Port Royal fort. About sixty of them were Micmac warriors, including their leader, Pasquitrois. The other forty were Acadians. Eighty of the men, headed by Pasquitrois, quietly surrounded the fort, while the other twenty, headed by Trahan, moved towards the governor's residence about one hundred fifty meters away. Just as the sun came up, a work detail of four soldiers exited the fort with a wagon to gather firewood. These four soldiers were quickly and quietly taken. Word was sent to Trahan informing him of the capture. Trahan requested the four French soldiers be brought to him at the Bélisle residence.

Trahan rapped on the door of the residence, and when Bélisle emerged, he said, "Sir, an unfortunate incident has occurred that now requires your expert attention. When the Micmac heard that Wilfred Chiasson had been arrested, they became enraged. For many years, Wilfred has regularly visited their village and taught French to their children. He is beloved among the Micmac. As you can see, Governor, the Micmac have now taken four of your soldiers as prisoners. It is the custom of the Micmac to dismember their captives, burn the body parts, and feed the meat to their dogs."

Upon hearing this, the four soldiers became very pale and faint and sank to their knees. The Micmac warriors had difficulty keeping straight faces. They all wanted to laugh out loud.

Trahan continued, "Sir, with your permission, perhaps I can negotiate with the Micmac for the release of the soldiers. Perhaps a prisoner exchange. The release of the four soldiers in return for the release of Chiasson."

"Yes! Yes! I agree!" Bélisle boomed. "My assistant will get Chiasson right away."

Trahan, now speaking in the Micmac language, told the warriors to show some reluctance in releasing the soldiers and to release just two initially and to hold back the other two for a while.

A cheer was heard from both the Acadians and the Micmac near the fort as Chiasson emerged. When Chiasson arrived at the residence, Trahan motioned to the warriors to release the soldiers. Two were reluctantly released, but the warriors holding the other two refused to release them.

Trahan now said, "My Micmac friends, I implore you to release these poor soldiers! They are innocent and have done no harm to anyone. I vouch that these are good men and they do not deserve to die a cruel death. If you release them, I will forever be in your debt."

The two Micmac warriors, with scowls on their faces, reluctantly released the final two soldiers.

Trahan addressed Bélisle. "Sir, your suggestion of a prisoner exchange was pure brilliance. It has saved the day and averted a massacre. It is now obvious why Governor Grandfontaine appointed you to oversee the affairs of Port Royal. You are a clear thinker and able to make excellent decisions in difficult situations. I am very impressed, and I congratulate you!" With that, the Acadians and Micmac began leaving the area.

Bélisle was shaken by this incident and immensely relieved that it now appeared to be over. His initial view of the Acadians as ignorant, pliable peasants was forever changed.

Later, as the Micmac began loading their boats for the return trip to their village at Beaubassin, the Acadians thanked Pasquitrois and his men and brought them six sheep, two pigs, two large sacks of dried beans, and several hundred pounds of various other vegetables as a token of their appreciation for helping with the release of Wilfred.

After several more months of overly arrogant behavior by the French officials, the Acadians learned to avoid them as much as possible. On the plus side, no one else was arrested, and the French paid the going price for whatever farm products they got from the Acadians. The French, however, continued to complain bitterly of the self-serving, unpatriotic attitude of the Acadians.

Within one year of the French takeover, the five Acadian farms closest to the Port Royal village center, including that of Wilfred Chiasson, were abandoned. Three of these families moved further up the Dauphin River to put more distance between them and the French. Wilfred and his neighbor, after dismantling their houses and loading all aboard their boats, moved one hundred miles away to Beaubassin.

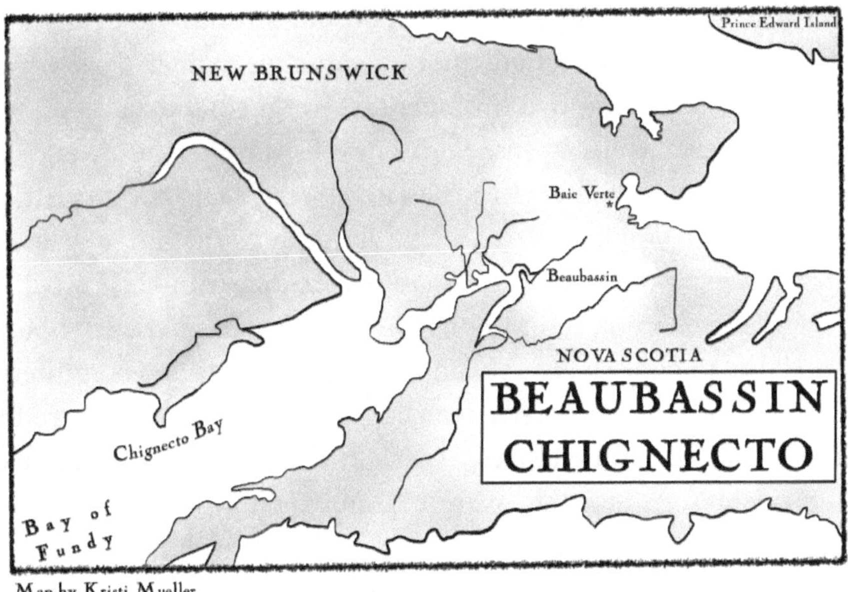



Map by Kristi Mueller

# CHAPTER 6
# BEAUBASSIN

Beaubassin lies at the northernmost end of the Bay of Fundy, on the Isthmus of Chignecto, about one hundred miles from Port Royal. The isthmus connects Nova Scotia with the mainland of what is today Canada. The farmland at Beaubassin was very similar to the land at Port Royal. Extensive meadows stretched many miles along the bay and tidal rivers. The land was soon diked by the Acadians, creating even more fertile farmland. The nearby Micmac village welcomed the early Acadian presence in Beaubassin.

Martin Aucoin, François's second son, moved from Port Royal to Beaubassin in 1671 with his wife, Marie Gaudet. He was strong-willed and didn't get along with his older brother Pierre. It seemed to Martin that his father favored Pierre, and that feeling fueled a never-ending resentment of Pierre. Martin was taller and stronger than his older brother. He was a better and more productive farmer, hunter, and fisherman as well. The two brothers often argued and came close to blows on several occasions. He saw his brother as weak and incompetent, yet his father clearly favored Pierre. Martin was frustrated and frequently complained to his wife about this situation. Marie tried but was unsuccessful at getting him to make peace with his brother. He loved his parents but, after giving this matter considerable thought, decided that moving to Beaubassin was in his and Marie's best interest.

Marie would have preferred staying put in Port Royal where they had many friends and relatives, especially since she and Martin had a one-year-old son. Starting over in Beaubassin would not be easy. Moving, however, was her husband's call. She knew him to be strong, smart and an excellent provider. She would follow and do her best to make the move a successful one.

Eighteen years later, in 1689, Martin and Marie, with their twelve children were well established with more acreage and farm animals than they ever had at Port Royal. They would eventually have a total of seventeen children. Their oldest son, Martin Jr., was nineteen years old.

Busy about the house, one day, Marie turned to her husband. "I'm so glad we moved here. I know your father still worries about us being so far away, but it's so much better here. The French don't bother us, and we are free to trade with Monsieur Nelson and the other New Englanders as we please."

"I agree," replied Martin. "Plus, the nearby Micmac village provides us with all the protection we need from both the French and the English."

"Any news on when we can sell our cattle?"

"Yes, I saw Jacques Bourgeois earlier today, and he asked me if I was ready to sell. I told him I had four steers that each weighed about 900 pounds. He said with my four, he now had twenty head ready to sell and he would plan with Monsieur Nelson for the pickup."

Jacques Bourgeois was one of the first Acadians to settle in the Beaubassin area. Besides his large farm and orchard, he raised cattle and operated a grist mill for the grinding of wheat into flour. He was a leader among the Acadians and the main contact with the New Englanders.

"Ah! Here comes Martin! That's our sailboat that just turned into the basin."

One week before, Martin Junior sailed the family sailboat from Beaubassin down to Port Royal to visit his grandparents. While Martin Junior looked like his father: tall, athletic and strong, with the same eyes, hair and cheek bones; his temperament was quite different. Whereas Senior was quick-tempered, opinionated, and slow to make friends, Junior was easy-going, loving, and quick to make lasting friends. After tying the boat to the dike, he made his way up to the house, carrying a large sack.

"Welcome back!" said his father. "How was your trip, and how is everyone in Port Royal?"

"The trip was great! I had fair winds going and coming, so no problems. All our relatives in Port Royal are fine. They said the French are as hard-headed as ever. One new thing I noticed, however, is that the New Englanders now regularly come to Port Royal to trade. The French officials in Port Royal might still be hard-headed, but they seem to have finally understood that waiting for the French supply ship makes no sense."

"What's in the sack?"

"Dried beans from your brother Joseph. Enough to last all winter! He said thank you for the carrots and winter squash you sent. He asked what else we were growing. When I said we only had a couple of rows of beans this year, that's when he decided to send you this sack. Oh, one other thing! It seems the latest Acadian families to leave Port Royal are now settling in Minas Basin, at a place called Grand Pré. Apparently, the land there is very similar to what we have here in Beaubassin but even more extensive."

•  •  •

For the next year, life in Port Royal, Beaubassin and Grand Pré was quite peaceful and pleasant for the Acadians. Martin Junior, married, was living on his own farm in Beaubassin. On a beautiful day, in the fall of 1689, he and his wife Paulette were having dinner at his father's house.

"How are your apple and pear trees doing?" Martin's wife, Marie, asked Paulette.

"Very well! Thank you again for the cuttings that got my little orchard started. Each tree is now about eight feet tall. I had blossoms for the first time this past spring and lots of small fruit. Unfortunately, ninety-nine percent of the fruit fell off the trees before they were even as big as the tip of my thumb."

"Don't worry. It's quite common for that to happen the first year the tree sets fruit. If the trees are healthy, you can expect a wonderful harvest next year."

Martin Junior turned to his father, "Papa, while several of us were working on the dike this morning, we heard that the Abenaki, across the bay, were fully engaged in a fierce war with the New Englanders."

"Yes, I heard the same thing from Monsieur Bourgeois yesterday. The ongoing conflict between the two seems to have escalated into fierce atrocities and massacres on both sides. The Abenaki feel the New Englanders are encroaching on their land and are trying to reclaim it. They have attacked many English settlements north of Boston, killed many settlers, and burned their buildings. The New Englanders are now enraged and lashing out for revenge."

"That's terrible!" gasped Marie, "How can this conflict be ended?" Marie was the peacemaker in the family. She was of a gentle, forgiving nature and had difficulty understanding why people could not solve their differences amicably. She knew God had a plan for mankind and we must accept his plan. The atrocities, however, spoke of the Devil himself. If the Devil was involved, there was much to fear. The Devil was almost as powerful as God. She would say some extra prayers tonight, especially to Sainte Marie, to help find a solution to this conflict.

"It will probably get worse before it ends," replied Martin Senior. "Monsieur Bourgeois said that a few weeks ago, when he last spoke with John Nelson, Nelson reported the Micmac had joined the Abenaki in fighting the New Englanders. Apparently, the Abenaki moved their villages deep into the woods, and while the Abenaki and Micmac warriors strike easily at the fixed English settlements, the New Englanders have difficulty locating and retaliating against the Abenaki settlements. The New Englanders are very frustrated at not being able to strike effectively at their enemies. Nelson emphasized the New Englanders blame the French for supplying the Abenaki and Micmac with weapons and other supplies. It seems only a matter of time before the New Englanders bring this war to us!"

"We get along so well with the Micmac," replied Marie. "Why can't the New Englanders get along with the Abenaki?"

Martin Senior answered forcefully, "Because the New Englanders are greedy and two-faced! Even Nelson and the other traders, who come to us with smiling faces, look at our land with envy. Not so many years ago, they attacked us and took over all of Acadia. Now that we are even more prosperous, why wouldn't they do the same again? We treat the Micmac fairly. The Acadian settlements are on reclaimed saltwater marsh land of little value to them. We do not present a threat to their hunting grounds. We have always made it a point to not engage in the trapping of fur animals. We trade with them to get the furs. This arrangement makes for a win-win situation. That's how a good neighbor behaves. The New Englanders are expanding into the Abenaki hunting grounds with new villages and extensive trapping for furs."

• • •

Eight months later, on May 19, 1690, Sir William Phips sailed an armada of six warships and over seven hundred men into the Port Royal basin. Phips, originally from Maine, had gained much experience and success in fighting against the Abenaki. He was fierce and brutal in combat and therefore won considerable respect from his fellow New Englanders. Earlier in the year, the Massachusetts Governor's Council appointed Phips to lead an expedition against Port Royal. The top French official at Port Royal was Governor Meneval. His garrison at the fort had about eighty men.

A loud knock echoed through Governor Meneval's residence. When he opened it, he saw a young, frightened soldier.

"Sir, several English warships have just entered the Port Royal basin and appear to be on their way here."

"Return to the fort and tell Captain Croteau to prepare for battle."

Ever since his appointment several years earlier, Governor Meneval had repeatedly requested more soldiers, larger cannons, and more funds to expand and strengthen the fort. All of his requests were ignored by his superiors in France. He rushed to the fort.

While the larger English warships remained in the basin with their powerful guns aimed at the fort, a smaller ship sailed up close to it so the French could hear the English lieutenant in charge of the ship calling out, "If you surrender, you will be granted honors-of-war! The entire garrison along with all French officials will be provided with safe passage to your choice of either Québec or France!"

Governor Meneval came out of the fort and said, "Take me to your commander. I want to negotiate directly with him."

After boarding the command ship, he was cordially greeted by Phips. "Welcome, Governor Meneval. I am Sir William Phips, commander of this expedition. Please follow me to my cabin."

On the way to his cabin, Phips told one of his assistants to bring a fresh pot of tea and a platter of sweets. Once they were comfortably settled, Phips said, "Governor Meneval, you and I both know you cannot win this fight. If you don't surrender, the guns from my warships will quickly destroy your fort. The seven hundred soldiers I've brought will then come ashore and quickly overpower your men. We will each lose some men in the fighting, but I daresay you will lose many more than I. If you surrender, your garrison may march out of the fort with their arms. You, your officials, and the entire garrison will then be loaded aboard one of my ships and taken to your choice of either Québec or France."

"What about the Acadians?"

"No harm will come to the Acadians or their possessions. I give you my word as an officer and a gentleman."

"And what of their church?"

"Again, I give you my word, no harm will come to their church or its contents."

Governor Meneval quickly decided he really had no choice other than to surrender. "I accept your terms, Commander Phips, and I now wish to return to my fort to prepare my men."

"Excellent! You have made a wise decision that will save many lives. Shall we say, two hours from now, your garrison will march out of the fort? If you need more time, speak up."

"Two hours will be fine."

"Very well! I will prepare to receive your complement aboard one of my ships."

Two hours later, the entire garrison marched out of the fort and some of Phips's men entered it. As soon as Phips's men had control, they disarmed the French soldiers and took them as prisoners. Governor Meneval and his officials were likewise made prisoners. All were forced aboard the English ships and stowed below decks. With the French soldiers out of the way, the New Englanders stripped the fort of all valuables and set fire to it. They plundered the warehouses. Anything of value was taken aboard the ships. Phips laughed as he entered Meneval's residence and took possession of his personal items: silverware, clothing, books, money, and everything else of value. He saw Meneval as a naïve bug that deserved to be crushed. In his mind, the Acadians were French, and all actions against the Indian-loving French were justified. This was war, but the fool didn't know it.

The New Englanders then turned their attention to the Acadians and their church. The church was stripped of everything of value and then set on fire. At the same time, the New Englanders attacked the Acadian farms. At the first one, they slaughtered all the farm animals, stripped the house of everything of value, and set fire to the barn.

Governor Meneval was outraged at the treachery by Phips. He vowed revenge and told his men this cowardly act would not go unpunished.

"Papa, they are killing Monsieur LeDoux's animals and have set fire to his barn!" Joseph Aucoin exclaimed to his father, François.

"I see! Take your sons and all the sheep and pigs deep into the woods and stay there until we come for you."

François's wife, Yvette, cried out, "What madness is this? Why are they attacking us?"

When the New Englanders arrived at François's farm, they killed his two milk cows, stripped his house of all valuables, and then set fire to his barn. The destruction of the Acadian farms at Port Royal continued for three days. Only the farms far up the Dauphin River escaped the wrath of the New Englanders.

Phips ordered that all Acadian adult males sign an oath of allegiance to the English king. He sent messengers to Beaubassin and Grand Pré informing them they must sign the oath of allegiance, otherwise he would destroy their farms. With fury in their hearts and curses under their breath, the Acadians signed the oath. "Papa, let me take my knife and kill them," said one young lad. "Hush," said his mother. "Do you want to sleep on the ground this winter? Your father is doing what he must."

Phips returned to Boston and was widely cheered for his successful and heroic campaign against Port Royal. Governor Meneval, his officials, and all the French soldiers were thrown into prison in Boston. Flush with the easy victory at Port Royal, the authorities in Massachusetts decided the time had come to attack the French stronghold in Québec and win there. In August 1690, Phips, commanding a flotilla of thirty-four vessels and 2,300 men, sailed up the St. Lawrence River. When he reached Québec City, he sent one of his lieutenants to demand that Governor-General Louis de Buade de Frontenac surrender, much as he had demanded Meneval's surrender. Unlike Port Royal, however, Québec City was well fortified with natural cliffs and experienced, determined defenders. Frontenac's answer to the lieutenant was widely reported to have been, "I have no reply to make to your general other than from the mouths of my cannon and muskets." These words inspired his men and lived on long after the battle. Phips spent several weeks ineffectively shelling the fortress city from his ships. He was then struck with a smallpox epidemic and forced to retreat to Boston with the loss of over four hundred men.

Frontenac is a controversial figure in the early history of Canada. Born in France on May 22, 1622, to a wealthy, well-connected family in the town of Saint-Germain-en-Laye, a rich suburb of Paris, he quickly became used to the good life. After reaching adulthood, he regularly lived beyond his means, amassing a huge debt by the age of fifty. With his creditors closing in around him, he sought and received from King Louis XIV the appointment to New France as its governor-general. On June 28, 1672, he sailed from La Rochelle, France, for Québec City. His appointment and departure placed all actions by his creditors in abeyance.

The king's appointment made Frontenac the military commander for all New France. Frontenac, however, was far more interested in the fur trade. He used a good portion of his military budget to create fur trading posts in the Great Lakes region to benefit himself and his cronies, much to the dismay of the civil authorities in Québec who knew the funds were needed to strengthen Québec's defenses. He died in Québec City on Nov 28, 1698, at 76. His critics claim he was largely a spoiled playboy who squandered the colony's funds on himself and lavish parties for his friends. But in 1690, in Québec City, when Phips came calling and his country really needed him, Frontenac came through with flying colors. He was in charge, so he therefore deserves the credit. The English would not attack Québec City again for another generation.

The following year, in 1691, the English crown appointed Phips as Governor of Massachusetts, a position he held until his unexpected death in 1695. The French captives from Port Royal remained in the Boston prison for over a year until they were finally released and returned to France in a prisoner exchange. When Meneval arrived in France, he complained angrily to the French authorities regarding Phips's behavior at Port Royal. The French authorities listened with sympathy and respect but, unfortunately, had other concerns and were not persuaded to pursue any direct actions against the English.

•　　•　　•

But before Phips's death, his appointment as governor, or even before he attacked Quebec, the Acadians had to deal with the aftermath of his treachery. "You must never trust the English," François's wife, Yvette, told her grandchildren. "They are in league with the Devil and do his bidding. They are evil and will surely burn in hell for all eternity. I wish them all an early, painful death. You must promise me you will never, never, trust them!

"We know," replied fourteen-year-old Paulette, the oldest of the seven grandchildren in the house.

"They are always ready to trade with us," said Yvette. "They get our cattle and wheat and in return provide us with goods like pots, pans, silverware, and farm implements. But after a few years of trading, they raid us and steal back all the goods they provided."

"We know, Grandma! We have seen this with our own eyes."

•　　•　　•

After Phips's departure, many boats from Beaubassin arrived at Port Royal loaded with lambs, piglets, calves, and other items to restart Port Royal. Martin Aucoin Junior's boat was among them. He sailed up to his grandparents' farm and saw his Uncle Joseph and his boys at the dike to receive him.

"Uncle Joseph!" cried Martin, "I'm so happy to see you. I can't believe what the New Englanders have done!"

"They are among the most evil men on earth. They are godless and brutal to the extreme. They laughed as they slaughtered our animals and set fire to our barns. Do they care if our children go hungry? They say the Micmac are savages, but in my mind, the New Englanders are the savages. Next time, and I'm certain there will be a next time, we must be better prepared to defend ourselves."

In addition to destroying the fort, the church, many barns and killing the farm animals, the New Englanders burned some homes and killed two Acadian fur traders who tried to protect their property in the village warehouse. Many of the Acadians witnessed the murder, and it stilled their hands—for the time being. After killing the two Acadians, the marauders stole all the furs as well as everything else in the warehouse before burning it down.

Martin Junior found it difficult to grasp the enormity of this carnage. The destruction stretched as far as the eye could see. Dead animals lay pitifully among the burned rafters. It was as if the farms he remembered had been swallowed by monsters and vomited up again. He knew this sight would forever haunt him. He'd heard his grandfather, François, speak of the *maudits Anglais* who burned his fields so long ago in France. Here they were again, doing the same thing, only worse, to an Acadian settlement. His view of the English was forever changed. He had never known quite what it meant to have a heart that was "hardened," but now he did. He felt it stiff and proud in his chest when he thought of the marauders. Like his Uncle Joseph, he would never again trust them.

"I brought some lambs and piglets for you," he said quietly. He did not know yet whether his grandparents had suffered as much as those whose devastation he could see.

"Thank you. Our sheep and pigs were all spared thanks to your grandfather's quick thinking. He sent me and the boys into the woods with the sheep and pigs before the New

Englanders arrived at our farm. Your Uncle Pierre, across the river, was not as lucky. All his farm animals were slaughtered. We'll give him the lambs and piglets you've brought."

"What about the house? Did the New Englanders damage it?"

"No, thank God, but they stole everything of value in it. They took everything made of metal—pots, pans, knives, spoons, everything. Even all our farm implements are gone—shovels, hoes, axes, and our scythes. Without the scythes, it will be very difficult to harvest our wheat and cut our hay this fall."

As they walked up to the house, Joseph continued. "I suppose it could have been worse. They left the dikes alone and didn't burn the houses, except for two."

"I see your two milk cows were killed. Who is that cutting them up?"

"Our Micmac friends arrived two days ago and are helping us salvage as much meat as possible from the slaughtered animals. They are cutting the meat into strips and drying it on those wooden racks over there. Very few of our knives survived the raid, so the Micmac help is much appreciated."

François and Yvette were 72 and 71 years old respectively during the Phips attack and their farm survived. Many of the Port Royal farms, however, did not survive the devastation. Some Acadians were so discouraged they simply gave up and moved away. Replacing so many barns at once was impossible. Trees had to be felled, timbers and boards cut, and then assembled into barns. All this while continuing to farm the land, replace the livestock, maintain the dikes, and feed the family. It would be many years before the farms returned to their previous routines.

The death rate in Port Royal for the next few years was significantly above normal, especially for the very young and very old. There wasn't enough to eat.

•   •   •

With Phips back in Boston, trading with the New Englanders resumed, and life for the Acadians gradually returned to normal. The Acadian distrust and, in many cases, hatred of the English, gave way to the necessity of trading. Some were stubborn and did without, but not many. Something was always needed, and they had no other people to trade with. For the next few years, neither the French nor the English took much interest in Acadia. Neither power established a presence in Port Royal other than the steady stream of New England traders.

Martin Aucoin Senior was horrified by the events in Port Royal. He could easily visualize the same thing happening in Beaubassin, perhaps even worse since Beaubassin had no soldiers or garrison to protect it. He was responsible for his large family, and his current home was no longer safe. In April 1691, after considerable discussions with his wife, Marie Gaudet, Martin informed his children, including Martin Junior and his wife, of his decision to move away from Beaubassin.

"Your mother and I have decided the location of our farm here in Beaubassin is no longer safe. We are too close to the basin and therefore very vulnerable to attack by the English. Martin, you and Paulette are much safer since your farm is four miles from here and up the Missaguash River. My friend René Comeau visited me a few months after the Phips attack at Port Royal. He lives at Rivière-aux-Canards in Minas Basin, near Grand Pré. He says Rivière-aux-Canards has excellent farm plots available and is much safer than either Grand Pré or Beaubassin. He said he would be happy to help us get settled there."

"Papa, if we move there, can we still trade with the New Englanders?" asked one of the children.

"Monsieur Comeau said he brings his produce to Grand Pré to trade with the New Englanders. The village of Grand Pré is about seven miles from his farm, a short trip on his sailboat."

Two months later, Martin Senior and his family settled in their new house in Rivière-aux-Canards. He and his wife had thirteen children, with four more to come.

.   .   .

Throughout this period, continuing attacks on New England settlements by native warriors and French-Canadian fighters so enraged the New Englanders that in 1696 the Massachusetts General Court condemned all trade with the Acadians and offered a bounty of fifty pounds each for the scalps of native enemies. Scalping, of course, was a common practice of the native warriors; it was not a European practice. But the Massachusetts authorities needed something to change the dynamic of this war in their favor, and men have always been willing to acquire new weapons, both material and psychological. The scalping reward seemed like a good tool to add to their war procedures. It had a unique ability to instill terror and was a handy way to ensure that a bounty seeker had indeed killed as many as he claimed. The Boston and other newspapers advertised the new reward. The fifty-pound bounty caught the attention of Major Benjamin Church of Rhode Island. He sailed to Boston in search of a commission to pursue the native enemies.

Church was born in 1639 in Plymouth, Massachusetts. Throughout his childhood, English relations with the local Indians were generally peaceful, but as he reached adulthood, those relations became more and more hostile as the New Englanders expanded their settlements into Indian territory. He became a strong, active leader in the local militia and fought bravely and effectively against the Indians. He rose quickly in the militia through the ranks of captain and major. He would eventually retire as a colonel. He was a large man, over six feet tall and 250 pounds, yet agile and strong. He led his men from the front. Throughout his long military career, his reputation was that of a fair and just warrior and an especially good tactician. He planned every engagement carefully, made sure his men were properly equipped, and used friendly Indians as scouts. As a captain, he commanded a ranger battalion and the historic predecessor of the U. S. Army Rangers. In 1992, in honor of his innovative tactical methods, Church was inducted into the U. S. Army Ranger Hall of Fame. A bronze Ranger Tab was affixed to his tombstone as a mark of this honor. He died January 17, 1718, in Little Compton, Rhode Island, which he called home for much of his adult life and where he is now buried alongside his wife.

"Sir," said Church to Massachusetts Lieutenant-Governor William Stoughton, "I've had considerable success in defeating the native warriors in Rhode Island and Massachusetts. I propose to do the same for you in your fight against the Abenaki and Micmac warriors."

"I welcome your help," replied Stoughton. "Striking directly against these native devils, however, will not be easy. If it were easy, we would have accomplished it ourselves by now. These native savages are supported and well-supplied by their French-Canadian allies. They strike our settlements and then melt back into the woods. By the time our reinforcements reach the settlements, the enemy is long gone. What we find are dead and scalped fathers, mothers, and children!"

"Are we strong enough to mount an attack directly against the French-Canadians?"

"Unfortunately, no. My predecessor, Governor Phips, tried a few years ago and was repulsed when his ships reached Québec. It will take major support from England to overcome the French-Canadians, and I'm not aware of any such campaign being in the works. A better approach, for the time being, would be to attack the Acadians at Beaubassin. We believe there is a large Micmac village near this Acadian settlement. The vicious cycle we're currently in is: New England traders freely trade with the Acadians. The Acadians then trade with the Micmac. The Micmac use their supplies to attack, kill and scalp our fellow men, women, and children in our outlying settlements. We need to break this cycle!"

"What about the recent court decree outlawing all trading with the Acadians? Won't that help break the cycle?"

"The scalp bounty in the decree was widely approved in Boston and surrounding towns. Not so the trading embargo. The Boston merchants are up in arms. They say this embargo will ruin our economy. And there are hundreds of New England traders who do business directly with the Acadians. At best, my patrol ships might be able to stop ten percent of them."

"I see the problem."

"I have two frigates and several transport ships for you. A force of four hundred to five hundred men should be more than sufficient for this mission, and you should have no difficulty in raising such a force. Our men are outraged at what the native devils are doing to our countrymen in the settlements. I need you to make the Acadians aware of our displeasure with them. Regarding the Micmac, we will pay the fifty-pound bounty on all scalps!"

"All?"

"Yes, all!"

•    •    •

On September 20, 1696, Church sailed his warships into Beaubassin. He was met at the dock by a lone Acadian man.

"Major Church, my name is Germain Bourgeois. I am the spokesman for the Acadians here at Beaubassin. I have with me a copy of the oath of allegiance all Acadians signed a few years ago at the request of Sir William Phips. We have not violated that oath. When the French warships have visited us here, we have always proclaimed our neutrality in the ongoing conflict between France and England. Our goal is to remain neutral. We are simple people. We only wish to tend our farms and raise our families in peace."

Germain was the son of Jacques Bourgeois, the Acadian founder of Beaubassin. The family still had the largest farm in the area and a large herd of cattle. The destruction at Port Royal was well known to Germain and all Acadians. Ever since then, his main fear was that something similar would happen to Beaubassin. In anticipation, for the past few years, every male over the age of fifteen trained regularly with the local militia. They practiced with their muskets, loading, firing, and reloading for many hours. Grazing lands, about twelve miles away, were found for the cattle and other farm animals to protect them from the would-be marauders. On that day, however, Germain knew his militia would be no match for the angry, well-trained, New England fighters.

"You Acadians have nothing to fear from me or my men," replied Church. "Trading with the Micmac devils, however, is another story. My goal, Mister Bourgeois, is to put an end to that trading. My men will relieve you and your friends of all goods that might be traded with the native devils."

"Major Church, I beg you to please reconsider. Our lives depend on our trading with the Micmac. We provide them with pots and pans in return for furs we then trade with you New Englanders for crucial items needed for our survival, such as medicine and winter clothing. Your anger at the Acadians and Micmac here in Beaubassin is misplaced. We are not your enemy."

"Misplaced? I don't think so!" With that, Church's men fanned out and began slaughtering the farm animals and plundering the Acadian homes. Everything of value was taken. The church, *Notre Dame du Bon Secour*, was plundered and then set on fire. Every barn was burned. The devastation at Beaubassin was very similar to what Phips's men had done at Port Royal a few years earlier.

While the plundering was going on, a detachment of Church's men searched for the Micmac village. When they returned, they reported they were unable to find any sign of a Micmac settlement. What they didn't report is that they were deathly afraid of venturing very far into the woods. They did all their searching along the basin and major rivers in the area. Church sent one of his men to fetch Bourgeois.

"Mister Bourgeois," demanded Church, "where is the Micmac village? If you don't tell me, I will burn all your homes!"

Bourgeois turned pale and fell to his knees.

"Major Church, please don't burn our homes. None of us can tell you where the Micmac are. If we betray the Micmac, they will surely slaughter all of us."

Church gave orders to one of his men who quickly set off and set fire to the nearest home and then the next and the next. Bourgeois was enraged but knew he could not betray the Micmac. He saw Church as the devil incarnate. The destruction at Port Royal a few years earlier taught him how evil the English could be. He now saw with his own eyes that same evil invading his own settlement. His worst fear was realized. How could this be happening? Was there no justice in this land? Who was making these terrible decisions? The term *maudits Anglais* was far too gentle to describe these evil people. Neither he nor any of the Beaubassin Acadians would ever again trust the English. They might trade with them, but they would not trust them. Church's man, after setting the fourth house on fire, returned, and no more homes were burned.

Before leaving Beaubassin, Church had every Acadian man sign a new oath of allegiance to the current English monarch. His parting words were: "If any of you violate this oath, I will return and kill every man, woman, and child in Beaubassin."

Church's words struck fear into the heart of every Acadian in Beaubassin. They were farmers with families doing their best to survive and prosper in a harsh environment. They knew they would never be able to defend themselves effectively against enemy warships and soldiers. Their fear, distrust, and hatred of the English became deeply embedded and would be passed down to subsequent generations.

•   •   •

The following year, in 1697, King William's War, which had started in 1688 between France and England, finally ended with the signing of a treaty at The Hague. This treaty officially returned Acadia back to French control. The peace between France and England, however, did not last long. In 1702, war resumed in what is commonly referred to as Queen Anne's War.

Martin Aucoin Senior, now fifty-one years old, was enjoying a rubescent sunset after a hard day in his fields in Rivière-aux-Canards.

His second son, twenty-four-year-old Michel, was relaxing with him on the porch. He said, "Papa, Colette and I have decided to move to Grand Pré after we marry in the spring."

"Have you told your mother?"

"*Non*, I wanted to tell you first."

"Grand Pré is fine with me, and I'm sure your mother will agree. She and I would prefer, of course, that you stay here in Rivière-aux-Canards, but it's your decision, and Grand Pré is a fine choice and not very far away."

"Thank you, Papa! Your support means everything to me."

"We have many friends in Grand Pré. You and Colette will fit in nicely there."

The devastation at Port Royal in 1690 and Beaubassin in 1696 was not forgotten by the Acadians. They had a long memory. The stories of English treachery were often repeated in most, if not all, Acadian households around the kitchen table. The children were taught the English were not their friends. Out of necessity, the Acadians continued to trade with the New Englanders, but friendships were rare, distrust common. Going forward one day at a time was the only practical option for most Acadians in this increasingly hostile land.

In Rivière-aux-Canards, the year 1702 was a good one for the Aucoin family. All seventeen of Martin Senior and Marie Gaudet's children had been born and were doing well. The next-to-last child was Jean, born in 1698. He was four years old and destined to take over the family homestead and produce a long line of Aucoins.

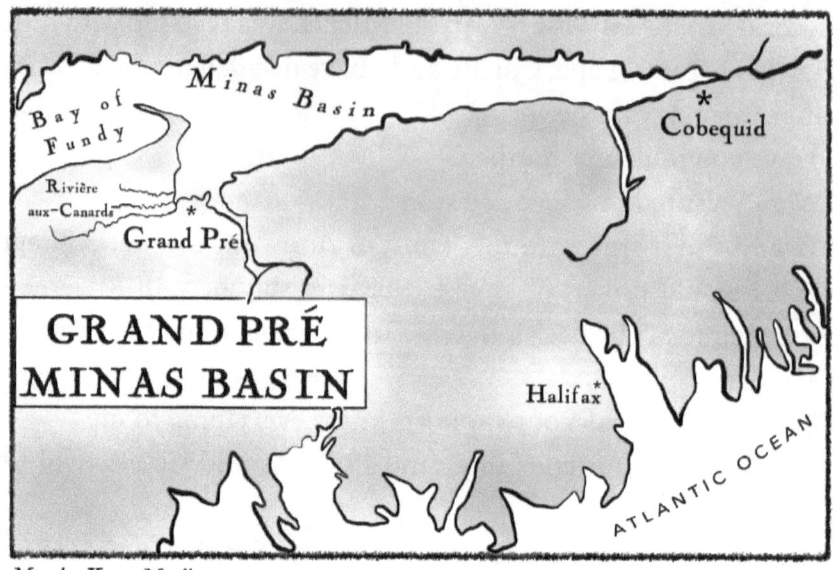


Map by Kristi Mueller

# CHAPTER 7
# GRAND PRÉ

Grand Pré (meaning large meadow) lay in the Minas Basin about one hundred miles northeast of Port Royal and about fifty miles east of Beaubassin. The fertile meadow along the basin at Grand Pré stretched for over eighteen miles.

"Can you direct me to the residence of Monsieur Pierre Melanson?" Michel asked an Acadian man upon his arrival to the village center of Grand Pré.

"Based on the animals, fruit trees, and furniture on your boat, can I assume 0you are moving here?"

"Yes, that is our intent. My wife, Colette, and I are from Rivière-aux-Canards. I am Michel of Martin of François Aucoin."

"Welcome! I know your uncle Joseph very well. I am Raymond Dusseault. Your uncle and I were neighbors in Port Royal. To find

Monsieur Melanson, keep going until you arrive at the river Gaspereau. It's the next river you'll come to. Go up the river, and his is the fifth farm on the right. He has a large oak tree next to his barn. Good luck, and I hope to see you again soon."

Before leaving Rivière-aux-Canards, Michel was well-briefed by his father in what to look for in a farm plot. The attacks at Port Royal and Beaubassin were still fresh. Any farms along the basin and nearby tidal rivers would be easy prey for the English. Michel needed to find not only a fertile plot but one that would be difficult for the English devils to find. He quickly saw that the Gaspereau River was too close to the center of Grand Pré and would be an easy target for the enemy. Arriving at the Melanson farm, he explained why he was there.

"Monsieur Melanson, my wife, Colette, and I wish to settle here, but we're very concerned about being too close to the basin or major rivers. We prefer a plot that would be further and safer from the plundering English, even if that plot is perhaps less fertile than the nearby ones. I hope you can help us find such a plot."

"I see your father has prepared you well," said Melanson. "All our new farms now take the English into consideration. From the last consecutive farm on this river, we have left four miles of vacant land before creating any new farms and then only a few. The bulk of our new farms are on several smaller rivers further down the basin and several miles up those rivers. And at the very end of this basin, about twenty miles from here, we have more new farms at a place called Cobequid. I'm sure we can find a suitable site for you."

•　　•　　•

Two years later, in January 1704, on a cold and blustery gray day, Jean-Baptist Hertel, the French-Canadian commander of the local militia, left Montreal with a force of nearly three hundred men. Their target was the English settlement of Deerfield in western Massachusetts, about three hundred miles to the south. His force included fifty French-

Canadian militia, with the rest being Abenaki, Mohawk, Pocumtuc, and Pennacook warriors.

Canada was a safe refuge and home for that force of three hundred warriors. The name "Canada" was coined by the French explorer Jacques Cartier in 1535 when he asked two Iroquois boys for directions to their village. In their answer, they used the word "Kanata" in describing the route to their village, which is the present-day site of Québec City. Cartier used the word "Canada" to describe not only the village, but the entire area controlled by its chief, Donnacona. The name was soon applied to an even larger area. Maps in 1547 designated everything north of the St. Lawrence River as Canada.

Hertel was born in 1668 in Trois-Rivières, the third largest town in Québec, after Montreal and Québec City. His father Joseph-François Hertel was also born in Trois-Rivières. Both father and son were successful, professional soldiers for the French in Canada throughout their adult lives. Both rose in the military ranks and assumed command of significant militia forces. Although usually assigned to different parts of Québec, they sometimes fought side-by-side in battles against the English. Both knew the value of cultivating Indian allies and did so effectively with solid respect for, and results from, the native warriors.

The three-hundred-mile trek to Deerfield was not overly cumbersome for these seasoned warriors since it mostly involved easy travel over frozen rivers and through several friendly Indian villages on the way. On February 28, 1704, with their target in sight, Hertel made final plans with Wattanummon, the chief of the native warriors.

"Chief, as we previously discussed, this attack on the English settlement has two purposes. First, to discourage the English from expanding their settlements into Indian hunting grounds, and second, to take as many captives as possible back to Canada with us."

From Hertel's point of view, taking prisoners back to Canada was the primary purpose of the attack. Those prisoners would later be used as bargaining chips in prisoner exchanges or ransom payments. Any ransom payments would be shared with the key Indian leaders. Deerfield was chosen because it held several hundred residents and was poorly defended. A swift attack and withdrawal could easily yield over one hundred captives with few casualties on the French and Indian side. The scalping of women and children, however, was a major concern for Hertel. He understood and accepted the scalping of men—but never women and children. He did his best to restrain such barbaric practice but had little control once the battle started.

"Yes, I understand the purpose, but 'discourage' is too weak a word! We need to crush these expansions and force all the English back to the sea! This is our land, and they will pay a heavy price for trying to steal it from us."

Hertel had worked with native warriors for many years on many occasions. He valued their skill as warriors and their friendship. He and his men respected their native allies and worked well with them during both war and peace. Many of his French-Canadian troops were married to native women. These mixed marriages were even more common in Québec than in Acadia, due principally to the dominance of the fur trade and the abundance of single, French-Canadian *coureurs de bois* (fur trappers), coupled with a relative shortage of native men because of their constant wars against each other and the English. Native women were plentiful and the *coureurs de bois* did their best to re-balance the situation.

"With regard to scalping, please remind your warriors that only men are to be scalped. I understand scalping has a long tradition in your culture and plays an important part in your battles. The killing and scalping of women and children, however, is an abomination that only serves to enrage the English against us."

"I have mentioned your concern to my warriors, but I make no promises."

Hertel's force attacked just before dawn on February 29, 1704. Of the 291residents of Deerfield, forty-seven were killed and 112 were taken captive. Many of the remaining 132 survivors were wounded but able to hold off the attackers successfully until mid-morning when reinforcements arrived from other nearby English settlements. Hertel and his forces withdrew. More than half of the forty-seven killed were women and children. About twenty of the captives, mostly old, sick, or wounded, died on the way back to Montreal. Hertel's losses were about thirty men.

Later that same day, twenty-one-year-old Jason Collins, who had helped fight off the raiders, volunteered to ride his horse to Boston to inform Governor Joseph Dudley of Massachusetts of the raid. This was Collins' first battle and the first that he knew of in the western settlements. His training with the militia during the past few years paid off. He was able to load and fire his musket rapidly for several hours until he ran out of powder and ball. Everything happened so fast. The enemy was everywhere. His parents were unharmed, but his favorite uncle, William, and his wife, Clara, were killed. When he found their bodies, he vomited. His uncle had been scalped. His Aunt Clara, miraculously, was not scalped.

"Governor!" said his assistant when Governor Dudley answered the rap at his door, "A messenger is here with terrible news about Deerfield."

"Deerfield, you say? Bring me the messenger!"

Dudley, born in 1647 in Roxbury, Massachusetts, a suburb of Boston, was already fifty-seven years old when the Deerfield raid took place. He was a descendant of the Puritan founders of Plymouth Colony and held increasingly significant positions of authority in Massachusetts politics from his early adulthood. The key positions were all appointed by the crown in England. To ensure his steady advancement, Dudley always supported the crown's position even when it was directly opposed by the colonial legislature, especially concerning taxes. He was never an advocate for the colonists, and his fellow colonists soon came to despise him. His focus was his own advancement. Queen Anne appointed him Governor of Massachusetts on April 1, 1702. For his living expenses, he received a stipend from England but was told by the London authorities to seek a regular salary for the governor position from the Massachusetts legislature. He, and all succeeding royal governors, however, were unsuccessful in gaining that concession from the colonial legislature. The annual salary request became another constant source of friction between the representatives of the crown and the colony right up to the American Revolution. Dudley died in Roxbury on April 2, 1720, a wealthy landowner.

"Sir, my name is Jason Collins. I'm a resident of Deerfield. This morning, we were attacked by a large force of French militia and their Indian allies. Over thirty of our women and children were killed in the raid as well as twenty or so of our men. In addition, over one hundred of our men, women, and children were captured and taken with the enemy when they retreated."

"This is an abomination!" exclaimed an outraged Dudley. "Were your men able to pursue the enemy during their retreat?"

"Yes, after the fighting in the village was over, we sent a party of about fifty well-armed men in pursuit. The enemy was easy to follow with all the snow on the ground. Unfortunately, our men were ambushed, with six of them killed and several others wounded. That ended the pursuit."

"Thank you for coming, Mr. Collins. I assure you this cowardly act will not go unpunished!"

The next day, based largely on the Deerfield raid, the Governor's Council increased the bounty on native scalps to an astounding one hundred pounds each, the equivalent of an average worker's wages for an entire year. The new bounty again caught the attention of Major Benjamin Church. Any bounty was welcome and would be shared with his rangers. Church was financially stable and well settled in Rhode Island. Money was not his main motivation. But he was a professional soldier and very good at his craft. He enjoyed the action and had a clear conscience. He was helping his fellow colonists rid themselves of the weak and conniving French and the Indian devils. In his opinion, any who allied with savages was asking to be slaughtered.

•   •   •

"Sir," said Church to Governor Dudley, "permit me to return to Acadia and exact revenge for the cowardly raid against Deerfield."

Dudley knew the Acadians had nothing to do with the raid on Deerfield. It was also unlikely the Micmac were involved in a raid so far to the west. None of this mattered. Since striking at Canada was not workable, Dudley readily agreed Acadia would pay for what happened in Deerfield. The Massachusetts people expected him to do something, and he most certainly would. No matter the Acadians were innocent of this specific act. They were surely guilty of others that had gone unpunished.

"I want you to strike them and strike them hard!" Dudley demanded of Church. "Kill their animals, burn their houses, barns, and churches, destroy their dikes, and bring back a good number of captives. Regarding the natives, I will pay one-hundred pounds each for all scalps!"

The Acadian captives in this case were to be used in an expected prisoner exchange to regain the Deerfield prisoners.

•   •   •

In Acadia, the women typically planted and tended the fruit trees— mostly apple, but also pear, plum and cherry. In Grand Pré, From the age of six, Louise Benoit had helped her mother tend their five apple trees. At eighteen, Louise was the primary caretaker for their nine-tree orchard—seven apple, one cherry and one plum. She loved working in her orchard—pruning and fertilizing in the late fall and picking off the caterpillars in the spring and summer. She considered her trees to be her babies and gave each one a name. Apples have a long shelf-life and kept her family in delicious pies all winter long.

In July 1704, Church arrived in Acadia with a force of 550 fighting men. He sent two of his warships to Port Royal and took the rest to Grand Pré. In both places, the Acadians fought back and were able to kill several of their attackers.

Grand Pré, with no fort or garrison, was no match for Church's men. After firing a few rounds, most Acadians scattered into the woods as best they could. The New Englanders slaughtered all the farm animals, plundered and then burned all the buildings, and destroyed the dikes. When they reached the Benoit farm, they found Louise and her father guarding the orchard, Louise with an axe and her father with a musket. Her father had pleaded with Louise to run into the woods with the rest of the family. She refused and told her father to go. He stayed with her. When the New Englanders arrived, they killed the father. Laughing at her tears, they easily disarmed Louise. With her watching, they used her axe to chop down all nine of her trees. Along with Louise, many Grand Pré Acadians were captured and taken prisoner.

Port Royal was a different story. The French had rebuilt the fort and now had it garrisoned with about two hundred French soldiers. Church's men were able to enter the basin at Port Royal and capture several Acadians in the village and burn their houses, but they were not able to get past the fort to attack the Acadian farms. The Acadian militia, along with Micmac warriors, fought alongside the French soldiers in repelling the New Englanders.

Beaubassin was a disaster for the Acadians. After Grand Pré and Port Royal, Church turned his full attention on Beaubassin.

Frank Temple was the eighteen-year-old New Englander who shot Louise's father in Grand Pré. It was his first kill, and he was very proud of himself. He was aware of the atrocities committed by the French and Indians in the outlying New England settlements—this was pay-back time, and he was more than ready for the task.

"I don't want a single building left standing!" Church instructed his men. "Kill all their animals, break open their dikes, take as many prisoners as possible, and kill all who resist!"

Like Grand Pré, Beaubassin did not have a fort or garrison of soldiers. The Acadian militia fired a few rounds and then scattered into the woods with their families. Only a few Beaubassin Acadians were captured, but the devastation was complete.

Upon hearing of the campaign's success, Massachusetts Governor Dudley was ecstatic. He happily reported this wonderful victory to his superiors in London. The British government praised him for a job well done.

Marcel, the son of Joseph Aucoin from Port Royal, sailed his boat to Beaubassin to help his relatives. His was one of many boats from Port

Royal that went to Beaubassin or Grand Pré. When he arrived at where his cousin Martin Junior's farm should be, there was nothing but destruction. The house and barn were gone, and many animals were slaughtered and lay decaying in the fields. He saw a man walking through the fields and hailed him.

"Monsieur," called out Marcel, "can you tell me where I can find my cousin Martin and his family? This is his farm."

"You must be from Port Royal. Thank God you fared better. As you can see, *les maudits Anglais* (the damn English) outdid themselves here. The men who did this will burn in hell for all eternity. I suspect they're still singing and dancing in Boston over our destruction. I wish them all an early, painful death."

"I share your sentiments. The English are evil and never to be trusted. Anyone who kills innocent Acadians and burns our settlements deserves the same and worse. Do you know where I might find my cousin?"

"If he wasn't captured, he's probably at Sylvain Croteau's farm or one of the other two farms just past his. Those three farms, about five miles from here, escaped the burning. Go back down to the basin, turn right and keep going down the basin until you reach the Tantramar River. It's the second river you'll come to, on your right. Go up the river and you'll find the Croteau farm. Good luck!"

Along the way, Marcel saw Micmac cutting the slaughtered animals and drying the meat. When he arrived at the Croteau farm, he noticed many boats from Port Royal tied up to the dike. As he made his way up to the house, he heard more than one Acadian man exclaim, "*Les maudits Anglais!*" He soon found his cousin.

"Martin, thank God you're safe. Is everyone okay?"

"Yes, hello, Marcel! It's good to see you, too. My wife, Paulette, and all our children are fine. We received word yesterday that my father, who moved to Rivière-aux-Canards two years ago, is also okay. When the New Englanders entered the basin, most of us fled into the woods with some farm animals and what little we could carry from our homes."

"That's great news. Your uncles in Port Royal were terribly worried when they heard what the Bostonians did here."

"Yes, our militia was no match for the New Englanders, but they were able to fire a few rounds and buy the rest of us some time to get deeper into the woods. Come! Let me show you our new quarters. Monsieur Croteau, who owns this farm, is letting us use his barn. About twenty families are staying here, so it's a bit crowded. Another twenty families or so are staying at each of the next two farms. The Micmac are likewise housing several families in their village."

"I brought some lambs and piglets for you and several sacks of corn and dried beans."

"*Merci*! All of that is much needed here. There's no room in the barn for the animals, so as you can see over there, some of the men are building corrals. The rest of our men are in the woods cutting trees and making boards to rebuild our houses. Rebuilding the houses is a priority! We hope to have them all rebuilt before winter. The cellars, of course, survived the burning, so there's no need to dig new ones, which will speed up the home building process."

At Grand Pré, like Beaubassin, several farms far up the rivers escaped the burning, and those homes then served as a magnet for the displaced Acadians. Michel Aucoin, the son of Martin Junior of Rivière-aux-Canards was one of those lucky ones, thanks to following his father's advice.

"Welcome!" Michel said to all arriving Acadians. "Please make yourselves at home. My wife, Colette, and I will get you whatever you need."

"Hello, Michel! I'm glad to see your farm was spared."

"Ah! Monsieur Melanson, I'm so glad to see you. We heard that many Acadians were captured and taken prisoner. I was afraid you might have been taken."

"Two of my sons and their families were captured, but my wife and I were lucky and escaped."

"Monsieur Melanson, my wife and I will move to the barn. I want you and your wife to take over our house. As our leader, it will be more appropriate for you to live in the house."

"Thank you, Michel, but the barn will suit us just fine. We need to discuss and plan many things, and being in the barn with everyone else will make things easier."

．  ．  ．

For the next three years, Acadian life at Beaubassin and Grand Pré slowly regained its customary routine. Homes were rebuilt, dikes were repaired, farm animals multiplied, and crops were planted and harvested. At Port Royal, two French privateers (privately owned warships) were now home-ported there and had been decimating New England shipping for the previous two years.

One of the privateers was captained by Bernard-Anselme d'Abaddie de Saint-Castin, from France. The other was captained by Louis-Pierre Morpain, from the West Indies. The New Englanders had no ships able to challenge either of these French vessels. The privateers therefore found easy pickings in the northeastern waters. They each captured dozens of New England trading ships and fishing boats. They even raided several New England coastal towns.

In the spring of 1707, Massachusetts Governor Joseph Dudley met with his council.

"Governor," addressed one of the attendees, "we must do something about those French privateers. The residents of Boston are up in arms regarding the lack of goods and supplies. Shortages of sugar, beef, tea, wheat, and cotton are getting worse."

"Our ships are in mortal danger as soon as they leave port," added another attendee. "They are no match for those French privateers who easily run them down and then strip them of all supplies. The privateers then head back to their haven at Port Royal."

"Something must be done to destroy Port Royal and deny the privateers their evil nest!" stated another attendee.

"I agree something must be done." replied Dudley.

•   •   •

On June 17, 1707, Colonel John March of Newbury, Massachusetts, arrived at Port Royal with three warships and 1,000 men aboard some twenty transports. The then-Governor of Acadia was Daniel d'Auger de Subercase. His garrison at Port Royal had about 250 French soldiers. The ensuing battle was a disaster for March. Over one hundred New Englanders were killed. Before leaving in defeat, March's men burned all the buildings in the Port Royal village and desecrated the graveyard, even digging up several graves and scattering the bones.

"Sir," said Governor Dudley's assistant, "Colonel March is here."

"Send him in," said Dudley.

"Governor," said March, "as I'm sure you already know, the affair at Port Royal did not go well."

"What happened? You had the superior force! The French warships were not there to impede you. How could you possibly lose?"

"After landing my men, as they were approaching the fort, they were suddenly attacked from all sides by Acadian militia and Indian warriors. The French soldiers then joined in. In very little time, scores of my men were lying dead. We were not able to regroup and mount an effective counterattack. We were in a killing field and had to retreat to avoid a complete slaughter of what was left of my men."

"Incompetence! Colonel, you are guilty of incompetence! You are relieved of command, effective immediately. Get out of my sight and consider yourself under house arrest! I will deal with you later."

The next day, Dudley again met with his council.

"We must destroy Port Royal!" exclaimed an exasperated Dudley. "Three warships and 1,000 fighting men should be more than enough to overcome a garrison of 250. What we need is a competent commander."

"Sir, I know of such a man," volunteered one of the council members. "Colonel Francis Wainwright of Salem has led several successful campaigns against the murderous French and Indians who attack our settlements. I believe he is the right man for an attack against Port Royal."

   •  •  •

Two months later, on August 20, 1707, Colonel Francis Wainwright, at the command of 1,000 men and three warships, sailed his fleet into the Port Royal basin. Although briefed on March's tactics and failure at Port Royal, Wainwright basically made the same mistake, only worse.

Wainwright's ego was enormous. He believed in himself and no one else. He paid little attention to his briefing on Port Royal for he knew from experience how bad such information could be. He would rely on his own proven skills and leadership to win this battle.

Whereas March had landed his men about two miles from the fort, and therefore out of range of the fort's cannons, Wainwright landed his men well within range of the fort's guns. As soon as most of Wainwright's men were on the ground, the fort's cannons opened and cut the New Englanders to pieces. The Acadian militia and Micmac warriors joined in from the nearby woods and brought down many more New Englanders. Wainwright's force was in total disarray from the very beginning and was not able to regain control of the situation. He soon left Port Royal in defeat with more dead and wounded than March had suffered.

"Sir, Colonel Wainwright has returned."

"Send him in."

"Governor," said Wainwright, "the enemy was far stronger than I was led to believe. The garrison at the fort was at least five hundred strong with larger and more powerful cannons than we expected. Hiding in the nearby woods were several hundred more Acadian militia and Indian warriors. When the bombardment from the fort started, the Acadians and Indians pounced on us from several sides. I lost over one hundred men in the first few minutes. No one could have fought harder than my valiant men and officers."

"You expect a medal? Is that it! You fool! You blundering, incompetent fool! We have spies at Port Royal and know for a fact the garrison has under 250 men. Before you left Boston, you were told to expect Acadian militia and Indian warriors. You still blundered into an ambush and wasted all the precious resources I gave you. And now you come and lie to me. Get out of my sight! You are a disgrace, and I expect you to resign your commission first thing in the morning!"

The next day, Dudley again met with his council.

"Wainwright was an absolute disgrace!" exclaimed Dudley. "Whoever among you recommended him to me, I want you to keep your mouth shut as we continue to search for a solution to Port Royal."

For the next three years, Dudley was not able to find a solution while the privateers from Port Royal continued to plunder the New England shipping. Dudley and many other New England officials complained bitterly to London that they needed British help in destroying Port Royal.

In May 1710, London finally responded.

"Sir," said an attendee at the Governor's council meeting. "Samuel Vetch arrived here today with letters from London requesting that we provide him with warships and men to mount an attack on Port Royal. If he captures Port Royal, the Queen has promised to make him Governor of Acadia."

"Vetch, the Scotsman? He's been nothing but trouble for us in the past! He left Boston for England in disgrace several years ago. He obviously has friends in high places. Well, if London believes in him, I suppose that's good enough for me. Since we now have the Queen's direct blessing, we should be able to attract even more men for the expedition."

•   •   •

On October 5, 1710, a force of thirty-six ships and 2,000 militia led jointly by Samuel Vetch and Francis Nicholson entered the Port Royal basin. Nicholson was a career soldier who rose through the ranks to become Governor of Virginia. His second in command was Major Paul Mascarene, another competent career soldier who was a native French speaker. On the first day of fighting, the fort's cannons caught the New Englanders off guard as they assembled ashore. Twenty or so were killed. Nicholson ordered a controlled retreat until the men were just out of range of the fort's cannons. There he ordered the men to dig trenches while he brought up his artillery pieces. The artillery was able to reach the fort and started a steady bombardment. After several days, Governor Subercase was forced to sue for peace. Nicholson granted him honors-of-war. Subercase, all French officials, and the entire garrison of soldiers—a total of about 250 men—were provided free passage to France. Whereas Sir William Phips had previously shown himself to be treacherous, a liar, and of poor moral character in dealing with the Port Royal defenders, Nicholson showed himself to be an honorable man who kept his word. Major Paul Mascarene took over as commander of the Port Royal fort.

Vetch, born in 1668 in Scotland, joined the British military and did well—rising quickly through the ranks. His unit was sent to Panama in the New World to quell a disturbance. That venture ended in defeat for Vetch and his unit. He recovered in New York where, in 1700, he married into the prominent Livingston family, who made their fortune as merchants and traders. As part of the Livingston group, Vetch started a lucrative but illegal trading business with New France. He eventually moved to Boston and in 1705, at the request of Governor Joseph Dudley of Massachusetts, embarked on a prisoner exchange mission to Québec to secure the release of the Deerfield prisoners. The mission was successful, but Vetch spent much of his time in Québec making contacts to pursue his trading business. Bostonians eventually uncovered Vetch's illegal trading with the enemy, including the sale of guns to the Québec militias. The New Englanders, including Governor Dudley, were outraged. Vetch was tried and convicted of trading with the enemy and deported to England where the ever-resourceful Vetch successfully appealed his conviction. He convinced the British authorities that the French in Canada could be defeated, and he was the man to lead such an expedition.

Vetch, now Governor of Acadia, wanted to deport all the Acadians, but he received clear instructions to the contrary from Queen Anne. She knew the English garrison now at the fort would need steady supplies from the Acadian farms to feed themselves.

In honor of the Queen, Vetch changed the name of the town from Port Royal to Annapolis Royal. He changed the name of the Dauphin River to the Annapolis River, and the fort, to Fort Anne. He also required all Acadians to sign a new oath of allegiance to the Queen.

The Acadians largely ignored the name changes and continued to refer to the town as Port Royal for many years to come.

At Grand Pré, Pierre Melanson was addressing the assembled Acadian heads of household.

"As many of you already know, the English have taken over Port Royal. They attacked with 2,000 men. Governor Subercase and his French soldiers were simply overwhelmed and have since been deported back to France. The new governor is Samuel Vetch, a Scotsman. The fort was heavily damaged during the battle, and the English are now rebuilding it, so it looks like they intend to remain in place."

"What about the Acadians at Port Royal? What happened to them?"

"As far as we know, no harm was done to any Acadian. They are being allowed to stay on their farms with all their possessions, providing they sign an oath of allegiance to the Queen. They all signed but added a clause that they would not bear arms against anyone."

"What about us? Can we expect similar treatment from the English?" The anxiety level in Grand Pré was very high. Everyone remembered their disastrous encounter with Benjamin Church just a few years earlier. That no Acadians were harmed in the recent Port

Royal takeover was welcome news but did little to reduce the overall anxiety level of the Grand Pré Acadians.

"We can expect them to contact us in due course. At a minimum, we will all need to sign the new oath of allegiance."

A few weeks later, Major Paul Mascarene arrived at Grand Pré aboard an English warship to deliver Governor Vetch's demands.

"All Acadians—anywhere in Acadia—are now considered prisoners-at-discretion," stated Mascarene to Melanson and the other assembled Grand Pré representatives. "You now hold all your possessions and properties out of the goodwill and mercy of your conquerors. If you defy us, we will crush you!"

Mascarene was unknown to the Acadians, but his message was in perfect French which surprised and pleased the Grand Pré residents. In the past, all serious discussions with the British were conducted in the English language with Melanson translating for the Acadians. Here was a British officer who was also, clearly, a native French speaker. The unusual dialogue gave a measure of hope to the Acadians. The English officer was all business. There was no warmth in his words, even so, the words were in French and that was something.

"Major," replied Melanson, "none of us here will defy you. We are simple farmers who only want to continue farming and raise our families in peace." Like everyone else, Melanson was surprised at Mascarene's fluent French. His mind was spinning as to what this encounter might mean. He would get to know this man as well as possible.

"Governor Vetch has ordered that this Grand Pré settlement is to pay a war fee of 600 pounds, and every male over the age of fifteen is to sign an oath of allegiance to the English monarch."

"Major, in all the households put together here at Grand Pré, we do not come close to 600 pounds. Such an amount is impossible for us. If you could convince the governor to cut this amount in half, we would forever be in your debt. Before your return to Port Royal, I believe we can collect perhaps one hundred pounds in cash and beaver pelts. The balance we will pay over time."

When Mascarene returned to Port Royal, Vetch was very pleased with the one hundred pounds and readily agreed to reduce the total to three hundred pounds. In successfully cutting the war fee in half, Melanson again showed himself to be a master at negotiating with the British authorities.

The signing of the new oath, however, proved to be a very thorny issue. Vetch insisted the oath be unconditional. In all prior oaths signed by the Acadians, they had added a clause that they would not bear arms against anyone. The stated intent of the Acadians was to remain neutral in the ongoing dispute between France and England. They refused to sign an unconditional oath.

The Acadians were first required to sign oaths of allegiance to the British crown in 1654 when the New Englanders took over Acadia. For the next one hundred years, as Acadia switched repeatedly from English to French control and back again, the English demanded the signing of an oath to the then British monarch. Whenever a new oath was required, the Acadian heads of household discussed this matter at length. In the early years, the clause added to the oath by the Acadians that they would not bear arms against anyone, was generally accepted by the local British authorities, if not the authorities in London. As the years went by, however, the British authorities insisted more and more on an unconditional oath. The Acadians refused. Some Acadians were willing to sign the unconditional oath, hoping for an end to conflict, but the majority opinion was that the conditional oath was better. The conditional oath had served their fathers well, and that path would be continued. In this matter, the majority opinion prevailed, right to the end. If only the Acadians had known that this solid resistance to an unqualified oath would eventually lead to their complete downfall, the history of Acadia might have evolved differently.

As to Vetch, he had amassed considerable debts in England and saw the Acadians as a source of revenue. Over the next few years, Vetch devised several schemes to squeeze more and more money from the Acadians. These schemes led to steady complaints from the Acadians, which eventually found their way to England. The British colonial authorities saw the schemes as self-serving on Vetch's part and inappropriate. As a result, Vetch was replaced as governor and recalled to England. In England, with no revenue stream, he continued to amass more debt. At the behest of his creditors, he was placed in the King's Bench Prison in London where he died on April 30, 1732, unable to pay his debts.

In April 1713, the War of Spanish Succession between France and England ended with the signing of the Treaty of Utrecht. England was awarded all of Acadia except for Ile Royale (Cape Breton Island), Ile Saint Jean (Prince Edward Island), and several other smaller, nearby islands. The French king sent Philippe Pasteur de Costebelle to take over as Governor of Ile Royale and to begin building a major fort to be named Louisbourg.

# CHAPTER 8
# LOUISBOURG

The key strategy of the French in Ile Royale in 1715 was to convince all the Acadians in Nova Scotia to move to Ile Royale. Such a move would deny the English garrison at Port Royal of vital Acadian provisions, especially wheat and beef. The English occupation would soon fail without the Acadian supplies, and the French could then regain all of Acadia. To this end, Governor Costebelle sent word to all the major Acadian settlements to send representatives to Ile Royale to hear his proposal for resettlement.

When the Acadian delegates arrived at Ile Royale, Michel Aucoin of Grand Pré and his cousin, Martin Aucoin Junior, of Beaubassin, were among them. The Acadian delegation totaled about thirty men.

"Welcome to Ile Royale," greeted Costebelle. "Your king, Louis XIV of France, the longest reigning monarch in all of Europe, has instructed me to inform you of his wish that all of you move from Nova Scotia to Ile Royale as soon as possible. We have much to offer you here. There is much land available. The land is very fertile, and you will be under the direct protection of Louisbourg, the king's fort, now nearing completion. The fort will be the largest and strongest on the entire American continent."

"Thank you, Governor," replied Jean Melanson of Grand Pré. "None of us here wishes to displease the king. Leaving our current homes, however, is no simple matter. Most of us have been on our land for three or more generations. Our Micmac friends have made it very clear they want us to stay where we are and will not allow us to leave."

"The king has requested all the native people, who are friends of the French, move to Ile Royale as well."

"Sir, the Micmac consider all the land in this part of the world theirs. They hate the English and fight them whenever the opportunity arises. Their hatred is especially deep ever since the English placed a bounty on all Micmac scalps—including women and children. They refuse to be bullied from their land by the English."

"Time will tell. Several of my ministers are now visiting the nearby Micmac villages. They have gifts for the chiefs and promises of many more such gifts if the Micmac move to Ile Royale."

"We wish you success with the Micmac, Governor. May we now see the farmland that is available?"

"Yes, if you'll climb aboard the wagons, my agricultural minister will show you the farmland."

When they arrived at the farmland, the Acadians were not impressed.

"Michel, look at the grass!" Martin said to his cousin.

"It's only about half the height of the grass in our meadows back home," replied Michel.

"And look at all the large rocks! This meadow is filled with them!"

"This land will not be easy to plow. All the rocks must first be removed."

Melanson addressed the agricultural minister. "Sir, Governor Costebelle told us the farmland here is very fertile. As the agricultural minister, can we assume you conducted tests to determine the fertility of this land?"

"Tests! How dare you ask such a question! If the governor said the land is fertile, it is for you to accept that fact and not question it. I was informed you Acadians were insolent and arrogant in the extreme. I now see it for myself!"

"Forgive me, sir, I meant no offense. The decision to move here is difficult for us. We are trying to gain as much information as possible."

"Your king has directed you to move here. That should be more than enough!"

Before returning home, Melanson again met with Costebelle.

"Governor, thank you for providing us with the farmland tour and the tour of the construction site for Fort Louisbourg. We appreciate your hospitality and are impressed with all that is happening here at Ile Royale. We now need to return home and discuss this matter with the Acadian heads of households."

"Before you leave, what is the status of that oath of allegiance the English insist you sign?"

"Sir, the English continue to insist we sign an unconditional oath. That will never happen. The only oath we will sign is one that allows us to not bear arms against anyone. If the English force the unconditional oath upon us, we will all quit our lands and move to Ile Royale. This, I promise you!"

On the way back to their homes, the Acadian representatives all agreed the Ile Royale farmland was poor compared to their current farms and if they did move, they would find themselves under the thumbs of the French officials. They agreed not to move unless forced to do so by the unconditional oath. The English deadline for the Acadians to sign the oath kept being extended because the Acadians simply refused to sign an unconditional oath.

•   •   •

On April 17, 1720, Colonel Richard Philipps, the new Governor of Nova Scotia, arrived at Port Royal. One evening, he summoned Major Paul Mascarene to join him for dinner.

"Welcome to my residence, Major. I trust your accommodations at the fort are adequate and comfortable for both you and your men."

"Yes, sir. The fort is in good condition, and we are well-supplied with all the necessities."

"I have many questions regarding the current situation here at Port Royal and the surrounding settlements. I'm particularly interested in the mindset of the Acadians regarding their refusal to sign an unconditional oath. I've been told you know more about the Acadians than any other Englishman in this colony."

"I'll do my best, Colonel, but the Acadians are a complex group that defy easy explanation. They have been here for over one hundred years and during that time have developed a unique culture. Most of them no longer consider themselves French. They still share language and religion with the French, so of course there is still a connection. That connection, however, is quite loose. In the past, they generally viewed the French officials who were sent here to rule them as oppressors."

"Oppressors! The Acadians belong to the peasant class. They owe allegiance to their superiors, whether they be French or English. The relationship between peasant and lord is natural, one might say God-given."

"I agree, Colonel, but during the many conflicts between the French and the English, the Acadians often found themselves adrift, with no lords over them. They were forced to fend for themselves. They developed their own form of self-governance and, in this process, became quite independent. They now value their own counsel more than the counsel of any other group, be it French or English."

"This Acadian independence cannot stand! I will not allow it. They will sign an unconditional oath to the English King or be banished from this land."

"The French buildup on Ile Royale, sir, is a major concern. If you force the Acadians to sign an unconditional oath, they will surely quit their lands and move to Ile Royale. The arrival of the Acadians would benefit the French and strengthen their Fort Louisbourg."

"Major, you said the Acadians don't particularly like the French. Why would they quit their lands and place themselves at the mercy of another 'oppressor'? Here, at least, they have their land."

"The Micmac Indians play a major role in this matter, Colonel. The Micmac and the Acadians share a long history. They depend now on each other. The Micmac do not want their relationship with the

Acadians to change. They insist the Acadians remain in place and will not allow them to leave."

"That seems to benefit us. If the Acadians sign the unconditional oath, they can remain on their land. It seems like a win-win-win situation for the Acadians, the Micmac, and us. What am I missing?"

"The missing piece, Governor, is the deep hatred the Micmac have for the English ever since the Bostonians placed a bounty on all Indian scalps. The Micmac have threatened to cut the throats of any Acadians who sign an unconditional oath. They will tolerate a conditional oath whereby the Acadians may remain neutral and not bear arms against anyone, but that's as far as the Micmac will go."

"This makes no sense! How can a crude, illiterate bunch of savages dictate terms to a superior people?"

"Sir, the relationship between Micmac and Acadian is quite complicated. Many Micmac warriors have Acadian fathers or grandfathers, while many Acadian farmers have Micmac mothers or grandmothers."

"So, they are part savage themselves, eh? Major, what counsel do you have for me going forward?"

"Sir, I firmly believe the Acadians will never become good, English subjects, regardless of the type of oath they sign. The only solution is to remove all the Acadians and replace them with English settlers."

"Thank you, Major. You have given me much to think about."

Paul Mascarene was born in 1684 to a Huguenot family in the Languedoc region of Southern France on the Mediterranean Coast. The Huguenots were a religious group of French Protestants who followed the Calvinist form of Protestantism. The word "Huguenot" appears to be derived from one of their early leaders, Bezanson Hugues, in the early 1500s. They suffered severe persecution at the hands of the Catholic majority. Many thousands, including the Mascarene family, emigrated from France, settling in non-Catholic Europe—the Netherlands, Germany, Switzerland, Scandinavia, and even Russia. About 50,000 took refuge in England—bringing the word "refugee" into the English language. The Mascarenes went to Switzerland where young Paul grew up and was educated. Moving to England, he embarked on a successful military career as an engineer, serving with the British forces throughout New England and Atlantic Canada from 1710 through 1740, often as a fluent negotiator with the Acadians and Indians. Mascarene rose to the rank of major-general and was appointed Governor of Nova Scotia from 1740 to 1749. He was fair in his dealings with the Acadians, but never forgave the French for the persecution of his family. His loyalties were clearly English not French. Retiring in Boston, Massachusetts, he died there on January 22, 1760.

The years went by with little change in the Acadian situation. The English continued to insist on an unconditional oath but kept extending the deadline for signing such an oath. Governor Philipps's instructions from London made it very clear he was not to do anything that would force the Acadians to move to Ile Royale.

•   •   •

In 1730, after ten years of trying through his lieutenant-governors, Philipps finally got the Acadians to sign an unconditional oath. The Acadians at Port Royal, Beaubassin, and Grand Pré all signed, and the Acadian settlements celebrated finally resolving the issue. Philipps sent copies of the signed oath to London. He did not inform them, however, of the oral concession he made with the Acadians acknowledging their neutrality.

For their part, the Acadians would have preferred the concession be in writing, but Philipps was a powerful commander in both Acadia and England. The Acadians believed the oral concession was valid, especially since many other English officials in Acadia, including Paul Mascarene, had witnessed it. The London officials soon learned of the oral concession and decided the best course, for the present, was to wait and do nothing.

The next nineteen years, regarding overall peace and prosperity, were the best for the Acadians. Throughout this period, however, skirmishes between the Micmac and the English—often deadly for both sides—persisted. The French-Canadian militias attempted to retake Nova Scotia. The New Englanders, assisted by several English warships, attacked Louisbourg and captured it on June 28, 1745. The Acadians, as usual, were caught in the middle of these battles with both sides insisting the Acadians join them.

With the signing of a treaty between France and England on October 18, 1748, at Aix-la-Chapelle, the War of Austrian Succession, better known as King George's War, formally ended. As part of the treaty, France was awarded Louisbourg.

In 1749, at Rivière-aux-Canards, Jean Aucoin (of Martin of François), now fifty-one years old, sat on his porch with his wife, Marguerite Pitre, after a hard day in his fields. They had married in 1721 and had three daughters and two sons. Jean's parents, Martin Senior and Marie Gaudet, lived well into their seventies and died peacefully.

"I'm glad we stayed here at Rivière-aux-Canards," said Jean. "My brothers, Michel and Alexis, seem happy in Cobequid, but for me, here is the best. I've lost count of the number of times they asked me to move there and join them."

"I agree. Our daughters are all settled on farms here with their husbands, and our two boys are getting bigger every day. Before we know it, they will leave us. I sometimes wish we could keep them as they are now forever, especially five-year-old Joseph, *mon doux* (my sweet one)."

"That would be nice. At thirteen, Pierre is my right arm on the farm. My plan is for him to take over this property, so if all goes well, we may be able to hang on to him forever."

•   •   •

In July 1749, Colonel Edward Cornwallis arrived as the new Governor of Nova Scotia. He was the uncle of Charles Cornwallis, who would surrender the English army to the Americans at Yorktown in 1781.

Cornwallis landed at Chebucto Harbor on the Atlantic side of Nova Scotia, where he decided to make his headquarters and build a town. He was accompanied by over 2,000 English settlers. He named the town Halifax, after his superior, Lord Halifax in London.

The Acadians at Grand Pré sent a delegation to Halifax to greet the new Governor. Claude Leblanc, Jean Melanson, and his brother, Philippe Melanson, were chosen for the trip. Each of them was a head of household with several children, well respected in the Grand Pré community, and could speak English. The distance over land between Grand Pré and Halifax was about fifty miles, a leisurely day's ride on horseback.

"I wish we knew more about Cornwallis," said Claude on the trip to Halifax.

"I agree," said Jean, "and what little we know is not good."

"His conduct in Scotland where the English sent him three years ago does not bode well for us," added Philippe.

"He burned the Scottish churches and tortured the civilians in crushing a Scottish rebellion," said Jean. "God help us if he is still the same man!"

After arriving in Halifax and making their presence known, they waited two more days before being summoned by Cornwallis.

"Governor," greeted Jean, "welcome to Acadia. We hope you had a pleasant passage."

"Thank you for coming," replied Cornwallis. "You have saved me the trouble of summoning you from your settlements. I have here a royal declaration written by Lord Halifax that requires all Acadians to sign an unconditional oath of allegiance to King George II. You have three months to sign the oath. All who do not shall lose all their property and be forced to vacate this province."

"Sir," replied Jean, "signing such an oath means a death sentence for us. The Micmac Indians will cut the throats of any Acadians who sign. They will tolerate a conditional oath that allows us to remain neutral."

"There will be no conditional oath!" exclaimed Cornwallis. "My assistant has several French translations of the declaration for you. Return to your homes, inform your friends, and return here in two weeks with representatives from all the Acadian settlements." Feeling defeated, the Acadians returned home to share this upsetting ultimatum.

The Acadian representatives from Port Royal, Beaubassin, and the Grand Pré area arrived in Halifax on August 11, 1749.

"Governor, I am Prudent Robichaud from Annapolis Royal. I have with me a letter signed by over 1,000 heads of household expressing our gratitude for the privileges granted us by General Philipps after we signed the oath of allegiance to his Majesty, King George I. We have abided by our oath and lived in peace for the past twenty years. Your requirement that we now sign an unconditional oath is not possible for us. Such an oath would place us in mortal danger from our Micmac neighbors. If you force this oath on us, we will all quit the province."

"You are not at liberty to negotiate with the King of England!" exclaimed Cornwallis. "The general who granted you a concession did so in error! You are a conquered people and have no rights other than those we choose to grant you. The deadline of October 25 for signing the oath, however, may be a bit too soon. I hereby grant you an extension until the spring of 1750."

"We have another tyrant in charge of us," thirty-six-year-old Joseph Aucoin said to his cousin, thirty-two-year-old Edouard Aucoin on their way back to their settlement.

"Yes," replied Edouard. "Besides, with all those English settlers, it seems clear Cornwallis intends to replace us with his own kind. It may be time for us to move to French-held territory."

"You may be right! Where would you go—Ile Royale, Ile Saint Jean, or Canada?"

"Ile Saint Jean, for sure! I don't want to trade one tyrant for another."

Joseph and Edouard were the sons of brothers Michel and Alexis Aucoin, formerly of Rivière-aux-Canards. That branch of the Aucoin family had moved to Cobequid (modern-day Masstown near Truro, Nova Scotia), at the northeastern end of the Minas Basin. In 1750, Cobequid was a growing community with over one hundred Acadians. Joseph was married, had eight children, and farmed a productive twenty-acre piece of land. His wife, Pauline, happily tended their four apple trees. Living there was easy. The land was fertile, the adjacent waters full of fish, and the nearby Micmac Indians good neighbors. The forest, rivers, meadows, and bays were a well-known and comforting part of their community. They knew where the fish bit and the deer grazed, when to expect the first snow and the spring thaw. It was home.

The arrival of Cornwallis severely alarmed the people. That generation of Acadians knew well the history of cruelty at the hands of the English. Cornwallis' reputation as the "butcher of Scotland" had spread and struck fear in the population.

Talk of relocation was rampant after the Acadian representatives returned to their settlements and informed the populace of Cornwallis' demands. Some Acadian families decided to move to Ile Saint Jean or Ile Royale as soon as the harvest was completed. Relocations started in earnest in the early spring of 1750 when hundreds of Acadian families moved to Ile Saint Jean or Ile Royale. All had friends or family in the new locations, so the move was easier than it otherwise would have been.

In Halifax, the governor's assistant brought him the bad news. "We have received word the Acadians are moving in great numbers to both Ile Saint Jean and Ile Royale."

"What? I gave no such order! How dare they leave without my express permission! Send word to Annapolis Royal for Fort Anne to send two companies of soldiers, one each to Beaubassin and Grand Pré, to put an end to these illegal relocations. And send Lieutenant-Colonel Lawrence to me at once!"

Lieutenant-Colonel Charles Lawrence had been garrisoned at Louisbourg and was transferred to Halifax along with five hundred English soldiers after the recent French takeover of Louisbourg. He was born in 1709 in Plymouth, England. His father was a general in the English army. Following in his father's footsteps as a career soldier, Charles entered the army in 1727, served in the West Indies and Belgium and joined the 45th Regiment at Louisbourg in 1747.

"How may I help you, sir?" said Lawrence.

"Colonel, I want you to take four hundred men and march to Grand Pré, where you are to build a fort suitable of controlling the inhabitants. You are then to do the same thing at Beaubassin. These Acadians need constant reminders as to who their superiors are. Since they accuse us of governing with fire and sword, we will not disappoint them!"

Lawrence's initial trip to Grand Pré and Beaubassin was more of a reconnaissance. The Acadians were alarmed when they saw the British regulars among them. They met with Lawrence and did their best to keep things peaceful. On his return to Halifax, Lawrence informed Cornwallis that Grand Pré did not need a fort, but Beaubassin direly needed one. Cornwallis agreed, and all efforts were then directed to building a suitable fort at Beaubassin.

During this time, the Isthmus of Chignecto, connecting Nova Scotia with the mainland, was controlled by the French. Beaubassin was on this isthmus, on the Missaguash River. In 1750, on a ridge on the western side of the river, the French built Fort Beauséjour.

Antoine Landry had a twenty-acre farm on the eastern side of the Missaguash. He was overjoyed when he first heard the French would build a nearby fort. "Rita, the French are finally coming to our aid," he told his wife. "If the English ever attack us again, they'll be in for a big surprise."

"Antoine, that fort will be much too close to our farm and will surely generate a response from the English," replied Rita. "They probably already know of the French plan. There will not be any surprise."

The English response was to build Fort Lawrence on the eastern side of the river. Soon, the village of Beaubassin was no more. The

French burned the Acadian homes and all other buildings on the eastern side of the river, including Antoine Landry's farm, denying the use of those buildings to the English and forcing the original occupants to flee to the western side. The Missaguash became the de facto boundary between French-controlled and English-controlled land on the Chignecto isthmus.

Cornwallis' harsh measures continued for the next two years. That tactic, however, had little effect on the tide of Acadian relocations. His superiors in London became alarmed that the French forces in the area were being strengthened by the added population. The cost of the English settler initiative had grown excessive, with little to show for it. Many, if not most, of the original settlers had moved to New England.

Cornwallis was ordered to use a different approach with the Acadians—one that would not force them to quit their lands, and he was told less money would be sent regarding the settler issue. He needed to economize and make do. Cornwallis saw this change in policy as a reprimand and loss of faith in his leadership. He resigned in the summer of 1752 and returned to London. His replacement was Colonel Peregrine Hopson.

Hopson had been the British governor of Louisbourg from 1747 to 1749 and had a good understanding of the Acadian situation. He saw the Acadians as critical for the efficient operation of the British garrisons and British government in Nova Scotia. In time, he believed the Acadians would become good British subjects. To ease the situation, he reversed the harsh policies of Cornwallis and instead took a much more conciliatory approach with the Acadians. Unfortunately for the Acadians, Hopson suffered a serious eye infection in the fall of 1753 and had to return to London.

With Hopson's departure, Lieutenant-Colonel Charles Lawrence was appointed Lieutenant-Governor of Nova Scotia. Lawrence's character, beliefs, and inclination were far closer to Cornwallis than to Hopson.

In Boston, upon hearing of Lawrence's appointment as Lieutenant-Governor of Nova Scotia, Governor William Shirley of Massachusetts sensed a comrade-in-arms and made plans to visit Lawrence in Halifax to discuss the final solution to the Acadian problem.

# CHAPTER 9
# THE DEPORTATION (LE GRAND DÉRANGEMENT)

"Governor Shirley, welcome to Halifax. I hope you had a pleasant trip."

"Thank you, Governor Lawrence, the trip was very pleasant. I've always enjoyed coming here, especially in the summer where your temperature is cooler and more comfortable than ours in Boston."

Shirley was born in 1694 in Preston, England. He arrived in Boston in 1731 with the intention of practicing law. Ten years later, he was named Governor of Massachusetts. He despised the Acadians, referring to them as, "the most obnoxious French inhabitants of Nova Scotia." He strongly believed the Acadians would form a fifth column against the English forces in the region. Because of their proximity to New England, he saw them as a major threat.

"Governor Shirley, you are always welcome here. Your dispatch mentioned a serious business you wanted to discuss with me."

"Yes, I'm concerned the Acadians in your colony are far too many and pose a serious threat to the peaceful existence of our English settlers. We know them to be closely allied with the Micmac savages that brutally attack our settlements, both here and in New England."

"I share your concern. The Acadians and Micmac are a significant threat to the stability of my government and the success of my English settlements. I am surrounded by this enemy! They profess to be peaceful and neutral, but the Acadians quickly help the French, and the

Micmac attack my English settlers on every occasion. There can be no peace with French agents entrenched in our midst."

"With our two colonies working together, I believe we can finally put an end to the unacceptable threat represented by these Acadians and savages within our borders."

"Your words are much appreciated. I have long sought an ally to assist me in ridding this colony of Acadians."

"Have you read the plan prepared by Captain Charles Morris for the removal of the Acadians?"

"No, I'm not aware of any such plan."

"Morris is another dedicated ally of ours. He currently serves as surveyor-general for your colony. In his work during the past five years, he has become very familiar with every bay, basin, river, stream, and tidal flat in your colony and has mapped the location of every Acadian village, hamlet, dike, and pathway used by them."

Lawrence's eyes lit up. "That information would be very useful."

"I'll see that a copy is delivered to you. This plan must not fall into the wrong hands. Secrecy and stealth are of the utmost importance."

"I'm intrigued. I must see this plan as soon as possible."

"You won't be disappointed. The plan provides details on how to disarm the Acadians and separate the men from their families—all without raising undue alarm. It even specifies how many boats will be needed to complete the extirpation and where the boats might come from. The Acadians are to be scattered among the other British colonies in North America, a few here, a few there. None are to be sent to French-controlled land. All that makes a community and a culture— thus a rebellious horde—will vanish."

"Amazing! That plan seems like a godsend."

"I agree, and in due course, I suggest the two of us meet in person with Morris to put the finishing touches on his plan."

"I look forward to that meeting with great anticipation."

"Thank you, Governor Lawrence. I would now like to discuss another proposal with you, specifically, the destruction of Fort Beauséjour in Chignecto."

After Shirley returned to Boston, Lawrence summoned Lieutenant-Colonel Robert Monckton to join him. Monckton was the commanding officer of the English garrison in Halifax. He was born in 1726 in London to a prominent English family, where his father was a member of Parliament. Entering military service in 1741, at fifteen, he rose rapidly through the ranks, was promoted to lieutenant-colonel in 1752 and posted to Nova Scotia in 1753.

"How may I assist you, sir?" asked Monckton.

"Colonel, I have an interesting assignment for you. Governor Shirley and I have just agreed on a plan for the destruction of Fort Beauséjour. You are to play a major role in that plan. Shirley will raise a force of 2,000 men and provide the vessels needed to transport them to Chignecto. You will train these men in Boston, and in the spring, when the firearms and ammunition for this campaign arrive from London, you will take your men to Chignecto and destroy Fort Beauséjour. One other thing, you will carry a letter of credit and provide it to Governor Shirley. The letter of credit will state that I will pay for this entire campaign out of my provincial funds."

"I am honored by this assignment. When do you want me to leave for Boston?"

Monckton was a career soldier with significant experience earned in several military campaigns in Europe and the West Indies. He was a solid, competent, and effective officer who took his new assignment in stride. He would prepare his men well, plan the attack appropriately, and succeed in due course. Failure was not an option.

"Perhaps in a month or so. Shirley will need time to raise the 2,000 men. He has given that assignment to Lieutenant-Colonel John Winslow, a well-decorated and well-liked soldier whose family arrived in Massachusetts on the *Mayflower*. Winslow will be your second-in-command on this campaign."

"I've heard favorable things about Winslow, and I look forward to having him at my side."

Winslow was born in 1703, in Marshfield, Massachusetts, twenty-nine miles southeast of Boston. He belonged to one of the most prominent families in New England. His great-grandfather, Edward Winslow, and grandfather, Josiah Winslow, each served as governors of Plymouth Colony. In 1755, at fifty-two, Winslow was twenty-three years older than Monckton, and although both held the same rank of lieutenant-colonel, Monckton clearly outranked him. Winslow's rank was awarded by provincial authorities with less exacting standards. Monckton's was awarded by senior British army officers who reported directly to the king. The British officers at every level often looked down on their counterparts in the local militias.

Winslow was aware of the superiority complex of the Redcoats. They always wanted to integrate his troops with their regulars. Winslow fought to keep militia soldiers under their own officers, fearing the hard discipline, including floggings and hangings, that was part of the regular army. His militia soldiers appreciated his efforts to protect them from Redcoat officers. True to his calling, Monckton tried to annex Winslow's troops under his direct command, but Winslow would have none of it. He stood his ground, leading to considerable discomfort between the two officers. They did not like each other but were still able to work together to achieve the common goal.

•   •   •

On June 16, 1755, Fort Beauséjour fell. The French officers and Canadian militia were granted honors-of-war and transported to Louisbourg.

At Rivière-aux-Canards, at midnight on June 2, 1755, while the battle of Fort Beauséjour was in progress, a sharp strike sounded on the door of Jean Aucoin's home. Jean and his eighteen-year-old son, Pierre, answered the door together. They were surprised to find a British soldier at the door.

"By order of Governor Charles Lawrence, you are ordered to surrender your firearms and ammunition," said the soldier.

"Why?" replied Jean.

"You must surrender them immediately! Otherwise, my men will enter your home and take them."

Jean and Pierre could then see four other soldiers standing just behind the first with their firearms pointed at the door.

"We need our firearms to protect our farm animals from wolves and other beasts," stated Pierre.

"You must surrender them now! This matter is not subject to debate. My orders are explicit!"

"Pierre, give him our firearms. We will discuss this matter later with our neighbors."

All the Acadian firearms and ammunition at Rivière-aux-Canards and in the greater Grand Pré area were simultaneously confiscated by the English starting at midnight on June 2, 1755. This confiscation of firearms was a key element in the deportation plan prepared by Charles Morris.

"Papa, the English have taken all the Acadian firearms throughout the Minas Basin region. What can this possibly mean?" asked Pierre of his father.

"No one seems to know. I met yesterday with the Melanson brothers in Grand Pré, and they were unable to shed any real light on this matter. The prevailing thought is the confiscation is related to the ongoing battle at Fort Beauséjour. Whatever is happening, it can't be good."

"Perhaps it's time for us to move to Ile Saint Jean," said Jean's wife, Marguerite. "Henri and Patrice have repeatedly asked us to join them."

"I'm not yet willing to abandon this farm. It would be a good idea, however, for Pierre and Mondou to join your brothers until our situation here becomes clearer. Pierre, how do you feel about taking your brother to Ile Saint Jean?"

"Whatever you think best, Papa. Getting to Ile Saint Jean should be simple. First, I would go to Beaubassin and stay with Uncle Martin, then to Baie Verte. From there, I would catch a boat to Ile Saint Jean."

"Keep in mind that Beaubassin will probably be in turmoil with the nearby battle for Fort Beauséjour. I will send a letter to Martin and let him know you and Mondou will visit him shortly."

In Halifax, a messenger arrived at Governor Lawrence's home.

"Enter," said Lawrence.

"Sir, we just received a dispatch from Chignecto. Fort Beauséjour has fallen!"

"Fallen? So soon? This is excellent news!"

"Colonel Monckton has deported all the captured French and Canadian fighters to Louisbourg. He says several hundred Acadians took part in the fort's defense. They all claim they were forced by the French to take part under pain of death. He asks what your orders are."

"Pain of death? Nothing could be further from the truth! I'm certain those damned Acadians willingly took up arms against us. They have violated their oath of neutrality. Now is the time to finally rid ourselves of those disloyal Acadians! Come back in an hour's time, and I'll have some dispatches for you."

"Yes, sir."

In Chignecto, while Colonels Robert Monckton and John Winslow were enjoying a leisurely dinner in Monckton's quarters at Fort Beauséjour (renamed Fort Cumberland in honor of King George II's son William Augustus, Duke of Cumberland, also known as Butcher Cumberland for the part he played in suppressing a Jacobite uprising in the Scottish Highlands in 1746), a tap came at the door.

"Enter," said Monckton.

"Colonel, a special dispatch has just arrived from Halifax."

"Thank you, Captain. That will be all."

"Well, now! Let's see what Governor Lawrence has in store for us!" Monckton said to Winslow.

Monckton read through the letter twice without saying a word. Winslow watched the color drain from Monckton's face as he read the dispatch. When finished reading, Monckton handed the dispatch to Winslow, with a smile on his face.

"My god! He plans to rid the entire colony of Acadians—men, women, and children, starting here in Chignecto!" said Winslow.

"Yes! This business is long overdue," replied Monckton. "The Acadians should have been removed years ago. These orders make it clear you are to observe the deportation process here and then proceed to Minas Basin, where you will perform the same there."

"I understand my orders," said Winslow stiffly. He did not say he was used to fighting men—not women and children. He realized now, as he had not quite before, that Monckton relished the part he was about to play in getting rid of all Acadians, seeing them not as adversaries but as vermin.

•   •   •

Eighteen-year-old Pierre Aucoin and his eleven-year-old brother, Joseph (nicknamed Mondou), sailed to Chignecto on an Acadian boat with several other passengers heading for Ile Saint Jean. As soon as they entered Chignecto Bay, their small boat hugged the coastline to avoid detection by the many English ships in the bay. The passengers, including Pierre and Mondou, disembarked about ten miles from Beaubassin and proceeded on foot.

"How will we find Uncle Martin's house?" asked Mondou.

"His farm is on the Missaguash river in Beaubassin. If we have trouble finding it, we will simply ask someone for directions. Uncle Martin has lived here for a long time. I'm sure he is well known, and people will know where he lives."

"Do you think Papa's letter reached Uncle Martin?"

"It should have. Papa sent the letter a full week before we left."

As they rounded a turn in the trail, Pierre and Mondou stumbled into a British patrol.

"Well, what have we here?" asked the soldier. Neither Pierre nor Mondou could speak English, and they understood very little.

"I asked you a question, boy, and you'd better answer!"

Pierre answered in French, which angered the soldier, who then struck him in the mouth with the butt of his rifle.

"Conway, for God's sake, leave him alone!" cried another soldier. "Our orders are to prevent any Acadians from leaving, not to assault them! Jenkins, I want you to take these two back to the captain. Take Williams and Adams with you and then return."

•   •   •

"By order of Colonel Monckton, all Acadian males aged sixteen years or older are to come to Fort Cumberland tomorrow at 10:00 AM to hear a message directly from the Colonel," said the English officer to the assembled Acadians. This message was repeated in every Acadian hamlet in the Chignecto region.

"Once the men are in the fort and under our control, the women and children will stay put and not try to run away with their farm animals," said Monckton.

This step to separate the Acadian men from their families was well detailed in the overall deportation plan prepared by Charles Morris that Shirley and Lawrence had previously studied. The age of sixteen in the Morris report, however, proved to be a mistake. It should have been younger. Many families with strong fifteen-and fourteen-year-old sons saw this ploy for what it was and escaped into the woods with their farm animals. Winslow would not make this mistake. At Grand Pré, he ordered all males ten years or older to assemble at the church.

"Seems like a brilliant plan," replied Winslow.

"We'll soon know if it's going to work."

"Governor Lawrence's dispatch stated that the ships for the removal from Chignecto are on their way from Halifax, and since the Chignecto Acadians have been the most rebellious, they are to be deported to the furthest of the British colonies in America."

"Yes, it will be most difficult for them to find their way back from our southern colonies," said Monckton. "This exercise should cause the end of any Acadians in this land for a very long time. Good riddance!

If they ever come back, they will find well-established English settlers on their old properties."

"The Governor's dispatch mentioned that the ships for the deportations from Minas Basin and Annapolis will be supplied by the Thomas Hancock Company in Boston. I know Hancock quite well. He is English, through and through, and has little love for the French. He will be happy to play his part in this exercise."

"You New Englanders have been, and continue to be, critical to the overall success of this plan. I know your Governor Shirley has played a major role in getting this project going. You are supplying the bulk of the manpower and ships for the deportation."

"We are happy to do our part in ridding this colony of our common enemy. The real threat, however, lies with the French in Canada and Louisbourg. I fear this extirpation of Acadians, especially the women and children, will come back to haunt us."

"This is a savage country, Winslow," said Monckton. "The wise soldier fights the battle at hand."

Winslow said nothing.

•   •   •

On July 4, 1755, fifteen Acadian leaders from the Minas Basin area arrived in Halifax after being summoned there by Governor Lawrence. They soon found themselves in front of Lawrence.

"I need all Acadians to swear an unconditional oath of allegiance to King George II," demanded Lawrence.

"Governor, we cannot swear an unconditional oath. For us to do so would mean our death at the hands of the Micmac."

"Silence! You Acadians have been using your Micmac friends as an excuse for far too long. This charade ends here today! If you refuse to swear to an unconditional oath, you will be removed from this province."

"Sir, we need to consult with the other Acadian heads of household to determine the will of the majority."

"Quiet! I'm certain you already know the will of the majority. For the moment, forget about the majority. I need to know if you fifteen will sign an unconditional oath."

"Sir, we can only sign an oath that allows us to remain neutral."

"Despicable! You will pay dearly for your outrageous and disloyal behavior. Captain, escort these prisoners immediately to our prison on George's Island."

•   •   •

On July 25, 1755, an additional seventy Acadian leaders from Minas Basin and Annapolis Royal arrived in Halifax after being summoned there by Governor Lawrence. The net result of this meeting was basically the same as the July 4 meeting. All seventy Acadian leaders refused to sign an unconditional oath and were then imprisoned on George's Island.

"Excellent! Excellent!" exclaimed Lawrence. "This matter is moving faster and better than I could have imagined. With their leaders now imprisoned on George's Island, the remaining Acadians should be easy to control, especially since they've all been disarmed."

"Governor, we just received word from Boston, the ships you ordered from the Hancock Company are on their way."

"More good news! Captain, come back in an hour's time, and I'll have two dispatches for you, one for Major Handfield in Annapolis Royal and the other for Colonel Winslow at Minas Basin."

•   •   •

"Where are you boys headed?" asked the English captain to Pierre.

"My brother and I are going to visit our Uncle Martin in Beaubassin."

"Beaubassin? Does your uncle's land border the Missaguash river?"

"Yes, his farm is about two miles up the river from the basin."

"Most of those farms were destroyed during the fighting for Fort Beauséjour. I doubt you'll find anything there. Where are you coming from?"

"Fighting? We know nothing of any fighting at the farms!"

"Where are you coming from?"

"We're from Rivière-aux-Canards in Minas Basin. The boat we were on was supposed to take us all the way to Beaubassin, but the owner of the boat became alarmed when he saw all the English ships in the bay. He refused to go any further. He put us ashore and then turned around."

•    •    •

"Colonel Monckton, a captain has asked to speak to you. He says he may have important information regarding the current campaign."

"Send him in."

"Colonel, thank you for seeing me. My men and I were assigned to guard the roads south of here and to stop any Acadians from leaving. While no Acadians came south to our position, we captured two Acadian boys who were coming north into Chignecto. They said they arrived on a boat from Minas Basin headed for Beaubassin, but the boat owner became alarmed upon seeing the English ships in the bay. He put them ashore and headed back to Minas Basin. It seems likely he'll warn the Minas Basin Acadians as to what he saw here."

"Thank you, Captain. Did you bring the boys with you?"

"Yes, sir."

"Place the boys with the rest of the Acadian men being held here. That will be all."

The next morning, on August 11, 1755, Monckton addressed the assembled Acadian men in the fort.

"You are all declared to be rebels! All your lands and goods are now forfeited to the king. You and your families are to be deported out of this province."

The Acadians were dumbstruck. It took several moments before anyone could voice their outrage. Several of them then came forward to Monckton to protest such an illegal and immoral pronouncement. They were immediately met with fixed bayonets by the soldiers around Monckton. He refused to debate the matter with them and was not interested in their complaints, withdrawing to his quarters instead.

"He cannot be serious!" exclaimed Joseph Babin to the other Acadians near him. "My family has farmed here for three generations. I have a wife and ten children under the age of fifteen. Deported where? What can this possibly mean?"

"Thieves and murderers," said another man softly. "Pa was right."

"My last-born is buried on the hill," said another. "It will kill the wife to leave her."

• • •

In Minas Basin, Colonel Winslow's dinner with his two top subordinates was interrupted by a messenger.

"Colonel, we just received an urgent dispatch from Halifax."

"Thank you, Captain. That will be all."

After reading the letter, Winslow informed his subordinates, "Governor Lawrence wants us to allow the Acadians to harvest all their fields before we proceed any further with this exercise. The harvest will supply the ships for the deportation. Their farm animals will likewise supply the ships with meat. This information is not to leave this room!"

• • •

After the fall of Fort Beauséjour, New England rangers were sent by Monckton to torch the Acadian hamlets north of the newly named Fort Cumberland. Lawrence had urged using every method to distress the Acadians, especially those who refused to surrender. Happily, Monckton complied with a campaign of terror. The rangers streamed across the countryside plundering all in their path, burning all homes and other buildings, capturing Acadians, and killing those who resisted. What happened to the girls and young women was equally traumatizing. In advance of this marauding army, hundreds of Acadians fled north, up the Petitcodiac River to several settlements far up the Petitcodiac. So far, all those lower Acadian settlements had proven to be soft and easy targets for the pillaging New England rangers.

The village of Petitcodiac, however, about sixty miles up the river from where it emptied into Chipoudy Bay, was the home of fifty-three-year-old Joseph Broussard, nicknamed Beausoleil (beautiful sun). He had an intense hatred for the English and for many years had been involved in raids against English settlers and British patrols in Nova Scotia. In late August 1755, he had gathered over one hundred of his like-minded men to his side in Petitcodiac, evenly split between Micmac warriors and angry Acadians. In addition, at his request, a French-Canadian militia force of about two hundred men commanded by twenty-eight-year-old, Québec-born, Charles Deschamps de Boishébert, arrived at Petitcodiac. Together, Beausoleil and Boishébert planned the defense of the village.

"It's amazing, the stupid Acadians don't even fight back," stated Private Frank Robinson, aboard one of the two New England sloops making their way up the Petitcodiac River. Their assignment was to lay waste to all Acadian settlements along the way.

"They deserve everything they get," replied his buddy, Private John Gates. "They're all cowards and will not receive any mercy from me."

The two sloops were commanded by Major Joseph Frye of Massachusetts. He had two hundred New England rangers with him. On September 2, 1755, after looting and burning several villages on the way, he disembarked fifty of his men to continue their campaign of terror against the village of Petitcodiac.

"Frank, I bet you a mug of beer that I kill an Acadian in this village before you do," said a laughing John Gates to his buddy.

"You're on!" replied a smiling Robinson. Both were in the party of fifty, and for them, this was a party very much to their liking.

After ransacking and burning a few homes near the river and making their way further into the village, the fifty terrorists were themselves terrorized when some three hundred well-armed Acadian, Micmac and Canadian fighters burst out of the woods, screaming their war cries and firing their weapons. The stunned New Englanders fell back in panic. By the time they regained their sloop and Frye ordered a retreat, twenty-three rangers lay dead and another eleven were seriously wounded. The dead included privates Robinson and Gates.

That brief battle on the banks of the Petitcodiac River further enhanced the reputations of both Beausoleil and Boishébert as dedicated and effective protectors of the Acadians. Both continued to engage the enemy decisively in many more battles. Of the two, Beausoleil's hatred of the English was more intense and led him to use harsher methods, including the scalping of the English soldiers and settlers that he killed. His Acadian and Micmac fighters would continue to strike terror into the hearts of many English soldiers and would-be English settlers for the next four years.

•   •   •

At Grand Pré, a wedding engagement was being completed at the home of Raymond Ladouceur. Ladouceur was a widower whose wife had died giving birth to their daughter, Andréane, just over seventeen years before. Ladouceur had never remarried. Andréane was his pride and joy. She had grown up to become a strikingly beautiful young woman, yet sweet and humble, with an immense love for everyone around her, especially young children. The entire village loved her. Many were the young men who hoped to catch her eye. The bravest among them even came calling. Andréane, however, had eyes only for Marcel Bergeron, her neighbor's son. Marcel and Andréane had grown up together. He was two years older than she, but when she was five years old, she knew she would someday marry Marcel. The parish priest as well as René Leblanc, the long-time notary for Grand Pré, were present and had now given their blessing for the proposed union. Both recorded the data into their official records, one religious and the other civil. Also present were Marcel and his father, Jean Bergeron.

All six enjoyed a savory dinner of roast pork, potatoes, carrots, sweet corn, and fresh bread and butter, with apple pie waiting for dessert—the entire meal prepared by Andréane. Her spinning wheel lay in the room's corner. Andréane was an accomplished seamstress, adept with both flax and wool. She made all of her and her father's clothing.

"Raymond, have you heard anything more why the English are here?" asked Jean.

"Nothing specific, but I was working with several men this morning on the dike, and the consensus seems to be that the English are here to purchase our produce after the harvest."

"If that's the case, why all the secrecy? Why not simply tell us they intend to purchase our harvest? And why do they need 300 soldiers to purchase it?"

"Excellent questions, my friend." replied Raymond. "Monsieur Leblanc, you are by far the most traveled and most learned of all the Acadians here in Grand Pré. Can you tell us why the English are here?"

"That question has troubled me ever since they arrived four days ago and took over the church as their barracks. That they confiscated all our weapons in June and are now holding many of our leaders in Halifax is a major concern. I don't have a good answer, but since the harvest is just about complete, we should know soon."

Two days later, on September 4, 1755, while Raymond Ladouceur was admiring his harvested fields, several soldiers rode up to him and told him all males ten years old and older were ordered to report to the church by 3:00 PM the following day to hear a message from Colonel Winslow.

"Papa, why do they want the ten-year-olds to attend?" asked Andréane. "It makes no sense!"

"We all agree it makes no sense. The entire community is alarmed, but what choice do we have? Some men think the English purpose is to evict us from our land and keep the harvest for themselves. The majority, however, believe Winslow's message at the church will be that we must sign an unconditional oath. We will, of course, refuse to sign such an oath, regardless of the consequences."

The following day, after 450 Acadian men and boys had entered the church, Winslow ordered the doors barred and the church surrounded by soldiers. He then read the orders he had received from Governor Lawrence.

"Gentlemen, I have received from his Excellency, Governor Lawrence, the following message: your lands and tenements, cattle of all kinds, and livestock of all sorts are forfeited to the Crown with all other of your effects, save for your money and household goods. And you yourselves are to be removed from this province." Winslow's message continued for several more minutes, but the above cruel and heartless words formed the core of his message.

The Acadians in the church couldn't believe their ears. None of them said anything for several minutes. They were dazed by what they had just heard and had great difficulty in digesting the repulsive message.

As the Acadians recovered from Winslow's hateful words, "*Les maudits Anglais!*" reverberated throughout the church as the Acadians found their voice. Alexandre Landry, a large, muscular, father of eight became enraged. With his fists closed tightly and the veins throbbing visibly in his thick neck, he began moving towards Winslow.

The five or six soldiers in the church with Winslow quickly realized they were in mortal danger and no match for the 450 angry Acadians. With bayonets pointed at the Acadians, they all swiftly backed out of the church and barred the door.

The men and boys were held in the church for thirty days while waiting for the deportation vessels to arrive. During this time, the women brought them food daily and a change of clothes as needed. Winslow prepared a list of the 450 males in the church. The name Aucoin appears eighteen times.

• • •

At Fort Cumberland, in Chignecto, Pierre Aucoin and his brother Mondou searched among the captives for their Uncle Martin.

"Monsieur, excuse me, but do you know our uncle, Martin Aucoin?" asked Pierre to an Acadian man in the fort. "His farm is on the Missaguash River in Beaubassin."

"Yes, I know your uncle very well. He lived on the Missaguash for many years. My farm was near to his."

"Do you know if he's here in the fort?"

"He's not here. After the French burned his home, barn, and fields because they were on the English side of the Missaguash, he and many other Acadians left Chignecto for Ile Saint Jean. I should have done the same. The French burned everything on the English side of the Missaguash, including my property." His head was in his hands, but he looked up at the young boys. "What happened to your face?"

"After my brother and I were captured, the English soldier hit me in the face with the butt of his rifle."

"*Les maudits Anglais!*" exclaimed the man.

•　•　•

In early October 1755, the loading of the transports began in Chignecto. As the men were loaded aboard, their wives and children joined them. Pierre and Mondou soon found themselves aboard one of the ships.

"Pierre where are they taking us?" asked Mondou.

"No one whom I've spoken with seems to know. The English are keeping our destination a secret."

"How will Mama and Papa find us if we don't even know where we're going?"

"I don't know, but at least we're not alone. There are many Acadians here who know our family. Somehow Mama and Papa will find out where we are and know what to do. The main thing is for us to stay together and hope for the best."

Pierre was doing his best to remain strong, but he was terribly concerned. He knew the English were the enemies, he had grown up with that story, but he hadn't really understood what it meant, that things could happen so suddenly, without explanation, to him, to his family. It was a break from everything his life had been, and his brain scrambled to put the pieces together. The one thing he knew for sure was that he was responsible for his brother, and that knowledge was his lifeline. He vowed to himself that they would survive and eventually find their way home again.

•   •   •

At Grand Pré, Andréane Ladouceur was filled with anguish. Her father and her fiancé were now imprisoned. How could God let this happen? What had started as one of the happiest days of her life had now turned into one of the worst.

Also in early October, the transports finally arrived in Minas Basin and the loading of the Acadians at Grand Pré began in earnest. Chaos reigned throughout the loading process. Those eighty-five Acadian leaders remained prisoners on George's Island for the next seven years. Their wives and children were deported without their husbands and fathers. The men were never informed by the English authorities where their wives and children were sent. With their husbands and fathers still imprisoned in Halifax. The women and children of those men refused to get on the transports without their men. The men, however, were clearly not coming back. Screaming women and children were forced onto the transports at bayonet-point. The English loaders soon lost patience with any effort to keep families together. Husbands and wives found themselves aboard separate transports headed for different destinations. Parents and children were separated—the mothers screaming for their young children. Mostly, the English hatred for the Acadians was absolute. No compassion, no mercy, no kindness was shown to the defenseless, captured Acadians. Terror reigned. As soon as the Acadian homes were emptied of their occupants, the soldiers ransacked them, stealing anything of value and destroying everything else. Livestock was butchered in place. All was done in full view of the former Acadian occupants.

"Papa, where is Marcel?" Andréane asked her father as the two of them were herded aboard one of the transports.

"We were together in the church, but the soldiers placed us in separate groups prior to our exit. My group came out first. He may still be in the church."

Upon hearing those words, Andréane was gripped with a terrible fear that she would never again see her beloved Marcel. Raymond Ladouceur heard a wailing sound escape from his daughter that he had never heard before. Her wail silenced everyone around them, both Acadian and English. It carried all the way to the church, and when Marcel Bergeron heard it, he knew it was Andréane. He screamed her name as loudly as he could, but the low pitch of his voice was no match for her high one. His scream, though loud, was not heard by his beloved Andréane. Marcel and his father were in the last group to leave the church. Their transport was destined for Pennsylvania, whereas Andréane's went to Connecticut.

•  •  •

On October 13, 1755, eight transports loaded with the Chignecto Acadians left for Annapolis Royal. The flotilla was accompanied by several British warships. The plan was for the Chignecto transports to remain in Annapolis Royal until joined by those carrying the Minas Basin Acadians.

On October 21, 1755, fourteen transports carrying over 2,600 Acadians left Minas Basin for Annapolis Royal. Each transport was overloaded well beyond its official carrying capacity. Still, there remained another 800 captured Acadians in the Grand Pré area that the English could not fit aboard the boats, including one hundred men and boys still imprisoned in the church.

On October 27, 1755, the twenty-two transports (fourteen from Minas Basin and eight from Chignecto) left Annapolis Royal for points south. They carried over 4,000 Acadians. While still in the Bay of Fundy, the flotilla was hit by a severe storm that battered the transports and scattered them onto the open sea. Two of these boats, the schooner *Boscawen* and the brig *Union*—bound for Philadelphia with 580 Acadians—were never heard from again and presumably went down with all hands.

On November 5, 1755, after only ten days at sea, six of the storm-battered transports limped into Boston Harbor for repairs. An investigation by a committee of the Massachusetts Assembly found the Acadians were severely overcrowded and suffering badly with insufficient food and clothing and very poor water. The death rate aboard two of the six transports was staggering. *Endeaver*, which left Minas Basin with 166 Acadians, arrived in Boston with only 125 alive. *Ranger*, with 263 exiles from Minas, arrived in Boston with only 205 survivors. The survival rate was better on the other four boats, but they were still severely overcrowded and under-provisioned.

The *Cornwallis*, not part of the six transports in Boston, departed Acadia with 417 Acadians and arrived in South Carolina with 207 alive.

On December 8, 1755, another seven transports left Annapolis Royal for the British colonies carrying 1,650 Acadians originally from the Annapolis Royal area.

In mid-December 1755, additional transports arrived in Minas Basin, and all remaining captured Acadians were finally loaded aboard. As soon as the loading was completed, the soldiers set fire to all the homes, barns, and mills in the Grand Pré area, including the church. The Acadians could see the flames from the boats.

Governor Lawrence's orders regarding this matter were very specific: All Acadian homes, barns, mills, and churches were to be burned to the ground to deny any refuge for any escaped Acadians. Colonel Monckton saw to the burning in the Chignecto region, while Colonel Winslow did the same in the Minas Basin area. Annapolis Royal was last and met the same fate.

By the end of December 1755, just under 7,000 Acadians had been deported from Nova Scotia. Over 1,000 of these deportees died in the process.

In his journal, during the deportation of Grand Pré, Colonel Winslow termed the business "Very Disagreeable to my natural make & Temper." He died comfortably on April 17, 1774, in Hingham, Massachusetts, just south of Boston, surrounded by his loved ones.

Many Acadians escaped the deportations of 1755. Ile Saint Jean housed over 4,000 Acadians, Ile Royale about 1,500, and modern-day New Brunswick also 1,500. Another 1,000 escaped into the woods of Nova Scotia and found shelter in the Micmac villages. The deportations, however, were just beginning.

# CHAPTER 10
# MASSACHUSETTS TO GEORGIA

The findings of the Massachusetts Assembly regarding the deplorable plight of the Acadians had very little impact in creating any goodwill towards the Acadians. The allocation of Acadians to the Massachusetts colony totaled about 1,000. These were assigned in small groups throughout Boston and the surrounding towns and villages where they were deeply hated and seen as enemy agents. Many of these towns refused to provide any help to the Acadians. They were left on their own to find food, shelter, and clothing to survive the winter. Many of the Acadians assigned to Massachusetts perished during that first winter. The overall treatment of Acadians in the other colonies was no better, and sometimes, worse. When the Acadian parents could not pay any rent, it was common to take their children forcibly and assign them as servants in wealthy British homes or as workers in various enterprises. The parents would not see their children again for many months.

"Pierre are we there?" asked Mondou as the two of them were finally allowed their turn on the deck of their transport.

"I don't know if this is our destination. I don't recognize that large town. I've never been here before."

An Acadian man standing nearby overheard them and said, "We are in Boston Harbor, but this is not our destination. I overheard two sailors yesterday say we're headed for Virginia."

"Virginia! I've never heard of Virginia. Why are we going there?"

In mid-November 1755, word came to Governor Robert Dinwiddie of Virginia. "Sir, six transports carrying 1,200 Acadian neutrals have arrived at Hampton Roads. The British commander in charge of these transports intends to disembark the Acadians there. He has provided this letter to you from Governor Lawrence of Nova Scotia."

"What? I know nothing of any Acadians coming here. Give me the letter!"

After reading the letter, Dinwiddie told his assistant to inform the British commander he was not to disembark any Acadians. He then called for an emergency meeting of the Virginia Assembly.

"Governor, we cannot allow these treacherous Acadians to settle among us. As we speak, their French countrymen with their native devils are murdering and scalping our brothers and sisters in our western settlements."

"I agree," replied Dinwiddie. "None of these repulsive Acadians will touch the soil of this colony! No governor may send such numbers of enemies to another colony. I will not permit this outrageous act to proceed!"

The Assembly initially refused to provide any provisions for the Acadians, but when informed by the British commander that he was out of supplies and the Acadians would all starve to death, they reluctantly agreed to provide some food and other necessities. Otherwise, the death of the Acadians would be blamed on the Assembly. What to do with the Acadians was hotly debated for several months with no clear solution. In the meantime, the transports remained at anchor in Hampton Roads. During this time, Dinwiddie's position towards the Acadians softened a bit after he considered how his superiors in London might view this situation. He suggested to the Assembly that the Acadians be allowed to disembark and then be allocated only to the eastern towns and villages. The Assembly vehemently opposed his suggestion and determined it was England's responsibility to decide what to do with the Acadians not Virginia's. They overwhelmingly agreed to send the Acadians to England.

In the spring of 1756, the transports carrying the 1,200 Acadians originally destined for Virginia, including Pierre Aucoin and his brother Mondou, turned east for England.

Previously, on November 15, 1755, aboard HMS *Syren*, Commander Charles Proby entered the final stage of his dreadful voyage from Nova Scotia. He was accompanying six transports destined for South Carolina and Georgia.

"Lieutenant, signal the transports to come about and enter the harbor before us."

"Aye, Captain."

As the transports and the *Syren* entered Charles Town Harbor in South Carolina, their unannounced arrival caused quite a commotion among the townspeople. When they finally realized the boats carried Acadians destined for South Carolina, the townspeople were dismayed. A messenger was immediately dispatched to the home of Governor James Glen of South Carolina.

"Governor," said the messenger, "six transports have arrived in Charles Town Harbor carrying Acadians. The British commander is in the process of disembarking them on Sullivan's Island."

"What? Acadians? What nonsense is this! No one may disembark any Acadians here!"

"The commander has a letter for you he says explains everything. He insists on delivering this letter to you personally."

"Jeffrey!"

"Yes, sir."

"Saddle my horse and inform Major Jones to meet me at the harbor with a platoon of soldiers."

"Governor Glen, thank you for coming so quickly. My orders are to offload four transports here carrying about 600 Acadians. The remaining two transports, with about 400 Acadians, are destined for

Georgia. Here is a letter from Governor Lawrence of Nova Scotia explaining this unusual situation."

"Commander, neither Governor Lawrence nor you may offload any Acadians here. I insist you reload the Acadians aboard your transports!"

"Governor, many Acadians aboard these six transports—men, women, and children—died on the way here. The survivors are all sick and in poor condition. Many more will die if they remain aboard the transports, and I have no intention of being responsible for any more deaths. My orders are to deliver four transports here. I have done that and will now be on my way. These Acadians are now your responsibility."

The following day, Glen met with his council.

"Governor, having these Acadians here is an abomination!" exclaimed one of the members.

Another added, "Let them fend for themselves on Sullivan's Island. They will not receive any help from us!"

"Unless we give them provisions, they will all die, and their deaths will be blamed on us," replied Glen. "Until we can figure out what to do with them, we will confine them to the island and provide them with the means to survive."

•  •  •

After leaving South Carolina, the *Syren* with its final two transports entered the harbor on the Savannah River in Georgia and began offloading the Acadians on Tybee Island at the river's mouth. The townspeople sent word to Governor John Reynolds.

"Governor," said the messenger, "a British warship and two transports filled with Acadians have entered the Savannah River. The commander is currently offloading the Acadians on Tybee Island."

"What? No one informed me of this!"

"Sir, the commander says he is following very specific orders."

"Governor Reynolds, thank you for coming so quickly. My name is Charles Proby, and I am the commander of the *Syren*. My orders are to offload two transports, carrying about 400 Acadians, in your colony. Here is a letter from Governor Lawrence of Nova Scotia."

After reading the letter, Reynolds said, "Commander Proby, I forbid you from disembarking any Acadians in this colony! Those that are already ashore must be immediately reloaded onto your transports."

"Governor, with all due respect, that will not happen. Many Acadians died on the transports on the way here and were buried at sea. If they remain on the transports, many more will die. I have no provisions for them. They are now your responsibility!"

Later that day, Reynolds convened his council to discuss the matter.

"Let them rot on Tybee Island!" said a member. "We owe them nothing!"

"I agree," said another. "We must keep them on the island. They cannot be allowed to settle in our midst."

After considerable discussion, the council agreed the Acadians would remain on the island, but they agreed to supply enough provisions for the Acadians to survive. Otherwise, they would die, and the council would be blamed.

At every subsequent council meeting throughout the winter months, the Acadian situation was thoroughly discussed with no solution in sight.

Life on the island was not pleasant for the 386 Acadians who landed there—all of whom were suffering from malnutrition and various illnesses, especially the youngest and oldest among them. Fortunately, several abandoned buildings stood on the island, including a large warehouse formerly used to store cotton bales for shipment overseas. The warehouse and surrounding buildings were in disrepair with large holes in their roofs but provided some protection from the elements. The provisions provided by the Georgians included mostly dry food items, such as beans and rice, and some blankets and old clothes. The Acadians were not familiar with rice but quickly learned how to cook it.

At the end of their first week on Tybee Island, twelve of their group had perished and were buried in the nearby field. Jacques Maurice Vigneau, thirty-two-years old, emerged as their leader, mostly because he could speak English and was reasonably healthy.

"Monsieur Vigneau, my wife Louise is very sick," implored Maurice Boudreaux, one of the island Acadians. "She has lost a lot of weight, has difficulty breathing, and needs a doctor. She's seven-months pregnant with our first child."

"I'll do my best to get help for her," replied Vigneau. "The supply boat, however, won't be here for another four days, and we have no way of communicating with the English except through that weekly supply boat."

On the day the supply boat arrived, twenty-one-year-old Louise Boudreaux was buried in the little island cemetery. But the weekly supply boat was a small sailing vessel that provided Vigneau with a tremendous idea.

In early March 1756, he approached Governor Reynolds's office.

"Sir, an Acadian man from Tybee Island is here and has asked to speak with you."

"An Acadian, you say? Send him in."

"Governor, forgive me for intruding. My name is Jacques Vigneau, and I am the spokesperson for the Acadians on the island. We pooled what little money we had and were able to purchase several small sailing vessels. What we need now is your permission to leave this colony. We intend to sail north until we reach our homeland."

Reynolds was stunned. Finally, here was the solution to his problem. He readily agreed to Vigneau's request and issued him a passport dated March 10, 1756. The passport stated that Vigneau and the other Acadians had proved peaceful and respectful inhabitants during their four-month stay in Georgia and were now free to depart the colony.

Only about half the island Acadians joined the sailing group. The rest decided to stay put on the island for various reasons—too sick, too old, not willing to take a chance on the open sea. When the sailing group left, the island cemetery had already grown to forty-eight graves.

At the end of March, Vigneau's flotilla arrived at Charles Town, South Carolina, where it caused quite a stir. The townspeople sent a messenger to summon Governor Glen.

"Governor, more Acadians have arrived in the harbor, but these are on their own sailing vessels."

"What? Their own sailing vessels? What nonsense is this?"

"They carry a passport signed by Governor Reynolds of Georgia giving them permission to leave his colony."

"Passport? Jeffrey, saddle my horse!"

"Yes, sir."

"Sir, thank you for seeing me," said Vigneau. "Here is my passport. We do not wish to inconvenience you. Several of our vessels, however, cannot go any further without repairs, and all our vessels need food and water. If you can assist us, we will be on our way as soon as possible and will cause you no more trouble."

Glen quickly endorsed Vigneau's passport and gave instructions to assist him with repairs and provisions. He then called a council meeting.

"Gentlemen, we finally have the solution to our Acadian problem. We will provide them with several sailing vessels, some provisions, and a passport to leave our colony."

Glen's proposal was unanimously approved by the council. Vigneau's flotilla heading north grew by several more sailing vessels.

In May 1756, several boats from the flotilla came ashore in Hampton, Virginia, for repairs and supplies.

"Sir," said the messenger in the governor's office, "several vessels with Acadians have landed in Hampton."

"Acadians? Who sent them? And why are they here?" questioned Virginia Governor Dinwiddie.

"They have passports signed by governors Reynolds and Glen giving them permission to leave their colonies. The vessels are here for repairs and provisions on their way north."

After meeting with his council, Dinwiddie agreed that the best course of action was to assist the Acadians and see them on their way as quickly as possible. No one wanted any Acadians in Virginia.

In early July 1756, in Halifax, a lieutenant arrived to see Governor Lawrence.

"Governor," said the lieutenant, "hundreds of Acadians in boats have been spotted off the coasts of Maryland, New York, and Rhode Island. They are all sailing north."

"What? The Acadians were supposed to be dispersed in small groups throughout the towns and villages of the colonies."

"It seems, sir, that some colonies refused to accept them."

"Damnation! Before you return to your regiment, Lieutenant, I will have several dispatches for you."

"Yes, sir."

Lawrence wrote letters to the governors imploring them to arrest any Acadians they found on their shores or sailing off their shores. He reminded the governors that stopping the Acadians was a key step in ending the French and Indian attacks on their settlements.

The first arrests took place at Sandwich on Cape Cod, Massachusetts, where Jacques Vigneau himself and one hundred Acadians had come ashore for supplies. They were all captured and taken to Boston where they were distributed to several towns.

A few weeks later, in August 1756, about eighty Acadians were found camping on a Long Island beach in New York. All were arrested and subsequently dispersed to several locations. The arrest order came from New York Governor Charles Hardy after reading the Lawrence letter.

In late August 1756, a flotilla of nine vessels containing several hundred Acadians and headed by Raymond Girouard entered the Bay of Fundy.

"Raymond, how should we proceed up the bay?" asked Paul Leblanc, his second in command.

"Signal the other boats to follow us, single file, up the western side of the bay. We want to keep as much distance as possible between us and the Nova Scotia coastline. Our goal is the *rivière* Saint Jean, another two hundred miles north of here."

"We are very low on food and water, but no one wants to stop. Two more days of sailing will bring us home!"

"Yes, if all goes well."

The trip from Georgia and South Carolina took four months aboard the small, cramped sailing vessels. During the voyage, to avoid the English authorities, they only came ashore at night to refill their water containers, dig clams, and gather whatever edibles they could find to supplement the fish they caught. At sea, they stayed far enough out that detection from shore would be difficult. The voyage was not pleasant, they all lost weight they could ill afford to lose, and several died, but their spirit was strong. They all yearned for their homeland and family.

All went well. Just under three hundred Acadians sailed up the *rivière* Saint Jean into modern-day New Brunswick. They went far up the river, near present-day Fredericton, where they were welcomed by other Acadians and Micmac friends. In reaching their homeland, they achieved a small victory over the maddening, deplorable and hateful deportation.

•   •   •

"Papa, do you know this town?" asked Andréane as their transport docked in the harbor.

"*Non*, I have never been here before."

"We are in New Haven, Connecticut," said a nearby Acadian man. "I heard the sailors talking as I came on deck. This is our destination."

"Connecticut? I have never heard of this place," said Andréane. "Papa, we must find Marcel! Perhaps his boat landed here."

"We will see. I will do everything in my power to help you find him."

Andréane and her father were forced to remain in Connecticut for two years before being granted a passport allowing them to leave the colony. During her two years in New Haven, she visited many

Connecticut towns in search of her beloved Marcel. A typical inquiry went:

"Monsieur, have you seen a young man named Marcel Bergeron? He is my fiancé. We're from Grand Pré."

"*Non*. I'm sorry. Have you seen a girl named Marie Dusseault? She is my daughter. She was fourteen when we left Port Royal aboard different transports."

From Connecticut, Andréane and her father went to New York. As soon as they arrived, she asked an Acadian lady, "*Madame*, have you seen my fiancé, Marcel Bergeron? We're from Grand Pré."

"*Non*. I don't know him. Have you looked through the ads?"

"Ads? What ads? I don't understand."

"The newspaper has a French page containing many ads from Acadians looking for lost relatives. The ads are cheap—just one cent, so many Acadians place ads in the paper. The newspaper makes money by then selling the papers. The same ad will appear in the major newspapers in Boston, New York, and Philadelphia, so they are very effective. Many Acadians have found their lost relatives through these ads."

Andréane was very excited. "Where can I get one of these newspapers?"

"The newspaper building is three blocks that way. Before you get there, you will probably find a boy on a corner selling the papers. Good luck in finding your fiancé."

The French page took up three full pages in the newspaper. It contained well over one hundred ads. She and her father recognized several families mentioned in the ads but read nothing of Marcel.

"Papa, even though there is no ad for him, there's a good chance he's here in New York. We must continue our search."

"Yes, my daughter. I will help you as long as I can."

The years slowly went by. Andréane and her father visited most, if not all, the towns in New York with no hint of Marcel.

"Papa, we must go to Philadelphia. The last Acadian man we spoke to said several transports from Grand Pré were sent there. That must be where Marcel is."

Two weeks later, at seventy-four, Raymond Ladouceur, the former master of a prosperous thirty-acre farm in Grand Pré, passed away and was buried in a pauper's grave just outside New York City. Andréane was forty-five years old. She grieved the passing of her father and then proceeded to Philadelphia, where she searched unsuccessfully for several more years for her Marcel. She joined a convent and spent the rest of her years tending to the sick and poor of Philadelphia. Marcel was never seen again and was presumed to have gone down at sea aboard one of the missing transports that never arrived.

# CHAPTER 11
# HUNT TO THE DEATH
# (CHASSE À MORT)

Twenty-four-year-old John Simons and his twenty-two-year-old wife, Janet, lived in a rented, two-room tenement on Front Street, in Watertown, Massachusetts, just across the Back Bay, west of Boston. John worked as a laborer for the Watertown Brick Manufacturing Company—work he did not like. Both he and Janet yearned to farm their own land.

"Janet! You won't believe what I saw today at the butcher shop," exclaimed John when he got home from work. "A flyer offering free land to settlers willing to move to Nova Scotia. Since the Acadians were deported last year, there's lots of free land."

"Nova Scotia?" questioned Janet. "That's so far away. Free land sounds good, but I was hoping we could find something nearby."

"Nothing nearby is safe. The men at the butcher shop were talking about a raid two days ago in Shrewsbury, not twenty miles from here. The savages slaughtered three families and burned their homes. With the Acadians gone, all of Nova Scotia has been pacified. We'll be much safer there than on any nearby farm."

Their boat left Boston Harbor in mid-May 1756. The voyage took two full days for the thirty-one families heading for their own farm plots at Annapolis Royal in Nova Scotia. Two months later, all thirty-one families were well established on the former Acadian farms. More families arrived every other week from the same boat.

John Simons couldn't believe his good luck. The five acres of corn he had planted were already knee high. The rest of his twenty acres were also doing well. The harvest that fall would help put him and Janet on easy street.

•   •   •

Beausoleil, who earlier repulsed the English at Petitcodiac, was born and grew up in Port Royal on one of the very farms occupied by those soon-to-be-dead New Englanders. He was enraged at the sight of them. Gathering over sixty Acadian and Micmac fighters, they spread out in the woods above the houses, just out of sight. All New Englanders, male or female, thirteen years or older, were to be killed.

Beausoleil launched the attack himself by bursting out of the woods and screaming, "*La mort aux maudits Anglais!*" (Death to the damn English!) The battle lasted only fifteen minutes. After all targeted New Englanders, including John and Janet Simons, were dead, the warriors set fire to the homes and other buildings. By the time the soldiers at the fort saw the smoke and came running, nothing was left to find but dead and scalped settlers and traumatized children. Sweaty and blood-soaked, Beausoleil had four scalps attached to his belt.

•   •   •

On May 18, 1756, England declared war on France. That date was the official start of the Seven Years War, better known in North America as the French and Indian War.

The war in 1756 and 1757 favored the French with major victories at Fort Oswego on Lake Ontario and Fort William Henry on Lake Champlain.

In London in December 1757, Sir William Pitt, the British war minister, summoned Major General Jeffrey Amherst. Amherst was then thirty-eight years old.

"How may I help you, your excellency?"

"General, what can you tell me about the losses at Fort Oswego and Fort William Henry? I've read the dispatches as I'm sure you have. I need to know what's not in the dispatches. Why did we lose?"

"Those losses are very disappointing. The campaigns were led by capable British officers, and each included a regiment of well-trained British regulars. The bulk of our forces, however, comprised colonial militia. The militia consists mostly of poorly trained farmers who sign up for the campaigns based entirely on the promised pay. The pay is often several times more than they can make on their farms."

"How are they when the fighting starts?"

"They are typically good for one volley. After that, if there is much resistance from the enemy, the militia turn tail and run for cover."

"That is treasonous behavior! Do you ever hang these defectors?"

"In the early days we tried, your excellency. We hanged several to encourage the rest. The result was that the militias refused to assist us on subsequent campaigns, regardless of the pay."

"I see. And how do you propose solving this problem?"

"There is no easy solution. The militia are farmers, not soldiers. Whatever commander depends on this militia during a major battle will have a tough time. One volley is all he can expect."

"I have decided, General, we will reverse these losses in North America. Based on your comments, I see now that the regiments involved must be comprised mostly, if not entirely, of British regulars. The next campaign, in which you will lead the troops, will be to take Louisbourg. You will be accompanied by twenty British ships-of-the-line, and your army will comprise well-trained British soldiers."

"I look forward to this engagement, your excellency. When do you want me to launch it?"

"I want you to spend the winter planning the destruction of Louisbourg! And you need to decide how best to gain mastery of the St. Lawrence seaway after Louisbourg falls. The twenty ships-of-the-line will remain at your disposal, and Admiral Boscawen is eager to assist you with the planning. You sail in the early spring."

•   •   •

"I love my new job in Monsieur Richard's store," exclaimed Jeannette Terriot to her husband Joseph. "The customers are nice, and I enjoy waiting on them."

The two escaped from the Cobequid area, near Minas Basin, during the deportations of 1755 and made their way to Louisbourg. For the first year, they lived in a tent provided by the French commander of the fort. During that time, hundreds of Acadians poured into the area and housing was in short supply. Tents filled the gap till permanent housing could be built. Two years later, twenty-one-year-old Jeannette and twenty-three-year-old Joseph lived in a small cottage on the edge of town with their one-year-old daughter, Annette. Joseph worked as a laborer in the fort.

"Are you sure Monsieur Richard doesn't mind you bringing Annette with you to work?" asked Joseph.

"He loves her almost as much as I do, so it is not a problem," replied Jeannette. "The town is growing so fast there's a shortage of workers. I know of twelve shops in town with more in the works. Most of them are short of workers."

"Three of those twelve shops are taverns, you know."

"Yes, and that's fine. The taverns attract the soldiers into town, and they spend their money in various shops, not just the taverns."

"Speaking of soldiers, another two hundred French soldiers arrived today. They moved into the new barracks my work group helped build. There must be over 3,000 soldiers stationed here, and the fort is indestructible. Its walls are so thick that no cannon balls can breach them. If the English are foolish enough to come here, they will be destroyed—not the fort."

•   •   •

General Amherst sailed for America on March 16, 1758. After arriving in Halifax, the army and navy units spent most of May training together as the massive invasion fleet came together. His army totaled 14,000 soldiers, all regulars except for four companies of well-trained American rangers. These troops were divided into three divisions, one each for brigadiers James Wolfe, Charles Lawrence, and Edward Whitmore. His invasion fleet, comprising over two hundred warships and transport vessels, anchored in Gabarus Bay, three miles west of Louisbourg, on June 2.

The French commander and governor of Ile Royale, the Chevalier de Drucour, had 3,500 soldiers under his command at the fort, as well as an additional 3,000 marines and sailors aboard the French warships in the harbor.

The English came ashore on June 8 under heavy artillery fire from the French. The English suffered substantial casualties but were able to secure a beachhead that allowed the rest of the troops to land and begin the siege of Louisbourg. To their credit, both General Amherst and Admiral Boscawen, his second-in-command, gave orders that the town of Louisbourg was not to be shelled. All fire was to be directed at the fort, its outside fortifications, and the warships. Those orders were followed. The town of Louisbourg suffered very little damage.

The French warships, in particular the seventy-four-gun *Prudent* and sixty-four-gun *Bienfaisant*, were anchored in the harbor and proved to be major impediments to the taking of Louisbourg. Those final two were captured on July 25, allowing Admiral Boscawen to enter the harbor with his warships. The end was in sight. The English warships began a bombardment of the fort it simply could not withstand.

The following day, July 26, 1758, Governor Drucour asked for terms. Amherst and Boscawen replied he must surrender unconditionally, otherwise the town would be attacked by sea and land. After some painful discussions with his French officers, Drucour accepted, and the British occupation of Fort Louisbourg began on July 27. A month later, afraid that a subsequent treaty with France might again return Louisbourg to the French, the English forces destroyed it. All walls and other structures within the fort were reduced to rubble.

The Acadians on Ile Royale, including Joseph, Jeannette, and Annette Terriot, and the Acadians on Ile Saint Jean were now defenseless and were rounded up in large numbers and deported. By November 5, 1758, over 3,100 Acadians from Ile Saint Jean were shipped to France—France because the British colonies refused to accept any more. Another 1,500 from Ile Saint Jean fled to Canada. Of the 3,100 shipped to France, at least 1,649 died at sea. British and French registers of arriving passengers in France recorded the loss of 780 Acadians from disease and exposure. The *Duke William* and the *Violet* went down in the mid-Atlantic with 756 Acadians, while the transport *Ruby* ran aground in the Azores, and 113 Acadians drowned. To add further insult to these deportations, the captain and crew of the *Duke William* survived in two lifeboats that carried them to safety. In doing so, they violated maritime laws by abandoning their Acadian passengers to the fury of the sea. All the Acadians under their control drowned while they saved themselves.

•  •  •

"Governor Lawrence, I appreciate the part you played in our successful campaign against Louisbourg."

"Thank you, General Amherst. Louisbourg has been a thorn in my side for the past four years. I was most happy to assist in the removal of that thorn!"

"As you may know, the next goal for me is to secure the Gulf of St. Lawrence to prepare for our assault on Québec, planned for next year. I need to remove all Acadians from Ile Saint Jean and the shores of the gulf, to eliminate the least possibility of resistance. What can you tell me of these Acadians?"

"I assure you, General, I will provide whatever help I can, including the troops under my command, to support your continuing exercise. We estimate about 4,000 Acadians are on Ile Saint Jean with much smaller numbers scattered in various hamlets along the gulf. This map I've prepared for you shows where the Acadian hamlets are."

"Thank you. How well-armed and led are these Acadians? How much resistance can we expect?"

"They are mostly farmers and poorly armed. You should have very little difficulty in capturing the bulk of the Acadians. Once captured, we will deport them then burn all their homes, barns, and churches to discourage any escapees from returning."

"I've heard of several armed resistance groups operating in the area. What can you tell me of them?"

"They comprise a combination of Acadian and Micmac warriors. Their leader is an Acadian named Beausoleil. They are well-organized and armed, and they frequently attack my patrols and English settlements, murdering and scalping everyone. Because of their terror tactics, I've been unable to place new settlers on the land vacated by the Acadians in 1755. I have placed a bounty of ten pounds each on the scalps of these terrorists. I intend to fight fire with fire."

•   •   •

After his successful defense of the Petitcodiac village and his ouster of new English settlers, Joseph Broussard, nicknamed Beausoleil, and his brother Alexandre were involved in many other raids against the invaders. They were active and vigorous hunters of the English. The brothers had seven grown sons as lieutenants, and that leadership team was supported by about fifty other fighters—half Acadian and half Micmac warriors. Beausoleil's hatred of the English knew no bounds. Growing up, he had always had a close relationship with the Micmac, his best friend since early childhood, being a Micmac boy. When they were both seventeen, the boy and his entire family, including his eight-year-old sister, were murdered and scalped by the English. As far as Beausoleil was concerned, the English were the savages. He always remembered the Micmac had been there first and the Acadian settlers depended on their friendship as much as on their own hard work. The politics of Europe did not concern him. This was his home, and he would protect it. "That one was born to be a hero or a criminal," his mother used to say.

Joseph was the strategic thinker and charismatic leader, while Alexandre focused on woodcraft. All the men learned to move like the Indians did, silently and without trace, to read the weather and animal signs, to hide in plain sight. They were a team, but they also knew how to decide on the fly, to choose whether attack or retreat was in order. They had contempt for the regimented English troops who fought for nothing but their pay. Alexandre was also the one the men came to if they disagreed with a choice Joseph made; he listened better, and if he thought the concern had merit, he knew how to put it to his brother.

•   •   •

Oliver Jenkins, an English bounty hunter from Halifax, used paid informers to gather intelligence about Acadians. "I know a fur trapper who was working his traps about thirty miles from here. He reported seeing three Micmac and six Acadians across the river from where he was. The Acadians were a man, a woman, and four children. The oldest child was about ten. The woman and all four children have blond hair."

The Halifax government paid the bounty on all scalps, regardless of color. No questions asked. Jenkins and his five cohorts became full time bounty hunters early in 1756. In just over two years, they collected the bounty on over 200 scalps. The bulk of them were Acadian, who were far easier to kill than the Micmac. Families with children were the easiest of all: few of the children could fight or would run if their mothers were near, and the women always screamed.

Unknown to Jenkins, the informer's information was a setup. About a week earlier, the Micmac came across the fur trapper's trap line and informed Beausoleil. A plan quickly emerged whereby an Acadian family would be used as bait to lure the bounty hunters to that location. Beausoleil was tired of seeing his people treated as prey; it was time to turn the tables. The Micmac let the trapper see the Acadian family by the river, which was shallow at that spot. The Acadian family was then safely whisked away from the river and guarded by several Micmac warriors. The biggest danger to the family was that the trapper might open fire on them. Such an event, however, was highly unlikely with the presence of three Micmac warriors. The trappers were usually just the informants, and if the trapper fired, it would mean his certain death.

"Maurice, I'm frightened! What if something goes wrong? We are all exposed here, especially the children," exclaimed the blond woman.

"We have to put our faith in Monsieur Beausoleil," replied her husband. "We are the bait, so there is some risk, but I believe the risk is small. Imagine if we did not have these men to protect us and fight back against the bounty hunters. Those monsters would kill our children without pity. It is far better to eliminate them now."

"Beausoleil, six English are heading this way," reported a Micmac scout.

"How far are they?"

"About three miles from here."

"Good. Light the campfire."

As the bounty hunters moved toward the river, they squabbled about how much to pay the informers. The hunters were the ones whose knives parted scalps from skulls, who risked their lives; didn't they deserve most of the bounty? Jenkins reminded them the game had changed: the prey was warier; scalps weren't so easy to find. He might have been talking about animals—and indeed, game was scarcer than it had been—except for the excitement in his voice at the prospect of murder. Not all the hunters were so bloodthirsty. For many, it was the only way they knew to make a living. They were rough men, solitary by nature, yet easily led.

"That river is about a mile from here," said Franklin. "Let's spread out and approach slowly and quietly."

When they reached the river, the bounty hunters gradually came together and waited patiently for a half hour. They were well-concealed and on full alert for any signs of activity. Soon they all smelled the smoke and, from the direction of the wind, knew a campfire was burning somewhere across the river. Jenkins gave the order for them to spread out again, wait another five minutes, and then slowly cross the river.

As the killers reached mid-river, the Micmac warriors rose. Four copper-tipped arrows found their mark. Musket balls from Beausoleil and his son downed the other two. Hatchet blows finished the would-be scalp takers. The blond woman covered her children's eyes, but the oldest boy wiggled free. He watched solemnly as the bounty hunters' scalps were taken and their scalps affixed to the waists of Beausoleil and the Micmac warriors.

His parents thanked the warriors profusely and invited them home for a victory feast: river trout, quail eggs, cornbread, and huckleberry jam. The boy watched the men eat, and his eyes traveled to the scalps still hanging from belts. He wondered if it was a bad thing to take pleasure in the deaths of enemies. He would not ask his parents about this.

•   •   •

"You called for me, sir," reported Colonel Monckton.

"Yes, with the impressive success of General Amherst in clearing the Acadians from Ile Saint Jean, I don't want to lose the initiative," Governor Lawrence said. "We know many Acadians are hiding far up the rivers on the mainland. I want you to take four hundred New England rangers and sail up the river Saint Jean."

"Sir, do you want me to arrange for transport for the Acadians we capture?"

"Colonel, I'm not interested in any more captives. I want you to kill everyone you find and burn all their homes and other buildings. The reason for the rangers, instead of our troops, is that the rangers are not at all squeamish in eliminating Acadians."

"As you wish, Governor."

Far up the river Saint Jean, near present-day Fredericton, New Brunswick, lay the parish of Sainte-Anne des Pays Bas. Many of the boat people who sailed from Georgia and South Carolina made their homes there.

•   •   •

"Colonel, the scouts we sent up the river have located two Acadian guards, one on each side of the river."

"Thank you, Captain, have Major Rogers join me in my cabin," replied Monckton.

"You sent for me, sir?"

"Yes, Major, two Acadian guards have been located about two miles up the river from here. I need you to send several men up each side of the river to eliminate them quietly. Those guards can only mean their village is nearby. After you eliminate the guards, send scouts up to find the village. Send one hundred or so of your rangers on each side of the river in a flanking movement to encircle the village and prevent escapes. They are to remain concealed and not engage the Acadians. After they're in place, they are to send a messenger to us. We will then proceed up the river and engage the enemy."

"Sounds like an excellent plan. What about captives?"

"There will be no captives. All Acadians are to be killed."

"Colonel, some of my men are sensitive and dislike killing children. We have come to an agreement among ourselves, only children four years or older will be killed. Children younger than four will be spared."

Monckton laughed and replied, "I appreciate your men's compassion, Major. Your terms of engagement are more than acceptable."

The massacre at Sainte-Anne went as planned. The Acadians fought, screamed, and ran; the men were shot first, then women with children in their arms were cut down by musket fire, and boys and girls of eight and ten were grabbed in the rangers' strong arms and had their necks broken or heads dashed against a tree. It was a scene out of hell for the parents, though they had little time to suffer. No Acadian above the age of four survived the initial attack and many of the littlest also died, left to burn in houses set afire. The livestock were killed as well, animal screams mingling with the crackle of the fire and the wailing of toddlers hiding under beds. The stench of burning human flesh rose from the homesteads along with the smell of smoke, gunpowder, blood, and ruptured bowels. The rangers methodically collected scalps.

•   •   •

"General Amherst, a captain has arrived with news of atrocities."

"Atrocities? Send him in."

"General, thank you, for seeing me. My commanding officer, Colonel Pickering, sent me here to inform you of the atrocities committed on an Acadian village up the Saint Jean River."

"The Saint Jean? I was not aware of any military activity in that area."

"We heard rumors of atrocities and were able to locate an English fur trapper who saw the site and confirmed the rumors. Colonel Pickering sent me with twenty men up the river to see for ourselves."

"And what did you find?"

"We found eighty-two dead Acadians in what remained of their village. At least fifty of that number were women and children. Children as young as four or five. All were scalped. All the buildings were burned, and all livestock killed."

"Scalped! Is it possible the savages did this?"

"No, sir. The custom for the savages is to take the young children as captives and bring them up as their own. No arrows or hatchet wounds were found, and none of the dead livestock was butchered. If the savages were involved, they would have taken choice cuts of meat with them." The captain's voice was tight with outrage.

"If not the savages, then who?"

"We questioned some New England rangers, and they readily and proudly admitted to the action. They said they were led by Colonel Monckton, who was under direct orders from Governor Lawrence that no prisoners were to be taken."

"Lawrence! I thought him an honorable man. Perhaps he has spent too long among the savages; this is not the action of a true Englishman." The general looked away for a moment, his mouth set, then roused himself. "Captain, please return to your unit. I appreciate your bringing this matter to my attention."

General Amherst was disgusted by the indiscriminate violence that occurred up the Saint Jean River. If Lawrence had been a soldier under his command, he would have been court martialed and demoted to private—or worse—but Lawrence's power came not from him, and the rules in the New World were more slippery than he cared for. He steeled himself with the thought that colonization was a messy business, like war, and informed Lawrence in writing, "I will always disapprove of killing women and helpless children." Other than that single reprimand, the heinous action was put aside by the English authorities. No one was punished.

•   •   •

Admiral Boscawen, with his twenty warships, quickly established naval control of the Gulf of St. Lawrence. General Wolfe then attacked the Canadian settlements on the Gaspé Peninsula, while Colonel James Murray, his second-in-command, struck the Acadian and Micmac villages at Miramichi Bay on the gulf. Few Acadians were captured, but all houses and wigwams were burned, and all livestock killed.

In late fall of 1758, Generals Jeffrey Amherst and James Wolfe met with Admiral Boscawen in Halifax to plan the taking of Québec City.

"Admiral, our spies report about 4,000 French soldiers, 1,000 Canadian, and 500 Acadian militia at the fortress in Québec City," stated Amherst. "The militia units include many Indian fighters. Our 11,000 troops will give us the numerical advantage."

"What concerns me, Jeffrey, is that all our previous attempts to conquer this prize have failed. Why is that? What went wrong? What do you plan on doing differently?"

"For one thing, Admiral, all previous attempts were led by colonial militia. This time, the bulk of our troops are British regulars. I expect a far different outcome."

"On the contrary, I spoke with the British captains of several warships that took part in the failed endeavors. To a man, they all said the colonial troops accounted themselves well. They did everything asked of them. Even after suffering heavy casualties, they continued to charge the enemy positions as directed. The terrain prevents warships from effectively shelling the fort. To do so, the ships would need to advance to a position directly below the fort, placing them in mortal danger from the fort's cannons. Those cannons have the advantage of 1,000 feet of elevation. My transports will deliver your men and my warships will shell the defensive positions below the fort, but you two generals need to figure out how to win this battle."

The siege of Québec City lasted three months. The French stronghold was well-defended on all sides. Repeated attempts by Wolfe to land his troops and attack the enemy positions were repulsed. Sheer cliffs protected the stronghold. Above these cliffs lay a 300-acre plateau called "the Plains of Abraham." The site got its name from the original settler who owned part of the land—Abraham Martin, long deceased.

"General Wolfe, every approach to the city is well-defended. Our troops are forced into a killing field at every attempt. My scouts, however, may have found an unguarded approach."

"An unguarded approach? Please continue, Colonel."

"The cliffs at the base of the citadel are not as sheer as they seem from a distance. Up close, there are many cracks that allow a man to scale the cliff easily."

"Show me! I must see this for myself."

General Louis-Joseph de Montcalm was the commanding officer of the Québec City garrison. He was a seasoned master at defending the city. For many years, he repulsed every attempt by the English to take his stronghold. But he was facing his final battle.

"General Montcalm, I believe the English are ready to withdraw. We have killed many hundreds of them in their ill-advised frontal assaults."

"Thank you, Colonel. Their bombardment has likewise tapered off. I wish I could blast their ships out of the water but will settle for their withdrawal. Remain on high alert and send your scouts out to see what that devil Wolfe is up to."

"Yes, sir."

As soon as it became dark, Wolfe led 2,000 men to the base of the cliffs to the ten or more areas where they could scale them. Before dawn, all 2,000, including Wolfe, were on the Plains of Abraham. The date was September 13, 1759.


"General, the English are on the Plains of Abraham in large numbers!"

"What? How is that possible?"

"They scaled the cliffs during the night."

"Have Colonel Therrien ready the troops. We will meet this enemy and throw him off the cliffs."

The battle on the Plains of Abraham lasted only thirty minutes. Wolfe had his troops lined up in two ranks—one kneeling, one standing, and both ready to fire. Montcalm came out with his troops and lined them up in front of the British regulars. As soon as the French soldiers were lined up, both ranks of English fired. This initial volley decimated the French. More than half were immediately killed or wounded. The French never recovered. General Montcalm was fatally wounded and died the next day. General Wolfe also died during the battle. His body lay on the Plains of Abraham while his troops overwhelmed the French and took the city. Wolfe was only thirty-two years old.

The following year, Montreal fell to the English.

With the fall of Québec, Acadian resistance crumbled. Many freedom fighters, including the Beausoleil group and other Acadians who had escaped deportation all those years, surrendered. Before long, almost 2,000 such Acadians were imprisoned by the English. The Micmac sued for peace and were granted land on Ile Royale in a treaty with the English. They remain there today.

In the spring of 1760, Governor Lawrence was finally able to place English settlers safely on the land vacated by the Acadians. The initial group of 300 New England farmers was soon followed by nearly 10,000 more over the next few years.

•     •     •

In Halifax, Governor Lawrence's assistant approached him. "Sir, the resettlement minister for Annapolis Royal is here to see you."

"Send him in."

"Thank you for seeing me, Governor. All the dikes in Annapolis Royal are in serious disrepair. After five years of no maintenance, many have been breached by the sea. Much of the best farmland is flooded with seawater at high tide. All our efforts to repair the dikes have been to no avail. We have assigned skilled carpenters, masons, and other tradesmen to fix the dikes, but no one possesses the right skills. The New Englanders have never worked with dikes and have no clue how to make them work. The farmers are not happy. Many have threatened to return to New England."

"Dikes? If the lazy Acadians could build and operate them, surely our more industrious English farmers can manage them even better! What can be so complicated?"

"As you know, sir, the tides here are enormous and exert a tremendous pressure on the dikes. None of our people, even our best engineers, have any experience with them."

The 2,000 Acadian prisoners were mostly held in military prisons at the various forts: Fort Cumberland, Fort Lawrence, Fort Edward, Fort Anne, and the like. All of these were under the direct command of General Amherst, the conqueror of Canada.

"General Amherst, thank you for seeing me on such short notice."

"You will always find my door open, Governor. How may I help you?"

"A situation has come up regarding the captured Acadians. My plan is to deport them as soon as enough transports become available. In the meantime, with your permission, the Acadians can be put to good use as laborers on the farms. In particular, the dikes need to be repaired, and the Acadians are masters of this work."

"I like your idea. It will provide the Acadians with a productive alternative to sitting in prison. This farm work, however, must be voluntary, and the workers are to be paid for their labor. I will not allow any forced labor."

"As you wish, General," replied Lawrence. "But the Acadians are not to be trusted. I request you maintain armed guards over them whenever they are working on the farms."

Lawrence's mindset in dealing with groups he disliked was revealed in his own writings. After quelling a disturbance in the predominately German town of Lunenburg in 1753 Governor Lawrence wrote, "…tho the merciful part is always the most agreeable (particularly with Foreigners unacquainted with our laws or Customs) in disturbances of this nature, yet it is seldom the most effectual."

•  •  •

The dikes were gradually repaired by the Acadians. They did their best to keep their dike secrets to themselves, but once a dike was completed, the *aboiteau*—the one-way tunnel and key to the success of the dike— was there for everyone to see. Governor Lawrence, however, never learned of the *aboiteau*. In October 1760, he caught a cold that developed into something worse and died at fifty-one. Not a single Acadian tear was shed.

Sir William Pitt's goal of removing the French from North America was finally achieved, but at what cost? He had to borrow heavily to provide enough funds to prosecute the war successfully in both America and Europe. By then, England was heavily in debt. The British Parliament decided that, since the American colonies were the primary beneficiaries of the successful conclusion to the French and Indian War, they needed to help pay down the debt. Taxes on tea, textiles, rum, and other goods soon followed.

"Taxation without representation!" cried the soon-to-be Americans.

"Greedy and ungrateful hypocrites!" replied the Londoners. The die was cast. There would be no peaceful solution to such a disagreement.

The French suffered great losses in the French and Indian War and were treated poorly by the English in the subsequent treaty. In due course, their decision to aid the American colonists in their struggle against Britain was a natural and easy one.

# CHAPTER 12
# ENGLAND

"Pierre are we finally here?" asked Mondou as they disembarked their transport.

"Yes, I believe so, but I don't know where we are."

"We're in England," replied an Acadian man who overheard them.

"England? Why are we here? How can we go back home?"

"You can forget about home for now. You and your brother need to concentrate on surviving. I suspect conditions here will not be good for us. Do you see all those English beggars on the dock? We will soon be worse off than them!"

Pierre had been strongly loyal to his mother and father while growing up. Family meant everything to him, and he was willing to die to defend his parents, his sisters, or his brother. The destruction of his home and his deportation had magnified his feelings tenfold. The passion other eighteen-year-olds might put into building or dreaming about an individual future, he directed into the care of his brother and the determination to return. He and Mondou would survive; they would go home; they would do whatever was necessary to restore the family. Meanwhile, anyone who messed with Mondou would find Pierre at his throat.

During the crossing, the two brothers spent a lot of time talking about their family. What happened to their parents? Their sisters? Did they know that Pierre and Mondou had been captured and deported? So many questions and concerns with no answers. Little did they know they would never again see or hear from any of their immediate family.

For a child, Mondou was brave enough and never cried, but he was never over two or three steps from Pierre. Pierre was his hero, and he would do anything his brother asked.

• • •

Lord Halifax was meeting with his ministers in London when an assistant arrived with an urgent message.

"Yes, what is it?" questioned Halifax.

"My lord, six transports have arrived carrying about 1,200 Acadians."

"What? That's impossible! Why would Acadians be here?"

"They were sent here by Governor Dinwiddie of Virginia."

"Dinwiddie! Why?"

"I have a letter from him. He says he wanted to keep the Acadians in Virginia, but his assembly vetoed that idea and forced him to send them to us for final disposition."

"Forced him? That's ridiculous! He's the governor and can override his assembly. As my direct representative, he has the final say, and he knows that!"

"Yes, my lord. What of the transports?"

"About 1,200 Acadians, you say. Send three hundred each to Bristol, Falmouth, Southampton, and Liverpool. Provide some instructions for their upkeep. They need to be contained until we decide what to do with them. That will be all!"

"Thank you, my lord."

Halifax followed up with a blistering letter to Dinwiddie criticizing his handling of the Acadians.

• • •

At the Southampton dock, the Acadians were unloaded briskly from their overcrowded ship.

"Move along! Move along quickly there or you'll find my boot up your arse!"

"Peters, do you know why these Acadians are here?"

"Not the slightest! What I know is the last thing we need are these bloody, skinny Frenchies. We don't have enough work for our own laborers. And not enough food for our own poor. How are we supposed to keep them alive? Most of them don't even speak English. This is Southampton, for God's sake! A poor, working-class city! Why send them here?"

"Where are you taking them?"

"I've been told to put them in the old produce warehouses."

"What? You know as well as I do those buildings are condemned and not even fit to house produce, let alone people. They're scheduled for demolition!"

Frank Peters worked for the city of Southampton, and the docks were his domain. His duties included the hiring of day laborers to load and unload the ships. The ship owners would pay the city for services rendered. If they didn't pay, their ships would be impounded. But Peters was told by his boss the Acadians were now part of his domain. Fifteen officers from the local police force were on hand to assist him in controlling the Acadians.

•   •   •

"Is this where we are to live? This building has large holes in the roof, and I've never seen so many rats in one place before," said an Acadian.

"No matter how bad this building is, I'd much rather be here than back on that ship," replied another.

Claude Babineau was one of the few Acadians who spoke English and for this reason was chosen by the heads of households to be their spokesperson. He was thirty-six years old, born and raised in Beaubassin, but he was not a farmer. For many years, he operated the general store in the village. He often dealt with New England traders so gradually learned to speak English and to understand their ways. With a friendly, outgoing personality that made him a natural shopkeeper, everyone liked him.

The condemned produce warehouses comprised four large buildings. None of the police officers or other English officials overseeing the exercise spoke any French. They angrily shouted in English and pointed where they wanted their prisoners to go. Finally, all the Acadians were herded into the first building. Peters stood on a table and yelled, "Does anyone here speak English?"

"I do," replied Babineau.

"Thank God for small miracles. Come forward. What is your name?"

"My name is Claude Babineau, and I am the spokesperson for my fellow Acadians."

"Well, Mr. Babineau, I suspect you and I are going to get to know each other well. My name is Frank Peters, and I'm in charge of these docks. There are four buildings in this compound, and these four will be your home for the time being. Feel free to spread out among the four, but you are not to leave the compound without my permission. Anyone who violates this rule will be severely punished! And as you can see, we recently had these buildings renovated for you."

This comment brought howls of laughter from the policemen.

"Monsieur Peters, we very much appreciate this building regardless of its condition. It's far better than the ship we were on. Many died on the way here."

"I have no food or other supplies for you today. There's a well at the entrance to the compound with good water. Feel free to use that. Settle in as best as you can, and I'll see what I can do for you tomorrow."

"Thank you, Monsieur Peters. We are in your debt."

•  •  •

"Damn, damn, damn!" exclaimed Peters to his wife, Silvia, after arriving home. "You know those dilapidated produce buildings on the dock? The bloody Acadians thanked me for housing them there."

"Those buildings are not safe!" replied Silvia. "Didn't the entire roof cave in on one of them recently?"

"Yes, of course they're not safe. Everyone knows that. And of the 256 Acadians, less than one-fourth are men. The others are women and children."

A sad look came to her eyes. Peters and Silvia had no children. He knew Silvia blamed herself, but he didn't care which of them had a problem; he just wanted her to be happy. If he could, if it were possible, he'd bring two younger orphans into their home and let her mother them. But that was out of the question.

"Be careful, Frank," she said at last. "If you complain to your boss, things could go badly for us. We have a good life here, and you are respected."

"I hear you, and I will not risk our well-being. But I won't have women and children die under my care. I need to find food, clothing, and many other supplies. I was able to appropriate some items from the ships that brought them here but not nearly enough."

•   •   •

Maurice Boudrot was a carpenter. After examining the four buildings with many of the other heads of families, everyone agreed the first two warehouses were the best. Boudrot suggested that with proper tools and permission to cannibalize the two worst buildings, the first two could be made much better. All 256 Acadians easily fit into the first two buildings, and that's where they settled for the night.

"Babineau! Where are you?" yelled Peters. It was barely dawn, and Peters wanted to deliver what little food and supplies he had.

"I'm here Monsieur Peters. How can I help you?"

"You can distribute the food and supplies outside to your neighbors. It's not much but will have to do for the next few days."

"Thank you. Again, we are very much in your debt. Monsieur Peters, we don't want to seem ungrateful for your hospitality, but we have one small request."

"What is it?"

"One of our men is a carpenter, and he says with proper tools such as hammers, nails, and saws, we could repair these first two buildings by using material from the other two."

"That's an excellent idea. I'll get the tools for you, but you will do this work at your own risk."

"Thank you again, my friend."

•   •   •

"These tools are perfect," said Boudrot to the assembled men. "And the ladders he brought will come in handy. Our initial task will be to take apart the first of the bad buildings. We must start at the top and carefully remove all the individual boards. You will remove and save as many nails as possible. Once all the boards are removed, we will take apart the structural support beams. These will brace the support beams in the good buildings. Please work carefully. I don't want anyone to get injured."

"Pierre, can you ask Monsieur Boudrot if we can go up and knock the boards down? I'm tired of just knocking the nails out of these boards down here," said Mondou.

Mondou was doing his best to help his brother with the nails, but his attention span was short. After the first five minutes, the job had ceased to be fun. They'd been at it for several hours, and the pile of boards with nails kept growing bigger, not smaller.

"Mondou, what we're doing is a bit boring, but it's important work, and someone must do it. You need to learn patience. Monsieur Boudrot is counting on us to remove and save as many nails as possible. After the nails are removed, he wants us to stack the good boards over there and the broken boards in a separate pile. How about we take a break from pulling nails and stack the completed boards." Pierre couldn't help thinking of what he was doing at his brother's age. Plenty of chores, certainly, but also long hours roaming the woods and beach, playing with other boys, always knowing come nightfall, there would be a good supper with his mother at one end of the table—her auburn hair that glinted in the firelight, her sweet smile—his tall father at the other. He had not known how happy he was.

"Good work, boys," said Boudrot. "Your stack of clean boards is very impressive. We'll be able to put those to good use later. Even the broken boards will not go to waste. The women can use those as firewood in the kitchen."

"Thank you, Monsieur Boudrot," replied both Pierre and Mondou. Mondou then added, "I like what I'm doing, but I would like it even more if I could go up and knock the boards down."

Boudrot laughed and said, "I admire your willingness to try new things. For now, however, it's best if you and your brother work down here."

After the warehouse was completely taken apart, the reclaimed boards and timbers were sufficient to repair both good buildings. It was early summer, and the weather was good, but the Acadians knew winter would eventually arrive. Boudrot assumed they would be there for a long while. His goal was to winterize the buildings as much as possible.

•  •  •

"Silvia, those damn Acadians have got their two buildings in better shape structurally than they've been in for years," said Peters. "I'd say they've given those buildings another good ten years of life."

"That's amazing," replied Silvia. "They've only been here a month. Can you assign them other work to do?"

"I can't assign them the loading or unloading of ships on the dock. My current pool of workers has made it very clear they will not allow it. They have threatened violence against the Acadians and the docks if I take work away from them."

"Can you find some work for them in the city?"

"Come on, Silvia, you know the local economy's been depressed for the past two years. So many of our people are out of work and struggling to survive. These Acadians don't belong here, and the people strongly resent them. I feel sorry for them, but there's little I can do."

"Perhaps you can assign them work our people refuse to do or dislike doing. I know cleaning out the public outhouse near the shops is not popular work. The digging of graves is likewise not very popular."

"Hmm. Perhaps."

"Doesn't the public outhouse need to be emptied every three months? And wasn't it last emptied six months ago by inmates from the prison, leading to a near riot by the prisoners? You told me the warden will not force them to empty it again."

"I didn't realize you were listening so closely," he said, though in fact, she always did and had a terrifying memory. "Do you think the Acadians might be willing to clean the outhouse?"

"I suspect they won't be happy with the assignment, but it seems like the best opportunity to get them some work in the city."

•   •   •

"Mister Peters, thank you for stopping by," said David Wenners, one of the city officials.

"I'm at your service, sir. How may I help you?"

"I was skeptical when you assigned those Acadians to empty the outhouse, but I must say the results are extraordinary. Not only did they empty the outhouse, but they also enlarged it to three times its original size and added two more seats."

"I'm glad their work meets with your approval."

"Where did the lumber come from for the expansion?"

"They took the lumber from the condemned produce buildings on the dock."

"I heard they scavenged materials from one of the condemned buildings to fix the one they're in. They seem to be rather industrious for peasant farmers."

"They're mostly farmers, sir, but they have some tradesmen among them—a master carpenter, several apprentices, a cooper, and a mason."

"Peters, we need to dig a new well to service the east side of the city. I'm thinking your Acadians would be perfect for this work."

"They can dig a new well, sir, but won't this take work away from our own people?"

"I can't afford to pay the wages our people demand. The city treasury is largely depleted."

"The people will see the Acadians as taking away their livelihood and may become violent."

"Damn the people! They constantly complain the well is inadequate, and then they refuse to accept lower wages to dig a new one. I'm at my wits' end."

      •   •   •

"Babineau! Where are you?" yelled Peters.

"I'm here, Monsieur Peters, how may I help you?"

"The city wants a new well dug and has suggested I assign this work to you."

"That's wonderful news! Just about every man here has experience in digging and maintaining wells. This is work we can easily do."

"I understand that, but there's a complication. The city can't afford to pay its own workers for this work. That's why they want to give the job to you. In return for digging this new well, the city says they will continue to provide food and other supplies for you and do their best to increase these items."

"Food and supplies are critical for us. We do not need wages."

"Yes, I understand, but the local workers will resent your working in their space. They will see you as taking food out of the mouths of their babies. They may become violent."

"Monsieur Peters, I need to discuss this matter with the heads of household. I will have an answer for you later today."

      •   •   •

"Constable Ballard, thank you for seeing me."

"What can I do for you, Peters? Having trouble on the docks?"

"The docks are fine. But David Wenners has informed me the city council wants the Acadians to dig the new well on the east side of town. The city can't afford to pay its own workers, so they want the Acadians to do it for free."

"Acadians? That won't sit well with the likes of James Stewart and his thugs. Their lack of employment has not mellowed out that bunch!"

"That's why I'm here. I informed the Acadians of the strong resentment they could expect from the locals, including violence. They said they understood the danger but would still dig the well, if that's what I recommended."

"Seems like you're their best friend."

"If they dig the well, how much protection can you provide?"

"As I'm sure you know, I'm very short-handed and cannot adequately patrol the city. The best I can do is assign one officer full-time to guard the Acadians while they dig the well. If there's real trouble, one will not be enough."

•  •  •

"Pierre, digging the well seems like an excellent chance to get out of this prison for a while," said Mondou. "Can you ask the men if we can go, too?"

"I will. I agree it would be good to get out for a while."

Fortunately for Pierre and his brother, the men refused to let them go on the well digging project. A total of sixteen Acadian men were assigned to the work. The first day was uneventful with only a few local protesters. The assigned policeman was able to control the situation. On the second day, however, over thirty locals arrived. Their faces were covered, and they were all armed with clubs. Three of the ruffians tackled the policeman and held him down while the others tore into the Acadians. Robert Poirier, thirty-seven years old and the father of eight, was the first casualty. He died instantly from a crushing blow to the head. Within minutes, the battle was over, and the locals melted back into the neighborhoods. Maurice Deveau, twenty-five years old and the father of three, was also dead. The remaining Acadians were all injured. About half suffered broken bones.

When the locals attacked, the Acadians fought back but were outnumbered two to one. At least one attacker had a shovel smashed effectively into his face. That Acadian, however, was pounced upon by two other locals who broke both his arms and smashed his face with the same shovel. He lost several teeth, almost lost an eye, and would have scars and a crooked nose the rest of his life. Afterwards, the Acadians readily agreed that *les maudits Anglais* were not only in Acadia, but many of them were also in England, where they originated. "The Devil shits *les Anglais*," said one.

The policeman was uninjured. When he was questioned, he was unable to identify any of the perpetrators. Constable Robert Ballard had a pretty good idea who was behind the attack but had no solid evidence. Local sentiment was also not in his favor. It seemed everyone except Peters despised the Acadians.

Not just the wives and children of the fallen men were in grief. The entire Acadian group was closely related through marriages over many generations. All were cousins in one way or another and were now in deep mourning.

"Pierre, if the Devil shits *les Anglais*, why does God allow it?"

"Hush, Mondou. I don't think we should talk about the Devil. We're not smart enough to figure out that stuff."

As the months wore on, relations between the Acadians and the Southampton residents did not improve. Most locals believed the Acadians at the well "got what they bloody deserved!" The promised increase in food and other provisions never occurred. In the dead of winter, there was not enough food for everyone. All the Acadians had lost considerable weight and were continuing to do so. More deaths would have surely followed if it were not for Reverend Richard Powers, pastor of the Church of Christ the Redeemer. He convinced his congregation to make the Acadians their special project. As Christians, they needed to help their fellow men who were worse off than themselves.

"Reverend Powers, we are deeply indebted to you and your congregation for these wonderful provisions," said Babineau. "If we can ever repay this kindness, please let me know. We are very good at repairing structures. If your church or the houses of your congregation need repair, we would be happy to do that work at no cost to you."

"Thank you for the offer. The quality of your work is obvious from the repairs you've made to this old warehouse. I'll let my congregation know of your offer."

"Reverend Powers, we don't mean to impose on your kindness, but there is one other matter in which you may be able to help us."

"Of course! What is it?"

"We have no priest among us, and two of our young people are ready for marriage. In a case like this, our Catholic religion allows any one of our leaders to perform the marriage. If you agree, however, we would be honored to have you officiate at this marriage."

"You want a Protestant minister to perform a wedding in a Catholic ceremony? This is unheard of. And I readily agree! I would be honored to officiate at the wedding."

The wedding was held in Reverend Powers' church. Besides the bride and groom, only fifteen other Acadians could attend, but that number was acceptable. The remaining Acadians prepared as best they could for the reception to follow at the warehouse. Peters was able to provide a few musical instruments, including a fiddle. The feasting and drinking were subdued because of shortages, but the music and dancing were a joy to behold. The wedding was one of the few bright spots in the otherwise bleak Acadian situation.

"Pierre, can I have another piece of chicken?" asked Mondou, his eyes following the platters of food. "This is the most I've eaten in days, but I'm still hungry. I hope we can have more of these weddings. Is there any cake?"

"You're still very skinny, but you've grown at least five inches in the year we've been here. It looks like everyone's been served at least once, so I'm sure that pretty girl guarding the chicken will give you another piece. And yes, there is cake."

Several days later, Babineau asked Peters, "Monsieur Peters, is it possible for you to make a portion of the land just outside this warehouse available for us to grow vegetables?"

"Land? What land?"

"Let me show you. This lot behind the warehouse may be suitable for growing vegetables."

"I've been managing these docks for over ten years. This lot has been the dumping ground for many things since before my time. As you can see, in most places the lot is covered several feet deep with rocks, broken bricks, broken lumber, broken glass, and other debris."

"If you can provide us with a few wheelbarrows and shovels, we would like to clear a portion of the lot. Similarly, the ground under the warehouse we dismantled may also be suitable for vegetables. Most of us were farmers in Acadia before being sent here. We would just need seeds to plant."

"Yes, for the wheelbarrows and shovels. I have those in abundance here on the docks and will bring them tomorrow. The seeds, however, may take more time. I have no experience with vegetable seeds."

Joseph Leblanc, a long-time farmer from Beaubassin, took charge of the garden project. In consultation with the other heads of families, they agreed the dimensions of the vegetable garden would be roughly 100 feet by 200 feet. Maurice Boudrot, the carpenter, and Lucien Bois, a mason, were assigned the task of creating the perimeter walls. All agreed the walls would be seven feet wide and five feet tall and be comprised of all the debris within the designated vegetable plot. The completed perimeter wall was to be strong, stable, and pleasing to the eye. As the plot was slowly cleared, Acadians with pickaxes began digging the hard ground.

"Pierre, can I ride in the wheelbarrow?" asked Mondou.

"Sure, jump in!"

"Do you know where the seaweed is?"

"Monsieur Peters said there's a large pile of it on the beach at the end of the dock."

"Can you go faster? I like this ride."

As they came around the end of the dock, they ran into three local men.

"Well, what have we here?" said one of the men.

"Looks like two frogs and a wheelbarrow," replied the second one.

"Looks to me like they're stealing the wheelbarrow and trying to escape!" exclaimed the third.

Pierre had gotten taller during the past year. He was just over six feet and very wiry. His handgrip was unusually strong. He understood and could speak a bit of English.

"Monsieur Peters sent us," said Pierre in English.

The three men looked at each other with some concern. Peters was not a man to trifle with. These two helpless Acadians, however, were too much to pass up. The men were unemployed, bored, and in need of a little diversion. One of them produced a knife and said, "Let's see if they bleed if you stick them." The other two laughed derisively.

Pierre now swung his elbow into the nose of the man closest to him. The man fell to the ground with blood gushing from his nose. Mondou was closest to the man with the knife. He lunged at the man and clamped his teeth down on one of the man's fingers holding the knife. The man screamed and dropped the knife. Mondou did not let go. He bit harder. With his right hand, Mondou grabbed the man's testicles and squeezed as hard as possible. Pierre quickly subdued the third man by pounding his head into the edge of the wheelbarrow. All three men were now in agony on the ground.

"Mondou, run back and tell Monsieur Boudrot what happened. Tell him to get Monsieur Peters. I'll stay here until you return." He stood at a distance, watching the men writhe in pain. He felt no sympathy for them, but he was worried about the consequences. Peters was a fair man, but he was English. Pierre would like to trust him, but he knew better than trusting an Englishman. He could only do his best to behave honorably and hope that would be sufficient.

•   •   •

When Peters arrived, his scowl was directed at his fellow countrymen. Mondou looked unafraid, his pride in their victory barely controlled. Pierre relaxed a little.

"Mister Peters, we didn't mean any harm. We were just having a little fun," said the first man.

"These bloody Acadians started it!" exclaimed the second. "Before we ever touched them, they broke Edward's nose and nearly bit off Howard's finger."

"Why did you stop them?" asked Peters, his eyes cold.

"We thought for sure they were escaping. We did our civic duty in stopping them."

"Gentlemen, if you ever want to work on these docks again, this ends here and now. These two had every right to defend themselves. When you return home, do not blame the Acadians for your injuries. Do not stir up trouble. If this incident festers into a larger problem, I will hold you three responsible."

After the three local men left, muttering to each other, Pierre and Mondou filled their wheelbarrow with seaweed and delivered it to the new garden site. After many such trips, they ended up with two piles alongside the perimeter, one of fresh seaweed and the other of older seaweed. Old seaweed is an excellent fertilizer. When mixed into the soil, it will quickly decompose and release its nutrients. The men with pickaxes were digging the newly exposed soil to a depth of ten inches and removing all rocks larger than a chicken egg.

"*Merde*! This new garden is beautiful with that lovely wall all around," exclaimed an Acadian woman.

"*Merci*!" replied Leblanc. "It turned out better than I expected. The multicolored wall of rocks, bricks, and glass is very pleasing to the eye. A more important question though is, will this garden grow vegetables?"

•   •   •

"Mister Peters, what can I do for you?" asked Lance Williamson, the agricultural minister for the greater Southampton area.

"Thank you for seeing me, sir. As you may know, I'm in charge of the Acadians confined on the docks. To sustain themselves, they cleared a surplus lot of rubble and created a rather impressive garden that is now ready for planting. Unfortunately, we don't have any seeds. I'm hoping you can provide me with some appropriate vegetable seeds for their garden."

"Seeds? I have some, but most of our farmers simply save seeds from each crop for the following year. My department typically assists new farmers. We help them get started. So yes, I will provide seeds for your Acadians. What I have are turnip, beetroot, and cabbage seeds."

"Thank you very much. I'm sure those varieties will be just fine."

•　•　•

"Monsieur Peters, thank you so much for the seeds. Our entire community is very excited about this new garden. The initial garden with its impressive walls is complete, and our men are now digging a second one on the site of that old warehouse. There's very little rubble to clear, so the work is going much faster. The seeds will be more than enough for both sites."

"You're welcome. I hope your gardens are successful."

"Monsieur Peters, we've noticed you often have horses pulling wagons on the docks. I would like your permission to have our two seaweed gatherers, Pierre and his brother Mondou, take their wheelbarrow to the docks and gather the horse manure."

"That's an excellent idea and will do me a favor in helping to clean up the docks. There's quite a bit to pick up. I'll write a pass for them. If anyone stops them, they can show their pass."

"*Merci*, Monsieur Peters."

"Pierre, is it safe for us to venture that far out on the docks?"

"We'll soon find out. The pass from Monsieur Peters should help defuse any potential problems. The new gardens can use the manure, and it's our job to gather it, so let's hope for the best."

The gathering of the horse manure went better than expected. Several dock workers laughed and made fun of Pierre and Mondou, but no one interfered with their work. After many round trips, they built a large pile of manure by the entrance to the garden.

"This manure will work very well," said master gardener Joe Leblanc. "Most of it is well-aged and can be used right away in the garden. Much of the seaweed is likewise ready for use. If we can get enough rain and sun, we should have a very productive garden."

"Thank you, Monsieur Leblanc. Do we now have enough of both, or do you want us to keep gathering?"

"What we have here is enough for this garden but not enough for the second one. I'd appreciate it if you and your brother could keep gathering and build new piles of both seaweed and manure near the second garden."

"*Oui,* Monsieur Leblanc. We will continue."

"Pierre, I wish Mom and Dad could see us now! Without us gathering the seaweed and manure, the garden wouldn't be nearly as good. Mama always said feeding her family was her most important job, remember? That's what we're doing for everybody," said Mondou.

At that moment, Pierre could not be prouder of his brother. For a twelve-year-old child, he had a good understanding of what really mattered in life.

# CHAPTER 13
# HALIFAX

With the death of the despicable Charles Lawrence in October 1760, the Crown appointed the equally repulsive Chief Justice Jonathan Belcher as Lieutenant Governor of Nova Scotia.

"Congratulations on your appointment," said General Amherst. "Since the province has been at peace now for quite some time, I assume you will ease the restrictions against the Acadians."

"Ease the restrictions? Surely you jest, General. The greatest danger to the overthrow of this government continues to come from the Acadians. As long as they remain here, we can never lower our guard. They are filled with resentment and hatred for the English and will gladly slit all our throats to regain their lands."

"Perhaps in 1755, but not now. The Acadians are no longer able to overthrow this government. Of course, there are resentments, but in time, the resentments will pass. A better strategy would be to integrate the Acadians into the fabric of this province. They are hard-working and possess valuable skills, especially in diking and farming. With a little effort, they could be steered into becoming productive members of this colony."

·   ·   ·

Joseph Broussard surrendered to the English in Chignecto shortly after the fall of Québec City. He, along with his brother Alexandre, their sons, and their families were now in prison at Fort Cumberland. The Broussard group numbered over one hundred, including women and children.

"Beausoleil, I don't know how much more of this prison life I can take," said Maurice Richard, one of his men. "During the day, we work for a pittance under armed guards for the New Englanders now on our land. At night we are crowded back into this prison. It would not be difficult to escape and resume our former occupation—the elimination of *les maudits Anglais* (the damn English). What do you say?"

"Maurice, I appreciate your resolve and your courage. Together, we eliminated quite a few of *les maudits Anglais*. I don't regret a single one. We did our best to even the score and didn't surrender until France itself surrendered all of Canada. This battle is lost."

"So, we should just give up?"

"Who knows what the future holds? But I will not die for a hopeless cause. Not now."

Beausoleil knew the English were like an invasive species that had taken over the land. They were entrenched and too far established to be dislodged. The Acadian people, for many years, had suffered at the hands of the English and continued to do so. He was fifty-eight years old, and he felt every one of those years—his back ached, his hands were stiff, and he could no longer run at more than a hobble. Though he had done all he could, he felt like he had failed. His hatred of the English was a permanent part of him, a splinter in his soul he hoped his Creator would understand, but he knew patience was required. The way forward would reveal itself in due course.

•    •    •

In July 1762, the French counterattacked and took the port city of St. John's in Newfoundland. Two weeks later, the English forced the French to vacate Newfoundland. The ineffective French attack, however, had a profound effect on Governor Belcher. He saw the attack as a prelude to an Acadian uprising. He therefore ordered all able-bodied Acadian men in all of Nova Scotia be marched to Halifax.

At that time, nearly 2,000 Acadian men, women, and children were held in prison in Chignecto, Minas Basin, and Annapolis. From that group, all the able-bodied men, totaling about 600, were marched to Halifax. Upon arrival, they were put in prison on George's Island.

"Beausoleil, why have we been transferred from our prison at Fort Cumberland to this prison in Halifax?" asked one of his followers.

"*Les maudits Anglais* not only hate us, but they also fear us." replied Beausoleil. "I hope we give them nightmares. They have again separated all Acadian men from their families. This can only mean they intend to renew the deportations."

•   •   •

At the governor's residence, Belcher was dining with the Colonel in command of the English garrison in Halifax.

"Colonel, the safety and, in fact, the survival of this colony now rests in your hands. Among the over 600 Acadian men you now hold on George's Island are many of the worst cutthroats this colony has ever seen. I want you to double the guard on them. Do not give them an inch! Do not allow them any privileges! When the transports arrive, I want these evil men loaded aboard as quickly as possible—all under heavy armed guard."

"I understand, Governor. Do you know when the transports are expected?"

"The boats are coming from Boston and should arrive in another few weeks."

In August 1762, five transports loaded with the 600 Acadian men left Halifax. The men were being deported to Massachusetts, whereas their women and children were left in various prisons in Nova Scotia.

Six weeks later, the five transports returned to Halifax.

"Governor, the five transports have returned with the 600 Acadians still onboard."

"What? We've had fair weather. No storms! Why would the transports return?"

"Sir, the Bostonians refused to accept them. They said they took in enough Acadians in 1755. They want no more."

"This is an outrage and must be reversed! The survival of this colony is at stake. Bring me my writing materials. London will hear of this."

•   •   •

On February 10, 1763, the war between France and England ended with the signing of the Treaty of Paris. France ceded to England all its territory in Canada and the maritime region, except for the small islands of St. Pierre and Miquelon in the Gulf of St. Lawrence, about fifteen miles off the coast of the island of Newfoundland.

Regarding Belcher's letter, the London officials decided his overall handling of the Acadian situation was inappropriate and showed poor judgment. They removed him as lieutenant governor and appointed Montague Wilmot in his place. Wilmot was the former commandant of Fort Cumberland and, unfortunately for the Acadians, was of the same mind as Belcher. Despite the peace treaty, at the start of 1764, the 2,000 Acadians in Nova Scotia remained in prison and continued to work on the dikes for low wages.

In September 1764, the British crown informed Wilmot if the Acadians took the oath of allegiance, they could stay in Nova Scotia; if not, they were free to leave the province.

In the lower British colonies, several hundred Acadians left for French-held Saint Domingue (modern-day Haiti). Initially, they were happy to be together in French territory, but they found the land poor, and then came yellow fever and malaria. The Acadians had no immunity to yellow fever and other diseases common to the tropics.

Before the end of their first year in Saint Domingue, one-third of the newly arrived Acadians were dead.

Wilmot forced the Acadians who took the oath to live in the province's interior in small groups of no more than three families.

"Beausoleil, what do you think of this oath?" asked one of his followers.

"Despicable! *Les maudits Anglais* will always be at our throats. I would rather hang than sign this oath."

In November 1764, six hundred Acadians led by Beausoleil and his brother Alexandre hired vessels and departed for the West Indies. They arrived in Saint Domingue in January 1765 and soon hired other vessels to take them to Louisiana. For many decades, Louisiana had been a French territory, but in 1762, in exchange for Spain's help in the war against England, France secretly ceded the Louisiana territory to Spain. French officials, however, remained in a caretaker capacity until 1766.

When the Broussard group arrived in Louisiana, they received a warm welcome and were presented with an opportunity to own land and raise cattle at Poste des Attakapas, a developing frontier area west of New Orleans with large open grasslands. After a brief discussion with all the heads of families, the Broussard group accepted. The Attakapas area settled by the Acadians would eventually evolve into the parishes of Saint-Landry, Saint-Martin, and Lafayette.

In New Orleans, acting Louisiana Governor Charles Philippe Aubry welcomed Joseph Broussard as a French hero. His exploits against the English in Acadia over many years were well known by the French officials. On April 8, 1765, Aubry appointed him Captain of Militia and Commandant of the Acadians. His men commended the wisdom of Beausoleil, who had steered them to this agreeable place.

Soon after the Broussard group arrived at Attakapas, they were struck by an unknown epidemic that claimed many lives. In September 1765, Alexandre Broussard died, and a month later, his sixty-three-year-old brother Joseph, nicknamed Beausoleil, died at the Attakapas settlement known as Beausoleil. He was buried there on October 20,

1765, near the site of the present-day town of Broussard, a few miles south of the town of Lafayette.

By 1770, the Attakapas area was home to a growing population of Acadians, many of whom originated from the Chignecto area of Nova Scotia, where raising beef had been a way of life. The sons of Alexandre and Joseph Broussard were soon driving cattle to market in New Orleans.

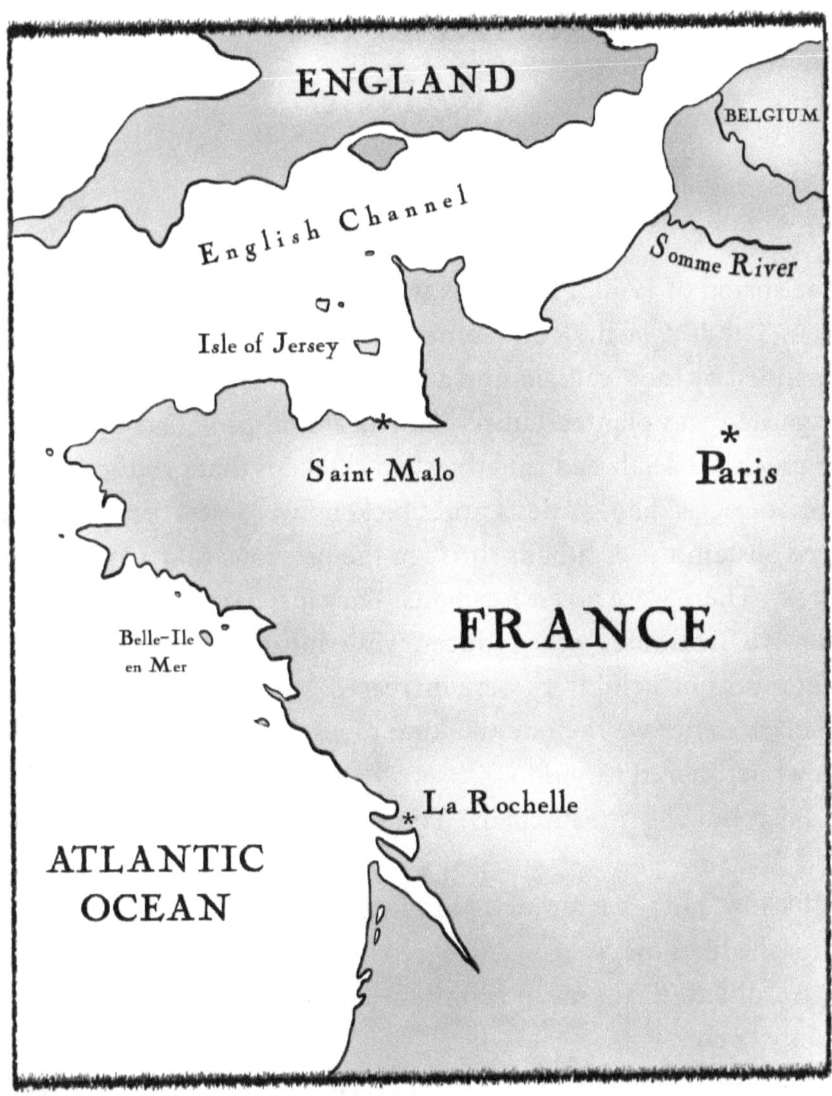



Map by Kristi Mueller

# CHAPTER 14
# FRANCE

In the spring of 1760, Pierre was twenty-three years old and Mondou fifteen. The last of the condemned warehouses had been completely dismantled by the Acadians and a third garden created in its place. The new garden was planted entirely in wheat and provided the Acadians with much needed bread, and they had chickens that produced a steady supply of eggs. The gardens and chickens were very productive and helped sustain the Acadians through the previous four years. Life was not easy. There were no fat Acadians. They just barely had enough food to survive. Birthrates were reduced while mortality rates, especially of infants and small children, were increased.

"Pierre, after we're done working today, can we go to the kitchens for a while?" asked Mondou.

"Sure, but why the kitchens? You know they can't give us any extra food."

"I know, but it's Antoinette I'm interested in. She works there, and I think she likes me."

"Antoinette? You mean Monsieur Landry's daughter? She's pretty but only twelve."

"She's fourteen. I asked her brother. He laughed when I asked about his sister, but he told me she was fourteen."

When they arrived at the kitchens, Pierre was struck dumb when he saw the profile of the most beautiful woman he had ever seen. She was in the back of the kitchen and walking from his right to his left. Her name was Félicité Leblanc. He surely had seen her many times before during the past four years but never in this light. She was twenty-one years old.

"Pierre! You're not listening to me. What do I say to Antoinette? Pierre! What's wrong with you?"

"Huh? Did you say something?"

"I said, what do I say to Antoinette?"

"Anything, tell her you like her hair."

"Her hair? She's wearing a cap. I can hardly see her hair."

"Mondou, tell her whatever you like. I can't help you."

When you and your intended are confined to a small area on the docks of Southampton, the courtship process is rather limited. Pierre took every opportunity to visit the kitchens and smiled at Félicité whenever she looked his way. It soon became obvious to everyone they liked each other. In the spring of 1762, Pierre was ready for the next step.

"Monsieur Leblanc, my name is Pierre Aucoin, and I would like your permission to marry your daughter Félicité."

"Pierre, we've lived and worked together for the past six years. There's no need to tell me your name. Yes, you have my permission."

"*Merci*, Monsieur Leblanc. Do you think she'll say yes?"

"Of course, she'll say yes. She is just as infatuated with you, perhaps even more so."

•   •   •

Pierre was generally very shy around women, but he found Félicité to be an exception. She was easy to talk to, was always pleasant, had a smile that melted his heart, and was the most beautiful woman he had ever seen. Once he had her father's permission, he was ready to commit himself to her.

"Félicité, will you marry me?" asked a very nervous Pierre when they were finally alone outside the kitchens.

"Yes, yes, I will," replied a relieved Félicité. "Pierre, I've been ready to say 'yes' for over two months. I'm so happy you finally asked."

"Thank you! You've just made me the happiest man in the world. This is so wonderful. I was afraid to ask. I promise to make a good life for you." Pierre hugged her and kissed her for the first time. When he released her, he saw the tears of joy in her eyes. He would devote the rest of his life to this woman.

One year later, in the early spring of 1763, their son Anselme was born in the renovated produce warehouse on the docks of Southampton, England.

After the signing of the Treaty of Paris on February 10, 1763, Louis-Jules Barbon Mancini Mazarani, the Duke of Nivernois, was appointed as the French ambassador in London. He contacted the Acadian prisoners and pledged to return them to France. In May 1763, 778 Acadians being held in England were transported to the port towns of Saint-Malo and Morlaix in Brittany, France, where they joined the Acadians deported directly to France in 1758.

Seven years earlier, 1,225 Acadian prisoners—men, women, and children, arrived in England. That only 778 returned was a testament to the horrible conditions under which the Acadians were held.

•   •   •

Pierre and his family, including his brother Mondou, settled into the town of St. Servan, near Saint-Malo. Although the treasury of French King Louis XV was severely depleted after the devastating losses of the Seven Years War, he made sure the Acadian exiles received an allowance that allowed them to survive. While in Southampton, Pierre had studied carpentry under the able tutelage of master carpenter, Maurice Boudrot. He now continued in this trade as an apprentice to Monsieur Boudrot in the greater Saint-Malo area.

"Mondou, Monsieur Boudrot has agreed you can assist us on our next job, which is to renovate an old chalet for a wealthy landowner."

"That's great! Did you explain to Monsieur Boudrot that I have extensive knowledge in wheelbarrow operation and in removing old nails from boards?"

Pierre laughed. "I suspect he is already well-aware of your wheelbarrow and nail removal skills."

Life in St. Servan was generally agreeable and certainly far better than their former life in England, but an undercurrent of friction existed between the Acadians and the local French. The locals were sympathetic to the Acadians for the harsh treatment they had received from the English. However, they resented the Acadians were now taking jobs away from them. And the Acadians spoke funny. Many of their words and pronunciation were different from the local speech. The locals saw the Acadians as belonging to a lesser subgroup of French, and this attitude colored all dealings between the Acadians and the locals.

"Félicité, I'm fed up with the condescending attitude of the locals," declared Pierre when he got home from work. "This afternoon, while waiting in line at the building supply store for materials that Monsieur Boudrot sent me to buy, two locals forced their way ahead of me in line. When I protested, they pushed me back and said they were here long before any Acadians, and they were not about to take a back seat to us."

'Pierre, you must be careful!" replied an alarmed Félicité. "You have three children now, and you cannot put yourself at risk. You must think of them."

"I know, sweetheart. I bit my tongue at the supply store, but I don't know how often I can do that. The French will never accept us as equals. We don't belong here. The sooner we go back to our own country, the better."

What Pierre was dealing with was a small-scale version of the significant rift that had grown, and would continue to grow, between the New World and Europe. After several generations, both the French and English in Europe viewed their cousins in the American colonies as belonging to a lesser group—useful certainly, and clever, but never as clever, loyal, or worthy as the Europeans.

By the start of 1764, almost 4,000 Acadian exiles were living in France. This large number of workers attracted the attention of French landowners looking to expand their estates with more tenant farmers, as well as government contractors seeking to populate their assigned colonies in Guiana, Saint Domingue, and other far-flung locations. King Louis was flooded with petitions from the landowners and contractors to approve their proposals for use of this Acadian labor. He approved several, including the resettlement of 1,500 Acadians to the province of Poitou in central France to jump-start a new farming community, but none of these ventures, except for the Belle-Ile project, proved successful. The target lands in Poitou were not fertile. Constant bickering and finger pointing between the government officials, landowners, and Acadians soon doomed the Poitou project. Funds dried up, and the Acadians were left on their own. Almost all moved to the port city of Nantes on the French coast, where they remained for the next ten years before moving to Louisiana in 1785.

Belle-Ile-en-Mer was a smaller project and better funded. Belle-Ile is a French island about eight miles off the coast of Brittany in northwest France. The initial Acadian leaders brought to the island to see its potential for resettlement were not impressed because of the poor soil, harsh climate, and exposure to British attack. To sweeten the pot, the Governor of Belle-Ile offered the Acadians not only land but a house, a horse, a cow, three sheep, 400 *livres*, and no taxes for five years. Starting in September 1765, Acadians began arriving at Belle-Ile. By the end of that year, seventy-eight Acadian families, totaling 363 men, women, and children had been transported to Belle-Ile. Many of their descendants are still there.

"Pierre, Monsieur Daigre's son Jean told me they are moving to Belle-Ile. Many other families are moving there. Others have already left for French colonies in Guiana, Saint Domingue, and the Iles Malouines (Falkland Islands) in the South Atlantic. It sounds so exciting! Where do you think we should go?"

"Mondou, my plan has always been to return to Acadia, where we belong. We are doing well here and saving money. As soon as we have enough to pay for our passage, we will return. Félicité agrees we belong in Acadia."

"Okay, return to Acadia, that's what I want too."

Mondou remained dedicated to his brother. He would stay at his side and follow Pierre wherever he led.

* * *

Saving enough money to pay their passage back to Acadia proved to be quite difficult. In June 1765, at twenty-one, Mondou married nineteen-year-old Marie Hébert. Marie and her family were captured on Ile Saint Jean in 1758 and deported directly to France.

On August 17, 1765, a second son, Pierre-Simon, was born to Pierre and Félicité. They called him Pierrot. And on March 31, 1771, a daughter, Marie-Félicité, was added to their family. They called her Marion. Mondou and Marie did not have any children.

The following year, while working with Monsieur Boudrot on a project in Saint-Malo, Pierre saw a flyer affixed to the door of a tavern in the center of town. Pierre could not read, but the flyer caught his attention because it contained a small map that showed France, the Atlantic Ocean, and Acadia with an arrow pointing from France to Acadia. He soon found a Frenchman who read the notice to him. "This flyer is from the Robin Company. They seek fishermen willing to move to the Gulf of St. Lawrence." Pierre had little interest in fishing but a lot of interest in moving to the gulf. The flyer gave the name of Charles Robin and an address in town. At the address, Pierre found an agent for the Robin Company.

"*Bonjour,* Monsieur, my name is Pierre Aucoin. I saw your flyer looking for fishermen, and I'm interested in learning more."

"Thank you for coming. Please have a seat. My name is Maurice Duval. I'm an agent for the Robin Company. Do you have any experience as a fisherman?"

"Not really. My brother and I sometimes go fishing off the docks in town, and sometimes in a small boat, but we are carpenters by trade, not fishermen."

"That's not a problem. The skills needed to become a full-time fisherman are easy to master. I can tell from your speech that you are Acadian. Where are you from?"

"I grew up in Rivière-aux-Canards, near Grand Pré in Acadia."

"I've never heard of Rivière-aux-Canards, but I have heard of Grand Pré. It's terrible what the English did to you there."

"Yes, it's more than terrible. What can you tell me about this Robin Company?"

"The company is owned by Monsieur Charles Robin and his two brothers. They are all from the Isle of Jersey. Men from Jersey have been fishing the Grand Banks for many generations. The company is well run and well respected. The only shortage they have is fishermen, hence the flyer. If you sign on, you'll be required to work as a fisherman for the Robins for three years. In return, your passage will be free, room and board for the first three months will be free, and you'll be paid a good wage."

"I have a wife and three small children. Does the free passage and room and board include them?"

"Yes, your family is included. You mentioned a brother. Is he interested in becoming a fisherman?"

"I believe so, but I need to speak with him and my wife. Thank you very much for this information."

When he arrived home that evening, Pierre was very excited and told Félicité and Mondou what he had learned from the Robin agent.

"Pierre, the Jerseys are English. How can we trust them?" asked Félicité.

"I agree we cannot trust the English. This opportunity, however, seems too good to pass up. Our children are young, and I want them to grow up in Acadia. After we're there and I complete my three years of service, we'll free ourselves from the English."

"I'm ready to go! I've always wanted to be a fisherman," added Mondou.

# CHAPTER 15
# CHARLES ROBIN AND COMPANY – RETURN TO ACADIA

The Isle of Jersey, the largest and southernmost of the British Channel Islands lay twelve miles off the coast of France. From the early 1200s, the island was largely populated with French-speaking Normans and Bretons. The island eventually became a British possession, but the French-speaking inhabitants remained.

Charles Robin was born in 1743 in St. Aubin, Jersey, the youngest of three brothers. One of his brothers spent time as a fisherman in the crowded fishery off the coast of Newfoundland. He became convinced that better, less crowded fishing could be had off the coast of Cape Breton Island and in the Gulf of St. Lawrence.

In 1765, the three brothers purchased a brig, the *Seaflower*, and Charles and his brother John sailed to Cape Breton to investigate the potential of the old French fishing settlements near Louisbourg. They found many Acadians eager to sell their catch. That Charles and his brother spoke fluent French helped to facilitate the transactions with the Acadians. In the fall, they returned to Jersey with their ship filled with dried cod. The Charles Robin and Company was formed, and they soon bought two more ships.

"Charles, how can you be sure we can fill our three ships with cod?" asked one of his brothers.

"I have no doubt we can fill a lot more than three ships with cod. There are many Acadian fishermen who currently don't have a market for their catch. By providing a market, we will encourage them to increase their catch. On top of that, almost every fisherman we've dealt with asked if we had extra fishing hooks, line, utensils, and the like that they could buy. We need to build and operate supply stores in each of the major fishing villages. Revenue from those stores should provide an excellent supplement to our fishing business."

The following year, the Robins expanded their operations to the Gaspé Coast in the Gulf of St. Lawrence. They chose the tiny port of Paspébiac, in the *Baie des Chaleurs*, as the North American headquarters for their fishing enterprise. Paspébiac's well protected lagoon was too small for their large boats but ideal for the small boats used in the inshore fishery. The nearby anchorage proved safe for large boats from even the worst storms. The main attraction of Paspébiac for the Robins was the availability of a large open area near the shore for the drying of fish. The Robins soon built a large warehouse for the storing of dried fish, a general store, and a manager's house in the village.

For the first few years, the Robins did not do any of the fishing themselves. They simply acquired the fish from the local Acadian and Micmac fishermen. A routine soon evolved whereby in the spring the local fishermen would get their fishing supplies and other goods from the Robins' general store on credit. In the fall, the fishermen would pay off their accounts with their catch. Cash did not change hands. This barter system continued for over sixty years until 1831, when it was abolished in England with the passage of the Truck Law. Employers were then required to pay their employees in cash.

"Charles, although the nearby fishing grounds are full of cod and the fishing is exceptionally good with calm weather, the Acadians refuse to fish today. They say that it's a religious holiday, the feast day of Saint So and So, someone I've never even heard of. They're all celebrating in the village," said John to his brother.

"I suspect the saint has nothing to do with it. They simply want a day off from fishing. One day off is not a disaster, but as you and I both understand, the fishing season is short. We should not waste any days."

"So, what do we do?"

"I've been thinking of bringing over our own fishermen from Jersey, young apprentices who are looking for a start. We would need to build a barracks for them and figure out how to pay them, but I believe this venture would pay off. The fish they catch should be more than enough to cover all expenses relating to them."

The Robins' apprentice program proved to be quite profitable. Soon, however, a shortage of workers developed in Jersey. Charles expanded his search for fishermen to the Saint-Malo area as opposed to an English area. French was the native language of the Robins. They therefore preferred French-speaking workers.

In March 1773, Pierre Aucoin, his wife Félicité, their three children, his brother Mondou, and his wife Marie sailed from the Isle of Jersey aboard a Robin boat. Their destination was Paspébiac in the Gulf of St. Lawrence.

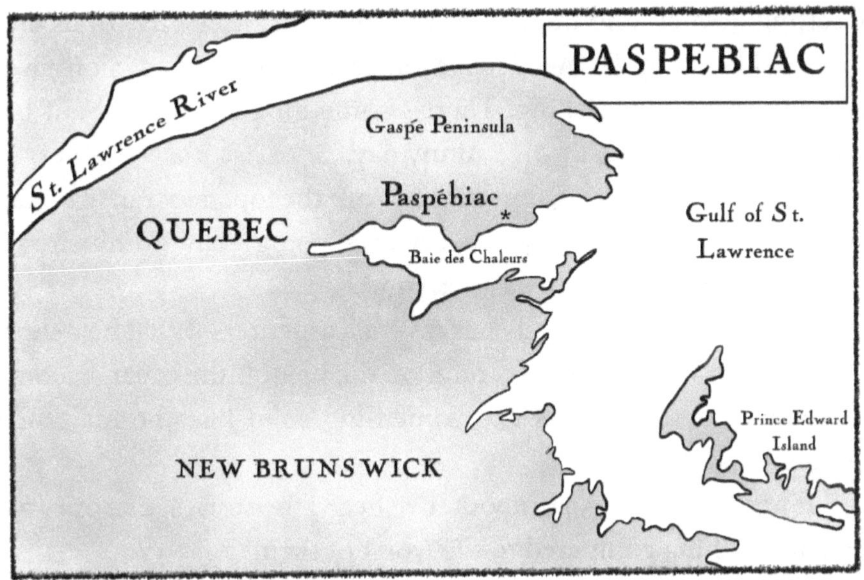



Map by Kristi Mueller

# CHAPTER 16
# PASPÉBIAC

The *Baie des Chaleurs* (Bay of Warmth) in the Gaspé area of the Gulf of St. Lawrence was so named by Jacques Cartier on one of his explorations in the 1500s when he noticed the unusually warm water of the bay. The heat came from a warm ocean current that entered the bay from the larger gulf to create what many have called the warmest ocean water on the Atlantic coast north of Virginia.

"Pierre, this company house we live in is small but more than adequate," said Félicité. "The Robins have kept their word. I'm surprised to be saying anything nice about the

English, but so far, they've been very good to us."

"I agree," replied Pierre. "Fishing is hard work, harder than I had imagined. But every man on the boat, even the captain, shares the work of setting the nets and then pulling them back in. The five of us on the boat are like a family. We depend on each other and get along well. I look forward to the fishing. There's something splendid about being out on the sea, especially on a sunny day."

"I know you like it, but fishing on the open ocean can be so dangerous. I worry about you every time you go out. I'd much rather you were a carpenter than a fisherman."

"Monsieur Robin already has several carpenters. What he's short of is fishermen. We're all very careful on the boat. If the ocean becomes a bit rough, we tie ourselves to something solid like the mast or the hatches."

"It's the storms I worry about. I've heard the stories. The ones we've seen are nothing compared to the worst of them!"

"Yes, storms come, and they are dangerous, but I'm not sure those stories don't exaggerate a bit. You know how it is."

"I also know there are fishermen's widows. Clotilde, Anne, Madelaine. You know how they struggle. If your boat goes down, Marie and I will join their company. The thought terrifies me. I need you, Pierre. At the first sign of danger, you must convince the captain to sail back."

"Clotilde's husband drank and took risks. Everyone agrees about that. I don't know about the others, but Captain Gosselin has a wife and three young daughters. He's a long-time Robin employee and does not take any unnecessary risks. The other two crew members, Roger Breton and Paul Normand, are both nineteen and apprentices like me and Mondou. None of us will do anything to put the boat or any of its crew in danger."

Félicité held her peace for a while, but she was always afraid and vigilant. Every year, on average, one fishing boat with all hands is lost at sea in the gulf. Those tragedies struck throughout the year but typically occurred in October through December when the gales and hurricanes arrived. The fishermen soon learned, during this period, it was not safe to venture too far out to sea. Privately, she thought they learned too slowly but understood they had to work.

•  •  •

By the start of 1776, business for the Robins was very good. They owned over a dozen general stores and fishing stations at various locations in the gulf. The American Revolution, however, brought turmoil even to Paspébiac.

"Charles, we just received word our fishing station at Thunder River on the north shore of the St. Lawrence was just raided by the New Englanders," shouted John to his brother. "They took all the cod and cleaned out the general store."

"Damn! That's the third attack this month. Did they burn the buildings?"

"No, nothing was burned. It's as if they're daring us to refill the warehouse and general store so they can rob them again."

Throughout the American Revolution, it was common for New England privateers (privately owned warships) to raid the coastal towns and villages of Nova Scotia and the Gulf of St. Lawrence. The New Englanders had gained considerable experience in this practice from their many years of persecuting the Acadians. The privateers typically received a commission from the American Navy that allowed them to disrupt enemy shipping. Although the intent of the commission was clear and limited—-the New England privateers were adept at stretching their commissions to include raiding coastal villages.

The Continental Navy was formed on October 13, 1775, when the Continental Congress in Philadelphia ordered the purchase of two armed ships to attack British supply ships to keep their supplies from reaching British soldiers in the colonies. Building or even purchasing warships was a decidedly slow process. Crews then needed to be found and trained to operate the ships. A much faster and less expensive approach was for the Navy to enter into contracts with private vessels to act on behalf of the Navy. These vessels and their crews came in all sizes and were known as privateers. The commission they received generally exempted them from the piracy laws. Without the commission, they could be charged with piracy and be subject to prosecution. A captured enemy ship was considered a prize. The proceeds from the sale of the prize and its cargo were then shared by the ship's crew and the Navy under a pre-arranged contract. During the American Revolution, nearly 800 vessels were commissioned by the American Navy as privateers.

·   ·   ·

One night when they were in bed, the children all asleep, Félicité spoke to Pierre. "I know how much you like fishing, but this new war makes it too dangerous. Look how many fishing boats have been captured by the New Englanders and taken to Boston. The fishermen lost their boats and all their belongings. They were lucky to return alive. Your three years of service are over. There's nothing to hold us here. My relatives on Ile Saint Jean have been asking us to join them. It's time!"

"I agree. Things were going well until this war broke out, but everything has now changed. Mondou also agrees. He and I were headed for Ile Saint Jean in 1755 when the English captured us. Perhaps we'll make it this time."

·   ·   ·

The move to Ile Saint Jean (modern-day Prince Edward Island) was uneventful. Pierre, Mondou, and their families landed near what is now Charlottetown, the capital of Prince Edward Island. They soon contacted Félicité's relatives and settled into a farming community comprised mostly of Acadians. Pierre missed the *Baie des Chaleurs*, but he did not say so. His wife was so much happier surrounded by cousins and no longer afraid.

# CHAPTER 17
# PRINCE EDWARD ISLAND

In 1775, when the American Revolution finally boiled over into armed conflict, only one-third of the colonists wanted to secede from Britain. Another third was strongly against secession and elected to remain loyal to Britain. That group soon became known as the Loyalists. The final third, as with most political issues, then and now, was undecided. They didn't much care either way. Many Loyalists soon began emigrating to Halifax.

The surrender of the English General Charles Cornwallis to the Americans at Yorktown, Virginia, on October 19, 1781, had a profound impact on the migration of Loyalists to Halifax. What had been a trickle then turned into a flood. The previous governors of Nova Scotia, starting with Charles Lawrence, had already allocated all the best land in Nova Scotia to favored contemporaries, military officers, government officials, friends, family, and some actual English settlers. Except for the settlers, the awardees largely held their lands as investments.

●　●　●

"Pierre isn't it lucky we ended up here!" exclaimed Félicité. "We have a large, productive parcel of land. I'm especially happy there are so few Englishmen on this island. No one bothers us. We are finally at peace."

"Yes, I agree. We have a bounty from land and sea. Our boat is a hardy vessel; now I'm a boatbuilder! I think we could live on cod alone if we had to."

"No thanks! I like our handsome chickens and our vegetable garden."

"Still, Mondou and I appreciate your efforts, and those of Marie and the children, in drying the fish. We can even sell our excess to the Robins."

"Speaking of Mondou, do you know if he and Marie have decided to keep the baby?"

"He says it's up to Marie. She wants her own, of course, but it's been so many years. I found out the father is an Irish boy who has since left the island. Poor Lisette is so young. When she gave the baby to Marie, she asked just one favor—that she keep the baby's name, Cyriac Roach."

"That's a strange request. Is Roach the father's family name?"

"Yes, it's the boy's family name, or at least the name he told Lisette. She says they were very much in love and wanted to make a go of it but, after the baby came, realized they didn't have the resources. I'm not sure Monsieur Roach was as interested as she was, but who can say? These things are always difficult. In any case, the baby is lucky to have Marie and Mondou, and Lisette may have more children."

Cyriac Roach thrived under the loving care of Marie and Mondou. They had no children of their own, so Cyriac proved to be a blessing for them. Mondou, who had always kept some of his younger-brother spirit, looking up to Pierre in every way, turned out to be a kind and sympathetic father. Cyriac grew up with stories of his father's and uncle's days in England, both the adventure and the grinding struggle, and was very aware of his privilege in living in Canada among his own people. As a man, he became a well-respected member of the Acadian community and continued to assist his adoptive parents well into their old age. He left a long line of descendants on Cape Breton Island, several of whom continue to hold leadership positions in the area.

•  •  •

In 1783, in Halifax, a messenger rapped on Governor Edmund Fanning's door. Born on April 24, 1739, in the Town of Southold on Long Island, New York, Fanning graduated from Yale College and became a lawyer and politician in North Carolina in the 1760s. As a Loyalist when the American Revolutionary War broke out, he was driven out of his home in New York and joined the British Army, eventually rising to the rank of general. At the end of the war in 1783, he settled in Nova Scotia and was appointed lieutenant governor, a position he held until 1786 when he was appointed lieutenant governor of St. John's Island (Ile Saint Jean). He held this new position until 1804. Ile Saint Jean was renamed Prince Edward Island during his tenure. He retired to London in 1813 and died there in 1818.

"Enter", said Fanning.

"Governor, three recently arrived Loyalists from New York have requested an audience with you."

"Send them in."

"Sir, thank you for seeing us. My name is Robert Cummings, and these two are James Rollings and Richard Graves. We're with a group of thirty-six New Yorkers who fled the traitorous rebels now in control of that colony. We hope you will grant us some land so we might reestablish ourselves here."

"Gentlemen, welcome to Nova Scotia. I applaud your loyalty to our king and will do what I can to assist you. I know of land on St. John's Island. Much of the arable land on the island currently consists of Acadian farms. The Acadians, however, do not hold title to their lands. They are simply squatters. If this land is suitable to you, I'm willing to make grants to you and your friends."

"Governor, that would be wonderful. Thank you so much!"

Shortly after the mass deportations from Ile Saint Jean in 1758, the island was completely surveyed and mapped by government surveyors from Nova Scotia. Governor Fanning used those surveys to make the land grants to the Loyalists.

.  .  .

"Papa," exclaimed Anselme to Pierre, "some Englishmen are here to see you."

"English? What do they want?"

"I don't know. Please come. They're waiting by the barn."

As Pierre and Anselme approached, Robert Cummings asked, "What is your name?"

"My name is Pierre Aucoin, and this is my land."

"You are sadly mistaken," replied Cummings. "This is my land, and if you want to remain here, from now on you will pay twenty percent of your harvest to me. Here is a copy of my grant from the governor for this specific piece of land."

This encounter took place in the fall of 1783, just prior to the harvest. When Félicité heard the bad news, she cried out, "*Mon Dieu!* How can this be?"

Her brothers and all the other Acadian settlers on the island met the same fate—pay the English or leave.

"*Les maudits Anglais!*" bellowed Pierre. "After all this time, they're again at our throats."

The next day, the Acadian heads of families met to discuss the situation. Germain Boudreau, who was the most fluent in English, was chosen to negotiate with the English. Everyone agreed twenty percent rent was too high. The immediate goal was to lower the rent to no more than ten percent. The longer-term goal was to obtain titles to their land.

After two full days of negotiations in Charlottetown, where the Loyalists each had their residences, the rent was finally agreed at twelve percent.

"Germain, thank you for your efforts. We all know how difficult your job was in negotiating with the English," expressed an Acadian when Germain returned.

"After the first day, they agreed to lower the rent to fifteen percent but refused to budge from there," replied Boudreau. "It was only after I told them we would burn all our buildings and leave that they lowered the rent to twelve percent. One other thing. While in Charlottetown, I noticed a garrison of about fifty British soldiers."

When Pierre relayed the information to Mondou, he had one question. "Pierre, does the twelve percent rent include our cod?"

"*Tabernacle*! I hope not. I forgot all about the cod. I'll meet tomorrow with the other fishermen and work out a unified position if the Loyalists insist on the cod."

•  •  •

"Thank you for coming," said Pierre to the fishermen. "My brother asked me yesterday if the English rent includes the fish we catch. My initial thought was no! I see the fish as being like the deer, rabbits, and game birds we catch in the woods, but we need to be prepared."

"The fish we catch have nothing to do with the land," called out Lucien Poirier. "I have no intention of paying them any portion of the fish."

"I agree the fish should be exempt from the rent," replied Marcel Gaudet. "Pierre is right though—we need to be prepared with a common position. When the Englishmen came to my farm, they noted all the cod drying in the open area by the shore. I saw them make notations on their paper."

"I suppose they could say without their land, we would be unable to dry or store the cod," added Raymond Doucet.

"None of us wants to pay rent on the cod," declared Pierre. "It seems likely; however, they will force us. What argument can we use to pay less than twelve percent?"

Try as they might, the Acadians were not able to avoid paying the full rent on their dried cod. The landlords simply included it as part of the overall produce. For the first harvest, the English arrived with their wagons and armed soldiers to collect their twelve percent.

In the spring of 1784, twenty-year-old Anselme Aucoin married nineteen-year-old Rose Chiasson. Since there were no priests on the island, Germain Boudreau officiated at the wedding. Later that summer, Anselme sold eight full barrels of dried cod to the Robins at Paspébiac. His father and uncle had decided that by selling the cod in the summer, they might avoid paying the percentage rent on it in the fall.

The Robins also had no love for the Loyalists, who had arrived earlier in Paspébiac with similar land grants. The Robins told Anselme that their fishing station in Chéticamp on Cape Breton Island had lots of land available and invited him to move there or to another of their fishing stations.

Upon returning home, Anselme excitedly told Pierre about the Robin's invitation. "The Robins told me Cape Breton has several fishing stations and general stores. It has few people, and the fishing is excellent. There are no Loyalists!"

"Cape Breton is a possibility," replied Pierre. "The percentage rent arrangement here is maddening. Monsieur Boudreau met several times with our landlords in Charlottetown this summer. They refuse to even consider selling their land to us."

"Papa, if you agree, Rose and I can go to Cape Breton and see what it's like. I can then report back, and we can decide if moving there is worthwhile."

"That seems like a good idea, but let's meet first with the heads of families and get their suggestions."

After discussing the matter for several hours, the heads of families agreed that Anselme Aucoin and his wife, Rose, would move to Cape Breton the following spring, work for the Robins, and then come back home in the fall to make their report.

# CHAPTER 18
# QUÉBEC

British General James Murray served as the Governor of Québec from 1760 to 1774. Throughout that period, most non-Indian inhabitants in the province were native French-Canadians or Acadian refugees. When Murray took over, the economy was in shambles. During the war for the conquest of Canada, many homes, barns, mills, and other enterprises had been destroyed. Many inhabitants had been killed or seriously wounded, which Murray had contributed to, as Wolfe's second-in-command. But once the war was over, and he was in charge, Murray's main task was to rebuild the area and revive the economy. He soon realized the French-speaking inhabitants were hard-working and the key to revitalizing his province. He needed more of them, but from where?

•   •   •

Jean Trahan, his wife, and three children were deported from Port Royal in December 1755 to Massachusetts. They lost relatives in the massacres and more to the disease and deprivation of the journey. They were assigned to the village of Lexington where they lived for the next eight years——working hard, often hungry, often cold. With the signing of the Treaty of Paris in 1763, they moved to Boston. Jean was the spokesperson and leader of about 250 Acadians who lived in Boston or its nearby towns.

"Jean, the war's been over for almost two years. Why do the Bostonians keep us here?" questioned Pauline, his wife. "I'm so tired of living among enemies."

"I don't know," replied Jean. "I'm meeting this evening with the other heads of families to discuss this very issue. You know, I'm not an unreasonable man. I mourned our dead and tried to get on with life. But after ten years here, we are just barely surviving. The English keep us down, and I don't see them changing. They refuse to let us get ahead."

"Where are you meeting?"

"We're meeting in the middle of Boston Common, next to the pond."

•   •   •

At the common, just as the meeting was getting underway, a group of English preteens walked by and yelled, "Look at all the frogs. They must have just come out of the pond." Laughing, they went on their way.

"*Les maudits Anglais,*" declared an Acadian. "The young ones learn that rude and insulting behavior from their parents."

"Thank you for coming," began Jean. "As you all know, the Bostonians continue to harass us at every opportunity. Life for us in this colony is not pleasant or easy. We're allowed to work for low wages in various enterprises but may not move up to higher positions. After discussing this matter with several of you over the past few weeks, what I propose is that we make a formal petition to the Massachusetts governor, Francis Bernard, to let us leave this colony for Saint Domingue."

"I agree!" shouted Marc-André Lepage, father of ten children—five born at Port Royal and five in Boston. "My children are bullied everywhere they go. I know little of Saint Domingue but I'm willing to take a chance. Life there must be better than here. At least we'll be rid of the English."

After considerable discussion over the next hour or so, the group agreed Jean would write a petition to the governor requesting permission for the Acadians to leave the colony for Saint Domingue.

•   •   •

In early January 1765, Trahan made his appeal to Governor Bernard.

"Sir, an Acadian is here and wishes to speak to you," stated the governor's assistant.

"An Acadian? Send him in."

"Thank you for seeing me, sir. My name is Jean Trahan, and I'm the spokesperson for the Acadians in this area. First, I'd like to wish you and your family a Happy New Year."

"Thank you, Mister Trahan. How may I help you?"

"I have a petition here signed by thirty-two heads of families representing over 250 Acadians living in Boston and nearby communities. We request permission to leave this colony for Saint Domingue."

"Saint Domingue? Mister Trahan, I assure you the climate there will not suit your group. White people simply don't live long in that region. There are many diseases that neither the French nor the English understand. I will read your petition, but I can tell you now, I will not grant your requested move to Saint Domingue."

After Trahan left, Bernard thought that an even more solid reason for denying the request was that he did not want to provide the French king with 250 settlers and deny his English king those same 250 settlers.

The Acadians were not happy with the rejection of their petition. The following year, however, they received a pleasant surprise from an unexpected source.

In the spring of 1766, Governor Bernard received a letter from Governor Murray in Québec.

The letter was extraordinary in that he requested Bernard inform all Acadians in his colony that they were welcome to move to Québec.

All settlers would be given free plots of land along the St. Lawrence River. Since the settlers would remain under the English king, Bernard quickly agreed to Murray's request. He sent his assistant to round up that fellow Trahan. When the man arrived, looking wary, the governor informed him of this new development. He could have taken credit for giving the Acadians what they wanted, but since he didn't care, he simply presented him with the information.

After Trahan rushed home that evening, he happily exclaimed, "Pauline, Pauline, you'll never guess what happened today!"

"What? Tell me!" declared an equally excited Pauline.

"The British Governor of Québec wants Acadians in the lower British colonies to move to Québec, where he will grant us free land. Governor Bernard has agreed to let us go. Isn't that wonderful?"

"That's amazing! Are you sure?"

"Yes, while I was at work this afternoon, the governor's assistant came to fetch me. I met with the governor, and he informed me of this new development."

"Jean, please be careful. Isn't the Governor of Québec the same Murray who burned and pillaged the French settlements from the Gaspé Peninsula all the way to Québec City and beyond? How can we trust him?"

"I didn't say we should trust him——you know I don't trust Englishmen. We need to be careful. I'll meet as soon as possible with the heads of families to discuss this new development."

During the meeting with the heads of families, all agreed that a delegation should proceed to Québec to meet with Murray and visit the land in question. Trahan and two other Acadian men were chosen.

•   •   •

In Québec City, Governor Murray's assistant informed him three Acadians had just arrived from Boston and requested an audience with him.

"Send them in," stated Murray.

"Governor Murray, thank you for seeing us. My name is Jean Trahan, and my associates are Paul Doucet and Raymond Poirier. We're here in response to your invitation for Acadians to move to your colony. We represent a group of about 250 Acadians in Massachusetts. I have a letter for you from Governor Bernard." Trahan was nervous, looking at this devil in the flesh. He was also angry, the memories of the deportation suddenly raw, and he did his best to conceal it. It wasn't difficult. He had the feeling no matter what he said, Murray didn't really notice him. Trahan was certain the governor didn't wonder if the men in front of him had lost parents, siblings, and other loved ones to his savagery.

"Thank you for coming. I hope your trip was a pleasant one. My goal is to convince you to move here. We have much fertile land available between here and Montreal and far too few settlers. I promise each settler a twenty-acre plot and no fees or taxes for five years. I will also provide some farm implements, a cow, and some chickens to each settled family."

"What about homes?" asked Jean.

"There are none. You will have to build your homes from scratch. I will provide some manpower to assist you in digging your cellars, felling trees, and splitting logs. The building of homes, however, will be largely your responsibility."

*And you will burn them down if you want to*, thought Jean. But perhaps there would be no reason for Murray to want to.

"Are there any Acadians already settled on or near the available lands?" asked Paul Doucet.

"Yes, there's a small group of Acadians as well as French-Canadians settled in a village called Trois Rivières (Three Rivers). The Acadians have been there for several years."

"What is the process for us to get legal title to this new land?" inquired Jean.

"You will be required to clear and farm at least three acres per year for each of the first three years. At the end of three years, if you are farming at least nine acres, you will be given a clear title to your twenty acres."

"Can we see the land available? We are especially interested in the land at Trois Rivières."

"Certainly. My settlement minister, Captain Frank Williams, will accompany you."

After viewing the land and meeting with the Acadians in Trois Rivières, Trahan, Doucet, and Poirier were sufficiently impressed to recommend to their associates in Boston that moving to Trois Rivières was a good idea. Within two years, 4,000 Acadians were living in Québec along the St. Lawrence seaway, between Montreal and the Gaspé Peninsula. Over 3,500 of those Acadians moved from the lower British colonies.

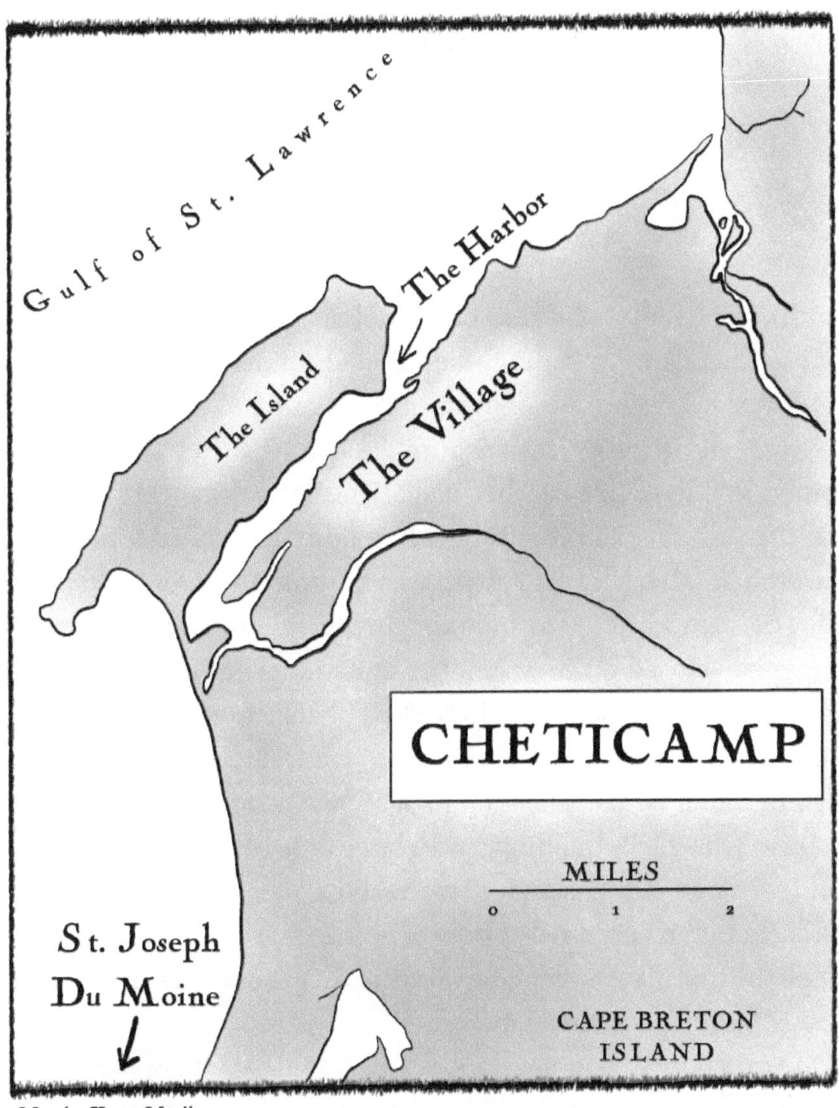


Map by Kristi Mueller

# CHAPTER 19
# CHÉTICAMP

In April 1785, twenty-one-year-old Anselme Aucoin and his wife Rose arrived in Chéticamp, a fishing station on Cape Breton Island operated by the Robins. The Robins arrived in Chéticamp in 1770. During the early years, the fishing station purchased all its cod from Micmac fishermen who lived in a nearby village. The fish were plentiful, and the station thrived. By 1785 the Robins had built a large dock on a small cove at the southern end of what was commonly referred to as the island. The island was a two-mile-long peninsula that formed one side of a large bay closed off by a sandbar at its northern end. At low tide, the sandbar was exposed and blocked all boats from entering. At high tide, the sandbar was covered by four to five feet of water and allowed passage of small boats. The Robins also had a general store, a large warehouse, a barracks building, and a large area of fish-drying racks on the southern end of the island, near the dock.

"Anselme, I'm surprised at how nice our quarters are," said Rose.

"Yes, the Robins are very good at what they do. My mother was very pleased with our house in Paspébiac."

"Do you know the other two Acadian families that are here?"

"*Non*, Monsieur Luce, the Robin manager, told me Monsieur Pierre Bois and Monsieur Joseph Richard arrived here three years ago, in 1782, with their wives. They've been fishing for the Robins ever since. I look forward to meeting them. They're out fishing now and won't be back for a few days."

"Their houses are not far from here. Perhaps we can visit their wives while waiting."

"Their wives work for the Robins. Monsieur Luce said that today they're working in the drying racks, turning the fish over. When the boats come in, they help cut the fish and place them on the racks. They also work in the warehouse storing the dried fish."

"That sounds like a full-time job. Who takes care of their children?"

"The Robins provide a nursery room for the children. A young, injured fisherman currently watches over them. The mothers have ready access."

"That's amazing!"

"Yes, like I said, the Robins are very good at what they do. Perhaps this evening, after they finish their work, we can visit the wives."


"*Bonjour, Madame*, I am Anselme Aucoin, and this is my wife, Rose. We hope we are not disturbing you. We are newly arrived and plan to settle here and work for the Robins."

"Please come in," replied *Madame* Bois. "My husband is out fishing and not expected back for a few days. This is our son, Régis. He's five. We also have two daughters, Denise and Nicole—they're three and one."

"*Merci*, we need to learn as much as possible about this place. We're from Ile Saint Jean, and the English landlords there have made life very difficult for us. We need to move."

"I understand. My husband and I came here from Gaspé. The farming and fishing were good. We were happy to settle there, but the English made life unbearable. The Robins suggested we join them here."

"My father worked for the Robins in Paspébiac for three years before moving to Ile Saint Jean. The Robins were good to us. How is your life here?"

"My husband and I are very satisfied. We both work for a good wage, and the Robins's store provides all the necessities. Regarding the store, however, you need to be careful. The store is well-stocked with merchandise you'd love to have but don't really need. It's easy to buy too much and get into debt. Several Micmac families who started out as independent fishermen, selling their catch to the Robins, bought way too much from the Robins's store. To settle their debt, they had to sell their boats to the Robins. They now work directly for the Robins as employees, for less money."

"What can you tell me about your neighbors, the Richard family?"

"They're very nice. They came here with us from Gaspé, but *Madame* Richard is not happy here. She's from Arichat and still has many relatives there. She keeps pestering her husband to move back to Arichat. I suspect he'll soon give in."

Arichat was an Acadian village in the southern part of Cape Breton Island, about one hundred miles from Chéticamp.

"What about farming? Does anyone grow crops here?" said Anselme. "How fertile is the land?"

"I'm not aware of any farms in this area, but the land is well-watered though with several brooks and small rivers. I know the grass in the meadows grows waist high in the summer, so the land seems fertile enough."

"*Merci, Madame* Bois. When your husband returns, please tell him I'd like to continue this discussion."

Both Anselme and Rose worked for the Robins that entire season. Anselme on the fishing boats, Rose on shore with the drying racks. In the fall, as promised, they returned to Ile Saint Jean. Anselme was tall and wiry, much like his father Pierre. well over six feet but only 140 pounds. His wife Rose was petite, just over five feet and perhaps 100 pounds. Anselme enjoyed being with people. He got along well with the Robins, and that positive relationship helped soften his views towards them. He saw them as being only half English. Their nationality and brains were English, but their blood and especially their hearts were obviously French.

"Papa," exclaimed Anselme. "The Robins have plenty of work available for all of us. The fishing is excellent, and there are no English, other than the Robins."

"What about the land? What can we grow there?"

"The land seems fertile enough. Several large meadows could be cultivated without too much effort, and we spotted enough space for twenty or more forty-acre farms. Very few trees need to be cleared, and I didn't notice any large rocks in the meadows. On top of that, several small rivers and brooks water the area, and the shoreline has lots of old seaweed piled up."

"Is anyone growing any crops?"

"Yes, but very little. Three Micmac families live in the area. I visited them. The men work for the Robins on the fishing boats. Their wives do the farming. They grow corn, beans, beets, turnips, and a few other crops. All seem to grow well."

"What about farm animals?"

"My entire time in Chéticamp, I didn't see a single cow, pig, chicken, or any other farm animals. The grass in the meadows is thick and appears sufficient to raise lots of cattle. There would be enough hay in the fall to fill many barns. Papa, I have not yet told you the best part. Two Acadian families are already settled there. One of them, Monsieur Pierre Bois, was approached by a government official seeking permanent settlers. The official told Monsieur Bois if he could convince at least a dozen families to settle in the Chéticamp area, the government would provide land grants."

"Land grants? How can we trust this government official?"

"About a month ago, Monsieur Charles Robin himself came to Chéticamp. Monsieur Bois and I met with him to discuss a possible land grant. Monsieur Robin vouched for the Cape Breton officials. He said that unlike the rest of Acadia, Cape Breton found it very difficult to attract settlers. The Cape Breton officials would be overjoyed to have permanent Acadian settlers to work the land. The grant would require us to cultivate a certain number of acres per year for a certain number of years before acquiring clear title to the land."

"*Mon Dieu!* This land grant seems like the answer to our prayers."

"I agree. While some of us work on the land, the rest can fish for the Robins. Surely, we can succeed and prosper in Chéticamp."

"We must inform the heads of families. It's too late today. We'll meet with them first thing in the morning."

• • •

In the spring of 1786, seventeen Acadian families moved from Ile Saint Jean to Chéticamp. The move involved substantial risk. On Ile Saint Jean, they at least had houses, food, and the means to make a living. At that point, Chéticamp provided only promises, and none of the Acadians trusted the English. Given the uncertainty, many Acadian families decided it was better to deal with the devil they knew than the devil they didn't know. They stayed put on Ile Saint Jean and reaped an unanticipated benefit. The Loyalist landlords became alarmed at the many tenant defections and lowered the rent for the remaining Acadians.

In anticipation of the move, the Robins constructed two additional barracks buildings to house the Ile Saint Jean Acadians and brought another fishing boat from the Isle of Jersey.

Anselme and his father Pierre were not only similar in physique, tall and lean, but quite similar in outlook and temperament. Both had many reasons to hate the English and would never trust them. The Robins, however, seemed to be an exception. They treated the Acadians well. The Robins, of course, were businessmen and business came first. But it seemed clear to both Anselme and Pierre that the Robins business was a win/win situation for the Robins and the Acadians. Chéticamp seemed like an excellent place to put down permanent roots.

"Papa," said Anselme, "even from here on the Robins's dock, you can see the forest above the meadows that I spoke of. The forest has many sugar maples, oaks, white pine, and birches. I also saw many signs of rabbits, deer, and moose. The forest will provide well for us."

"I'm impressed," replied Pierre. "I'm pleased that the Robins agreed to let us stay in their buildings rent-free for two months. We will fish for them, but a high priority for us must be to build our houses."

"Before I left in the fall, the Robins's manager told me we could build our houses all along the basin here. Our boats can easily enter and leave the basin at high tide."

"I doubt that location will be acceptable. It's too close to the shore and provides no protection against an English raid. We must discuss this matter with the other heads of families."

The decision was unanimous. Building their houses close to the shore was unacceptable because of the risk of attack from the English. Instead, they built about a mile inland from the basin at a place they called *le platin,* a flat area behind a low hill. The hill blocked their homes from the sight of any passing ships. As time provided, they dug their cellars and built their homes. Before leaving Ile Saint Jean, they dismantled their houses and barns and brought the lumber with them so, after the cellars were dug, construction of the new homes went quickly.

•   •   •

In Sydney, the capital of Cape Breton Island, about 100 miles from Chéticamp, Colonel Joseph Frederick Wallet Des Barres, the Lieutenant Governor of Cape Breton lived. Des Barres previously served as aide-de-camp to General James Wolfe during the French and Indian War.

"Sir, we've just received word from the Robins that fifteen or so Acadian families have moved from Prince Edward Island to Chéticamp," explained Des Barres's assistant, Thomas Peterson. "The Robins say they appear to be good candidates for permanent settlement."

"Really? That's excellent news! God knows for the past several years I've done all that I bloody can to attract settlers with little to show for my effort. We must do what we can to keep these Acadians."

"Sir, do you want me to send a message to the Robins?"

"No, better yet, Thomas, I want you to go to Chéticamp and meet directly with the Acadians. I want you to offer them in person the land grant we previously discussed. They can't just fish for the Robins. They must build homes and farm the land to qualify for a grant. You know the details."

"Yes sir, I'll make arrangements for a ship and depart as soon as possible."

•   •   •

"Pierre," whispered Félicité, "this store is even better supplied than the one in Paspébiac. We'll need to be careful not to buy more than we can afford."

"I agree," responded Pierre. "Yesterday, I noticed two foreign fishing boats—one Portuguese and one Basque—pull in to the Robins's dock. The crew spent all their time in the store. They came out with many purchases. It seems this store serves much of the fishing fleet on the Grand Banks."

•   •   •

In August 1786, Thomas Peterson arrived in Chéticamp. On the day he arrived, the Acadian men were out fishing for the Robins. The next day, the boats returned and offloaded their catch onto the dock. That evening, Peterson met with the Acadians.

"Gentlemen," stated Peterson, "I bring you greetings from Governor Des Barres in Sydney. He wishes you well and will provide you with land grants if you meet certain criteria."

"What criteria?" asked an Acadian.

"For one thing, you must be settlers, not speculators. You must build houses and farm the land. It's not enough to be a full-time fisherman."

"How much land do we have to farm?" asked Pierre Bois.

"You must farm three acres per year for every fifty acres granted. That means in year two, you must cultivate six acres, and in year three, nine acres per fifty acres granted."

"Providing that we comply with these terms, when would we receive the actual grant?" asked Pierre Aucoin.

"If all goes well, you should receive the grant in about four years. We need to see that your houses are built, and you are cultivating the land."

"Monsieur Peterson, thank you for bringing this offer to our attention, and please thank Governor Des Barres for us," said Pierre Bois. "We are very interested in settling here. Many of our homes are already completed just beyond that small hill closer to the meadows. I would be honored to show you the community we have built and have you join me and my family for supper at my home this evening."

"Thank you, Monsieur Bois. I would be very pleased to join you."

The Acadians were overjoyed at the thought of owning their own land. That night, in many homes, the Acadians got on their knees: fathers, mothers and children, and thanked their favorite saints, especially Saint Christopher, the patron saint of travelers, for having led them there and making the grant possible. They could see the light at the end of the long, dark tunnel—a 150-year-long tunnel.

• • •

The following year, in 1787, Des Barres was called to London to settle some financial claims and remained there for sixteen years. He returned to Acadia in 1804 to become the Lieutenant Governor of Prince Edward Island, a position he held until 1812 at the age of 90. He retired to Halifax and died there at 103. He was replaced, in 1787, as Lieutenant Governor of Cape Breton by Colonel William Macarmick. On September 27, 1790, Macarmick signed the document granting "Lands at Chetican (sic) to Pierre Bois and Associates 7,000 acres." The document listed fourteen Acadian heads of families who became known as the founders of Chéticamp. Dividing the land grant among the Acadians was left to the Acadians. Squabbles between families pertaining to the land divisions soon followed, but the main takeaway was that the Acadians, for the first time, held clear title to their own land.

# CHAPTER 20
# RESCUE AT SEA

On a pleasant, mild day in late-February 1800, five Acadian boys from Chéticamp were playing by the shore. Every winter, their fathers hunted seals on the ice. The boys were therefore familiar with the seal hunting process. They knew the mother seals came onto the ice to give birth. The sea froze from shore out for a mile or two to the open water. The seal hunters dragged their small boats over the ice to reach the open water. They then sailed or rowed near the edge of the ice looking for seals on the ice. Once they were spotted, they did their best to block the seals from returning to the sea, using clubs to kill the seals. The seal meat helped the Acadians survive the harsh winters, and the seal skins provided shoes and water-proof boots.

"Jean-Paul, look over there!" cried nine-year-old Robert Poirier, one of the five boys playing by the shore.

"Where? What do you see?" replied Jean-Paul Deveau. At ten, Jean-Paul was the oldest and the leader of the five. Two of the remaining boys were eight, the other was seven.

"Over there," Robert pointed. "Do you see the black spot?"

"Yes, I see it!" exclaimed one of the boys. "It must be a seal."

"Let's get some clubs and go get it," replied another.

The boys, now spread out and in a crouched fashion approached the black spot. With their backs to the land and perhaps 100 yards out from shore, they did not notice the wind had picked up and was blowing from land to sea. Their focus on the black spot probably prevented them from hearing the loud "crack!" as their one-mile square ice sheet parted from shore and was pushed out to sea.

As Rose Aucoin was peeling potatoes for the evening meal on that February day, their neighbor, Edward Leblanc, burst in.

"Anselme, we need you and your boat," shouted Leblanc. "Five children have been blown out to sea on an ice sheet. It's getting dark, and we must go at once to find them."

"*Mon Dieu!*" exclaimed Rose.

Eight Acadian boats set out to find the ice sheet and the boys.

"Darn, it's just a piece of wood!" exclaimed one of the boys as they neared the black spot on the ice sheet.

"No seals today," replied Jean-Paul. "It's getting dark. Let's go back."

As the boys turned around, they realized the shore was much further away than it should be. They ran towards home and soon saw the open water—close to a mile of it between them and land. Terror now gripped the boys. The open water was terrifying enough, but worse still, their ice sheet was breaking up. Their piece of ice was now no larger than a football field.

•　•　•

Each of the eight boats set off in a different direction to search the many ice sheets in the gulf. While the wind pushed the sheets in a certain direction, the tide and ocean currents then carried the sheets in diverse directions. Each boat carried three men, many torches, and a gun. The torches were made of three-foot long hardwood sticks covered at one end with pitch from the pine trees. The pitch was embedded into the hardwood. Each torch would burn brightly for about half an hour. A gunshot was the signal that the boys were found. Darkness, the men's biggest enemy in the search, was quickly overcoming the light.

"Denis, please light the oil lamp," declared Anselme. "I have clear water in front of me and will continue in this direction, but I'll soon need a torch to help me see forward."

Besides the many ice sheets, icebergs populated the gulf. The icebergs originated in the north and flowed down into the gulf. Running into an ice sheet was typically a minor problem—the boat would either slice through the relatively thin sheet or slide up onto the sheet. Hitting an iceberg, however, would typically result in a major catastrophe—the boat would be demolished.

Two hours after darkness won its battle with light, Anselme's boat was on its fourth torch. The men prayed and especially invoked Saint Peter and Saint Christopher to assist them. Saint Peter was the patron saint of fishermen while Saint Christopher was the patron saint of travelers. The men saw the boys as travelers on the ice sheet.

"Crack!" A loud gunshot carried over the water. The men in Anselme's boat were overjoyed and tried to orient themselves in the gunshot's direction. As agreed, the first gunshot was followed by another and another every three minutes or so, to allow the other boats to find them.

Anselme steered towards the sound of the gunshots, but as they began moving in that direction, all three men on his boat heard another sound off to their left. The sound was muffled, indistinct, and frightening. Each man instinctively knew what caused that sound but refused to admit or say it.

"It could just be driftwood scraping up against an iceberg," whispered Denis.

Anselme had already turned the boat in the direction of the new sound. Fifteen minutes later, they saw the broken wood in the water, but it was not driftwood. They soon saw several unlit torches in the water and knew for sure they were looking at the remains of a Chéticamp boat. They found two bodies floating and pulled them onto their boat. For the next hour, they searched all around the iceberg but were unable to locate the third body. Each of them knew in this cold water, a man could not survive for over five minutes.

"Perhaps they left shore with only the two of them," wondered Denis.

"I wish it was so, but these two are the Doucet brothers, André and Paul, and I saw them leave shore with Claude Leblanc as the third hand," replied Anselme. "All three are married. André and Paul each have two small children, while Claude has five."

The rescue boat with the five children, safe and sound, was the first to dock at the Chéticamp pier to the immense relief and joy of everyone on shore. Five boats soon followed, and everyone waited for the final two. Almost two hours later, Anselme's boat arrived with the sad news. He and his crewmates were relieved to hear of the safe children but, like everyone else in the village, heavily distressed over the loss of the three men.

The sea provided well for the men of Chéticamp, but she was a hard mistress. She took as well as she gave. It was good that two of the three bodies were returned, but it was not always so. In due course, many more fishermen would find watery graves. Returned bodies were a rare gift from the vastly productive but unforgiving sea.

·  ·  ·

In late-March, as the days noticeably got longer, winter's grip appeared to lessen.

"Anselme!" exclaimed Rose after supper. "I can't imagine a better place than Chéticamp for us. It's been fifteen years and still no English to bother us."

"Yes, I agree. We have legal title to our land. Our farm produces well, and the fishing is excellent, but the price the Robins pay for our cod is too low. The price is much better in Sydney, but we can't take our fish the 100 miles to get there. Sydney is too far."

"Keep in mind, *mon chéri*, that the Robins were the key to our coming here. They invited us, gave us free lodging while we built our homes, employed us, gave us a way to live, and have always provided a market for our fish."

"They have their good side, but also their bad. Take Fidel LeFort, for example—the Robins surely knew he was buying far more than he could afford from their store. They let him get way over his head in debt. To settle that debt, Fidel had to sell his boat to the Robins. He now fishes for them on his old boat for a lot less money."

"What happened to Fidel is unfortunate, but the Robins are not entirely to blame. Fidel was his own worst enemy. His wife, Lucienne, tried to make him stop buying. She even tried to return some of the items back to the store."

"Fidel is not the only one. There are many Acadians here unable to clear their Robins' debt fully in the fall. Each year, they drop further behind. The Robins control the price for our fish and the price of the goods in their store. They control everything."

"Perhaps, but we have seen and endured much worse from the English. At least the Robins speak French, don't interfere with the free practice of our religion, and are not a threat to the morality of our community, especially our young people. Things could be much worse."

Rose knew from talking to the other women in town that, many times, the debt owed to the Robins was largely caused by the men purchasing too much rum and other alcohol products. Drinking was a common problem in Chéticamp and led to many heated arguments between husband and wife, including between Anselme and Rose. The men were generally hard-working and good providers for their families, but many seemed to be addicted to alcohol, to the chagrin of their wives. The men saw alcohol as one of the few pleasures in their otherwise difficult and dangerous lives. While they loved their wives and children, sometimes they needed more. The alcohol provided the "more."

# CHAPTER 21
# LOUISIANA

The first Acadians to arrive in Louisiana were four interrelated families from Georgia in 1764. They were followed in 1765 by about 200 members of the Beausoleil group from Halifax. Several hundred more Acadians arrived in 1767 from Pennsylvania and Maryland. The largest group to arrive was 1,600 Acadians from France in 1785. This group was offered free passage, free land, and free farm tools by the Spanish king, who was very interested in populating his newly gained colony with experienced and proven settlers. These initial Acadians, totaling about 2,500, took lands upriver from New Orleans or on the prairies and bayous west of the Mississippi River.

François Robichaud, his wife Marie, and their six children, all under the age of ten, were part of the 1,600 that arrived in 1785.

"François, I'm so happy to be on land again," declared Marie after arriving in New Orleans. "I'm sorry I was so sick during the crossing."

"I'm glad you're feeling better. It's lucky the children and I were hardly sick at all. Can you imagine if I had been as sick as you were—and they were not? As it was, the little ones got into all sorts of mischief."

"I know," she said fondly. "I could hear them. Anyway, it's over now."

"Unfortunately, we still have some distance to go by boat. Our destination is on the Bayou Lafourche. To get there, we must continue up the Mississippi River to where it connects with Bayou Lafourche and then down the bayou another forty miles."

"A river is not the sea. I will be fine. But what is a bayou? I'm not familiar with that word."

"A bayou is what the locals call a slow-moving waterway. It's like a canal or lazy river. Some are quite long. The Bayou Lafourche, for example, is over 100 miles long. It empties into the Gulf of Mexico."

"Is that where the Acadians that came here earlier are settled?"

"*Non*, the earlier Acadians settled in the Attakapas region, about 100 miles west of here. The Attakapas are an Indian tribe."

"Indians? Are they friendly?"

"I've been told there are very few left. Smallpox and other diseases have decimated their numbers. Hundreds of Acadians are settled there, so it seems safe."

"That is sad, isn't it? It was their land, even if they are heathens. But I admit, I would be uncomfortable if there were a lot of them. How do the Acadians live in Attakapas? What do they grow?"

"Monsieur Amarro, the Spanish governor's agent, explained to us that the Beausoleil group, led by Joseph and Alexandre Broussard, settled into the Attakapas region about twenty years ago. Their main product is beef, and their cattle number in the thousands."

"Is that what they want us to do—raise cattle?"

"*Non*, they want us to grow rice, corn, and other crops."

"Rice? Why rice? We have no experience in growing rice. Why not wheat?"

"The agent told us wheat does not grow well here, whereas rice grows very well. We must learn all we can about this new land, its climate, and its people. This is our new home. It will be a challenge, Marie, but we must succeed so our children may flourish here."

"Of course, we will succeed. We are Acadians, and we know how to work."

The parcel of land assigned to François and Marie Robichaud on Bayou Lafourche had about forty acres with an unusual shape. The parcel had about 400 feet of frontage on the bayou. The rest of the parcel stretched straight back for almost a mile. The parcel was a long, narrow rectangle anchored on the bayou. This type of land division provided all parcels with access to water and was the common practice in the area. Homes were typically built on the bayou end of the property.

Because the water table was so high, the Acadians soon learned that digging cellars for their homes was not only impossible but unnecessary since the ground didn't freeze in the winter. Building their houses along the bayous progressed very quickly. The Spaniards provided the lumber, and François and his family were soon settled in their new home.

"François, come quick!" cried Marie one morning. "There's a monster in our yard!"

"Monster? Where?" replied François.

"He's there, next to the shed."

"*Tabernacle*! What is that?"

François, Marie, and the children were looking at their first seven-foot alligator. François, with the help of neighbors, killed the beast and skinned it. The children looked on, at first afraid and awed, and then, once it was dead, investigated it thoroughly, teeth to tail. For months, the older ones teased the younger ones with stories of alligators in the privies. Finally, Marie put a stop to it with a serious threat of no pies or cakes for a season.

Alligators were plentiful, then and now, in the South Louisiana bayous and swamps and soon found their way onto the Acadian menu where they proved to be popular, tasty, and an excellent source of protein.

•    •    •

By 1790, François and Marie's farm was well-established. The rice they grew produced a surplus they were able to sell or exchange for other items they needed. All their children worked on the farm. Their fourteen-year-old son Jean-Paul was a major contributor to the farm's success.

"Papa, I stopped by Monsieur Hébert's farm this morning and noticed he is growing cotton," declared Jean-Paul.

"Yes, I heard the same from Monsieur Landry today when he came by to exchange his beans for my rice. Apparently, there's a significant demand for cotton. We may grow it someday, but I'm not yet ready."

"Why not, Papa?"

"The large planters who are growing cotton all use slaves. Without the slaves, it's unlikely it could be grown for a profit. Picking ripe cotton is very labor intensive. You then must remove the seeds from the picked cotton—another labor-intensive process. I have no intention of acquiring any slaves." With a smile, François added, "Unless you and your siblings will be my slaves."

"Mama has us working all the time!" piped up their daughter Louise.

"And mama works harder than all of you put together," said François.

François and most Acadians from that first generation in Louisiana stayed out of the slave business. Not so for their children and grandchildren.

In 1800, twenty-four-year-old Jean-Paul Robichaud was married with two children on his own farm on Bayou Teche. Cotton was his main crop. He owned two male slaves. Jean-Paul and his slaves worked side by side and did much of the same work. During the harvest, his wife Paulette also picked cotton.

"Jean-Paul, the cotton has done very well this year. The bolls seem fuller than last year," said Paulette.

"Yes, I agree. Last year was good. This year is even better. Picking cotton is hard work, but growing it is very easy. It requires minimal fertilizer and comes back strong, year after year, on the same ground. It's a wonderful crop. Our rice, corn, and beans have also done well. This will be a comfortable year of plenty for us."

"Monsieur Doucet stopped by this morning and asked if we had any alligator hides to sell. I told him no and we'd contact him when we have some."

"His hide business seems to thrive. I saw him on the bayou last week heading for New Orleans with his boat full of hides. I'm sure he gets a very good price for them."

The land grants provided to the Acadians required them to erect dikes—called levees by the locals—to prevent the Mississippi River and the various bayous from flooding the farmland. The farms were contiguous along the rivers and bayous. Each landowner was legally responsible for maintaining the levee fronting his property. The word *levée* was French for "raised up" and referred to the mound of earth that held back the water. Whether called dikes or levees, the work was second nature for the Acadians. Once they became familiar with the makeup of the spring floods, the levees were easily constructed and maintained to contain the high water.

The early 1800s were good years for the Louisiana Acadians. Their farms prospered and adult children were able to get land grants of their own on the same bayou or other bayous not too far away. Some upwardly mobile Acadians moved into the upper class and became planters, growing cotton or sugar with their fifty or more slaves on ever larger estates. Most Acadians, however, belonged to the farmer class and managed their land with the help of two or three slaves. These second-generation farmers reached a standard of living very similar to that of their successful pre-dispersal ancestors at Grand Pré in old Acadia. Life was good, but foreign politics were at play that would soon alter the ideal and carefree life of the average Louisiana Acadian.

During this time, Louisiana society comprised four distinct groups, not counting the Spanish government officials. The Creoles, the Anglo-Americans, the Acadians, and the Black slaves made up these four groups. The Creoles—white descendants of the original French settlers—dominated the highest rung of society. A close second were the Anglo-Americans, many of whom were the sons of rich plantation owners from Virginia and the Carolinas who came there to replicate their plantation way of life. The Acadians formed the middle and lower classes, with the Blacks, the largest group of all, at the very bottom.

# CHAPTER 22
# BAYOU TECHE

On April 30, 1803, President Thomas Jefferson purchased Louisiana from the French. The territory purchased included all of modern-day Louisiana, Missouri, Arkansas, Iowa, North Dakota, South Dakota, Nebraska, and Oklahoma. It also included most of modern-day Kansas, Colorado, Wyoming, Montana, and Minnesota. The land gained totaled 828,000 square miles and doubled the then-size of the United States.

The Louisiana Purchase triggered a flood of new Anglo-American settlers into Louisiana. In general, these new settlers were far more affluent than the resident Acadians and were able to acquire considerable land from those Acadians struggling to make ends meet.

• • •

Cotton remained king but was seriously hampered during the War of 1812 when British warships blockaded Louisiana in the Gulf of Mexico. Traders in New Orleans typically shipped the cotton down the Mississippi River to the gulf and from there to their customers on the U.S. East Coast and Europe. The blockade ended all shipping down the Mississippi and soon caused a glut of cotton in New Orleans. The lack of sales to final customers resulted in a severe cash flow problem. The money to pay growers soon dried up.

"Monsieur Thibodeau says *les maudits Anglais* have put an end to the cotton business," declared Jean-Paul Robichaud to his wife when she asked when they would get paid for their cotton. "The British are patrolling the gulf and capturing and confiscating all American ships and goods."

"Why are they doing this? What have we done to them?" questioned Paulette.

"They are English. They don't need a reason. They do what they want. You've heard my father's story regarding *le grand dérangement* (the great upheaval). The English are not to be trusted."

•　•　•

The War of 1812 officially started on June 18, 1812, when the Americans declared war on Britain for repeated violations of U.S. maritime rights—particularly the impressment of American sailors into the British navy. For the first two years of the war, the British were clearly in control. They won most of the major battles and burned Washington, D.C. to the ground, including the White House. The British, however, subsequently lost a major battle at Lake Champlain in Vermont pulled their forces back into Canada. The war basically ended in a draw with the signing of the Treaty of Ghent on December 24, 1814. Word of this treaty did not reach America in time to prevent the Battle of New Orleans on January 8, 1815.

Paul Aucoin and his neighbor Robert Chiasson, each twenty years old and lifelong friends, were members of the Baton Rouge militia. Their 500-member battalion consisted entirely of Acadians and was known as the Baton Rouge Demons. Since the start of the war, their unit had been placed on alert multiple times and had undergone extensive training but had not yet seen any combat. All the battles, so far, were naval engagements on the lower Mississippi or in the gulf.

"Paul, do you think we'll ever see any action in this war?" exclaimed Robert. "I'm bored to death with all this target shooting, marching, and other training they force us to do. I'm also tired of the constant guard duty we must pull at night."

"I'm just as bored and tired as you," replied Paul. "Major Mouton has finally returned from New Orleans. I saw him disembark at the dock this morning. Perhaps we'll hear something soon."

A few days earlier, in New Orleans on December 23, 1814, Major Gabriel Villeré discussed the situation with Major General Andrew Jackson.

"The British have taken over the Lacoste Plantation on the Mississippi about nine miles south of here," Villeré reported. "I was in my nearby residence when the British arrived."

"What? My ships are constantly patrolling the river many miles south of there. No enemy ships came through."

"The enemy troops came overland from the east, possibly from Lake Borgne."

"Damn! How many troops did you see?"

"At least 1,000, possibly as many as 2,000. I also counted twelve large artillery pieces."

"Thank you, Major. Return to your unit and place them on high alert."

Jackson immediately called a war council comprising his key commanders. A plan quickly emerged and was implemented. That very night, under cover of darkness, Jackson led a force of 2,000 men, including pirate Jean Lafitte commanding fifty of his experienced fighters, to attack the encamped British at the Lacoste Plantation.

The attack caught the British completely by surprise. Jackson then pulled his troops back to the Rodriguez Canal, about four miles south of New Orleans. The Americans suffered twenty-four killed and 115 wounded, while the British reported forty-six killed and 167 wounded.

"Gentlemen, this is where we will make our stand," declared Jackson. "We will transform this canal into a heavily fortified earthwork. If the enemy is foolish enough to attempt a frontal assault, he will enter a killing field and pay a heavy price."

•    •    •

The Rodriguez Canal was four miles long and ran from the Mississippi River on its western end to a large swamp on its eastern end. The canal averaged four to five feet deep and was about ten feet wide.

Jackson created a fortified six-foot high earthen berm on the north side of the canal over its entire four-mile length. He placed his artillery pieces behind this berm with a clear field of fire over the entire open approach to the canal. He also placed an artillery battery across the Mississippi to protect his flank. Major Mouton and his Baton Rouge Demons were assigned the task of protecting this battery from British assault. The Demons, including privates Paul Aucoin and Robert Chiasson, had been in their defensive positions on the western side of the Mississippi for a week.

"Paul, do you think the British will come?" asked a weary Robert as dawn broke on January 1, 1815.

Before Paul could answer, they both saw and heard the start of the British bombardment of the American line at the canal across the river. The American cannons immediately returned fire.

After three hours of constant bombardment, British General Sir Edward Pakenham ordered his troops to cease fire.

"General Pakenham, our forward Indian scouts say the American line has been seriously damaged by the bombardment," reported infantry Colonel Jonathan White. "Many of their cannons have been destroyed, and our shells have opened large holes in their line. I'm certain my troops can overrun their position."

"I envy your optimism, Colonel. My artillery commander, however, has informed me our artillery ammunition is largely depleted. We will wait for the rest of our 8,000 men and supplies to join us before continuing the attack."

· · ·

At dawn on January 8, 1815, Pakenham launched his main frontal attack against the entrenched American line. The previous night, he ordered Colonel William Thornton with a force of 800 men to cross the river in small boats to attack the American artillery position on the western side of the river. The plan was to capture the American artillery and then use those guns to fire into Jackson's line across the river.

"Colonel Thornton, sir, the canal that was dug to get the boats to the Mississippi has collapsed," reported one of his captains.

"Bloody hell! Did any boats make it to the river before the collapse?"

"Yes sir, five or six."

"Damn! That's not enough. We need at least twenty-five boats to launch this attack. Have the men drag the boats to the river."

By the time the required boats were on the river, Thornton was already twelve hours behind schedule. Crossing the river caused a further delay. The current was stronger than expected and pushed the boats several miles downstream from where they intended to land.

"General Pakenham, the heavy fog this morning surely means Providence is on our side," said Major General Samuel Gibbs. "Our troops will be upon the Americans before they can see us and react."

"I hope you're right General. We'll soon know."

Across the river, the Baton Rouge Demons came under fire from Colonel Thornton's well-trained British troops. Paul Aucoin, Robert Chiasson, and the other Demons returned fire, but it soon became obvious to Major Mouton that his position could not be held. He ordered the artillerymen to render their cannons inoperable. Once the cannons were inoperable, he ordered a retreat upriver.

Just as Thornton's troops took control of the enemy battery and began turning the guns to point across the river, the fog lifted, and Jackson's guns opened on the British troops exposed in the open field. The battle lasted less than thirty minutes. Both Generals Pakenham and Griggs were shot off their horses and lay dead on the battlefield along with over 1,000 other British troops. British Major General John Lambert, whose brigade was held in reserve, took command and quickly ordered his brigade to advance and ordered the withdrawal of British forces. His brigade was used to cover the retreat of what was left of the British army.

Colonel Thornton's success on the western side of the river was the only win for the British that day but had no bearing on the overall outcome of the battle. The British suffered over 2,000 dead, wounded or captured to less than 100 for the Americans.

Winning the Battle of New Orleans catapulted Andrew Jackson to national fame and led to his successful campaign for the U.S.

presidency. This battle ended the War of 1812 and business soon returned to normal.

Within a few short years, however, a cotton blight struck and devastated all cotton in Louisiana. "*Merde*! Look at our fields. The cotton plants are all rotting," exclaimed Paulette Robichaud.

"It's the same throughout the parish and beyond," replied Jean-Paul. "Monsieur Leblanc says all the cotton on Bayou Teche and Bayou Lafourche is rotting. We need to switch to another crop."

"Papa, while I was catching crawfish the other day along the bayou, I noticed Monsieur Poirier is growing sugarcane," replied Jean-Paul's seventeen-year-old son Henri. "Perhaps we can grow sugarcane."

"Sugarcane is a possibility, but the growing, harvesting, and manufacturing process is complicated—much more complicated than cotton."

"How so, Papa?"

"For one thing, it takes two years for the canes to grow. You then need to cut them off at ground level without disturbing the roots so new shoots can grow. Cutting the canes is not easy. The leaves have very sharp edges that will cut your arms as you swing the machete. The canes are sold to the middleman, who will transport them to the mill. The mill washes the canes and crushes them to produce the liquid, and the sugar crystals are then extracted from the liquid. This raw sugar is light brown and looks like sand. The final step removes the impurities and results in pure white sugar and molasses."

"Wow! I didn't realize it was that involved."

Sugar soon replaced cotton as the major staple crop throughout Louisiana. In 1825, Henri Robichaud was twenty-seven years old and well-established on his own sixty-acre farm on Bayou Teche in Lafayette Parish. He and his wife Marcelle had four children. The oldest child, Raymond, was six years old. Henri, with the help of his four slaves, grew sugar cane on forty-five acres. On his remaining land, he grew rice, corn, beans, and sweet potatoes.

Henri and Marcelle's relationship with their slaves can best be described as business-like. Henri worked alongside his slaves and performed much the same work, but no question, he was the boss, and they were his property. He treated them well and assumed they were at least satisfied, if not happy, with their current position. The Robichauds, like most other slave owners, were not overly concerned with the feelings of their slaves. They assumed all was well. This happy illusion was shattered in 1831.

*   *   *

"Papa, Papa!" cried eleven-year-old Raymond as he flew into the house. "I heard Monsieur Richard talking to other men on the bayou about a slave rebellion. Many white people were murdered!"

"What?" replied Henri.

News of Nat Turner's rebellion reached the Louisiana parishes in September 1831 and forever changed the relationship between slaves and their white masters. The rebellion took place on a Virginia plantation on August 26, 1831, when a thirty-year-old black slave, Nat Turner, and about seventy of his co-conspirators went house to house freeing the black slaves and killing the white owners—men, women, and children. About fifty whites were killed by the slaves. The rebellion ended a day or two later when the rebel slaves were surrounded by an overwhelming force of white militia, including several artillery companies. Over two hundred Blacks were subsequently executed in the days that followed. The key conspirators, including Nat Turner, were beheaded. Their heads were then mounted on poles and placed at intersections along the local road. Many, if not most, of the executed Blacks appeared to have been innocent of any rebellion.

Because of Nat Turner's rebellion, the Lafayette Parish government, as well as most other Louisiana parishes, adopted increasingly repressive slave regulations. The new regulations forbade the education of Blacks, reading and writing. Preaching in Black churches was forbidden unless a White preacher was in attendance. All abolitionist material, pamphlets, flyers, letters, and so on were banned for both Whites and Blacks.

·   ·   ·

In 1851, thirty-one-year-old Raymond Robichaud had his own eighty-acre farm on Bayou Teche. His main crop was sugarcane. He and his wife Nicole had four sons and two daughters. The oldest boy, Philippe, was ten years old. Raymond owned four slaves.

"Nicole, have you seen my cap?" asked Raymond.

"It's on the peg by the stove. It was wet when you came in yesterday. I put it there to dry."

"*Merci*, looks like we're in for another rainy day, but I must get the lower five acres harvested today."

"Be careful and don't work the men too hard. We've had a wonderful year. Sugar prices keep climbing. There's no need to rush the harvest. It seems like the prices will be even better tomorrow."

"It's not the prices that concern me. I need to keep up with the growing schedule." The canes took about twenty months to ripen. The plantings were staggered about a month apart in five-acre parcels so there was always a parcel ready to harvest. "The rain has slowed us down, but we need to harvest and then fertilize the lower five acres. The real problem is the next field is ready to harvest and will soon develop over-ripe canes. Wish me *bonne chance, ma chérie* (good luck, my darling)."

All was well on Bayou Teche during the 1850s. Sugar had replaced cotton as king. The Acadian farmers were prospering and had reached a standard of living well above that of their ancestors from Grand Pré. As the 1850s ended, however, distant war clouds could be seen on the horizon. The Louisiana Acadians didn't know it yet, but their easy way of life was about to be torn apart.

# CHAPTER 23
# ISLE OF JERSEY

In September 1802, Charles Robin left Paspébiac for good. He retired to his home in St. Helier, the largest town on the Isle of Jersey. He left his nephew, Robert Robin, in charge of the North American operations of the Charles Robin Company. Charles continued to manage the overall affairs of the company from St. Helier until his death on June 14, 1824, at the age of eighty-one.

In 1810, the Robins were concerned with the dwindling number of young apprentice fishermen in their employ. The profit margin from an apprentice fisherman was considerably higher than the profit margin they earned from buying fish from independent fishermen.

"Robert, when you return to Jersey, please see if you can convince at least thirty apprentices to come back with you," said his brother, Francis Robin. "When their three years are up, most of the apprentices leave us. All our fishing stations, including here in Paspébiac, are short of apprentices."

"Yes, I know very well," replied Robert. "But on my last trip home, many parents refused to let their sons come with me because they feared the sons would become involved with local girls and perhaps even marry one. I need to convince the parents I won't let that happen."

"But how can we possibly stop that? It doesn't take long for the apprentices to find the local girls. We can't keep them locked up for three years. Boys will be boys. You can't stop nature."

"I agree. Perhaps Uncle Charles can figure out a solution. I'll explain the problem to him when I get back."

That winter, after Robert's arrival in St. Helier, Charles met with Paul Breton, an old friend from his teenage years. Charles knew Paul was well-acquainted with the ladies of the night in St. Helier and beyond.

"Charles, the lady for you is Marie-Thérèse MonPlaisir," declared Paul. "She's an extraordinary woman—very beautiful, popular, and bright, with a shrewd mind for business. She's by far the most capable woman I've ever met."

"Is she here in St. Helier?" replied Charles.

"*Non*, I wish it was so. She's the reason for my frequent trips to Saint-Malo. She lives there."

Marie-Thérèse was smart enough to have succeeded in many professions or enterprises, but being of low birth, few options were available to her in France, or anywhere else, in the early 1800s. She developed into a strikingly beautiful woman. From her mid-teens, her beauty attracted much attention—both male and female. At first, she was surprised by the constant attention. Her agile mind, however, soon saw that her beauty was a gift not to be wasted. She would use this gift to her advantage to gain a better life. She was familiar with the prostitutes plying their trade on the docks and saloons of Saint-Malo. That life was not for her. She aspired to much more and quickly achieved it.

"Paul, if I go to Saint-Malo, how will I find her?" probed Charles.

"She's easy to find if you know where to look," teased Paul. After a few seconds he followed up with, "She operates a flower shop called *la Plus Belle Fleur* (the Prettiest Flower) in the business district of Saint-Malo."

"How attached is she to Saint-Malo? Do you think she might be open to moving?"

"I know she refused to move to St. Helier even though she was very much in love with me," laughed Paul. "Her talents are such that she easily convinced me, for several years, that she loved me more than anyone else. I know of at least three prominent men today, from different towns, who each consider her to be his exclusive mistress. She is like no other woman you've ever met."

"I'm impressed, but the key for me requires her to relocate."

"With regard to moving, a recent development may push her in that direction. It seems the Duke of Orleans, while on a business trip to Saint-Malo, became infatuated with her. She soon became what he thought was his exclusive mistress. He lavished a lot of attention and money on her but could not convince her to move to Orleans. Eventually, the duke's contacts in Saint-Malo informed him of her other alliances. The duke became enraged and has vowed to destroy her."

In mid-January 1811, on a clear and calm day, Charles took the ferry from the Isle of Jersey for the twelve-mile trip to Saint-Malo.

"*Mademoiselle* MonPlaisir, I'm honored to meet you," said Charles. "I've heard much about you. You are even more beautiful than I was told. My name is Charles Robin, and I'm a friend of Paul Breton in St. Helier."

"Ah, Monsieur Robin, everyone has heard of you," replied Marie-Thérèse. "You are the big boss of the largest fishing enterprise in all of Europe. You catch and sell fish all over the world."

"I wish it were so," answered a smiling Charles. "I have many competitors. Several are larger than me."

"But they are not French-speaking gentlemen like yourself. That makes a big difference. How is Paul? I haven't seen him in a long time."

"He's well but suffering from gout. He sends his love to you."

"Oh! I'm sorry to hear that. Of all my acquaintances, Paul is by far my favorite. Are you here to buy flowers, Monsieur Robin?"

"*Non*, although I'm very impressed with your shop. You have a great variety of beautiful flowers and even prettier flower attendants."

"Has any flower attendant caught your eye, Monsieur Robin?"

"*Mademoiselle*, you and all your attendants have certainly caught my eye. I'm here to propose a business venture. Can we sit down somewhere?"

An hour later, after considerable discussion, Marie-Thérèse said, "So, you want me and several of my flower attendants to sail to America this spring and become part of your organization."

"Yes, you and eight of your attendants would be about right to start. Your passage, of course, would be free. Room and board at our fishing stations would also be free. Regarding the sale of flowers, 90% would be for you and 10% for me. After the first year, we would sit down and renegotiate these terms. My intent is that this arrangement be good for both of us."

"Monsieur Robin, as you can see here, I already have a thriving business. Your proposal is interesting, but I would need an additional incentive to make me leave."

"*Mademoiselle*, I'm familiar with your difficulties with the Duke of Orleans. I know also that the duke has considerably pressured the Saint-Malo police department to shut you down. You have been saved so far by Monsieur Henri Malouin, the Saint-Malo chief of police. The chief is also one of your favorites. However, it's only a matter of time before the duke has the chief removed from office."

"You are well informed, Monsieur Robin. I suspect we may soon do business together. Before you return home, let me provide you with a fresh bouquet of flowers—no charge."

After securing a tentative agreement with *Mademoiselle* MonPlaisir, Charles informed her of his intent to spend the next few days visiting his company's agents along the French coast. His plan was to offer the agents a bonus for each apprentice signed up. Marie-Thérèse volunteered that the Bishop of La Rochelle was also one of her favorites and might be helpful in securing additional apprentices. She wrote a note for Charles to deliver to the bishop.

Soon after his return to St. Helier, Charles met with his nephew Robert and informed him of the agreement with Marie-Thérèse.

"Uncle, this agreement is fantastic!" exclaimed an awestruck Robert. "If we can keep the apprentices' passions in check with professional women who won't form messy relationships, a big part of our problem will go away."

"That's the plan," replied Charles. "During our discussions, *Mademoiselle* MonPlaisir asked me about the community makeup at our fishing stations and whether there were any forts or soldiers stationed nearby. When I told her of the garrison in Charlottetown, her eyes lit up. She says the apprentices will be easily managed with enough extra time to allow her to expand her flower business."

"Flower business? Is that what she calls it?"

"Yes, and she in fact operates a very successful real flower shop in Saint-Malo. While there, I bought a boat that I'm having modified to suit her flower business. I changed the name of the vessel to *La Belle Fleur*."

"How do we manage her business? Who decides what fishing stations to visit? We now have fifteen permanent fishing stations, including stores, all over the gulf, with several more in the works."

"I've already worked out the details with her for the first year. She promised to enlist eight of her associates for this venture. Two each will be stationed at our three largest fishing stations. The remaining two, with Marie-Thérèse, will stay aboard *La Belle Fleur* and make the rounds of the smaller stations. Every month, the girls will rotate to a new station. This process will keep fresh faces at the stations and diminish the chances for any unpleasant relationships to develop."

"Who do you have in mind as the captain for *La Belle Fleur*?"

"Jean-Marc LeFrenier has agreed to sail the boat from Jersey to the gulf. After his terrible accident two years ago, he is now impotent but still an excellent sailor. I'm hoping his impotency will make him somewhat immune to the charms of his passengers. Even if that is not the case, no harm done. He is still the right man for this job. During the crossing, he will teach Marie-Thérèse and her girls how to sail and operate the boat. After they arrive in the gulf, Marie-Thérèse will captain the boat, and her girls will serve as first mates."

"Uncle, you are truly one of a kind. I have never seen, and never even heard of, a female captain of any boat the size of *La Belle Fleur*. If she can learn to master the boat across the gulf, she will quickly earn an impressive reputation throughout the region."

"I have no doubt that she will quickly earn an impressive reputation."

In late March 1811, Robert and his flotilla, including fifty apprentices, sailed for the gulf.

# CHAPTER 24
# THE BUSINESS OF
# MARIE-THÉRÈSE MONPLAISIR

Although she never attended any school, Marie-Thérèse was fluent in French, English, Spanish, and Italian. She could read and write French and English. By the time she was twelve, she had mastered basic mathematics. She was curious about the world and its opportunities for her. She never knew her father, but her mother sold flowers in the town square during the summer months and dug clams at low tide during the winter months. Marie-Thérèse helped as best she could, yet they barely made ends meet.

Shortly after she turned fifteen, an older, single, prominent gentleman from town met with her mother and asked if Marie-Thérèse could become his live-in maid. He offered a considerable sum to her. Mother and daughter discussed the offer and quickly agreed to accept. The old man was a blessing in disguise. He kept Marie-Thérèse off the mean streets, gave her access to books, and was gentle with her. A few years later, when he passed, he left her enough money to buy the flower shop in Saint-Malo.

When *La Belle Fleur* sailed into Paspébiac, Marie-Thérèse was at the helm with her mates lining the deck. They indeed caused quite a stir.

"Maurice, come quick!" exclaimed a recently arrived apprentice to his friend. "A beautiful woman has just sailed a large boat, filled with other beautiful women, into the harbor. I can't believe my eyes!"

"*Tabernacle!*" exclaimed his friend. "How can this be?"

A few weeks later, with Marie-Thérèse in charge, the routine was set with *La Belle Fleur* visiting the outlying fishing stations. The fees charged by the girls were within reach of the apprentices. Of the 150 apprentices, most refused this new service. Some were too shy or too religious. Others were too cheap to part with their hard-earned money. Regardless, the overall goal of keeping the apprentices from engaging with the local girls was largely achieved. The most passionate apprentices were kept in check.

The War of 1812 between the Americans and the English was again cause for concern for the Robins. The New Englanders raided some coastal villages in Nova Scotia, but the English fleet ported at Halifax kept them from reaching the gulf and the many Robin enterprises.

"Robert, do you think we should empty some of our stores and bring the merchandise here?" asked Roger, his younger brother.

"We have no way of knowing which stations, if any, might be attacked," replied Robert. "If we bring the merchandise here and the New Englanders find out, they will surely attack here. I think it's best to wait and see."

•    •    •

During the summer of 1814, the New Englanders raided two of the stations—Thunder River and Eskimo Point, both on the North Shore of the gulf. All the cod and merchandise from the stores were taken. At Thunder River, the New Englanders found two of Marie-Thérèse's mates. After figuring out why the girls were there, the New Englanders readily and happily gang raped them, beat them, and left them near death.

When Roger informed his brother Robert what the New Englanders had done, he was understandably upset.

"What? *Les maudits Américains*! I can understand stealing the fish and merchandise, but not hurting the girls. Does Marie-Thérèse know?"

"Yes, she sailed into Thunder River after the New Englanders left. She brought the girls back on her boat. She is enraged! I've never heard such cursing from any person before—man or woman. She vowed to castrate every man who took part in the rape. Before leaving Thunder River, she spoke with every person who had contact with the perpetrators. She took many notes and has a good description of the men and boat involved. The name of the Privateer is *Fire Maiden*. May God help its occupants!"

Business soon returned to normal and remained so through the end of the season. Late in the fall, Robert prepared for the return trip to Jersey.

"Marie-Thérèse, will you be joining me on our voyage to Jersey?" enquired Robert.

"*Non*," said Marie-Thérèse. "I plan to recruit new girls in Boston. If all goes well, I'll be spending the winter there."

•   •   •

In January 1815, shortly after receiving word that the war was officially over, Marie-Thérèse with three of her mates set sail for Boston. On a shrouded, overcast evening, Marie-Thérèse tied up *La Belle Fleur* in Boston Harbor, near to the famed Faneuil Hall. No one took notice of them with their bulky winter clothing. They quickly found rooms at a nearby inn and settled in for the night. The following morning, they fanned out along the harbor in search of the *Fire Maiden*. As arranged, they reconvened at a nearby restaurant for lunch.

"No luck," stated one of the girls. "We searched up and down all the piers south of here."

"Same for us on the north side," replied Marie-Thérèse. The girls were careful not to mention the name of the boat they were searching for—not even among themselves. "As planned, we will visit every shop in Boston, if needed. We will engage the shopkeepers in conversation and try to steer them into talking about ships and the recent war, but we must never mention the word *privateer* or the name of the boat. Someone here is surely familiar with our target. We just need to get them talking.

The girls visited many shops the rest of the day with no luck. At supper that evening, one of the girls suggested that visiting the taverns might be more fruitful. "Perhaps, but more dangerous for us," replied Marie-Thérèse. "So far, no one knows who we are. It's best for us if we can keep it that way. We still have more shops to visit tomorrow. If we have no luck with the shops, we will try the taverns."

The next morning, Marie-Thérèse entered a men's clothing store on Boylston Street.

"Good morning, miss," greeted the shopkeeper. "How may I help you?"

"*Bonjour* Monsieur," replied Marie-Thérèse. "My nephew is a student at your wonderful, but too far from home, Harvard College. I want to buy some dress shirts for him."

"You've come to the right place," smiled the shopkeeper. "We have an excellent selection. Are you visiting from France?"

"Yes, my nephew is a first-year student, and from his letters, we could tell he was quite homesick. My brother asked me if I could visit his son. I would have come sooner, but the war was frightening. Did Boston suffer much damage?"

"No, not at all. We have *Ironsides* to protect us."

"*Ironsides*? Is this a ship? I'm afraid I know little about ships or the waging of war. It seems, however, that Boston would need more than one ship to protect it."

"*Ironsides* is the greatest of all the American warships. She defeated many English warships during our recent war. Her official name is U.S.S. Constitution. In addition, we have several privateers on call in the nearby towns."

"Privateers? I'm not familiar with that term."

"These are privately owned warships that can be called on to assist our navy. The closest one, the *Fire Maiden*, is home ported in Ipswich, a few miles up the coast."

"*Mon Dieu*! You know a lot about boats."

"I spent five years in the navy before opening this shop. Do you know your nephew's shirt size?"

"Yes, he's a medium. His neck size is fifteen."

At lunch, Marie-Thérèse informed her mates of her success.

"I've never heard of Ipswich," stated one of the girls. "It can't be a very large place. How will we fit in?"

"Now that we know where they are," said Marie-Thérèse, "we must find out their names. The Boston navy has its headquarters within walking distance of our inn. If the *Fire Maiden* assisted the navy, the sailors will know the men and have records, including a list of the crew. That's what we need. It's time to visit the nearby taverns."

"Blow the man down! Well, blow the man down!" sang the patrons in the smoky and boisterous Silver Keg Tavern as Marie-Thérèse and Francine, one of her mates, walked in. The local girls were the first to notice them, and they were not pleased. Marie-Thérèse smiled at a sailor in uniform, and she and Francine were soon seated at his table.

"What are your names, and where are you girls from?" asked the sailor as he leaned into Marie-Thérèse.

"I'm Paulette, and this is my friend Louise. We're from Montreal," responded Francine. "The weather is so bad there. We decided to spend the winter in Boston."

"Very few people come to Boston for its mild winters," laughed the sailor. "But in your case, it makes perfect sense. Barkeep! Let's have a round here."

Later that night, back at the inn, the girls compared stories.

"Francine and I had a good time with four sailors assigned to the local navy shipyard. They were familiar with the *Fire Maiden's* captain, a man named William Reynolds, but did not know the names of his crew."

"As we sat down at the small restaurant attached to the Fox and Hound Tavern, Yvette and I were quickly approached by two ensigns in uniform. They joined us for dinner and then drinks in the tavern. When we told them the *Fire Maiden* saved us from capture by an English ship and that we'd like to thank the captain and his crew, my ensign said he could get a crew list for us. He works in the office. We have another date with them tomorrow night."

"That's great," said Marie-Thérèse. "After we get the names, we need to find out when these men visit Boston. One or more of them may even be here now."

The following night, Yvette reported back to Marie-Thérèse with the list. "My ensign said that William Reynolds, the captain of the *Fire Maiden*, frequents the Black Swan Tavern a few city-blocks from here. He's six feet tall and has red hair."


"Reynolds!" shouted a fellow patron in the noisy Black Swam. "Now that the war is over, what are your plans for that ship of yours?"

"I suspect the next war won't be too long in coming," responded Reynolds. "In the meantime, I'll be sailing down to the Caribbean this spring to pick up a load of rum."

"If you're short a crewmate, I'd be happy to assist on that voyage."

"I'll keep you in mind," replied Reynolds, but his mind was totally focused on the beautiful creature entering the tavern. Reynolds stood and did his best to make eye contact, but she sailed by, towards an empty seat at the bar. She ordered a glass of red wine from the bartender.

"Put that on my tab, John," exclaimed Reynolds. He looked Marie-Thérèse in the eye but, looking down, was unable to miss her cleavage. "I've never seen you here before. My name is William, what's yours?"

"My friends call me Louise. This is my first time in Boston. I'm from Montreal, and I'm visiting relatives in Cambridge. As I'm sure you know, there's not much to do in Cambridge once the sun goes down."

"You've got that right," laughed Reynolds. "I have a table by the window. Let's move there before someone steals it."

After settling in at their table, Reynolds continued, "What do you do in Montreal?"

"I run a flower shop, but as you can guess, the flower business in Montreal is quite slow in January. What about you? What do you do for a living?"

"I'm a privateer. I have my own boat and crew and have a commission from the navy to assist them. We split any prizes I might capture."

"Prizes? I hope you don't consider me to be such a prize. I would not like being split."

Reynolds smiled. "I would never consider splitting you with anyone."

"Is your boat here in Boston?"

"No, I'm from Ipswich, about twenty-five miles north of here. The boat is there. Three of my crew live aboard."

"Is that your entire crew? Seems like too few men for a powerful privateer."

"As far as privateers go, my boat is at the small end. I operate with a crew of five. The other two crew members are in Gloucester, between here and Ipswich. Last month, I got word that one of them lost an eye in a bar fight."

"An eye? That's terrible. I hope he can still be part of your crew."

"It shouldn't be a problem. His eye patch will probably make him more popular and famous than he deserves."

"Could I have another glass of wine?"

"Certainly."

As Reynolds walked to the bar, no one noticed as Marie-Thérèse mixed the powder into his drink. The powder originated from one of her favorites in France who owned an apothecary shop. The powder, when mixed with a liquid, rendered someone sleepy in half an hour and sound asleep within a full hour. After Reynolds finished his drink, Marie-Thérèse said, "Do you live near here, William?"

"Yes, perhaps we'd be more comfortable there. My room is a short walk from here."

"That would be fine. Please lead the way."


With Reynolds sound asleep on his bed, Marie-Thérèse produced a small folding knife from her purse. The blade was curved and razor sharp. She carefully slit open his scrotum and removed his testicles which she then dropped into the chamber pot next to the bed. She was surprised at the amount of bleeding. She pressed a kitchen cloth firmly against the wound and held it in place for ten minutes—long enough for the blood to clot. As she left his room, she met Francine on the corner of the street and together they walked back to their inn. An hour later, they were on *La Belle Fleur* and heading for Gloucester. They anchored near the dock in Gloucester Harbor and slept till noon.

"Yvette, you will row Francine and me ashore and then return to the boat. If all goes well, we'll return tonight and signal you to pick us up."

Marie-Thérèse and Francine found a tavern with a popular lunchroom. They settled at a table and were soon chatting with the waitress.

"We're on our way to Boston," said Francine. "We were told that Gloucester is the whaling capital of the world. Is it possible for us to see how the whales are processed? That would be very interesting."

"I don't know who you spoke with," replied the waitress. "But there's no whale processing here. The whaling ships return with barrels of whale oil. That's it. There's nothing to see other than warehouses with barrels of whale oil."

"That's a shame. There must be something for us to see. What about pirates? Do you have any of those?"

"Pirates? I'm afraid not, although we have a troublemaker who looks like a pirate. He lost an eye and now wears an eyepatch. Since losing his eye, he's calmed down a bit. I guess he doesn't want to risk losing his other eye."

"That's awful. How did he lose his eye?"

"He lost it in a bar fight at the Tar N Feathers Tavern. You'd think he'd stay away, but that's still his favorite spot. He's there most every night. His name is Bob Wilson."

In the early evening, Marie-Thérèse and Francine walked into the Tar N Feathers. As usual, they received ugly stares from the working girls and broad smiles from the men. They were soon seated at Bob Wilson's table.

"I'm Bob, and this is my shipmate Brent," uttered an excited Wilson. "What are your names?"

"I'm Louise and this is Paulette," replied Marie-Thérèse. "We're from Montreal on our way to Boston but stopped here for a day or two."

"Well, Brent and I are glad you did. What can I get you to drink?"

"Red wine for me," breathed Marie-Thérèse. The name Brent was on the list. She and Francine exchanged a knowing smile.

"Same for me," whispered Francine.

After another round of drinks, the girls discreetly mixed the powder into their partner's drink.

"Do you gentlemen live near here?" inquired Francine.

"Yes," replied Brent. "In fact, Bob lives just behind this tavern and has a large room. We could all be more comfortable there."

"Oh, that sounds nice, but it might be better if you and I went to your place," inhaled Francine as she pressed against Brent.

Bob and Brent soon met the same fate as William Reynolds.

As *La Belle Fleur* left Gloucester for the short trip to Ipswich, Francine mentioned, "I've never heard a more satisfying sound than the sound of his testicles hitting the bottom of the chamber pot."

In Ipswich, the girls followed the same routine. They anchored just short of the town pier and slept till midmorning. Their plan for Ipswich, however, did not involve any taverns.

As the three men aboard the *Fire Maiden* were playing cards on that miserably cold and drizzly January day, they heard a commotion on the pier near their boat.

"What's going on?" inquired James, one of the men on the boat.

"I don't know," said his shipmate Paul as he looked out. "It seems some women are fighting on the pier."

"Women? Fighting? Let me see."

As the three men exited their boat, they saw that several ships away, three women were indeed fighting on the pier.

"Hold on there!" shouted James as he tried to pull two of the women apart. The men soon gained control of the situation. "What's going on here?" asked James.

"This jealous bitch called me a cow," declared Marie-Thérèse. "Simply because her tits are so much smaller than mine."

"Who are you calling a bitch?" yelled Francine as she lunged for Marie-Thérèse.

"Hold on! Hold on! Let's get out of the rain and figure this out," exclaimed Paul as the three men led the women back to their boat.

The women slowly calmed down and became more social. They readily accepted the offered wine. The men relaxed and thanked their lucky stars for this wonderful gift of lovely women. After Marie-Thérèse verified their names were on the list, the men were soon asleep and missing their testicles. The girls carried the men onto the pier. They then dumped the oil from the boat's oil lamps all over the inside of the cabin, untied the boat, set fire to the oil, and pushed the boat free of the pier.

As they sailed out of Ipswich, the women were captivated by the beautiful torch the aptly named *Fire Maiden* made in the middle of the harbor.

Their next stop was Portsmouth, New Hampshire, where they found a nice inn and spent the rest of the winter. In early April, they set sail for their home in the gulf. With them were five young but well-experienced recruits for their flower business.

# CHAPTER 25
# THE GULF OF ST. LAWRENCE

As Marie-Thérèse entered the gulf in early April, she carefully steered around the icebergs that would linger well into May. Upon entering the *Baie des Chaleurs*, she saw clear water all the way to Paspébiac. Any iceberg that dared enter the bay would be quickly reduced to nothing by the warm water.

"Welcome back!" cried two of her land-based mates as *La Belle Fleur* tied up at the dock. "We missed you terribly. You must tell us everything that happened on your voyage."

"There's not much to tell," replied Marie-Thérèse, "other than finding these five beautiful flowers."

• • •

The Robins's business continued to thrive. In the summer of 1815, they had twenty fishing stations, with more planned—most with general stores. Marie-Thérèse was kept busy rotating her girls among the stations.

In 1828, while in the Robins's Chéticamp store, Marie-Thérèse was approached by a young Acadian girl.

"*Mademoiselle* MonPlaisir," implored the girl. "I don't mean to bother you, but could I speak with you in private?"

"Of course, *ma chérie*," replied Marie-Thérèse who led her outside on the dock. "What is your name, and how may I help you?"

"My name is Yolande Jolin, and I would like to work for you. I know I'm young and inexperienced, but you will find me a very willing and quick learner."

"How old are you?"

"I just turned seventeen. I have a good figure. The men all look when I walk by. I'm sure I can become a good worker."

"What about your parents?"

"My mother kicked me out of the house. She accused me of seducing her husband—my father."

"Did you seduce him?"

"No! Of course not," cried Yolande as she burst into tears. "My father started coming to my bed soon after I was fourteen. He fondled me and made me use my hand on him. He made me promise not to tell anyone. He visited my bed at least once per week, and the routine was always the same until a month ago. He tried to penetrate me. I screamed and jumped out of bed. My mother burst into the room, and that's when she accused me and kicked me out of the house. This happened in Margaree, about fifteen miles from here. I walked to Chéticamp and have been staying with friends ever since."

"You poor dear. No child should have to go through something like that. Yes, I will give you a job, but not here. We need to place more distance between you and your father. My boat is just over there. Please go aboard and wait for me. I still have some business to finish." Her hand closed around the small folding knife in her bag, but after a few moments' thought, she knew the knife was not the answer. She would discuss this matter with Robert Robin but take no further action against the father.

Marie-Thérèse always did her best to maintain good relations with the married women in the villages—not an easy task. She insisted her girls focus their attention on the apprentices. She discouraged and even punished sexual encounters between her girls and the married men who lived in or near the fishing stations. Encounters still happened, but she did her best to keep them at a minimum.

•  •  •

"Anselme," said Rose. "Chéticamp has been a blessing for us. There's very little crime. The worst crime in the past year was when the Cormier boy stole Henri Doucet's boat and sailed it down to Sydney. Even the Robins' lady, *Mademoiselle* MonPlaisir, keeps her business out of the village."

"I agree," replied Anselme. "Things are going very well for us. It's been a long time since we were bothered by the English. I hope that's all behind us. Our children don't know how good they have it."

"They all know. You keep reminding them whenever you get the chance," added a grinning Rose.

"It's important they know our history, where they came from, and how we suffered. I want a better life for them."

"Simon invited us over for supper tomorrow. That wonderful aroma you smell is the apple pie I have baking in the oven. We'll take it with us tomorrow."

Simon, at forty, was the oldest of their ten children. He fished with his father on the family boat. At supper the next day, Simon told his father, "Papa, if it's okay with you, I'll take the boat to Miquelon tomorrow. Louis Poirier just returned from there with several calves. He said there's a surplus of cows on Miquelon, and they're selling their calves at very low prices."

"That seems fine," replied Anselme. "Bring back as many as you can. I'm sure we can find buyers for them here."

Miquelon was a small French island just off the coast of Newfoundland, about 120 miles from Chéticamp. Soon after settling in Chéticamp, the Acadians sailed to Miquelon to purchase cows and other farm animals.

•  •  •

The next few generations of the Aucoin family progressed very well with no interference from the English. Simon fathered eight children, his son Christophe fathered ten, and Christophe's son Fulgence fathered eleven.

In 1867, Father Hubert Girroir was named *curé* (pastor) of Chéticamp. He, more than anyone else before or after, found a way to improve significantly commercial activity in Chéticamp that created real and ongoing opportunities for its resident Acadian population.

# CHAPTER 26
# LAFAYETTE

Bayou Teche and the Vermilion River form a large part of the Lafayette parish in Southwest Louisiana.

In late December 1860, forty-one-year-old Raymond Robichaud, his wife Nicole, and their seven children were well-established on their eighty-acre farm on Bayou Teche. Their oldest child, twenty-year-old Philippe, was engaged and planning to marry in June 1861.

"Papa, the men at the Vermilion store this morning were all talking of war!" exclaimed Philippe. "Is war likely? Will it impact us? How can I marry if a war is coming?"

"If war comes," replied Raymond, "it will likely pass us by. Our farm is far from any railroad, factory, city, or other major target for an invading army. My father's war in 1812 lasted just two years. I suspect this next one will be even shorter."

·   ·   ·

Regarding the coming Civil War, the Louisiana Acadians were generally in two camps. The rich Acadian planters and large farmers with upwards of fifty slaves were very much invested in the Southern cause. Several of them became generals and fought bravely for the South during the war. The typical Acadian farmer, however, was not overly concerned with affairs beyond his parish, especially the Acadians who lived west of the Atchafalaya River. In this regard, they were not much different from their ancestors at Grand Pré. The bulk of Acadians kept to themselves. They had little interest in the Southern cause and preferred to remain neutral during the war. Many, if not most of them, spoke only French and had a poor understanding of English. Unfortunately, just like their ancestors before them, neutrality was not an option.

At 4:30 AM on April 12, 1861, the Civil War officially started when confederate troops fired on Fort Sumter in South Carolina's Charleston Harbor. The war would last four years, and before it officially ended on April 9, 1865, over 600,000 men, women, and children would die because of the war.

•  •  •

"I, Philippe Robichaud, take you, Marie Thibodeaux, to be my wife."

War or no war, Philippe and Marie's wedding went on as planned on June 10, 1861. The war was far away and not a concern for the Acadians on Bayou Teche, at least, not yet. The wedding reception was held at Marie's home on the Teche, just a few miles from the Robichaud home. As was the custom, the neighbors and other invited guests brought food, liquor, and musical instruments to the reception. There was crawfish pie, many gumbos and *fricots* (stews), catfish *étouffée* (shredded and cooked with onions and small pieces of salt pork), and many other dishes. The feasting, drinking, and dancing went on well into the night. Philippe and Marie thanked their parents and the next day set off for their new home—a forty-acre farm about thirty-five miles further down the Teche.

•  •  •

In April 1862, two events occurred that forever changed the easy-going lifestyle of the Louisiana Acadians. New Orleans, the seat of the Louisiana government, fell to the Union Army, while in Richmond,

Virginia, the capital of the Confederacy, the Confederate Conscription Act was signed into law.

"Papa!" exclaimed Philippe to his father, "I don't know what to do. Marie is at her parents' home. We've abandoned our farm. We were too far down the Teche to be safe after all our neighbors abandoned their farms."

"I'm thankful you came back," replied Raymond. "You and Marie can stay here with us, or you can stay with her parents. Either way, you'll be much safer than way down on the Teche by yourselves."

"Papa, I'm concerned that Louisiana has moved the seat of the government to Opelousas. Opelousas is at the northern end of Bayou Teche, much too close to us. If not already, the Union Army will soon target the Teche."

"I know. Another concern is that Conscription Act. I spoke with Paul Landry yesterday. He says the act requires all males between the ages of seventeen and forty join the army. There's an exception for married men with children, but few other exceptions."

"What? This is the first time I've heard of this act. I don't want to join the army. I don't believe in this war. I have no intention of killing anyone."

Philippe was not alone in his distaste for the war and its disruption of his life. Most Acadians west of the Atchafalaya River saw the forced recruitment of their sons, brothers, and husbands as an intolerable intrusion into their lives. Regardless, grey-clad Rebel commanders soon made their presence known on the Teche and nearby communities. Their initial recruitment drive netted over 2,000 conscripts, including twenty-one-year-old Philippe Robichaud and his nineteen-year-old brother-in-law Roland Thibodeaux.

Brigadier General John C. Pratt of the Louisiana state militia was assigned the task of establishing a camp of instruction for the new recruits. In May 1862, he established his camp on the northern end of Spanish Lake in New Iberia, about one mile west of Bayou Teche. His training site soon became known as Camp Pratt, and it was a living hell for the Acadian trainees. From the very start, many deserted. Most of the conscripts simply wanted no part of the Rebel army. During this time, substantially all Louisiana-based military units were short of men and in dire need of trained replacements. The bulk of the trained Camp Pratt conscripts were subsequently assigned to the 18th Louisiana Infantry Regiment.

"Roland, where do you think we're going?" asked Philippe, as the two trained and armed recruits, now privates in the 18th Louisiana Infantry Regiment, were loaded aboard a vessel on Bayou Teche.

"I heard a sergeant say we're headed for the LaFourche district. I hope the fighting stays on that side of the Atchafalaya. I don't want the fighting to reach our families."

•    •    •

On October 27, 1862, the two friends had their baptism of fire on Bayou LaFourche in the Battle of Labadieville, about twenty-five miles west of the Mississippi River. Brigadier General Alfred Mouton, the son of former Governor and United States Senator, Alexandre Mouton, was in command of the Louisiana forces comprising the 18th Louisiana Infantry Regiment and elements from six other Confederate units. His total force was about 1,400 men. Brigadier General Godfrey Weitzel commanded the Union forces totaling about 4,000 men from the 8th New Hampshire Infantry, the 75th New York Infantry and the 13th Connecticut Infantry.

General Mouton arrived on site first and prepared defensive positions by dividing his force in two. He placed half on the west side of Bayou LaFourche and half on the east side—not a wise tactic, as he soon discovered. His force was simply too small to divide against a much larger enemy force. Philippe and Roland's platoon was dug in along the east side of LaFourche.

"Philippe, when the shooting starts, what if we alternate our shots?" said Roland. "You shoot first, and when you're halfway through reloading, I'll fire. That way one of us is almost always ready to fire."

"Sounds good," agreed Philippe. "I can't imagine that the Yankee soldiers are happy to be here, certainly not the privates, like us. These bayous are filled with snakes, alligators, and swarms of mosquitoes. Perhaps if we put up a stiff enough defense, they'll give up and leave."

"Keep in mind they defeated our best troops when they took over New Orleans. During our training at Camp Pratt, the drill instructors kept telling us how weak and cowardly the Yankees are. That any one of us could easily defeat two Yankees. So why did we lose New Orleans?"

The Yankee force of 4,000 men soon came down the east side of the LaFourche and ran into the 700 Rebels defending that side. The result was inevitable. After firing two shots each, Philippe and Roland, along with the rest of their unit, were quickly overwhelmed and retreating in full disarray. The Yankee soldiers did not pursue. Instead, they focused their attention on the west side of Bayou Lafourche. They built a pontoon bridge and crossed the LaFourche with enough men and equipment to displace and quickly rout the 700 Confederates on that side.

When the smoke cleared, the Yankees suffered 86 casualties versus 229 for the South—a decisive Yankee victory that gave the North complete command of the strategically important Mississippi River and its nearby tributaries.

After running down the LaFourche for well over a mile, Philippe and Roland found a rowboat and used it to cross the Bayou.

"Philippe, I'm done with the army," said Roland. "I don't understand what we're fighting for. Let's just go home."

"I agree. I want no part of this war. Let's go home and help our families survive this chaos."

Their goal was to return home. During the aftermath of the Battle of Labadieville, hundreds of Acadians did the same thing—deserted and tried to return home. Their Rebel officers and sergeants were unable to stem the tide of desertions. Several days later, however, Rebel cavalry units rounded up most of the deserters, including Philippe and

Roland, and returned them to the 18th Louisiana Infantry Regiment. With so many deserters, and being so short of men, General Mouton thought it best to not execute any of them. Instead, he chose five deserters at random and had them flogged in front of the assembled regiment. The flogging did little to change the minds of his French-speaking soldiers. Mouton and his fellow officers would be plagued with high Acadian desertions through the end of the war, even though they soon started the practice of executing deserters.

· · ·

Back on Bayou Teche in December 1862, Philippe's father was surprised to see a Confederate unit with several wagons arrive at his home.

"*Bonjour*, Captain, how may I help you?" said Raymond Robichaud to the Anglo-American officer.

"I'm here with a foraging detail," replied the officer. "We need to take some of your farm animals and produce to help feed our army."

As the officer spoke, Raymond noticed the soldiers were already loading several of his pigs and chickens into the wagons. Other soldiers emerged from his barn with bags containing several hundred pounds of husked corn, rice, and beans. The men tied one of his two milk cows to the back of a wagon and were off to their next target.

"*Sainte Marie!*" exclaimed his wife, Nicole. "How will we survive the winter? They've taken too much of our food. We are now forced to choose between saving our remaining corn to plant in the spring or eating it this winter to keep us alive."

"We'll manage, *ma chérie*. We both need to lose weight. This will be the winter for it."

In mid-January 1863, another Rebel foraging party arrived at their home. They took all their remaining adult pigs, including the pregnant sow, leaving them with two fifteen-pound piglets. Seven or eight chickens were taken—the rest scampered into the winter fields of stubble. Several large bags of rice and beans exited the barn and were loaded onto the wagons. The smiling Rebel officer thanked them for their cooperation as he moved on to the next farm.

At about this same time, Union Major General Nathaniel P. Banks launched a full-scale invasion of south-central Louisiana. Bayou Teche sat in the middle of that area. The Confederate Army was forced to retreat north to Opelousas, where they set up a defensive perimeter. Acadian soldiers took advantage of the confusion of the retreat to desert in droves and returned to their nearby homes along the Teche to help their families.

Many Acadians initially saw the Union soldiers as liberators and happily welcomed them. And Acadian deserters from the Confederate Army even volunteered as scouts in the Union Army. The Acadian scouts did all they could to keep the Rebel forces away from their families. All was well until the Union Army ran short of food. Union foraging parties were soon dispatched to gather food from the nearby farms. They were even more ruthless than their Confederate counterparts. They took everything. The Robichaud family lost their milk cow, two piglets, and all the corn, rice, and beans found in the barn.

"*Les maudits Anglais!*" exclaimed Raymond. "It doesn't matter whether they wear grey or blue uniforms. They're all the same. They treat us with contempt and laugh at our misery."

During their occupation of the Teche valley, the Union soldiers plundered many Acadian homes, stealing all valuables, and raping many women. As the war progressed, the Union forces eventually moved on from their positions in the Teche valley. Confederate troops soon refilled the vacuum left by the Yankees.

In August 1863, President Jefferson Davis of the Confederacy issued a blanket pardon for all deserters. The Acadian deserters readily returned to their former units. They now understood who the real enemy was and were ready to fight to keep their homes safe from the Yankee devils.

Try as they might, the war soon went from bad to worse for the Confederates. The North simply had more men, more factories, and more and better weapons, including the new repeating rifle. A Yankee soldier could fire seven shots for every shot from a Rebel soldier.

The Civil War officially ended on April 9, 1865, but deadly battles between Yankee and Rebel units would continue for many more months, especially in the outlying areas such as southwestern Louisiana.

With the war's end and the freeing of all slaves, the social order in the South was forever changed. About fifty percent of all slaves, now free, left their farms in search of a better life elsewhere. The other fifty percent, now considered freedmen, remained in the local workforce but required wages in return for their labor.

• • •

In late-April 1865, when Philippe was finally able to return home, he found his parents malnourished and sickly.

"Papa, I'm sorry I wasn't here to help you," cried Philippe. "Together, we'll get this farm going again."

"Your mother and I are happy to have you back safe from the war," replied Raymond, his father. "This farm is now yours. I'll do what I can to help you."

Raymond died the following year, at forty-seven. His wife, Nicole, Philippe's mother, died a few months later. She was forty-five years old. Philippe's two oldest siblings were killed during the war. His four youngest siblings were living with relatives.

"Philippe, what's to become of us?" inquired his wife, Marie. "We have a nice eighty-acre farm but no slaves to help us, no mule to pull the plow, and very little seed to plant. How will we survive?"

"We will survive and eventually thrive!" said Philippe. "I met this morning with our neighbor, Robert Cyr. He's in the same boat as us, except worse. He and his wife have three toddlers. He has a bit of money saved and so do we. Between us, we can afford to buy a mule. We'll share the mule and help each other with the farming. We agreed we'll each plow and plant five acres and share the harvest this fall. His land is wetter than ours. Rice grows very well there, so he'll plant mostly rice and beans, whereas I'll plant mostly corn which does very well here."

"I hope this plan works. We need a good harvest."

Fortunately for the Robichaud and Cyr farms, all went reasonably according to plan—not so for the larger Louisiana farming community. Years of neglect, because of the war, caused many levees to fail. The resulting flooding destroyed many farms—some under ten feet of water throughout the planting season. Following the annual spring floods came the armyworm invasions that decimated the cotton industry from the end of the war through the early 1870s.

The Civil War brought devastation to the South, including the Louisiana parishes. Roads and bridges were destroyed. Many boats were sunk in the bayous, making them impassable. Wholesale destruction of agricultural processing equipment, tools, and draught animals was everywhere. Sugar mills, cotton gins, and warehouses were destroyed, and the slaves were freed. All of this led to a drastic contraction of the local economy. Starvation became a real threat for many Acadians. The resulting depression in many Acadian parishes would last from 1865 until the start of World War II in 1941.

To survive this chaos, many Acadians were forced to become day laborers. They farmed their own land as best they could but also worked for a nearby sugar mill or other enterprise for an hourly wage. Prior to the Civil War, the Louisiana Acadians enjoyed a standard of living higher than the excellent one enjoyed by their pre-deportation ancestors in Grand Pré. After the war, the bulk of the Acadians were generally reduced to subsistence farming.

In April 1895, after a hard day working in their fields, fifty-six-year-old Philippe Robichaud, his wife Marie, and their five children were relaxing on the porch of their farmhouse overlooking their eighty-acre farm.

"Papa," said his twenty-year-old son Robert, "after Louise and I marry this June, we plan to move to Lake Charles. You've seen the flyers and posters in town. Lake Charles is booming with many new enterprises. The businesses are paying good wages to their workers. I think Louise and I could make a go of it there."

"I've seen the flyers," replied Philippe. "If I was a young man, I'd be tempted to move there myself. Your older brother Paul will inherit this farm. The rest of you need to find your own way in this world. Lake Charles seems like as good a place as any to make a new start. You have my blessing."

"*Merci*, Papa. Louise's brother moved there several months ago and is now working as an apprentice carpenter. He says there is more work than they can handle. Pipeline companies, timber companies, bakeries, repair shops, and many other operations are all begging for workers."

After a wonderful wedding in June, Robert Robichaud and his wife, Louise, were soon on their way to Lake Charles.

# CHAPTER 27
# CHÉTICAMP HARBOR

Father Hubert Girroir was born in Tracadie, Nova Scotia, and could trace his ancestry to François Girouard, who married Jeanne Aucoin in Port Royal in 1648. The family name developed several spellings over the generations such as Girouard, Girroir, Giroir, and Gerrior, among others. Regardless of the spelling, they were all descendants of that early union in Port Royal and therefore part of the same family.

In 1867, Father Girroir was named pastor of Chéticamp. For many years, prior to the arrival of Father Girroir, Chéticamp was served primarily by missionaries who stayed for a short time and then moved on. Some of these missionaries left much to be desired. They did little to help the Acadians other than saying mass and hearing confessions. They railed against the Acadians for drinking, playing cards, and dancing. The arrival of Father Girroir was like a breath of fresh air for the Chéticamp Acadians. He enjoyed playing cards with them and was an immediate hit with his parishioners.

"Father, we hope you'll decide to stay with us permanently," declared Patrice Chiasson, a spokesperson for the Chéticamp Acadians. "When you have some time, we'd appreciate it if you could look at the schools in Chéticamp. We're lucky to have them, and our children are learning, but many times, the teachers know very little. The children soon learn all they can and become bored when there is no more to learn from a particular teacher."

"Thank you, Patrice, for bringing this matter to my attention," replied Father Girroir. "I will investigate it. Schools are crucial in preparing our children to succeed in this world. Even the fisherman who loves his work and wants no other will do better as a fisherman if he can read, write, and understand basic arithmetic."

Father Girroir did more than just investigate the school situation. He made himself aware of and then an expert in the provisions of the Federal Free School Act of 1864. He obtained funds from the government for the building and maintenance of modern schools in Chéticamp. These new schools replaced the one-room schools then in place. The government also provided and paid for qualified teachers and books of instruction in French—a major accomplishment.

With his success in obtaining funds from the government fresh in his mind, Father Girroir then focused his considerable intellect on the economic situation in his parish. Fishing, of course, was the economic driver. The Chéticamp harbor was large, deep, and beautiful but inaccessible to large boats. If large boats could freely enter and leave the harbor, the economic situation would quickly improve. All that was needed was to dredge the mouth of the harbor. The mouth was currently blocked by a large sandbar that allowed only a few feet of clearance at high tide.

•   •   •

In late 1873, Father Girroir met in Sydney, Nova Scotia, with the land commissioner in charge of Cape Breton Island.

"Mr. Williams, thank you for seeing me," said Father Girroir. "It's an honor for me to meet with you."

"You're welcome, Father," replied Williams. "Are you here about the schools? I assumed that matter was well in hand."

"Thanks to you and your government, the schools are doing very well. We appreciate your efforts in that area. I'm here regarding a different matter—one that involves the economic growth of Chéticamp and by extension, all of Cape Breton."

"I'm all ears! Please proceed."

"I've brought a map of Chéticamp that shows its harbor. As you can see, the harbor is three miles long by half a mile wide, with an average depth of thirty feet. This harbor could easily hold and shelter fifty large boats, but its mouth is blocked by a sandbar. What I propose is that the government dredge the mouth and open the harbor to commercial shipping. The opening of the harbor would quickly lead to a significant increase in commercial activity. The entire province would benefit."

"Father, I'm impressed with your proposal and will recommend it to the governor. May I keep this map?"

"Yes, please do, and thank you for your encouragement."

"Father, I don't mean any disrespect, but if you ever decide to leave your current profession, I would be pleased to offer you a good position here in the government."

With a wide smile, Father Girroir replied, "Thank you, Commissioner, I will keep your offer in mind."

•   •   •

The dredging of Chéticamp Harbor occurred in 1874, and as predicted by Father Girroir, commercial activity soon followed. Father Girroir was an excellent fit for Chéticamp, and he loved his parishioners, but unfortunately, he was soon gone.

Parish priests exerted a lot of influence over their flocks. The parishioners often voted in government elections based on the preference of their *curé* (pastor). In the federal election of 1872, Father Girroir backed a candidate he thought best for his flock. The opponent, however, was a cousin of the bishop, his superior. As a result, in late 1874, Father Girroir was named to another parish in another county. He died there on April 25, 1884.

•   •   •

In the 1860s, Sam Lawrence, who owned a fishing business in Margaree, came to Chéticamp and started a new fishing business and store at the harbor, still blocked at that time. Initially, the Acadians were pleased to see someone compete with the Robins. They soon realized, however, that Sam Lawrence was no friend of the Acadians. His prices and practices were equally abusive as those of the Robins.

The processing of cod and other fish for the world market was relatively simple. The fish needed only to be cut open, washed, and then dried or frozen. The processing of lobster, however, was considerably more complicated and expensive. The lobsters needed to be cooked, shelled, and canned. For this, a lobster factory containing steam boilers, shell stripping equipment, and canning machinery was needed.

A Mr. MacFayden of Pictou, Nova Scotia, constructed the first lobster factory in Chéticamp in 1876. It was built near the mouth of the newly opened harbor. MacFayden's lobster venture failed after three years and was bought by Sam Lawrence. Lawrence ran the lobster factory for another eight years until it failed again. The site was subsequently demolished and replaced with other operations.

*   *   *

In 1898, Mister H. L. Foran of Portland, Maine, opened a lobster factory at L'Anse-du-Bois-Marié, about one quarter mile beyond the mouth of Chéticamp Harbor. This factory operated until 1921.

Finally, an Acadian, Fulgence (of Christophe, of Simon) Aucoin built a lobster factory at Cave-à-Loups (Wolf Cave) about one mile northeast of the Harbor. This factory also operated for many years.

Lobster factories and fish processing plants remained in operation in Chéticamp well into the 1980s.

Fortunately for the Acadians of Chéticamp, the replacement for Father Girroir, Father Pierre Fiset, proved to be another truly extraordinary priest. He was born on May 28, 1840, in the village of Ancienne-Lorette in Québec, and was appointed pastor of Chéticamp in 1875. He served as *curé* for thirty-four years until his death on April 18, 1909.

During his tenure, he accomplished many things. On September 8, 1879, he created a new parish, St. Joseph du Moine, about ten miles south of Chéticamp. Its church was built the same year. He built a convent for nuns and arranged for the *Filles de Jesus* (Sisters of Jesus), a teaching order from France, to come to Chéticamp, where they remained for many years beyond his death. He also convinced his brother, Napoléon Fiset, a doctor, to move to Chéticamp. Doctor Fiset was the first doctor in Chéticamp. Father Fiset did these and many other good works, but his two greatest accomplishments were the building of the new church in Cheticamp and the leveling of the playing field with the Robins.

The first church in Chéticamp was built in the winter of 1800 when English raids were still fresh in the minds of the Acadians. This church was therefore hidden from the view of the coastline. When completed, it was already too small. In subsequent years, a second, third, and fourth church replaced the previous ones. The fourth church, called *l'église du buttereau* (the church on the hill) was built in 1862 and it too soon became too small and no longer centrally located. The opening of the harbor caused a major shift in population. New homes, now clustered near the harbor, their owners were no longer afraid of English raids. Father Fiset decided a new, larger church, centrally located at the harbor, was needed.

·   ·   ·

"Father, we appreciate all you've done for us and continue to do for us, but most of us do not believe a new church is needed," said Antoine Poirier, a spokesperson for the Acadians. "The current church is not that old. It's made of solid stone and still has many years of life left. Perhaps we can enlarge it instead of building a new one."

"Antoine, I appreciate your opinion," replied Father Fiset. "I know that building a new church will be a major and expensive endeavor, but I believe it is necessary. Besides being too small, the current church is no longer centrally located. The homes, businesses, and population of Chéticamp are now centered on the harbor. The church needs to be here, too. We can use the stones from the old church to build the new one."

•   •   •

Father Fiset proved to be an excellent negotiator and convinced enough parishioners to move forward with the new church. From his own pocket, he purchased a centrally located piece of land, across the road from the harbor, that was large enough to hold the church, the rectory, a school, a convent, a hospital, and then some.

For five years, before beginning work on the church, he set a levy for his parishioners of six dollars per family per year. When the five years were up, he encouraged the parishioners to continue paying the six dollars or donate a day's catch of fish, which he would sell on his own to benefit the church.

Chéticamp Island, on the far side of the harbor, contained an excellent source of construction-grade stone. Father Fiset met with the Robins, owners of the island, and they graciously agreed to allow the Acadians to take all the stone they needed without charge. During the five-year levy period, in the summer months, the Acadians cut the stone from the quarry on the island and stacked the stones along the shore of the harbor. In the winter, with the harbor frozen, the stones were hauled across the harbor to the church site.

Construction started in 1892, and the interior of the church was completed in 1900. The parishioners furnished the homemade mortar, wood, and manpower to complete the church. The mortar, still good today, has withstood the test of time.

The architect was D. Ouellet of Québec. The contractor was Hubert Morin, also from Québec.

The total cost of the church was about $40,000. This amount was collected from the parishioners prior to and during construction, leaving the parish with no mortgage.

The completed church was named Saint-Pierre, after Saint Peter, the patron saint of fishermen. The church today measures 212 feet by 74 feet. It rises to a height of 166 feet. It is one of the largest and most beautiful churches in all of Cape Breton. This church remains the largest building and glory of Chéticamp as it overlooks the harbor. Father Fiset's body is entombed in the vault in the church basement.

A close second to Father Fiset's success with the new church was his expertise in competing directly with the Robins for the economic betterment of his parishioners. When Father Fiset first arrived in Chéticamp, he was appalled to see that the Robins held many, if not most, of the Acadians in economic slavery. The Robins controlled the market for fish, since the Acadians had no other buyers for their catch. And, of course, the Robins controlled the company store. Father Fiset vowed to fight fire with fire. He would beat the Robins at their own game. Fortunately, Father Fiset hailed from a prominent family in Québec and had access to considerable family resources, including cash.

•  •  •

"Your Eminence, thank you for seeing me," said Father Fiset as he kissed Bishop MacKinnon's ring in Arichat, Nova Scotia.

"You're very welcome," replied the bishop. "You've come a long way, Father. How may I help you?"

"I intend to free my parishioners in Chéticamp from the economic slavery of the Robin Company by competing directly with them in the wholesale fish and retail store markets."

"A worthy endeavor, my son, but an expensive one the diocese cannot afford."

"Your Eminence, I'm asking for your spiritual, as opposed to financial, support. My family in Québec has the financial means to assist me. What I seek today is your encouragement to proceed down this economic path that will immerse me in trade and business. While doing so, I promise to continue to administer to the spiritual needs of my flock. Freeing them from the Robins is critical to their economic as well as spiritual wellbeing."

"You have my support, Father. Now, let's proceed to the dinner table and that wonderful *fricot* (stew) my Acadian cook has prepared in honor of the parishioners you serve."

In 1883, Father Fiset bought a store in Chéticamp that he entrusted to the care of Michael Crispo, a capable manager from Fiset's previous parish who moved to Chéticamp at his request. The store soon became one of the largest and most popular at the harbor. As part of the store's business, Father Fiset began trading in fish and animals.

The huge stretch of land above the new church was soon covered in drying racks for the fish. Now competing effectively with the Robins, he gave the fishermen better prices for their fish and charged less for the goods in his store.

In 1888, he built a large wharf at the harbor. In 1904, he built another at La Pointe, the southern end of Chéticamp Island. He purchased the lobster factory that the Robins owned at La Pointe and purchased the flour mill at the head of Le Platin.

He also owned a large farm with five barns, eight horses and over one hundred cattle. He did his best to encourage his parishioners, by example, to do more farming and ranching—to diversify from fishing.

After selling their operations at La Pointe to Father Fiset, the Robins moved to the harbor and were no longer interested in Chéticamp Island. They sold their entire interest in the island to Fiset, except for the livestock on it, for $10,000.

Fiset also immersed himself in the mining ventures in the nearby mountains. In 1903, he created and became President of the Great Northern Mining Company, a gypsum-mine operation. Gypsum mining in Chéticamp went through many difficulties before finally closing its doors for good in 1939.

All this Father Fiset did to free his parishioners from the Robins and provide them with a more comfortable and humane existence. He succeeded very well.

Diversification into farming, ranching, mining, or other ventures was a worthy goal but a hard sell for the fishermen of Chéticamp. Fishing, far out on the open sea, provided the fisherman with an excitement and freedom that the farmer was hard-pressed to match.

# CHAPTER 28
# THE FISHERMAN

The open sea had served as a magnet for the boys of Chéticamp for many generations. Wives and mothers feared for their seagoing husbands and sons, for they knew, all too well, how cruel the sea could be. For the men who went to sea, however, the key emotion was not fear—it was the irresistible pull of the sea, the excitement, the anticipation, the unknown, the worthwhile risk that spurred them on. Their very blood seemed to rise and fall with the ebb and flow of the tides.

Joseph Wilfred Chiasson was born in Chéticamp in 1923. His parents were John Chiasson and Joséphine Aucoin. From the very beginning, everyone called him Wilfred because there were already two other boys in the village with the name Joseph Chiasson. His father and uncles were all fishermen. Wilfred grew up knowing he would follow in their footsteps and make his life on the open sea.

May 28, 1933, was one of the happiest days of Wilfred's life. He had just completed the fourth grade at the Chéticamp elementary school. He could read, write, and do basic arithmetic. He was ten years old, and his parents agreed there was no need for him to continue school. He was destined to be a fisherman, and his father and uncles were in a better position to teach him the basics and finer points of that profession than any school. For the next two years, he worked for the Robins in their fish drying racks. At twelve, he started going out to sea, fifty or more miles from shore, with his father and uncles, to reach the rich fishing grounds.

At eighteen, he had his own twenty-foot fishing boat, with a gasoline-powered motor, that he managed with two of his friends.

"Wilfred, how far out do you want to go today?" asked Joseph Leblanc, one of his mates.

"Only a mile," replied Wilfred. "We'll be catching mackerel today, and we should find a nice school of them not too far out. The three buckets of chum we have should be more than enough to attract all the mackerel we want."

Mackerel was a popular food item for the Acadians and was used as bait in the lobster traps, so the demand was steady and an easy source of revenue for a young fisherman like Wilfred. Mackerel was much oilier than most fish, and perhaps for this reason, served as a better lobster bait than the typical codfish head.

"When we return to the dock with our catch," said Wilfred, "we'll see what the other boats are bringing in and what's in demand. Tomorrow, we can fill the boat with mackerel again or perhaps go for flounder or haddock instead. We'll see where the best prices are."

Regarding the proceeds from their catch, the arrangement Wilfred had with his men was that each man and the boat received an equal share. The boat's share was used for maintenance and upgrades to the boat and motor. That arrangement served Wilfred and his mates well throughout their long fishing careers.

In 1951, at twenty-eight, Wilfred acquired a thirty-eight-foot fishing trawler he named *Stella Maris*—Latin for *Star of the Sea*. Our Lady, Star of the Sea, was an ancient title for the Virgin Mary, protector of seamen. *Stella Maris* was therefore a very appropriate name for a North Sea fishing vessel. His boat quickly rose to the top as one of the most productive fishing boats in Chéticamp and stayed there for many years.

The only weather instrument on Wilfred's boat was a barometer that used mercury to measure air pressure. A reading of thirty was normal. A rising barometer with a reading above thirty showed high pressure and an expectation of clear and calm weather. A falling barometer showed low pressure with a storm on the way. There was no radio.

In late August 1955, as Wilfred and his crew left Chéticamp for the fifty-mile trip to their favorite cod fishing grounds, the barometer reading was just over thirty and holding steady—a good sign.

"Wilfred, how many passes over the banks do you think it will take to fill our hold?" questioned his mate, Réal Boisvert.

"It took three last time. With a little luck, I believe we can do it in two," replied Wilfred.

"That would be great," chimed in his other mate, Joseph Leblanc. "Today is my wife's birthday. It would be nice to get home a little early."

In their first pass, their net was filled to the brim. The winch strained with the weight but brought in the catch. The second pass also went well, and it looked like they would indeed go home early, but all three men noticed the sea growing rapidly around them. There was no wind, but what a short time before had been a calm sea was now filled with large swells.

"Wilfred, the barometer is at twenty-eight and dropping!" cried Joseph.

"*Merde!*" exclaimed Wilfred. "Start the winch! We need to bring in the net!"

The wind then made itself known, and the swells grew much larger. A cold rain pelted the three men. A large wave broke over the vessel and washed all gear that was not tied down into the sea. The three men barely hung on. They tied themselves to the boat with the pre-positioned rope intended for such a storm. All three were thankful for the time they previously spent practicing that safety procedure.

Another large wave crashed over the stern and barreled its way into the galley, ripping the galley door off its hinges. Pots, pans, dishes, and their food were all flushed into the briny deep. The angry sea reclaimed much of their catch as the hold filled with seawater and flushed the cod out and back into the ocean. The *Stella Maris,* tied to the bottom by the full net, was unable to maneuver and began to flounder.

The ocean swells became towering over the boat. Waves, carrying thousands of pounds of water, continued to crash onto and into the boat. The railing was torn off the port side.

"Cut the net!" yelled Wilfred as he did his best to control the boat. His words were carried off by the wind and never reached the ears of his crew. He took out his knife, made eye contact with his crew, and slashed the air with his knife. He pointed to the stern, where the net lines were, and continued slashing the air with his knife. His crew understood. The winch had pulled the net up enough that cutting it loose with the knives was possible. Joseph and Réal tethered by their own safety ropes, and abused by the wind, rain, and crashing waves, applied themselves to cutting the ropes of the net. Finally, Wilfred felt the boat surge forward as the net was freed. He steered into the wind and waves—rising sixty or more feet up one swell and crashing down the other side into the trough until the next swell. The battle was not yet won. It would last another three hours, when the whitecaps finally diminished, and the watery mountains became mere hills.

The battered *Stella Maris* made it back to port that day with a bruised but safe crew. Not so for three other Chéticamp boats with all hands lost—nine men, including six fathers with young children.

The type of storm that hit that day was called a *suête* by the Acadians—a violent storm with winds from the southeast.

In late September 1958, after three days of stormy weather that prevented the Chéticamp boats from leaving the harbor, the fishing boats were finally able to go out to sea. About twenty miles out, the *Stella Maris* found itself in a field of floating fifty-five-gallon wooden barrels. After pulling one of the barrels onto their boat, Wilfred and his crew determined it was filled with flour. They pulled in about twenty more barrels and returned to Chéticamp. News of the flour barrels quickly spread, and boats of all sizes set off to share in this bonanza. The sea routinely took from the Acadians, but, as the flour barrels proved, she occasionally presented them with a gift other than fish. The Acadians knew nothing of the ship that gave up the flour barrels. Most likely, the barrels had been stored on the deck of a large ocean-going vessel and their lashings proved inadequate. Hopefully, the ship itself survived the violent weather. Regardless, many Acadians smiled as the sale of flour in the Robins' store was severely diminished for many months.

By the mid-1950s, besides its diesel engines and power winch, the *Stella Maris* had a sonar fish finder and radios for communication. The radios were a significant improvement in safety. The barometer, however, kept its place of honor aboard the boat. Regardless of weather reports, updates via radio, and other safety improvements, Wilfred and his crew checked the barometer several times per hour whenever they were at sea—it never failed them.

In the winter of 1958, while visiting relatives in New Hampshire during the off-season, Wilfred's young cousin asked about his life at sea. He responded, "I love the ocean and my place on it. Each day on the sea is an adventure. When we pull in the net, I'm always filled with excitement as to what we might find, besides the fish. Several times, the net has provided pieces of broken wood from boats that went down many years before. Pottery, old muskets, pistols, knives, and other items sometimes come up. All these items are treasure to me. Every time the net comes up, I'm like a kid with a new toy, even after all these years."

On November 21, 1960, Wilfred married Marie Lucie Aucoin, who went by the name of Lucie. They did not have any children. Wilfred's Lucie was the first cousin of my mother, Lucie Anne Aucoin.

During the 1960s, '70s, and '80s, Wilfred and his crew were at their peak. They were still occasionally caught in storms and sometimes lost fishing gear, fish, and supplies, but the good days far outnumbered the bad ones.

Wilfred died peacefully in his sleep on June 3, 2002, at seventy-nine—the sailor home from the sea.

# CHAPTER 29
# ST. JOSEPH DU MOINE

As the Aucoin family in Chéticamp grew, the descendants of Joseph, nicknamed Grannoume (big man), moved about ten miles south to an area that eventually became known as St. Joseph du Moine. Grannoume, born in 1776, was a younger brother of Anselme Aucoin, the early pioneer who first came to Chéticamp. The main attraction of St. Joseph du Moine was its miles of large meadows that proved to be excellent for growing crops—especially potatoes—and raising beef. The settlers of the new area relied more on farming than fishing. The village between Chéticamp and Margaree became its own parish, thanks to Father Fiset, with its own church serving a population of about 600 residents.

Lubin (of Dosithée of Michouque of Grannoume) Aucoin married Olive Levert on January 31, 1894. They had eight children. Their oldest child, William, nicknamed Willie, was born on February 26, 1895, and would see combat in France during World War I.

"Lubin, the water pump is leaking again," declared his wife, Olive, on a bright summer's day. "Perhaps you can buy a replacement part from the Robins' store next time you're in Chéticamp."

"Yes, I know the pump is leaking, but it's leaking into the kitchen sink, so it's not that bad," replied Lubin. "I'll see what the replacement part costs. If it's not too much, I'll get it next time I'm in Chéticamp."

The water pump in their kitchen was powered by hand-pumping the handle until the water came up. The pump was connected to a metal pipe that went through the kitchen floor into the cellar and then into the ground. When the house was first built, the pipe was driven into the ground just below where the kitchen would be. The men drove the pipe down until it reached water. They then drove it down another few feet. The water table in that area was quite high, and only ten feet of pipe was in the ground. When completed, the house had access to fresh water without needing to visit an outside well or stream—a major innovation in the mid- to late-1800s.

Their second child, Théophile, was born the following year, in 1896. He was a strong, healthy baby. He and Willie soon became best friends. They were inseparable playing together all summer and winter long. Their sister, Magdeleine Marie, nicknamed Minnie, was born in 1898, and another brother, Marcellin, in 1900. Four more children would eventually follow.

·   ·   ·

"Théophile, come quickly!" cried Willie. "There are baby rabbits in the field." The date was June 2, 1907. Willie and Théophile were twelve and eleven years old, respectively.

"Where are they?" said an excited Théophile as he came running. "Let's catch them." The boys were both running as fast as they could as the six or seven baby rabbits scattered in front of them.

Lubin smiled as he watched his boys chase the rabbits. He called after them, "Be careful not to damage the potato plants."

The rabbits were never in danger of being caught. Even a baby rabbit can easily outrun a twelve-year-old boy, but the chase was on, and the boys made a good effort.

Once the rabbits had located the tempting and delicious young potato plants, Lubin knew it was time for the snares. He set the snares in the usual places, and Olive soon added rabbit stew to the family's usual fare. The entire family loved rabbit stew.

In the fall, the harvesting of the potatoes was a family affair. Even five-year-old Catherine and two-year-old Angéline helped. They did their best to dig with their bare hands around the plants and pull the tubers out of the ground. The older children used hand tools to help loosen the tubers from the soil.

"Be careful not to cut or bruise the potatoes," cried Lubin. He knew undamaged potatoes could be stored in the cellar and feed the family all winter long. Damaged ones would not last and would need to be eaten soon. The soil around the potatoes was lightly removed by hand, and the potatoes were left to dry in the sun. They were then placed in burlap sacks holding about fifty pounds each. Lubin used his wheelbarrow to haul the filled sacks back to the house to store in the cellar.

•   •   •

In the spring of 1908, Olive was pregnant with her seventh child. In late April, on a pleasant day, Lubin told Willie and Théophile to split some firewood from the woodpile. The long winter had largely depleted the firewood for the house.

"Be careful with the axe," stated Lubin. "It's very sharp. It hasn't been used yet since I sharpened it during the winter."

Cutting and splitting firewood was a job the boys had done many times. They took turns. One would place a large piece of wood in position while the other swung the axe to split the wood. The sharp axe easily and efficiently bit into its target. It's difficult to say exactly what happened, but as Théophile swung the axe, something went terribly wrong. The axe bounced off the block of wood and embedded itself deeply into the side of his knee. Major blood vessels, including the artery, were severed. Willie rushed to help his brother and cried for his father, who was about 200 yards away in the field. Olive and the children poured out of the house but were helpless at stemming the spurting blood. Lubin came at a run, but by the time he arrived, Théophile was beyond help. He died while holding Willie's hand.

Two months later, on June 27, 1908, Olive gave birth to her seventh child, a boy. She and Lubin named him Théophile. With twelve years between them, Willie and the new Théophile were too far apart to become close. Even as adults, the two brothers were cordial with each other but never close. Olive's final child, a boy named François, nicknamed Francis, arrived two years later. Francis eventually took over the family farm.

For the next four years, the extended Aucoin family on Cape Breton Island continued to live comfortably, if not prosperously. Then, on June 28, 1914, Archduke Franz Ferdinand of Austria was assassinated in Sarajevo, Bosnia. His assassination set off a rapidly escalating chain of events that led to the start of World War I a month later on July 28, 1914. The initial combatants in this war were Russia, Belgium, France, Great Britain, and Serbia facing off against Austria-Hungary and Germany. It took a while for news of the war to reach St. Joseph du Moine, but it eventually did.

       •    •    •

"Papa, Papa, the English have declared war against Germany!" cried an excited nineteen-year-old Willie as he ran to his father in the field.

"I know," replied Lubin. "I heard it this morning when I was talking to the men by the road."

"The government will soon ask for volunteers. I want to go," stated Willie.

"Willie, this is an English war. It has nothing to do with us. You've heard the stories of the old ones. The English are not our friends. They are not to be trusted. No Acadian should fight in their war."

"Papa, the old days are over. We belong to Canada, and Canada belongs to England. Canada is my country, and if Canada is to fight in this war, I want to be part of it."

Such a battle of wills between father and son would go on for many more months, well into the next year. Willie was not especially patriotic. The main force driving him was boredom. At nineteen, he was ready for something more than St. Joseph du Moine. Joining the military had never occurred to him previously, but now seemed like a viable option. As an Acadian, he wasn't sure if the military would accept him. Acadians generally kept to themselves, did not trust the English and were not part of the Canadian military. Willie understood English, but only if spoken slowly, and he could not speak it. Quitting school after the fourth grade, he could read and write French and do basic arithmetic. Skilled with a gun, he shot a moose the previous fall that fed his family all winter. That should be more than enough for any military.

•   •   •

On August 5, 1914, in Ottawa, Canada, Prime Minister Sir Robert Borden addressed his cabinet.

"As you all know," stated Borden, "on July 28, England declared war against Germany, and yesterday, our own governor general declared war on Germany. The question before us is, how are we going to take part in this war? Our current military force comprises a regular army of 3,000 men and a militia of 24,000."

"Sir, we must raise a large force and send them to support England," replied General Willoughby Gwatkin, Chief of the General Staff.

"Yes, General, but how best to raise that force?"

After considerable deliberations, the decision was made to leave the regular army and the militia as they were. Instead, an independent Canadian Expeditionary Force would be created. This new force would report to a new ministry, the Ministry of Overseas Forces of Canada. The new force was quickly raised, but as with any such major government endeavor, the new force was rife with political patronage positions and a lack of qualified officers and noncommissioned officers. The troops would pay a heavy price for the lack of qualified leadership.

The Canadian Expeditionary Force eventually totaled five divisions. The 2$^{nd}$ Division, formed in Québec, was the first to deploy to Europe. It arrived in France in September 1915.

•   •   •

With the Canadian declaration of war, the Cape Breton Highlanders, the largest militia infantry regiment on Cape Breton, embarked on an island-wide recruiting effort during the winter of 1914–15.


"Who are you?" questioned Duncan Mcintosh, the large sergeant in charge of his unit's temporary recruiting office in Chéticamp.

"I'm Willie Aucoin, and I want to join your army."

"Sorry, I don't speak French. I'm only taking men who can speak English. If you want to join, you'll have to go to Québec to sign up. Québec is forming both English-speaking and French-speaking battalions."


"Papa, I need to go to Québec City to join the army," declared Willie after returning home. "That's the only place that has French-speaking units. I need to leave right away."

"Willie," his father said with a sigh, "your mother and I would prefer you stay home, but we know we can't hold you here. Since you are so determined, you may go to your war with our blessing. We have a little money saved that should get you to Québec. We will pray for you every day."

Late the following day, Willie arrived in Halifax and proceeded to the rail station to catch the train to Québec City. He was told the next train would be in three days. The train service between Halifax and Québec City, a 600-mile trip that took twenty hours, happened only once per week. He stayed in a nearby hotel for the first night and slept in a chair at the rail station the next two nights to save money. The train left early on that third morning.

After arriving in Québec City, Willie quickly found the French-speaking recruiting station. The date was February 27, 1915.

"*Bonjour*," stated Willie. "I'm here to join the army."

"You've come to the right place," replied the French-Canadian recruiting sergeant. "Please have a seat over there and fill out these papers. Next!"

Willie soon found himself in the army's hastily constructed basic training camp about ten miles north of the city. He quickly made friends with several of his fellow recruits.

Basic training lasted eight weeks. The first few days were spent receiving their military clothing, rucksack, and other equipment and a medical exam. More than anything else, the socks and underwear made a deep impression on Willie. While living at home, Willie owned two pairs of socks and two sets of well-worn underwear. The army gave him four pairs of socks and four sets of underwear. Willie was amazed and pleased at being on the receiving end of this bonanza.

The first hour of every morning was spent on calisthenics and then a slow run of one mile. By week eight, the run grew to three miles at a faster pace. Marching came next. "Right face! Left face! About face!" cried the instructors. At the end of the first week, the drill instructor, Sergeant Paul Lejeune, a tall, lean, wiry, no-nonsense man, told them they were by far the worst group of recruits he had ever seen. Lejeune foamed at the mouth a bit when he yelled at them. They all feared him.

The rifle range took up much of the recruits' time. Some of the men had never fired a gun. All learned the basics and were told their best friend was their rifle, not the man standing next to them. Before long, while blindfolded, they were able to take apart their rifles and put them back together in less than a minute.

Bayonet training came last and was the scariest of all. "Fix bayonets!" cried the instructor. After attaching the bayonets to the ends of their rifles, the recruits were then required to charge the scarecrow figures in front of them and plunge the bayonets deep into the hay-filled chests. "*Kill! Kill! Kill!* is the spirit of the bayonet," repeated the instructors, over and over.

At the end of the eighth week, on graduation day, Sergeant Lejeune faced the assembled recruits.

"Men," he began, "I am truly amazed at your progress. You started so far back from most classes that I never thought I would see this day. You have gone further and achieved more than any other class I have ever taught. I would be proud to serve with any one of you in combat. You have my respect and my compliments. Welcome to the army."

The basic training instructor's main job was to convert otherwise docile farm boys into effective killers on the battlefield. The instructors were very good at their trade.

In May 1915, the 2nd Canadian Division, including Willie, boarded troop ships in the St. Lawrence Seaway for England. The crossing took ten days. The division spent three months training in England and then boarded ships for the three-hour crossing to Calais, France. They arrived in September 1915 and were immediately moved up to a reserve area behind the front line. Willie was wounded twice during the war.

In April 1916, while Willie sat uneasily at the bottom of his trench, a German artillery shell landed about four meters from the edge of the trench. The earth was soft where the shell hit, and it buried itself into the soil a good four feet before exploding. The explosion resulted in a tidal wave of earth slamming into Willie's trench. Willie ended up flat on his back at the bottom of the trench with over a ton of earth pressing down on him.

Men frantically dug at the earth with their bare hands and shovels where they thought Willie would be. The first sign of Willie was when a burly soldier drove his sharp spade into the earth and struck Willie on the forehead, opening a deep five-inch-long gash. Willie was dazed and sputtering as his friends pulled him out with blood pouring from the open wound on his forehead. With a man on each side holding him up, they rushed one hundred meters down the trench to the first-aid station—a large room cut into the side of a hill. The room was reinforced with timber and wooden planks and contained about ten folding cots for patients.

The medics washed the dirt out of Willie's wound, added powdered sulfur to prevent infection, and closed it with ten stitches. They added more sulfur, a dressing to the wound, and wrapped gauze around his head to hold it in place. He was placed on a cot with his head slightly elevated and told to stay there. Willie soon recovered. Two days later, he was back in the trench with his unit.

His second wound was more serious. During the Battle of the Somme, a German machine-gun bullet caught him in the shoulder, shattering his collar bone. He was rescued from the battlefield and rushed to a hospital in the rear where he received excellent care.

After eight days of physical therapy, Willie soon regained full use of his shoulder and was sent back to his unit on the front lines. He continued fighting in France until the last shot was fired on November 11, 1918.

Canada's total casualties at the end of "the war to end all wars" stood at 67,000 killed and 173,000 wounded out of a total expeditionary force of 620,000—a casualty rate of thirty-nine percent.

In late December 1918, Willie was twenty-three years old and back in St. Joseph du Moine.

"Papa, I'm so thankful to be home and done with that war," declared Willie. "In the spring, I'll help you with the planting, but after that I'll be leaving. Farming is not for me."

"Where will you go?" asked his father, Lubin.

"I'm not sure yet—either Montréal or Waltham. Based on the flyers I've seen in Chéticamp, both places have lots of good-paying job."

In June 1919, Willie left for Waltham, Massachusetts, where he became a machinist, married Joséphine Aucoin, a distant cousin, bought a nice house with a big yard, had three sons, and became a loyal Red Sox fan.

Willie seldom spoke of the war. Instead, he much preferred talking about baseball or his job as a machinist with the Waltham Watch Company. He enjoyed watching his sons grow up. He lived out the rest of his life in Waltham, having seen more than enough of the world. He was eighty-one years old when he died in 1976.

# CHAPTER 30
# LAKE CHARLES

Lake Charles encompasses a five-parish area in Southwest Louisiana. The town was incorporated in 1857 as Charlestown. Ten years later, on March 16, 1867, it was renamed the City of Lake Charles. The city is on the banks of the Calcasieu River and is bordered by Lake Charles and Prien Lake. Several bayous also flow through the city.

The Calcasieu River is wide and deep and allows ocean-going vessels to sail up from the Gulf of Mexico, about thirty miles downstream from the city. This ready access to the gulf was the key factor in Lake Charles becoming a major port city. Petrochemical plants and a large oil refinery would eventually dominate the area—creating thousands of jobs. In 1895, however, when Robert and Louise Robichaud arrived in Lake Charles, there was no such thing as a petrochemical plant.

"Robert, have you ever seen a more beautiful lake?" exclaimed his wife, Louise. "My brother, Maurice, told me it was nice here, but his letters focused mostly on the job situation. He said little of these two beautiful lakes and the river."

"I agree," replied Robert. "This is probably the prettiest place I've ever seen. Let's find your brother and get settled. I want to find work and start making our own way as soon as possible."

•　•　•

Robert soon found a good-paying job in the lumber industry. Large stands of old-growth oak and pine trees populated the nearby countryside. Robert became part of a crew that cut and trimmed the trees. Other crews used horses to haul the logs to the nearest waterway, where they floated to the sawmill. The finished lumber was then shipped down the Calcasieu River to the gulf and the waiting customers.

"Louise, the foreman at work today called us Cajuns," declared Robert. "I didn't know if that was a good or bad word, so I asked one of my coworkers later. He said that 'a Cajun' is the same as 'Acadian'—just easier to say and no harm intended. At first, I was shocked, but the new word makes sense. We are now Cajuns instead of Acadians."

The following year, on August 12, 1896, Louise gave birth to the first of her six children—a boy named Roland. Next came four girls: Yvette, Claudette, Paulette, and Josette, followed by the final boy, Edouard, born on February 5, 1912.

In June 1930, Edouard became the first member of his family to graduate from high school. It was cause for a huge celebration at his home. Friends and family arrived with gumbos, *fricots*, crawfish pie, and more. His Uncle Maurice, now a master carpenter, took him aside and offered him a job as his apprentice.

"Uncle Maurice, thank you so much for the offer," said Edouard, "but I've decided to work with my dad in the lumber business. He still likes cutting and trimming trees, but I prefer working with machines, so he found a good position for me in the big new sawmill."

"It seems you already know what you want," replied Maurice. "I'm very proud of you and wish you well. If you tire of the sawmill, you can always come work for me."

After working at the sawmill for three years, Edouard became the top expert at keeping all the machines working. If a machine broke down, Edouard was who they called to fix it. At twenty-one, he married his high school sweetheart, Paulette Laverdière.

After fourteen years at the sawmill, he still liked his job. He was very good at it, felt appreciated, and believed he was well paid by his employer, until he met George Stevens.

In mid-1944, Edouard and Paulette had four children—three girls and a boy. They lived in a nice home on Henderson Bayou in Lake Charles. Edouard typically used his small motorboat to get to and from his home and the sawmill, enjoying commuting to work that way. He also owned an eight-year-old 1936 Ford automobile he used for other trips. While not rich, he and Paulette lived comfortably and were satisfied with their place in society.

•   •   •

One day, while buying meat at the butcher shop, a stranger approached him.

"Mr. Robichaud, I hope I'm not disturbing you, but, if possible, I'd like a few minutes of your time. My name is George Stevens, and I'm the superintendent for the Cities Service oil refinery currently under construction in Lake Charles. I've asked around for the names of men who are good with machines, and your name came up the most. I'm aware of your current position at the sawmill, and I'm ready to double your pay if you'll come to work for me."

Edouard was shocked. He knew nothing about the oil business, but if this man was offering double his pay, Edouard would listen.

"Mr. Stevens, your offer has taken me completely by surprise. I'm honored, but I know little about your company and nothing about the specific job you're offering. Perhaps we can meet again later, and you can provide more details. Now is not a good time. This meat is for tonight's supper. My wife sent me here to get it and is expecting me."

"I understand," replied Stevens. "We can meet tomorrow afternoon, after you finish work, if that's convenient for you. My office is in a trailer at the construction site. Ask anyone for Stevens, and they'll direct you to my trailer. I'll see you then, Mr. Robichaud. Have a good evening."

When he got home, Edouard told Paulette about his meeting with Stevens.

"Edouard, you must be careful," exclaimed Paulette. "You have a good position and many friends at the sawmill. You know nothing about this George Stevens. The big pay may be just to get you to help him get his operation running. Once everything is running smoothly, he might reduce your pay or even let you go."

"You're right," answered Edouard. "I'll try to find out about him, but I suspect no one will know much since he and his operation are new to Lake Charles."

The next day, after work, Edouard knocked on the door to the Stevens trailer.

"Come in," said Stevens. "Ah! Mr. Robichaud, thank you for coming. Please take a seat. I'm so glad to see you. Let me show you what the refinery will look like when completed. This chart shows the 1,200 acres of land we purchased. The refinery complex is here and the tank farm there. The rest of the land is for future expansion."

"The refinery complex is well-named," stated Edouard. "It seems very complex."

"Yes, to the untrained eye, the refinery seems very complex. It's like looking at a forest and not seeing the individual trees. The refinery comprises individual process units connected by pipelines. Each process unit is simple in its design and serves a specific purpose. The crude unit, for example, is where the crude oil is boiled. As the vapors rise in the tall crude tower, they cool and condense back to a liquid at different temperatures for each product. Trays are designed into the crude tower to catch the liquid and move it into product tanks, such as diesel or jet fuel, or to another process unit for further processing. What happens in the crude unit is not much different than what happens in the moonshiner's still. The physics are basically the same."

"If you say so, Mr. Stevens. My skills, however, deal mostly with the mechanics of machines, not so much the physics."

"Your skills are much needed to keep this refinery running smoothly. When completed, the refinery will contain hundreds of machines—pumps, generators, compressors, valves, and so on. I need a skilled man to keep all these machines running twenty-four hours per day and 365 days per year. Once we start up the refinery, it does not stop unless there's a serious problem or the process units are due for major maintenance, every few years or so. I'd like you to help install the pumps, generators, compressors so you'll know their size, location, and purpose. You'll need to organize the spare parts inventory for all these machines. Each of them will eventually need maintenance, and I want you to be their caretaker."

"How large a crew would I be part of?"

"Initially, you'll have three or four men under you who know how to turn wrenches. You'll be the boss. Your title will be maintenance manager."

"Mr. Stevens, I appreciate your confidence in me. I need to discuss your offer with my wife. If I say yes, I will need to give notice to my current employer and assist them in training my replacement."

"I need you here full-time in about three weeks. Until then, perhaps you can work part-time here and part-time there."

"That should work. I appreciate your flexibility. The sawmill has been very good to me, and I don't want to leave them in a lurch."

Edouard took the job at the refinery. The following year, on February 12, 1945, Paulette gave birth to their fifth and final child—a boy named Roger. Edouard thrived at the refinery. He soon earned the respect of his boss, his peers, his crew, and the operators for his work ethic and his knowledge of the overall refinery operation. He took care of all the machines, he listened to them, oiled them, repaired them, and replaced them as needed, with no slowdown in refinery operations.

•   •   •

On a fine, spring day in 1947, Edouard approached his boss, George Stevens's office. Stevens's secretary told him to go right in.

"Edouard," exclaimed Stevens, "thanks for coming. Please have a seat. I know you and your crew are in the middle of that compressor replacement. I assume everything is under control."

"Yes, all is well," replied Edouard. "We should be done by tomorrow afternoon."

"Great! The reason I asked for you is that a major project is planned for the refinery, and I wanted you to hear of it first. Since the war ended, the big bosses at headquarters have noticed that the returning soldiers bought and are continuing to buy automobiles in increasing numbers. All these extra cars on the road have caused a significant increase in the demand for gasoline, which is likely to increase even more. They want us to double the size of our reformer so we can make more gasoline."

A reformer is a process unit in an oil refinery. Its purpose is to convert heavy fuel oil into lighter petroleum products. It does this by subjecting the molecules of fuel oil to high pressure in the presence of a catalyst. As a result, a chemical reaction takes place. The molecule of fuel oil is cracked into several molecules of lighter products. One of these is called reformate and is the primary building block of gasoline. Gasoline is always a blend of several petroleum products. Starting with reformate, naphtha, butane, and other additives are combined to create the desired octane rating of the gasoline.

"Double? Wow!" exclaimed Edouard. "That's no simple matter. Our refinery is currently well balanced. We have customers for all the products we make, even the bottom-of-the-barrel fuel oil that we send to our asphalt unit. If we send all the fuel oil, instead, to the reformer to crack into reformate for gasoline, our asphalt plant will have to shut down. That will mean angry asphalt customers, especially the Lake Charles Paving Company that recently won the contract with the city to pave hundreds of miles of dirt roads. But I know the profit margin on gasoline is much higher than on asphalt. What I don't know is how bad this decision will be from a public relations standpoint."

"Good point, but even if we divert all fuel oil to the reformer, we won't come close to having enough. The plan is to build a large fuel oil tank near our refinery dock. We would then buy barge loads of fuel oil and have them delivered to our refinery dock for offloading into our tank."

"If that plan works, we can probably keep operating our asphalt plant."

"Yes, the additional fuel oil should be just enough to keep the expanded reformer operating at peak efficiency. The larger reformer will also allow us to buy cheaper crude oil containing more of the heavy fuel oil than the lighter products, such as diesel and jet fuel. On paper, this project looks like a money maker. You and I need to make it happen."

The reformer project was completed on time and on budget and led to increased profitability for the refinery. Even the asphalt plant benefited. Enough fuel oil was brought in to increase the production of asphalt. After seven years in his new job, Edouard was a key member of the refinery's management team and well-respected in the greater Lake Charles community. He recruited many fellow Cajuns to come work for the refinery. His entire maintenance crew as well as many refinery operators were of Cajun origin. The refinery paid higher than average wages, which allowed its workers to achieve a better-than-average standard of living.

Roger Robichaud, Edouard's youngest child, loved growing up in Lake Charles. With lots of kids his age in the neighborhood, he had no shortage of playmates. Baseball was his favorite. Every Saturday morning, the kids would play in a pickup game. The two captains would take turns picking their players from the kids, usually between six and twelve years of age. Everyone played. Typically, they had a total of around ten kids—boys and girls—so each side would end up with five players or so. Any ball hit into the bayou, even a grounder, was an automatic out, and the hitter was required to retrieve the ball. A nearby canoe was available for retrieval. No one kept score, but if it became obvious one team was dominating, a trade was made to even up the teams. The object of the game was to have fun and not to embarrass anyone.

Catching crawfish and catfish was very popular with the neighborhood kids. Alligators, however, are what really got their attention. The boys had homemade slingshots they used to shoot acorn-sized rocks at the alligators. Hitting a gator with a slingshot was the apex of fun. They could imagine no better way to spend the day.

•   •   •

Roger did well in school. With minimal studying, he easily got "A"s or "B"s in all his subjects. His junior year in high school, he fell in love with Madeleine LeBlanc, his classmate. They went to the junior prom together, dated all summer, and went steady in their senior year.

"Roger, what are your plans after we graduate in June?" asked Madeleine.

"I'm not sure," replied Roger. "College is a possibility, but I'll probably go to work full time at the refinery with my dad. What about you?"

"College would be great, especially if we went to the same one. You can always work at the refinery. Getting into college, however, requires planning. You need to take the SAT exam, apply to the college, and if accepted, make financial arrangements. You also need to figure out housing and food."

"So, college is the plan?"

"Of course, silly! We both have good grades. College will give us a chance to get away from Lake Charles for a while. I'm sure we can both get accepted to the Attakapas Community College and probably several other affordable ones that we'll apply to."

"You're the boss, *ma chérie*. College it is!"

•   •   •

Roger and Madeleine were both accepted at the four Louisiana colleges they applied to. They decided on Lafayette Business College. LBC offered bachelor's degrees in accounting, finance, marketing, and computer science. They also provided student housing and dining facilities. After graduating from high school with honors in June 1963,

Roger and Madeleine made several day trips to LBC to scope out their future school and its nearby town.

In early August 1963, Roger received the worst phone call of his life. His beloved Madeleine was dead, killed in an automobile accident. The news hit him like a gut punch. He doubled over and ended up collapsed on the floor. Later in the month, after the funeral, Roger walked into the army recruiting office.

"How can I help you?" asked the sergeant.

"I want to join the army," responded Roger.

"Well, then, you've come to the right place. Please have a seat and fill out these forms."

# CHAPTER 31
# NEW HAMPSHIRE

Théophile, like his older brother Willie, quit school after the fourth grade. He worked with his father in the fields but soon realized that farming in St. Joseph du Moine, or anywhere else, was not for him. He knew he would follow Willie to Waltham. At sixteen, he started working in the Cape Breton lumber camps during the off-season when it was too cold to farm.

Tall and thin, he would eventually grow to be five feet, eleven inches tall, but never weighed over 145 pounds in his entire life. His finger strength was above average. He could easily bend steel bottle caps in half using just his thumb and index finger, a feat most men could not perform.

The lumber camps had a barracks and dining hall for the men. Room and board were free, and the pay was good. Some men, including Théophile, would stay for the entire winter season, cutting pulp wood. Others would come and go every few weeks throughout the winter. Hygiene in the camps was minimal. Lice infested the barracks and the men.

When he first arrived as a sixteen-year-old, he was met with hard stares from some of the men.

"Who the hell are you?" questioned Charlie Deveau, a lumber camp worker and bully, if there ever was one.

"My name is Théophile Aucoin, from St. Joseph du Moine. I'm here to cut wood."

A broad sneer was on Deveau's face as he stepped closer to Théophile. "We don't need any children here. I suggest you go back to St. Joseph du Moine and stay there till you grow a pair."

Taller than Deveau, Théophile moved forward and got in his face. "I'm here to cut wood, but if I need to start with you, that's fine. I'll cut you!" declared a thoroughly angered, red-faced Théophile, his neck veins throbbing.

Deveau was caught off guard and took a step back. He forced a laugh and uttered, "Take it easy, the boss doesn't allow any fighting here."

From then on, no one picked on Théophile. They soon learned he had no fear of any man. When picked on, he always stood his ground and fought back. If faced with a fight-or-flight situation, fight was his immediate response. The bullies left him alone. He prided himself that, as a teenager, he could work as hard and produce as much as any man in the lumber camp.

Théophile saved the money he earned, and at twenty, said goodbye to his family in St. Joseph du Moine and left for Waltham. Willie welcomed him into his home and soon got him enrolled in a trade school where he learned the basics of the tool and die maker trade. After graduating, he was hired by the Raytheon Company as a trainee in their tool and die department. He quickly excelled at this trade and became an accomplished tool and die maker. He became a skilled laborer with many job opportunities open to him. His tool and die making skills were much in demand.

In 1932, at twenty-four, Théophile was in his prime. He had a good job and money to spend, and as a handsome, tall, blond-haired, and blue-eyed bachelor, had his pick of the girls. That summer, he met Lucie, and his remaining bachelor days were numbered.

Lucie Anne Aucoin was born on February 22, 1913, in Chéticamp, Nova Scotia. She left there in 1931 to join her eldest sister Catherine in Waltham. The summer of 1932, she was nineteen years old and in her prime. She was attractive, with a curvy figure that immediately caught Théophile's eye and heart. She was five feet, four inches tall, weighed

125 pounds, had brown, curly hair, and hazel eyes. They met at a popular dance hall on the Charles River in Waltham.

Théophile and Lucie were both descended from Pierre Aucoin, who spent those seven years as an English prisoner after the deportation of 1755. They were distant cousins separated by five generations of Aucoins.

They were married in Waltham on September 4, 1932. Soon thereafter, Théophile became aware of a better-paying job in Manchester, New Hampshire with the Anchor Manufacturing Company—a job he kept for the next seven years. He and Lucie moved to Manchester and rented a five-room, cold water tenement at 13 Laval Street on the predominately French-speaking west side of Manchester. The Merrimack River ran through the middle of Manchester, separating the east side from the west side.

Cold water tenements did not provide any piped-in hot water—only cold water. To take a comfortable bath, especially in the winter, one needs to heat the water on the stove and dump it into the bathtub.

A daughter, Jeanne Marie, was born on March 6, 1934. Next came a son, Lionel Joseph, on August 26, 1935, followed by another daughter, Claudette Cécile, on August 5, 1941.

The children kept Lucie busy, but she was not happy in Manchester. She missed being close to her relatives.

"Théophile," declared Lucie. "I just got another letter from my sister Marie, in Montreal. She says there are lots of jobs there. I want to move to Montreal."

For well over a year, she had pestered her husband with the request to move to Montreal. He finally gave in.

In 1944, he moved his growing family to Montreal, Canada. Besides her sister Catherine, who lived in Waltham, Lucie had four other sisters and a brother who lived in Montreal. Later that same year, 1944, when Lionel was nine years old, he was struck by a taxicab and sent to the hospital in critical condition. Lucie was pregnant at the time and prayed at the Shrine of Brother André on the backside of Mont Royal in

Montreal. She promised that if he saved Lionel, and her unborn child was a boy, she would name him André.

Lionel recovered, and a son was born on February 9, 1945. She dutifully called him André from then on, but two days after his birth, he was baptized Samuel André. Many years later, when brought to her attention, she insisted the baptismal certificate was wrong. It should have read André Samuel.

•   •   •

After two years in Montreal, Théophile moved the family back to Manchester and resumed his job with the Anchor Manufacturing Company. The final child, Dianne Yvette, was born on September 16, 1950.

Jeanne was the first to leave home. At seventeen, she answered an ad in the newspaper for a nanny position in Somerset, Pennsylvania. She eventually married William G. Kimmel of Somerset, and together they raised three sons: Lionel, Ronald, and Richard.

Lionel was next to leave home. In 1954, he quit school during his junior year of high school and joined the U.S. Marine Corps. They sent him to Camp Lejeune, North Carolina, for basic training.

Later that same year, his nine-year old brother André, nicknamed Andy, while riding a friend's bicycle, was hit by a truck about four miles from home. He suffered a concussion and severe lacerations to both legs. A policeman was first on the scene. When he saw the loss of blood, he applied tourniquets to each leg, placed the boy in his cruiser, and rushed him to the hospital. There was no time to wait for an ambulance. The driver of the truck was in shock and refused to come out, thinking the boy he hit was dead. At the hospital, while being wheeled down the corridor to the operating room, Théophile held Andy's hand. Their eyes met. No words were spoken, but an immense connection passed between the two.

Andy spent three weeks in the hospital. The policeman who drove him there came to visit, and Andy thanked him for saving his life.

Andy's mom, Lucie, visited him every day. She often wondered why her two sons, when nine years old, were each critically injured in traffic accidents. After his release from the hospital, Andy used crutches for the next six months to walk, gradually regaining full use of his legs.

When Andy entered Bishop Bradley High School in Manchester, he was asked to provide his baptismal certificate, and that's when it was pointed out to him that his first name was Samuel. This news came as a complete surprise. Going forward, Andy used Samuel as his first name on all official paperwork. His family and friends prior to high school continued to call him Andy, but friends from and after high school called him Sam.

His sister Claudette graduated from Saint Marie High School and won a full scholarship to the Notre Dame School of Nursing in Manchester. She completed the three-year nursing program and was awarded her Registered Nurse (RN) designation. After working as a nurse for one year, she joined the Air Force and was commissioned a 2nd lieutenant.

In August 1963, after graduating from high school, Andy tried to join the Navy, but the recruiter couldn't take him because Andy was born in Montreal and was not a U.S. citizen. The Navy recruiter suggested Andy go next door and join the Army. The Army readily accepted resident aliens with green cards.

"How can I help you?" the Army sergeant said as Andy entered the small office.

"I want to join the Army."

"Well, have a seat and fill out this form," replied the sergeant.

Andy was soon on his way to Fort Dix, New Jersey, for eight weeks of basic training, followed by eight more weeks of advanced individual training in one of the Army's military occupational specialties (MOS). All recruits were given aptitude tests to determine the best MOS for them. The Army decided the best MOS for Andy was that of a clerk typist. After eight weeks, he could accurately type sixty-five words per minute and knew how to complete many of the basic Army forms and reports, including the morning report. It was a daily report that stated how many men were present, absent with authorization, or absent without official leave (AWOL) for each unit in the Army. The morning reports were forwarded up the chain of command and eventually compiled into a total for the entire Army.

After graduating from the advanced training program, Andy and about 500 other recent graduates from various programs were ushered into a movie theater on base.

"Men, congratulations on completion of your advanced training," said Colonel Jonathan Emerson, commanding officer of the advanced training program at Fort Dix. "You'll next be hearing from several speakers of other opportunities available to you in the Army on a volunteer basis. Please give these speakers your attention and consider volunteering for one of these specialties. First up is Master Sergeant Frank Johnson from the Airborne School at Fort Benning, Georgia."

"Thank you, Colonel," said Johnson. He was wearing his Class A uniform with bloused boots and silver wings on his jacket. Only airborne-qualified soldiers could wear boots with their Class A uniforms. He was tall, confident, and captured everyone's attention.

"Men, I'm here today to offer you one of the most respected positions in the entire Army—that of an airborne soldier. We still have a few openings for the class that starts in late January."

Johnson went on for several more minutes, but Andy was already sold. Airborne was his calling. At the end of his talk, Johnson asked for a show of hands of those interested in joining the airborne. Andy was sitting in the fifth row of that theater and was afraid he'd be overlooked from the expected large show of hands. He jumped out of his seat with his hand high in the air. When he looked around, he saw a total of three hands were up, including his. Later that day, he completed and signed the application form for the Airborne School.

On December 22, 1963, after sixteen weeks in the Army, Andy received orders releasing him from Fort Dix and ordering him to appear at the Airborne School at Fort Benning by January 20, 1964. He spent the intervening month at home in Manchester with his family.

# CHAPTER 32
# VIETNAM

When Andy arrived home from Fort Dix, he was pleased that his sister Claudette had just joined the Air Force as a 2<sup>nd</sup> lieutenant. She was ordered to report to the Air Force officer training program in Montgomery, Alabama, not too far from Fort Benning. After spending Christmas and a relaxing month at home, they drove south together in their father's car. Claudette owned a 1954 Chevrolet that she had purchased for $200 a year before. It was a junker with no reverse. Their father, Théophile, insisted they use his 1962 Chevrolet Impala for the trip. In the meantime, he would use Claudette's car. She dropped Andy off at Fort Benning and proceeded to her base, just a few miles away.

His first impression of Fort Benning in January was the hundreds, if not thousands, of robins all over the base. Growing up in New Hampshire, he saw the robins fly south for the winter each fall. He now knew exactly where some of them went—Fort Benning, Georgia.

After reporting to the Airborne School, he was assigned to a barracks building and settled in. The next day, he saw a roster of the students in his class and noticed the name, Roger Robichaud, the only Acadian name on the list, other than his own. Roger was assigned to the same barracks building.

"Are you Roger Robichaud?" asked Andy, known in the Army as Sam.

"Yes, who are you?" replied Roger.

"My name is Sam Aucoin. When I saw the class roster, I recognized your name as a fellow Acadian. Do you speak French?"

"Not really. My grandparents spoke it well, but I grew up speaking English in Lake Charles, Louisiana. Almost all my friends were Cajun, but we spoke only English. I know a few words and phrases in French, but that's all. Where are you from?"

"I grew up in New Hampshire, but my parents are from an Acadian village in Nova Scotia. We spoke French at home. I learned English in school."

"Well, I'm happy to meet you. Where was your basic training?"

Roger and Sam spoke for the next hour or two and were well on their way to becoming good friends.

Paratrooper training started the next morning. Each day began with twenty minutes of calisthenics followed by a three-mile run. A full week was spent perfecting the parachute landing fall (PLF). Very few injuries occurred on the aircraft or upon leaving the aircraft. Most injuries happened on the landing. Some, however, occurred upon leaving the aircraft. Jewelry of any type on the hands or wrists was not allowed. Wedding rings, watches, bracelets, or the like had to be removed prior to the jump. Upon leaving the larger aircraft, such as a C-130, the paratrooper stood in the door on the side of the aircraft and pushed off by placing his hands on either side of the door. The C-130 was typically moving at about 350 miles per hour. A good push from the side of the aircraft was necessary to prevent the prop wash from slamming the jumper back against the side of the aircraft. Cases existed where a ring on a jumper's finger hooked onto an exposed rivet. The finger was ripped off when the man jumped.

Most accidents, however, occurred when the soldier landed. Sprained ankles or broken legs were the likely result of a bad landing. Hence the emphasis on the PLF.

"Hit, shift and rotate!" bellowed the instructors over and over as the students practiced this fall from a standing position on the ground. Next came practicing the fall from a two-foot-tall ramp. They were instructed to hit the ground softly with their boots, shift their bodies to one side, go into a roll on the ground, and come up standing. Of all the new skills they had to learn, this one, the PLF, took up the most time. The instructors would not let the students proceed until they had mastered this skill.

In a practice jump, if a jumper was caught landing upright on his feet, he was penalized. The chute used by paratroopers differed greatly from the one used by sky divers. In a combat situation, the paratrooper was a vulnerable target in the sky. His chute was therefore designed to get him safely but quickly onto the ground. As a result, the paratrooper typically hits the ground much harder than a sky diver.

Roger and Sam briskly mastered the required skills, made their five qualifying jumps, all from C-130 aircraft, and received their paratrooper wings at the graduation ceremony. To Sam's surprise, his sister Claudette, in her Air Force 2nd lieutenant uniform, was at the ceremony and presented him with his wings. He saluted her and then gave her a hug.

Later the next day, the orders stating where the graduates would go were posted on the bulletin board. Roger's name, along with the names of substantially all the graduates, was there, but not Sam's. All the men on the list were assigned to the 173rd Airborne Brigade in Okinawa. They left the next day. Sam was upset. He wanted to go with his new buddy, Roger, and he complained to the sergeant in charge to no avail.

"Aucoin, you need to be patient!" declared the sergeant. "The Army knows best. Your orders, and those for the other two waiting graduates, will arrive when the Army is good and ready."

One of his fellow waiting graduates was an Irish kid from Dublin. The other, an Englishman from Liverpool. From the Okinawa orders, Sam jotted down the mailing address for the 173rd.

Two days later, Sam's orders arrived. He was to proceed to the Navy yard in Brooklyn, New York. There, he boarded a troop ship for the eight-day crossing to Germany. He was assigned to an airborne artillery unit of the 8th Infantry Division located on the Rhine River in Biebrich, a suburb of Wiesbaden, Germany.

Roger and Sam corresponded with each other regularly. Roger said he liked Okinawa. It was tropical and reminded him of his home in Louisiana. His unit made at least one parachute jump every month into the countryside. They spent fifty percent of their time practicing jungle warfare—month after month.

In early June 1965, Roger reported that his entire battalion had been deployed to Vietnam. They were stationed at Bien Hoa Air Base, near Saigon. Their initial mission was to protect Saigon from attack by the Viet Cong.

On August 20, 1965, his platoon sergeant, Ronald Stevenson, had a routine assignment for him.

"Robichaud, I need you to take the three-quarter-ton truck and go into Saigon for supplies," ordered Stevenson. "Take two men with you."

"Yes, Sarge," replied Roger. "Do I go to the same supply depot as before?"

"Yes, Sergeant Graham is expecting you. Make sure you stay on the main road—no detours."

Saigon was about sixteen miles from Bien Hoa. The night before, the Viet Cong buried a large mine into the road about halfway between Saigon and Bien Hoa.

"Hey, Rog, do you think we'll have time for a little R&R in Saigon after we pick up the supplies?" asked Private Pulaski, one of the two men selected for the trip.

"Not after," replied Roger. "After we get the supplies, we need to guard the truck. If we get there early, I think a quick stop at the Velvet Cat Lounge would be in order."

The three doomed men ate an early breakfast in the mess hall and set off for Saigon at 6:00 AM.

The Viet Cong who placed the mine in the road were planting rice in the nearby rice paddy. They watched as the three-quarter-ton truck with its three occupants approached.

"Boom!" The explosion was enormous, deafening, and deadly. All three men were instantly killed.

A month later, Ronald Stevenson, Roger's platoon sergeant, wrote to Sam and informed him of Roger's death. He would not be the last.

•   •   •

Roger's death hit Sam hard. Not only did he lose a friend, but it meant one less Acadian to keep the Acadian story alive. As a Cajun, Roger, along with most Cajuns, had already lost his French language. The assimilation of Cajuns into the prevailing Anglo culture throughout south-central Louisiana was well underway—not that assimilation was entirely bad. Learning the dominant language was usually necessary to enter the work force successfully and provide jobs for young people. Conforming to the prevailing culture, however, always comes at a price—a reduction in one's own ethnic culture.

The Vietnam War had a profound impact on Sam. It was his war. More than a few of the men he trained with were killed or severely wounded there. He served in the army from August 1963 to August 1966. Several of his friends from elementary and high school, drafted into the army, were killed in the jungles, cities, and rice paddies of Vietnam. Why were the U.S. forces there? The civilian politicians in charge told them to go there——that's why. That's all that they, at the tip of the spear, knew. The American troops, for the most part, did their best to accomplish their assigned tasks or die honorably. What they didn't understand is that they were basically caught in the middle of a civil war between the North and the South. The mission, from the North's perspective, was very clear—to unite the country and expel all foreign troops. This mission was easily communicated, understood, and accepted by substantially everyone in the North. Failure was not an option. The mission from the South's perspective, "to stop the Communists," was harder to communicate, explain or rally behind, especially when the corruption and mismanagement in the South became clearer.

At first, the focus of the Americans was to train the South Vietnamese Army and pacify the countryside—win their hearts. That soon changed to search and destroy missions with the detestable and misleading body counts. According to the body counts, the Americans were way ahead and should easily win the war in due course. The bad guys would soon run out of men. The Americans had air superiority, napalm, agent orange, and the carpet bombing of the North, to no avail. Losing the war was traumatic and make no mistake—the Americans lost the war. Returning soldiers were spat upon. That spit should have been aimed at the politicians that sent them there and kept them there.

•   •   •

After his tour of duty in the Army, Sam returned home and took advantage of the G.I. Bill to complete four years at the University of New Hampshire in Durham, NH, where he earned a Bachelor of Science degree in Business in 1970. While in college, he quickly learned to keep his military service to himself. His fellow students were predominately anti-war and anti-military. His honorable discharge was anathema to them.

Over the years, he made several visits to Chéticamp, where he saw for himself its transformation from a quaint Acadian village to a thriving hub of tourist activity. On his most recent visit in 2010, he was greeted by his cousin, Lucienne LeFort, who lived in Chéticamp and worked as a hostess in an Acadian restaurant.

"André, I'm so happy to see you again!" exclaimed Lucienne. "It's been too long since you were last here."

"I'm happy to be here," replied Sam. "I'm surprised at how busy everything seems in the village."

"Yes, during the tourist season, we have difficulty filling all the jobs—waiters, waitresses, maids, tour guides, you name it. Since you were last here, we now have an eighteen-hole golf course, and I'm sure you've noticed all the new motels, rental cabins, and restaurants."

"I've also noticed your English is much improved since my last visit."

"Of course! The tourists speak mostly English, and all the young people in Chéticamp speak fluent English. It's their path to a good job market, here and beyond. We also offer whale-watching cruises and deep-sea fishing charters. The captains of these boats are generally older and speak very little English. They hire our young people to serve as guides and interpreters on the boats. It's a win-win situation."

As I listened to my cousin, I found it difficult to find fault with all that progress, but I, for one, missed the sound of French as I walked through the village of Chéticamp.

# EPILOGUE

"Well, Chloe, what do you think of the story?" asked Sam Aucoin of his granddaughter. Hours had passed, and the two now sat on a park bench watching the sun set in the distance.

"It's a sad story, Grandpa, but I'm glad you told it to me. The Acadians sure had to struggle just to survive. So many of them perished for no good reason, including your friend Roger."

"Yes, Roger was only twenty when he died."

"I know you wanted to go with Roger after jump school, but I'm happy you didn't. I'm glad we have you here with us. Did you ever figure out why you weren't on those orders after jump school?"

"Yes, it took me about three months to find someone familiar with the pertinent rules. It turns out that although resident aliens were subject to the draft and could therefore be forced into the Army, they could not be sent to a combat zone. I volunteered for the Army and jump school, but the same rule applied to me. They could not send me to a combat zone even if I wanted to go. That was the rule in the 1960s. I don't know if it still applies today."

"That was a terrific rule. I'm happy about it. From my perspective, an Acadian finally got a good break."

Sam couldn't help but smile at his granddaughter.

"Chloe, the story of the Acadians is your story. I expect you to pass it down to your children."

"Don't worry, Grandpa. Your history will carry on with me."

"Many other ethnic groups including the Scots, the Irish, and the Indians were oppressed by the English during the eighteenth and nineteenth centuries. These were very large groups numbering in the hundreds of thousands, if not millions, as in India. By comparison, the Acadians were a tiny group who in 1755 numbered only 20,000, and a significant percentage of them perished during the deportation and its aftermath. Few people today have ever heard of the Acadians."

"You're right, Grandpa. Until you told me their story, I knew nothing about them. I'd heard of the Cajuns but never the Acadians. I look forward to learning more about them."

"Thank you, Chloe."

Chloe leaned over and gave me a big hug and whispered in my ear, "Thank you for giving me such a rich history. Don't worry, Grandpa. I'll keep the story of the Acadians, our story, alive."

I hugged her back. She'd made an old man very happy.

# APPENDIX A

The below genealogical chart traces the Aucoin genealogy from Martin Aucoin in the early 1600s to the author's grandchildren.

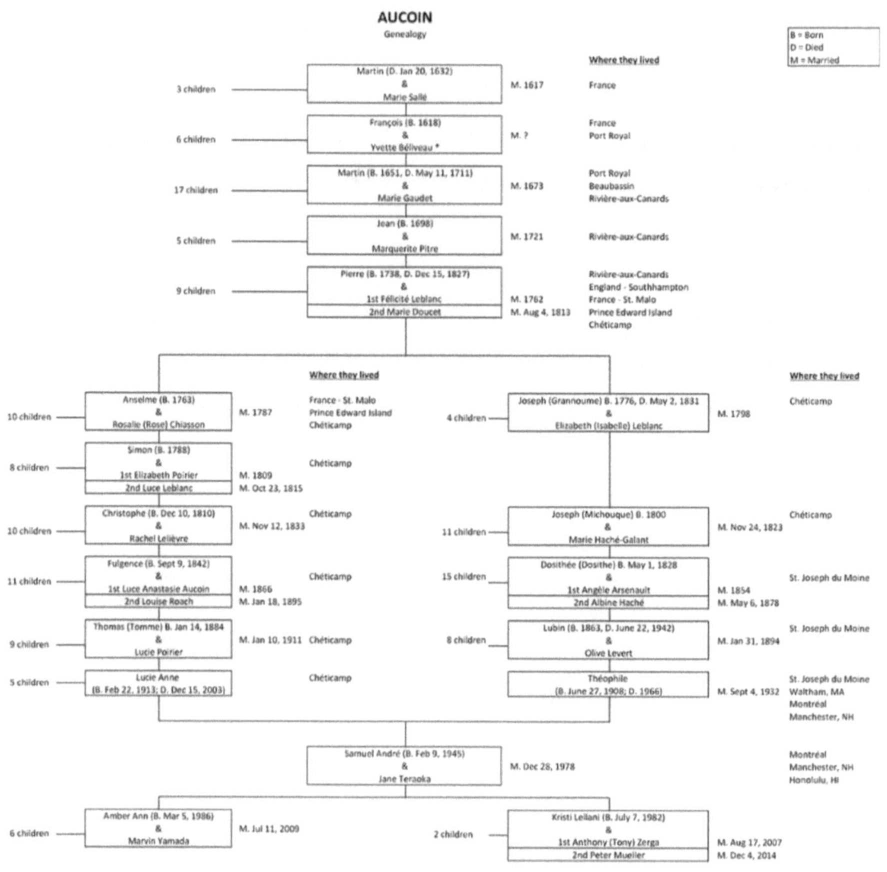


* Yvette Béliveau is a fictitious name. Real name of François' wife is unknown.

# APPENDIX B

Below document copied from the book "Nos Aucoin de Chéticamp ******* Our Aucoins of Chéticamp" with the permission of its author Charles D. Roach.

**The revalidation of the marriage of Anselme Aucoin and Rose Chiasson, Feb 1, 1787.**

Original French text

L'an mil sept cent quatreving (sic) sept—trois février, je soussigné ai marié en face de notre mère la St. Eglise, Anselm (sic) Aucoin, fils de Pierre Aucoin et de Félicité LeBlanc, avec Rosalie [1], fille de Paul Chiasson et de Louise Boudreau, les ci desus (sic) dé-nommés aiant (sic) auparavant été marié (sic) par Germain Boudreau en présence des quatre témoins soussigné (sic), en foi de quoi je leur ai délivré le présent certificat au Havre Sauvage[2] les jour et an que desus (sic).

Anselm AucoinLedru, curé de la
Rosalie ChiassonBay St Marie (sic)
Germain Boudreauet du Cap Sable [3]
Alexis Delaurier
Xavier Pitre
Pierre Aucoin
Amant Chiasson

---

1. Connue du nom de "Rose."
2. Présentement Savage Harbour, I. P. E.
3. Dans le sud-ouest de la Nouvelle-Ecosse.

---

Translation of the original French text.

In the year one thousand seven hundred eighty-seven, on the third day of February, I, the undersigned have married before our Holy Mother Church, Anselm (sic) Aucoin, son of Pierre Aucoin and Felicite LeBlanc, and Rosalie [1], daughter of Paul Chiasson and Louise Boudreau, the above-mentioned having been married previously by Germain Boudreau, in the presence of the four undersigned witnesses, in testimony whereof I have given them this certificate at Havre Sauvage[2] on the day and year aforementioned.

Anselm AucoinLedru, pastor of
Rosalie ChiassonBay St Marie (sic)
Germain Boudreauand Cape Sable [3]
Alexis Delaurier
Xavier Pitre
Pierre Aucoin
Amant Chiasson

---

1. Known as "Rose."
2. Presently Savage Harbor, P. E. I.
3. In southwestern Nova Scotia.

---

# APPENDIX C

Below document copied from the book "Nos Aucoin de Chéticamp ******* Our Aucoins of Chéticamp" with the permission of its author Charles D. Roach.

**The transfer of land from Nicolas Jaquet to *Pierrot* Aucoin and Luce Babin, April 1, 1791.**

Original French text

*Lan Mille Sept Cent Soixante et onze (sic) Enpressence de temoint Jay Moy Nicolas Jaquet & Madelaine le bland mon Epouse Sousignont et Certifiont aVoir donne & abandonné à Luce babin Et pierre auCoin Sont Maris Cent Six Verge De Notre terre pour En jouire à Leur propre Volonté a la Reserve que Sy laditte Luce babin & le dit pierre auCoin Estest dans les Sentiment de l'an bandonner ne pouvent pâs La Vendre Ny Enfaire aux Cun trafique Sans Endonner la Preférance aux dit Nicolas Jaquet & à la dit Madelaine le bland Sont Epouse Et Leurs desandant Lequel terrain Ne leur Sera fait auCun Trouble par aucun de nos Enfants—Cette donation fait de notre prope Volonté Les dis Cent Six Verge aprende La profondeur suivant la ligne Suivante, lequel la dit luce babin Et pierre auCoin Seront aubligé dans payer la Rente de leur terrain que Nous Leurs aVont donné, Le tout fait Enpressence du Nommé Pierre Cauté & de Thomas Jaquet quy ont Sine aVec Nous Ce*
*Premier aVrille 1791 (sic)*

*Nicolas jaquetmadelaine lebland*
 *pierre + aucoinluce + babin*

*Thomas JaquetPierre Cotté*
 *temoint*

French interpretation of previous text:

L'an mil sept cent soixante et onze [1], en présence de témoins, je, Nicolas Jaquet, et Madelaine Leblanc, mon épouse, certifions avoir donné et abandonné à Luce Babin et à Pierre [2] Aucoin, son mari, cent six verges de notre terre pour en jouir à leur propre volonté, sous la réserve que, si la dite Luce Babin et le dit Pierre Aucoin décident de l'abandonner, ils ne pourront pas vendre cette terre, ni en faire quelque trafic que ce soit, sans d'abord en donner la préférence au dit Nicolas Jaquet et à la dite Madelaine LeBlanc, son épouse, et à leurs descendants, pour laquelle terre aucun trouble ne leur sera causé par aucun de nos enfants—cette donation faite de notre propre volonté, les dites cent six verges a prendre de notre terre et à s'étendre sur toute sa profondeur, pour laquelle terre la dite Luce Babin et le dit Pierre Aucoin devront payer la taxe, le tout fait en présence des nommés Pierre Côté et Thomas Jaquet, qui ont signé avec nous ce premier avril 1791.

---

1. Il s'agit sans doute d'une erreur. C'est plutôt 1791 qu'on a voulu dire.
2. Il s'agit de notre Pierre-Simon (dit *Pierrot*)

Nicolas Jaquet   Madelaine Leblanc
Pierre + Aucoin   Luce + Babin
Thomas Jaquet, Pierre Côté
Témoins

English interpretation of previous text:

In the year one thousand seven hundred seventy-one[1], in the presence of witnesses, I, Nicolas Jaquet, and Madelaine LeBlanc, my wife, certify having granted and abandoned unto Luce Babin and Pierre[2] Aucoin, her husband, one hundred six yards of our land to enjoy as they see fit, with the reservation that, if the said Luce Babin and the said Pierre Aucoin should decide to abandon this lot of land, they cannot sell it or make any other traffic of it without giving the first option to the said Nicolas Jaquet and the said Madelaine LeBlanc, and to their heirs, this lot of land to be free from all intervention from any of our children— this transfer made of our own free will, the one hundred six yards to be taken from our land and extending to its full depth, for which land the said Luce Babin and the said Pierre Aucoin will assume the responsibility of paying the taxes, this document drawn up in the presence of Pierre Coté and Thomas Jaquet who have signed with us this first day of April 1791.

---

1. This is obviously an error. The year was no doubt 1791.
2. This is our Pierre-Simon (known as *Pierrot*)

Nicolas Jaquet   Madelaine Leblanc
Pierre + Aucoin   Luce + Babin
Thomas Jaquet, Pierre Côté
Witnesses

# ABOUT THE AUTHOR

Sam Andre Aucoin was born in Montreal and grew up in New Hampshire. He is of Acadian descent and heard their stories first-hand from his parents and other relatives. He has degrees from the University of New Hampshire and the the University of Hawaii. He served as a paratrooper with the 82nd Airborne Division and currently resides in Honolulu with his wife Janie. They have two daughters and eight grandchildren.

# NOTE FROM
# SAMUEL ANDRE AUCOIN

Word-of-mouth is crucial for any author to succeed. If you enjoyed *The Acadians*, please leave a review online—anywhere you are able. Even if it's just a sentence or two. It would make all the difference and would be very much appreciated.

Thanks!
Samuel Andre Aucoin

We hope you enjoyed reading this title from:

# BLACK ROSE writing™

www.blackrosewriting.com

Subscribe to our mailing list – *The Rosevine* – and receive **FREE** books, daily deals, and stay current with news about upcoming releases and our hottest authors.
Scan the QR code below to sign up.

Already a subscriber? Please accept a sincere thank you for being a fan of Black Rose Writing authors.

View other Black Rose Writing titles at www.blackrosewriting.com/books and use promo code **PRINT** to receive a **20% discount** when purchasing.